Praise for the N[...] W9-CSP-268 [...]ies

"An absolute surfeit of weird, sometimes terrifying creatures."
                    —*Booklist* on *The Mirror of Worlds*

"Courage, ingenuity, and a bit of fancy wizardry."
                    —*Publishers Weekly* on *The Gods Return*

"Drake has a light touch with his characters, making them believable and serious without becoming overly ponderous or melodramatic. He employs the standard epic fantasy tropes of action, sorcery, and romance to great effect in this exciting, compelling read."
                    —*RT Book Reviews* on *The Fortress of Glass*

"Drake has wit. . . . Installments stand on their own feet, giving readers the luxury of jumping right into the action."   —*Starlog* on *The Fortress of Glass*

"Drake's grasp of large-scale action, as well as small dramas, makes him a superb storyteller. The sixth addition to his Lord of the Isles series belongs in most fantasy collections."

                    —*Library Journal* on *Master of the Cauldron*

"Great, gritty realism on both material and magical planes, and Hell quite literally breaks loose on occasion. The audience for this kind of fantasy saga should prove large and ongoing, and for this volume, at least, it will be well deserved." —*Booklist* on *Master of the Cauldron*

Tor Books by David Drake

The Gods Return

THE THIRD VOLUME OF
The Crown of the Isles

DAVID DRAKE

TOR®
fantasy

A TOM DOHERTY ASSOCIATES BOOK
NEW YORK

THE GODS RETURN

A Tor Book
Published by Tom Doherty Associates, LLC
175 Fifth Avenue
New York, NY 10010

www.tor-forge.com

Tor® is a registered trademark of Tom Doherty Associates, LLC.

ISBN 978-0-7653-5118-0

First Edition: November 2008
First Mass Market Edition: January 2010

Printed in the United States of America

0 9 8 7 6 5 4 3 2 1

TO DAN BREEN

As sort of a bookend, for making this series much better than it would've been without his help.

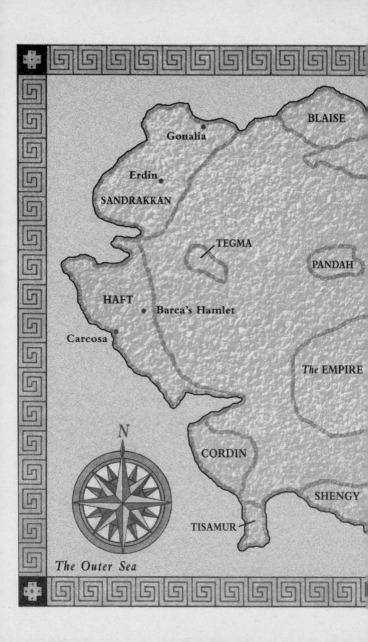

The
LAND

LAUT

ORNIFAL
• Valles

ATARA

KEPULAKECIL

BIGHT

CHARAX

TELUT

PARE

of PALOMIR

Saltwater Intrusion

KANBESA

SIRIMAT

SERES

DALOPO

BOWWKAN

Acknowledgments

W<small>HEN I'M DEEP</small> into writing a novel, everything else sort of blurs. On my own, I'd eat whatever's simplest to grab. I don't have much sense of serial time on my best day, and when the book takes over I'm likely to be off by a week or more on when things have to be done. The fact that things (this includes sending in the taxes and paying bills) *are* done and I'm fed excellent, healthy meals is due to the efforts of my wife, Jo.

Dorothy Day and my Webmaster, Karen Zimmerman, archived my rough and intermediate texts, so that if disaster struck central North Carolina the work would survive. (I might not, but that doesn't concern me. In that case, somebody else will have to sort out the problems.)

Dorothy helped with continuity matters (for example, what color was the Ornifal standard?), and Karen (a skilled cybrarian) researched all manner of questions, including finding books and images that my whim suggested might be helpful. (I have very clever whims, by the way.) I joke about "my trained staff," but in all truth Dorothy and Karen make the process smoother and the result significantly better than it would be without their help.

Dr. John Lambshead provided me with drawings of a large, vicious nematode which he discovered and named after his then girlfriend, now wife. (Hi, Val!) My version of the creature is bigger still but perhaps no more dangerous if you happen to be of the right size.

I had computer adventures. (Do you know anybody else who had the power button of his PC fall into the case? Mine did.) My son Jonathan and my friend Mark Van Name kept me going. All they get out of it is a fund of stories with which to astound their fellow geeks.

Thank you all.

Dave Drake

Author's Note

THE RELIGION OF the Isles is based on the Sumerian triad of Inanna, Dumuzi, and Ereshkigal. That fact is of more significance here than it has been in the previous books of the series.

The magic (which in the Isles series is separate from religion) is based on that of the Mediterranean Basin in classical times. Its core was probably Egyptian, but it borrowed heavily from other cultures (including Jewish elements). What I call words of power are the *voces mysticae* which were written or spoken to bring the request to the attention of demiurges.

I do not believe the magic of the Isles series or any other magic is effective in the waking world. I've been wrong about many other things, however. On general principles, I prefer not to pronounce the words of power when I transcribe them.

My background is basically that of a classical antiquary. There's a great deal to amuse other classicists in this novel besides the snatch of Ovid which I translated (and for more, check my Website, david-drake.com). I put in these references not as jokes but to give some of the texture of our wonderful real world to my fantasy creation. (Though, okay, the discussion of Pytheas and Strabo *is* a bit of a joke.)

I don't believe I've discussed style in print before. I'm going to do so here because of some recent questions.

Although this novel (and most of mine) is told in third person, I do not use an omniscient narrator: each section is written from a particular viewpoint and in language appropriate to that viewpoint. Ilna is more formal than her brother Cashel, but neither of them has the educated vocabulary to be expected from Garric or Sharina. In all cases this internal viewpoint involves the use of contractions that would not be proper in (say) an academic paper.

I believe this helps to put the reader in the character's own worldview. You may think I'm a fool to do this or that the technique doesn't work; we can discuss those matters. Please, though, don't assume that I and my erudite editor are ignorant of the rules of formal English prose.

One final note: we scattered the ashes of my editor and publisher Jim Baen in a grove on my property. I've put the grove into this novel. I can't say with Horace, *"Exegi monumentum aere perennius . . . ,"* but I felt that a little extra memorial to my close friend would be a good thing.

DAVID DRAKE
www.david-drake.com

The Gods Return

Prologue

Y OU WERE RIGHT, priest," said Archas grudgingly as he and Salmson stared at the jungle-covered building. He wore his blond beard in two braids, curving outward like the horns of a mountain sheep. "Though it doesn't look like any temple I've ever seen."

Before the Change that mixed all eras to re-form the Isles into a single continent, Archas and his men had been pirates scouring the seas off Sirimat and Seres. Now Franca the Sky God had use for them.

The under-priest Salmson shivered despite the muggy air and the runnels of sweat which had already soaked his robe. "Franca's revelation to Nivers His priest is always right, Captain Archas," he said. "Of course. Franca is lord of all existence; how can He not be right?"

Salmson looked up to mumble a prayer, but he couldn't see even a patch of sky through the layers of foliage. Nonetheless Franca was present, here and everywhere. *All power is Franca, and all serve Him.*

"Anyway, it's a temple and a prison both," Salmson said, wiping his neck where the robe chafed. Insects ringed the collar, not biting but drinking his sweat and making him itch. Other insects crawled into his eyes, though he kept blinking them away. "And it's your path to power, Captain."

Salmson had spent the past twenty years as steward and general dogsbody to Nivers, high priest of Franca, in the glittering ruin which was all that remained of the Empire of Palomir. It frightened him to have suddenly become so close to unthinkably great power. That was true even though the power was his to control.

The Gods of Palomir had returned. Deep in Salmson's fearful heart, he regretted his loss of the past when rats chittered in the crystal hallways of Palomir and the jungle inexorably devoured its margins. Those days were gone forever, though. Now Salmson spoke with the voice and power of Franca.

He grimaced and said, "Bring up the prisoners. It's time we got started."

The man-sized rat beside him turned and sent a clicking call back along the trail. A squad of rat men chivied the captives out of the jungle, each carrying a pack. There was no formal division, but Archas and his men had taken the lead during most of the journey from their base on the eastern coast of the seaway which penetrated the new continent.

The pirates didn't mix with Salmson's escort of rat men, but they wouldn't have mixed with another band of human cutthroats either. The pirates were a pack of wild beasts which Archas ruled by being the most savage beast among them.

Whereas the rats were certainly beasts, but not wild ones: they were the minions of Franca, raised by Nivers to serve the place of the human worshippers which depopulated Palomir could not yet provide. The rat men stood upright, carrying swords. They spoke their own language among themselves, but they took Salmson's orders and kept better discipline than most human soldiers; certainly they were better disciplined than Archas' pirates.

The rat men were as ruthless as the icy winter wind. Franca demanded that in His worshippers, and soon all the world would worship Him.

The prisoners staggered forward and set down packs before sinking to the ground. The six-year-old boy and handful of elderly people didn't have burdens, but even so the trek had exhausted them to the point of collapse.

This wasn't a clearing, but the canopy hundreds of feet in the air and the lesser canopy of saplings and palms thirty or forty feet up meant there were only ferns and fungi on the forest floor. Some of the captives stared fearfully at the rat men and the pirates, each band more savage than the other; most turned their eyes to the ground. Here flowers fallen from a giant tree threw magenta patterns across the leaf mold.

Only one prisoner, an old woman, bothered to look at the structure to which Salmson had drawn them. It was flat-topped, a massive table at least eighty feet long—both ends were hidden in the forest—and twelve high, built from the coarse red limestone which underlay the jungle's thin soil. The frieze along the top register seemed to alternate geometric designs with the heads of stylized beasts, though it was hard to be sure: fern fronds and the roots of major trees covered most of its length.

Archas prodded the alcove in the center of the structure with one of his pair of curved swords. "This isn't a door!" he said. "It's carved out of rock just like all the rest of the thing. Where's the real door, then?"

The altar block in front of the temple had a narrow ledge along the back side. Salmson looked up from laying out his apparatus there. A pair of captives had carried the chest holding his paraphernalia of wizardry.

It made Salmson uncomfortable to think of himself as a wizard. He felt even more uncomfortable in directing the powers of Franca, though . . . and that seemed to be the truth of the matter.

He rose to his feet. "That's as expected," he said curtly. "It's the door, or will be. Now, get out of the way while I remove the seal."

Archas gave him a look of cold appraisal, flicking his sword like the tip of a lion's tail. He stepped aside, though.

They were all on edge, even the chittering rat men. The journey along jungle tracks or no track at all, the heat, the insects—all these things were uncomfortable enough.

Beyond those normal miseries lurked fear of the un-known and the scraps of knowledge which were even more fearful.

There was no turning back; Salmson touched his ap-paratus, nerving himself to begin by raising his athame. That knife of art had been cut from a whale's tooth by a wizard of an age lost in dim time. Its yellowed ivory was inscribed with symbols which Salmson couldn't trans-late and with tableaux which were all too clear.

No turning back. . . . *"Abriaon orthiare,"* Salmson chanted, dipping the athame's point at each syllable. He hadn't scratched a figure on the altar as he normally would've done, but he thought he saw a pentagram glow-ing in the heart of the opaque stone. *"Lampho!"*

Wizardlight as blue as the heart of a glacier quivered along the edge of the alcove; it spluttered every hands-breadth as if igniting blobs of sealing wax. Only when it had described the whole rectangular course did the cold glare fade away.

"There!" Salmson cried. "Archas, get the shackle that I've freed. By Hili, man, don't lose it or you'll never con-trol the—Hell blast you, I'll do it!"

The priest scrambled around the end of the altar, trip-ping on tree roots because his eyes were focused on the wall from which a quiver of gold was drifting. He thrust his hand out against the stone and to his relief felt the ghostly caress of the gossamer which had held the portal closed beyond the strength of even a god to open. Care-fully, he began to wind the fetter onto a tourmaline min-iature of Fallin of the Waves.

"What is it?" said the pirate chieftain. He'd stepped back when Salmson shouted at him, his sword raised against whatever might be coming from the tomb. Now he approached again, keeping the blade slanted across his body with the edge outward. "Is it a hair? It looks like blond hair!"

"It's a hair," Salmson said slowly as he coiled the wisp

of gold on the finger-long tourmaline statue of Franca's
sibling. "It's supposed to be a hair of the Lady Herself."

Salmson knew everyone's attention was on him. There
were forty-odd pirates; two had died during the march,
one in a fight too disorganized to be called a duel and the
other screaming at the demons he'd swilled with his wine.
The twenty rat men groomed themselves as they waited.
Though they didn't wear armor for this expedition, the
jungle's mold and moisture had caused their harnesses to
chafe. They licked the sores in their coarse fur methodically.

"A god's hair?" said Archas. "That's impossible!"

He glowered, then added, "And anyway, didn't you say
the Gods were dead? The Lady and the Shepherd and the
Sister, all three?"

Nearly a hundred human captives had survived the
march, but they were too cowed even to run away. They
watched with the dumb apathy of sheep at the gate of the
abattoir.

The black rooster trussed to a handle of Salmson's
casket watched him with furious black eyes, though. Unlike the human prisoners, it hadn't given up.

Slavery is a state of mind, thought Salmson. *But we
are all slaves of Franca.* Even the cockerel.

"I said," Salmson said as he finished coiling the impossibly long strand of hair, "that since the Change this
world is without gods. As for what the hair is—perhaps
you know best. But I warn you, Captain, when I turn this
over to you—"

He raised the talisman to call attention to it. The filament was so clear that Fallin's carved features could be
glimpsed in the pale green stone.

"—don't lose it. Without it you won't be able to control the Worm. No one will be able to control the Worm."

Salmson's lips smiled, though fear froze his mind for
an instant at the thought behind his words. *No turning
back. . . .*

"But no matter," he said, walking back around the altar. He placed the talisman on the ledge among the other implements and raised the athame again. "Bring me the cockerel."

A rat man lifted the rooster. Instead of cutting the cord, he teased the knot open with delicate claws before handing the sacrifice to Salmson.

The priest held the cockerel to the center of the altar stone with his left hand. It wriggled and tried to peck him, so he shifted his grip slightly.

Salmson had noticed birds all the way from the seaway to here. They'd clattered and called in the foliage even when they couldn't be seen, but generally he'd seen them. Since he'd spoken the incantation to unshackle the portal of the Worm, the forest had been silent.

He sighed, took a deep breath, and intoned solemnly, *"Barbathi lameer lamphore. . . ."*

This wasn't as trying as the previous incantation. All he was doing this time was loosing the power of Franca. It was like lifting the trigger bar of a loaded catapult, childishly easy though it released a ball that could smash a gate or the hull of a ship.

"Anoch anoch iao!" Salmson said. He stabbed the rooster with his athame. The edge of the ivory knife wasn't keen enough to slice flesh, but its point could split a bird's chest. Blood followed as he withdrew the blade, splashing the stone and his arm to the elbow.

For a moment there was nothing but the thick smell of violent death. Then the rooster's blood began to steam from the altar, swelling into a misty figure the height of the sky. It didn't exist in the same world as Salmson and the jungle, but it was nevertheless visible.

The figure bent to grip the stone door slab. There was no single scale of sizes in what Salmson saw; though he closed his eyes in sudden terror, the figure remained. Lightning flashed within its dim outlines, but the portal remained shut.

"Bring me a prisoner!" Salmson said. Two rat men seized an old man by the arms and dragged him to the altar. The prisoners who'd been carrying packs merely shrank back, but several of the old men would've tottered off if pirates hadn't grabbed them. The child sobbed in misery; the old woman held him by the shoulders.

The rats threw the prisoner onto the slab faceup, gabbling in wordless terror. He was still wearing a tunic; Salmson gripped it with his left hand and pulled hard, but the cloth didn't tear. One of the rat men slid the tip of his sword under the collar and sliced the garment open without touching the skin beneath.

"Anoch anoch iao!" Salmson said, and stabbed. The prisoner's back arched. The priest tugged, but the ivory blade had stuck between ribs. He levered the athame back and forth till it came out with another spray of blood. The sacrifice continued to thrash convulsively, but his eyes had glazed before his heart ceased pumping.

The cloud-formed figure grew denser as it wrestled with the portal. When Salmson looked at it—his eyes were open again, since it didn't matter—he thought the figure stood in a cascade of planes which should've intersected but didn't, or didn't in the waking universe.

Still the portal remained closed. "Another!" the priest cried. "Bring me a sacrifice!"

Pirates held the prisoners, but none of them came forward at Salmson's command. The rat men who'd brought the first victim now flung his drained corpse off the slab and minced toward the remaining supply.

Before the rats could make a choice, the old woman shoved the boy toward them. He turned shrieking to run back, but the rats caught him and threw him onto the slab. The rats' limbs were slender by human standards, but they had the strength of whalebone.

"Anoch iao!" Salmson repeated. He stabbed again and the boy's blood gushed.

The cloud figure solidified into a black-bearded giant

whose legs spanned the cosmos. Lightning crackled from its hands as they wrenched at the portal. The stone came away with a crash and flew skyward.

The figure of Franca dissolved, but titanic laughter boomed across the sky. The portal was open.

"Sister take it!" Archas muttered. He was staring into the forest canopy with his sword lifted, as though expecting the giant to reappear. "Sister take it and take you, priestling!"

"Cap'n?" said a pirate holding a stout-shafted javelin. The weapon had a ring in the butt where a line could be reeved to grapple with a merchant vessel, but the barbed head was equally able to disembowel human prey. "What's that that's coming out of the hole now, hey?"

Salmson's eyes followed the pointing javelin. The square opening in the temple's face had been an empty blackness initially; now thin, violet smoke began to drift out of it. Archas took another step back. Salmson set down the bloody athame and raised the miniature of Fallin.

The Worm crawled through the interstices of the worlds. Salmson gripped the talisman and faced it, too frightened even to think of running. *We are the slaves of Franca. All power is in Franca.*

The portions of the Worm in the waking world were slate gray, pebbled, and colossal. A long tusk thrust from the circular mouth, then withdrew. The opened portal was ten feet square, but the Worm could never have passed through it in the natural course of things.

Sometimes Salmson saw a world beyond as though the Worm were squirming through a frescoed wall. In that other place cold, sluggish waves swept a rocky strand. Where the body of the Worm should have been was instead a purple mist, but it solidified as the creature writhed into the jungle.

Some of the pirates had fled. Archas held both swords out, and the man with the barbed spear cocked it over his shoulder to throw.

A fat, scarred pirate with one ear fell to his knees and began incongruously to call on the Lady. *How much mercy did you grant to the prayers of your victims, savage?* Salmson thought, but the past no longer mattered.

He held up the talisman. The skein of golden hair blazed brightly, though no sunlight penetrated here in the jungle's understory. "In the name of Fallin of the Waves!" Salmson cried. "Halt!"

The Worm reared, its blunt snout penetrating the treetops. Branches crashed aside, showering mosses and spiky airplants like a green rain. The creature was thicker than a five-banked warship and longer than Salmson could judge. Perhaps it was longer than the waking world could hold. . . .

Slowly the Worm settled back, shifting between the solidity of cold lava and the swirls of violet mist that Salmson had seen rippling in the world beyond the plane of this one. The great body didn't seem to touch the temple from which Salmson had drawn it, but swaths of the jungle beyond shattered at the touch of the gray hide.

A tree, its crown lost in the canopy two hundred feet above, toppled majestically; wood fibers cracked and popped for minutes. When the bole slammed down, the ground shuddered and knocked several pirates off their feet. The rat men chittered and squeezed closer together; most of the prisoners lay flat and wept or prayed.

The pirate with the barbed spear screamed, "Hellspawn!" and hurled his weapon into the Worm; he must've gone mad. The spearhead barely penetrated; the creature twitched, causing the thick shaft to wobble.

Salmson pointed with the talisman. There must be a demonstration; as well to use the pirate for it as the surplus prisoners he'd brought for the purpose.

"Kill," he said, though the God had revealed that he needn't speak aloud while holding the talisman.

The pirate who'd thrown the spear stood where he was, babbling curses. The Worm's mouth opened like a whirlpool yawning. Inside was a ring of teeth and a gullet the mottled red/black colors of rotting horse meat.

Black vapor belched from the creature's gullet, enveloping the pirate. His scream stopped in midnote. His bright clothing crumbled like ancient rags; his body shriveled as it fell.

The Worm quivered forward a few segments, furrowing the jungle like a warship being dragged onto the beach. Its maw engulfed the corpse with a cartload of soil and bedrock, then closed. The creature recoiled slowly to its previous position.

In a moment of trembling anticipation, Salmson felt an awareness of the power he controlled—the power to destroy anything, *everything,* by directing the Worm. He recoiled: if he went any further down that path in his mind, he wouldn't return. There would be nothing as valuable to him as the thrill of universal destruction.

He raised the talisman again. "In the name of Fallin," he said, "go back until you are summoned."

The Worm began to dissolve into glowing mist: patches here and there, spreading like oil over a ridged gray seascape, iridescent but with foul undertones. The sizzle that accompanied the disappearance was too loud to speak over.

At the end there was a violet speck in the air. It vanished with a *clack* like wood blocks striking. The forest was silent.

Salmson still shivered. There was a fetid odor which he hadn't noticed while the Worm was present.

He looked down the swath cleared by the monster's body, mashed vegetation from which a miasma rose. Birds hopped among the crushed branches, hunting for prey stunned by the catastrophe.

All this power. . . .

"Here, Captain Archas," Salmson said in a clear voice. "Take the talisman. By the grace of Franca, God over all

Gods, it is given to you to conquer the Kingdom of the Isles!"

Archas reached left-handed for the offered statuette. Before he touched it, he paused and said, "And what then? When I've conquered the Isles, what of your folk in Palomir?"

"We're all slaves of Franca, Captain," Salmson said. "When the whole world worships Franca, then He will decide our fate."

Archas hesitated a moment longer, then snatched the talisman. "There's nothing more to it?" he demanded. "I just—use it as you did?"

"The Worm is yours to command," Salmson said quietly. "But don't lose the talisman, or—"

He shrugged and gestured with his head toward the gouge in the jungle.

"—the whole world will look like this. Like the Worm's own world."

And will it be any different for mankind when Franca is God of Gods? Salmson wondered. *But there's no turning back. . . .*

Chapter

1

CASHEL CARRIED RASILE in the crook of his arm up the last few tens of steps to the top of the fire tower, the highest point in Pandah. The old wizard's people, the Coerli—the cat men—held the physically weak and aged in contempt even if they happened to be wizards.

Since the Change, Rasile had been helping the humans who'd conquered the Coerli; her life and health had improved a great deal. Still, the fire tower was a hollow pillar with many tens of tens of steps shaped like wedges of pie on the inside. Lots of younger people, cat men and humans both, would've had trouble climbing it.

Cashel didn't mind. Rasile scarcely weighed anything to begin with, and besides, it made him feel useful.

Cashel's friends were all smart and educated. Nobody'd thought that Garric would get to be king while he and Cashel were growing up together in Barca's Hamlet, but he'd gotten as good an education from his father, Reise the Innkeeper, as any nobleman's son in Valles got. Likewise Garric's sister Sharina.

Cashel smiled at the thought of Sharina. She was *so* smart and *so* lovely. If there was wizardry in the world—and there was; Cashel had seen it often—then the greatest proof of it was the fact that Sharina loved him, as he'd loved her from childhood.

Cashel's sister Ilna couldn't read or write any better than he could, and like Cashel she used pebbles or beans as tellers if she needed to count above the number of her fingers. But there was more to being smart than book learning, and nobody had *ever* doubted that Ilna was smart. She'd been the best weaver in Barca's Hamlet since she'd grown tall enough to work a loom, and the things she'd learned on her travels had made her better than any other soul.

None of that had made her happy. Her travels had been to far places, some of them very bad places. She'd come back maybe missing parts that would've let her be happy. Still, Ilna was much of the reason that the kingdom had survived these past years; why the kingdom survived and, in surviving, had allowed mankind to survive.

Cashel, well, he was just Cashel. He'd been a good shepherd, but nobody needed him to tend sheep anymore. He was strong, though; stronger than any man he'd met this far. If he could use that strength to help people like Rasile who the kingdom depended on, then he was glad to have something to do.

"I'm setting you down," he said, just as he'd have done if he'd been carrying a bogged sheep up to drier ground. The sheep couldn't understand him and the Corl wizard didn't need to be told. Still, a few calm words and a little explanation never hurt. "It's supposed to be the highest place in Pandah and—"

He looked around. The top of the tower flared a little, but it was still only two double-paces in diameter.

"—I guess the folks who said that were right."

Rasile stepped to the railing. From a distance the cat men didn't look much different from humans, but close up you saw that their hands and feet didn't use the same bones. As for their faces, well, they were cats. Rasile was covered with light gray fur which had a nice sheen since she'd started eating properly again.

Cashel grinned. If Rasile was a ewe, he'd have said she was healthy. Of course back in the borough she'd have been butchered years ago; there was only fodder enough to get the best and strongest through the winter before the spring crops came in.

"I'll never get used to the cities you beast-men live in," Rasile said. She flicked the back of her right hand with the left, a gesture Cashel had learned was the same as a human being shaking her head. "All those houses together, and so many of them stone. None of the True People ever built with stone."

"Well, you don't use fire, so you can't smelt metal," Cashel pointed out. "That makes it hard to cut stone."

He didn't add, "And you cat men aren't much interested in hard work, either," though it'd have been true enough. The Coerli were predators. All you had to do was own a house cat to know that most of the time it'll be sleeping; and when it isn't, it's likely eating or licking itself.

"Anyway . . . ," Cashel continued diplomatically. Rasile didn't mean anything by "beast-men" and "True People"; it was just the way the Coerli language worked. "I don't guess I'll ever get used to cities either. I was eighteen before I left Barca's Hamlet, and it wasn't but three or four tens of houses."

Pandah had been a good-sized place when the royal army captured it back in the summer, but that was nothing to what it'd become now. All around the stone-built citadel, houses were going up the way mushrooms pop out of the ground after the spring rains. There were wood-sheathed buildings, wattle-and-daub huts, and on the outskirts any number of tents made of canvas or leather.

Before the Change, travel for any distance meant travel by ship. The Isles were now the Land, a continent instead of a ring of islands about the Inner Sea, and Pandah was pretty nearly the center. It'd gotten to be an important place instead of a sleepy little island where ships put in to buy fruit and fill their water casks.

The Corl wizard cleared her throat with a growl that had sounded threatening before Cashel got used to it. She paced slowly sideways around the tower, seeming to look out over Pandah.

Cashel had spent his life watching animals and figuring out what was going on in their minds before they went and did something stupid. He knew Rasile hadn't asked to come up here just to view a city she disliked even more than he did. That was why he'd asked Lord Waldron, the commander of the royal army, to put a couple soldiers down at the base of the stairs to keep idlers out of the tower while Cashel and the wizard were in it.

"Warrior Cashel," Rasile said with careful formality, though she still didn't meet his eyes. "You are a friend of Chief Garric. As you know, the wizard Tenoctris summoned me to help your spouse Sharina while Tenoctris herself was occupied with other business."

"Yes, ma'am," Cashel said. "I know that."

"There is no wizard as powerful as Tenoctris," Rasile said, this time speaking forcefully.

Cashel smiled. It was a good feeling to remember a success.

"Ma'am, I believe that's so," he said. He could've added that it hadn't been true before Tenoctris took an ancient demon into her while Cashel watched. Risky as that was, it'd worked; and because it'd worked, the kingdom had a defender like no wizard before her. "Even she says that, and Tenoctris isn't one to brag."

"And now she has accomplished her other tasks," Rasile continued, turning at last to look at Cashel. "It may be that with a wizard of his own race present—and so powerful a wizard besides—Chief Garric may no longer wish to keep me in his council. Do you believe that is so, Warrior Cashel?"

Cashel chuckled, glad to know what was bothering the old wizard. "No ma'am, it's *not* so," he said, making sure he really sounded like he meant it. He did mean it, of course, but with people—and sheep—lots of times it wasn't the words they heard but the way you said them. "Look, Garric's job is fighting against, well, evil. Right?

The sort of evil that'll wipe out everybody, your folk and mine both. And the fight isn't over."

The sound Rasile made in her throat this time really was a growl, though it wasn't a threat to him. "No, Warrior Cashel," she said, "the fight is not over."

She gestured toward the eastern horizon. "A very great fight is coming, I believe. But—you have Tenoctris again."

"Ma'am," Cashel said, hearing his voice drop lower because of the subject, "what with one thing and another, I've been in a lot of fights. I've *never* been in one where I wouldn't have welcomed help, though. I figure Garric feels the same way."

Rasile gave a throaty laugh. "I am relieved to hear that," she said. "During the time I accompanied your spouse Sharina, Warrior Cashel, I became accustomed to not being relegated to filth and garbage. While I *could* return to my former life with the True People, I don't feel the need to reinforce my sense of humility to that degree. Wholesome though no doubt it would be to do so."

The laughed together. Cashel looked down at the city, holding his quarterstaff in his left hand. There were all sorts of people below, walking and working and just idling along. They made him think of summer days in the south pasture, sitting beneath the ilex tree on the hilltop and watching his sheep go about their business.

In the past couple years Cashel had gone a lot of places and done a lot of things, but he was still a shepherd at heart. He'd learned there were worse things than sea wolves twisting out of the surf to snatch ewes—but he'd learned also that his hickory staff would put paid to a wizard as quickly as it would to the sort of threats his sheep had faced.

He tapped the staff lightly, clicking its iron butt cap on the tower's stone floor. To his surprise, a sizzle of blue wizardlight spat away from the contact.

Rasile noticed the spark also. Her grin bared a jawful of teeth that were noticeably sharper than those of a human being.

"I told you the fight was not over, Warrior Cashel," she said. "I felt but I did not say that Chief Garric would be wise to keep me by him. I cannot do as much as his Tenoctris does, but I can do some things; and he will need many things done if he and his kingdom, *our* kingdom, are to survive the coming struggle."

Cashel nodded without speaking. From this vantage he could see birds fishing the pools that now dotted the plains where the Inner Sea had rippled before the Change. Most were the white or gray of seagulls, but there were darker shapes which flashed blue when they caught the sun right: kingfishers, he was sure.

"Would you mind staying here a little longer, Warrior Cashel?" the Corl wizard said. "I would like to work a small spell. Both our height above the ground and your presence will aid me, I believe."

"Whatever you want, ma'am," Cashel said. "And I'd appreciate you just call me Cashel. I'm not a warrior, you know. I'm just a shepherd."

Rasile snorted mild laughter as she squatted on her haunches. She took a handful of yarrow stalks out of a bag woven from willow withies, so fine and dense that Cashel thought it would shed water. The cat men were good at weaving; even Ilna said so.

"You see what you see, shepherd," Rasile said. "But I see what the world sees. If you do not want me to say 'Warrior,' I will not say the word. But the truth does not change, Cashel."

She tossed the yarrow stalks into a pattern on the stone, then began mumbling words of power. Cashel didn't pay much attention to her. He kept watching the sky and the land beneath, the directions that danger might come from.

He was a shepherd, after all.

* * *

SHARINA LOOKED AROUND the apartment in which
Tenoctris lived and worked. She hoped her shocked dismay didn't show in her expression. The small room had
been let into the outer wall of the citadel. The walls wept
condensate, and the only window was the small one in
the iron-braced door. In all, the place would've been
suitable for a prison cell—and had probably been used
as one in the past.

Besides being a friend of Frince Garric and Princess
Sharina, Tenoctris was the wizard who through advice and
skill had done as much to preserve mankind as had any
other single person. Though Pandah's population was increasing by the day, she could have any quarters she wanted.

"Oh, dear," Tenoctris said in obvious dismay. She
looked like a woman of twenty-two or three, pert and
pretty without being beautiful. Apparently Sharina *hadn't*
kept her face blank. "I'm sorry, dear. I chose this room
because it's what I'm used to. I didn't mean to suggest
that you wouldn't give me better or, well, anything. You
have to remember that for most of my life—"

She shrugged. Tenoctris had been a woman of seventy
when she'd washed up on the shore of Barca's Hamlet,
flotsam flung a thousand years forward in time by the
cataclysm which ended the Old Kingdom. She now appeared to be the woman she'd been in her youth, but
that was true only physically. She'd gained both knowledge and wisdom over a long life. She retained those
virtues and had now added power that few wizards ever
could have claimed.

"—I was considered rightly to be a wizard of very little power. I prided myself on my scholarship, again I think
rightly, but—"

Tenoctris grinned. Her cheerfully wry expression
would've been enough by itself for Sharina to identify her,
no matter what features she was wearing.

"—scholars aren't lodged or fed as well as wizards who can split mountains with an incantation and a gesture."

"Well, speaking as an innkeeper's daughter rather than as Princess Sharina," Sharina said, keeping her tone light, "I'd rather a friend of mine had better lodging. But I understand the attraction of the familiar. I wish I had the same freedom in what I wear."

She tweaked her silk robe. It was a relatively simple garment compared with full court dress weighing as much as a cavalryman's armor, but contrasted with the tunic she'd ordinarily worn in Barca's Hamlet—both an inner and an outer tunic for unusually formal occasions—it was heavy, hot, and confining.

A squad of soldiers talked in low voices as they waited outside in the passage. They were Blood Eagles, members of the royal bodyguard. Sharina had come to accept that, because she was a princess and regent in her brother's absence, she would always have guards.

She grimaced. It wasn't that she wanted to be alone—nobody in a peasant village expected privacy, especially in the winter when even a wealthy household heated only one room. She wasn't used to people actually *caring* what she did, however, day in and day out. Well, there was no help for it; and the dangers were real enough.

Sharina smiled faintly. Though she doubted men with swords would be any help against the wizardry which had been the worst danger to the kingdom these past two years.

"What's your opinion of Rasile, Sharina?" Tenoctris asked abruptly. She fluttered her hands, also familiar—though it seemed odd to see a young woman making the gesture an old woman used to make. "I know she's a powerful wizard; *that* I can judge. What sort of person was she to work with?"

Sharina took time to frame her reply. The room's low-backed chair was stacked with codices. The bed likewise, though there was room enough for a slim person to sleep along the outer edge. And the three wicker baskets of scrolls, though of a height to be sat on, struck Sharina as too flimsy for that to be a safe option.

There was room to squat, however. She squatted, just as she would've done back home while popping open peapods for dinner.

"Rasile doesn't waste words," she said. She grinned. "Or mince them. Which I actually appreciate. She's brave, calm, and good company."

Sharina met the gaze of the old/young wizard who'd seated herself on the edge of the low bed, putting their eyes on a level. "She wasn't you, Tenoctris," she said. "But you couldn't have left me with a better helper."

"No, she isn't me," Tenoctris said with a quirk of her lips, a smile that wasn't quite humorous. "She's a great deal more powerful than I *ever* was. And equally precise, which is why she hasn't precipitated a cataclysm the way so many powerful wizards have done in the past. Also, I don't think she cares much about her power."

"She isn't as powerful as you are now, though?" Sharina said carefully. She wasn't trying to be flattering, but she needed to understand the tools that preserved the kingdom. Tenoctris and Rasile were among those tools, just as surely as she and her brother and all those who took the side of Good were.

She was Princess Sharina. She *had* to think that way if she was to do the best possible work in the struggle with evil, and there was no margin for anything but the best possible work.

"Cashel is accompanying Rasile at this moment," Tenoctris said, looking squarely at Sharina. "I thought that might be a good pairing for the future, if the kingdom's safety required a wizard with suitable protection to act at a distance from the palace and army."

Sharina didn't mean to turn away, but she found her eyes were resting on the top codex of the pile on the chair.

It'd been bound with the pebbled skin of a lizard. There was no legend on the cover, but on the edge of the pages was written *Hybro* in vermilion ink. The word didn't mean anything to her.

She pursed her lips. "You mean the sort of thing you and Cashel did just now, while I led the army against Pandah," she said without emphasis. She looked at the wizard again. The young, pretty, very powerful wizard. "That went very well, I believe."

"Yes," said Tenoctris flatly, "it did."

She paused. "I always found Cashel impressive," she said. "I find him even more so now that I have—"

She twisted a lock of hair to call attention to her gleaming, sandy-red curls.

"—more capacity for appreciation."

This time it was Tenoctris who looked away. She cleared her throat and continued, "Sharina, I have powers that I wouldn't have, couldn't have, dreamed of in the past."

She smiled wryly. "In a very *long* past life. I hope that this power hasn't caused me to lose my judgment, however. Specifically, it hasn't caused me to miss what Cashel is: a rock which will stand though the heavens fall."

"I never doubted you, Tenoctris," Sharina said. She didn't know if that was true. Her lips were dry.

"If you're wise," Tenoctris said, smiling again, "then you never doubted Cashel. You never should doubt Cashel, Sharina. Though the heavens fall."

Sharina rose, feeling a trifle dizzy. That was common after squatting, after all. "I'm sure Rasile will find him a good companion and protector," she said. "If there's need, of course."

There would be need. Sharina was as sure of that as she was that there would be a thunderstorm. She didn't know when or how violent it would be—

But she knew that the storm was coming.

* * *

ILNA'S FINGERS KNOTTED short lengths of cord as she looked at the four people across the desk from her. She was angry, but that—like the fact the sun rises in the east—wasn't unusual enough to be worth comment.

Directly before her were a pair of plump young women, Carisa and Bovea, foster nurses employed by the Lady Merota bos-Roriman Society for Orphans; they were crying. A man of thirty named Heismat, originally from Cordin, sat to their left. He'd wanted to stand, but he'd obeyed when Ilna ordered him onto the third low stool. Despite his bluster and the angry red of his face, Heismat's eyes were cold with fear.

Ilna smiled, though nobody could've mistaken the expression for humor. Heismat knew he was in trouble, though as yet he didn't understand how serious the trouble was. It was hard to convince some people that they shouldn't knock children around, and even more people thought a Corl kit was an animal rather than a child.

Mistress Winora, the manager of the Merota Society, stood beside the door with her hands crossed at her waist; her face was expressionless. Winora was fifty, the widow of a merchant from Erdin who'd been killed in the chaos that followed the Change. She'd kept the books and managed the Erdin end of the business while her husband traveled, so she—unlike Ilna—had the skills required to run the day-to-day operations of the Society.

Carisa and Bovea were among the many other women who'd lost their spouses recently. There were even more orphans than there were widows, so it'd seemed perfectly obvious to Ilna to put the two together to the advantage of both, paying each pair of nurses a competence sufficient to care for a handful of children. She'd done so in the name of Merota, who'd been an orphan also until Ilna and Chalcus took charge of her.

Ilna's fingers knotted, forming a very complex pattern.

It calmed her to knot and weave, but she had a specific purpose this time. She was *very* angry.

Merota and Chalcus had died during the Change. If you believed in souls, then Ilna's soul had died with them—with her family. Ilna didn't believe in souls or gods or anything, really, except craftsmanship. And she believed in the death that would come to all things, though perhaps not as soon as she would like.

"Look, I'm sorry," Heismat snarled. He glared at his knotted hands. He'd been a laborer before the Change and had come to Pandah to work in the building trade. "I *said* I was sorry, didn't I? I didn't mean to do it!"

"Mistress," blubbered Carisa. Heismat was her boyfriend. "It was only because he was drinking, you know. He's a good man, a *good* man, really."

"Mistress Winora, how is the kit?" Ilna asked. Her voice was thin and as cold as the wind from the Ice Capes.

"She'll live," Winora said. Her face was bleak, her tone emotionless. Winora regarded this as failure on her part. "She'll probably limp for the rest of her life, but we may be lucky."

Ilna nodded. "Worse things happen in this world," she said.

It wasn't Winora's fault. It was the fault of Ilna os-Kenset, who'd created a situation which allowed a child to be injured instead of being protected as was supposed to have happened.

Worse things happened, as she'd said. She'd done far worse things herself. But this *particular* thing wouldn't happen again.

"There were other instances of Master Heismat hitting the kit," Winora said. "They weren't as serious, and I didn't learn about them until after this event. I'm sorry, mistress. I wasn't watching as closely as I should have done."

"People make mistakes," Ilna said quietly, her eyes on Heismat; he fidgeted under the cold appraisal. She thought,

At least you're aware that it was a mistake. If Winora had said the wrong thing—and it wouldn't have had to be very wrong, because Ilna was extremely angry—she'd have been next in line as soon as Ilna was done with Heismat.

"Mistress, please," Carisa said, mumbling into her kerchief wadded in both hands. "Heismat's a good man, only the cats killed his whole family. *Please,* mistress."

The rhythmic *ching! ching!* of iron on stone sounded from the courtyard. A mason was carving letters and embellishments for the lintel with strokes of a narrow-bladed adze. Ilna had been angry to learn that money was being spent on what she considered needless ornamentation when a painted sign would do.

She'd checked her facts before she acted, though; someone who got as angry as Ilna did learned to check the facts before acting. Lady Liane bos-Benliman, the fiancée of Prince Garric and, less publicly, the kingdom's spymaster, had ordered the carving. Liane was paying for the job from her own funds.

Ilna still thought the carving was an unnecessary expense, but she'd learned a long time ago that what she thought and what the world thought were likely to be very different. And Ilna also knew that she made mistakes.

Sometimes it felt like she made only mistakes, though of course that wasn't true anyplace but in Ilna's heart. She'd thanked Liane for her generosity.

"Mistress," said Heismat, glaring at his hands. "I didn't mean it, only I come home and there the beast—"

"Cloohe, mistress!" said Bovea. "Little Cloohe, and it's my fault, I'd shut her up when we saw it was getting on and Heismat wasn't home yet, but she must've slipped out while I was dozing."

"I seen the, the cat, and I thunk of my own three that the cats kilt and I couldn't stop myself, mistress," Heismat said brokenly toward his knotted fists. "I'd drunk a bit much. I *knowed* I shoulda kept away, but I wanted to see Carisa and, and I didn't think. I seed the, the kit, and I just flew hot."

"Mistress, it was the drink," Carisa said. "It's my own fault not to keep Cloohe locked up better when it got so late and Heismat not back."

"I've already split the women up and put them with stronger partners, mistress," Winora said in the same dry tone as before. "They're among the best caretakers we have. Though of course I've warned them that you may choose to dismiss or otherwise punish them."

Ilna shrugged. "I'm concerned with preventing a recurrence," she said, "not vengeance. I tried vengeance long enough to determine that it wasn't a satisfactory answer."

How many of the Coerli did I kill after they'd slaughtered Chalcus and Merota? Many, certainly. More than even Merota, who counted any number you pleased without using tellers, could've kept track of.

Ilna smiled. Bovea, who happened to be looking at her, stifled a scream with her knuckles.

"Mistress, I'm sorry," Heismat said, stumbling over the words in his fear. "I swear by the Lady it'll never happen again. *Never!*"

"It were just the drink, mistress," Carisa pleaded. "He's a *good* man."

Ilna looked at the girl; without expression, she'd have said, but from the way Carisa cringed back there must've been something after all. "As men go," Ilna said quietly, "as human beings go, I suppose you're right. Though I'm angry enough as it is, so I don't see what you think to gain by emphasizing the fact."

Carisa blinked. Her hand was over her mouth. "Mistress, I don't understand?" she mumbled.

Ilna grimaced. There were *sheep* with more intelligence than this girl—who was Ilna's age or older in actual years.

Still, Carisa was a good mother to orphans, which is

more than Ilna herself could say. While Ilna was caring for Merota, a cat man with a stone mace had dashed the child's brains out.

"Master Heismat, look at me," Ilna said.

Heismat's face twitched into a rictus. His eyes slanted to Ilna's left, then above her; he knuckled his balled fists.

"Master Heismat," Ilna said. She didn't raise her voice, but her anger sang like a good sword vibrating. "I'm offering you an alternative to being hanged and your body dumped in a rubbish tip, but I assure you that I *will* go the other way if you don't cooperate."

"Mistress, I'm sorry," the laborer said. Tears were dribbling into his sandy beard and the rank stain darkening his gray pantaloons showed that he'd lost control of his bladder, but he was looking directly at Ilna as she'd demanded. "It'll never happen again, I *swear!*"

Ilna raised the pattern she'd knotted. It was quite a subtle piece of work, though no one else in the world would've understood that. Her patterns generally affected everyone who looked at them. That was true here as well, but only Heismat had the *background* to be affected. His memories were the nether millstone against which Ilna's fabric would grind out misery and horror.

She smiled because she was *very* angry, then folded the pattern into itself and placed it in her left sleeve. She'd pick the knots out shortly.

"All right," Ilna said, rising. "Mistress Winora, you'll have business to go over with the nurses."

She looked at Heismat, who was blinking in surprise. "Master Heismat," she said, "you're free to go also."

She considered adding, "And I hope I never see you again," but that would've been pointless and Ilna tried to avoid pointless behavior. Given that all existence struck her as fairly pointless, the whole business was probably an exercise in self-delusion, another thing that she'd have said she tried to avoid. The train of thought made her smile.

"But what happened?" Bovea said. Heismat and Carisa were keeping silent, probably stunned by what they thought was their good luck. "Nothing happened, did it?"

"Bovea, be silent!" Winora snapped as she stepped aside from the door. "You're in trouble enough already, girl."

Ilna stopped and looked back. "Nothing happened unless Master Heismat takes a drink," she said, "which he's promised not to do. If he goes back on his word, he'll experience the slaughter of his family through the eyes of one of the Corl hunters involved. *Every* time he takes a drink."

"But . . . ," said Carisa. Heismat simply sat with his mouth open. "A drink? You don't mean he can't have a mug of ale? Mistress, the water's not safe in Pandah with all the people coming in and the wells so shallow!"

"I mean any drink," Ilna said. "Anything with alcohol in it. As for the water in Pandah, I quite agree. Your friend can find a place where the water's safer, I suppose."

She smiled.

"Or he can die," she added, eyeing the laborer critically. He stared back at her as blankly as a landed fish. "We all die eventually, and there's nothing in Master Heismat's behavior that makes me wish he was an exception."

Carisa lifted her apron and began sobbing into it. Ilna touched the latch lever to open the door; Winora put out her hand.

"Mistress?" Ilna said sharply. She didn't mean the anger; not exactly, at any rate. She very much wanted to be shut of this affair, and Winora was prolonging it.

"Mistress, do you wish me to continue in my position?" the older woman said. She met Ilna's eyes, but she was obviously frightened. *She's terrified!*

"Yes," said Ilna. *Am I as terrible as that?* "You caught the business as quickly as reasonably could be done."

She felt her lips lift in a cold smile again. Ilna *was* that terrible, of course; but not to this woman whose only mistake was that she hadn't been perfect, that she hadn't foreseen *all* the things that could go wrong. A Corl kit had been crippled; worse had happened to a child named Merota because of Ilna's own mistakes.

"And you told me at once instead of trying to hide it," she added. "That was wise."

"Thank you, mistress," Winora said, shuddering in relief. She glanced over her shoulder, drawing Ilna's attention also. Heismat had his arms around Carisa and was trying to murmur reassurance to the blubbering girl. He probably *was* a good man, as humans judged such things.

"It would have been a mercy to have killed him instead," Winora said without emphasis.

"Yes," said Ilna. "But this way he's a better example to others."

She opened the door. Gilla, Mistress Winora's chief assistant, was standing in the hall with her back to the panel. When it opened she jumped aside and said, rattling the words out all together, "Mistress-Ilna-this-gentleman's-come-to-see-you! I told him you'd said not to be disturbed and you wouldn't be, not while I had life and breath!"

"Thank you, Gilla," Ilna said. From the way the plump woman was wheezing, she had very little breath left. Ilna felt a touch of real amusement that didn't reach her lips. Still, it lightened her mood. "Lord Zettin? As a matter of fact, I was hoping to see you today. Can we speak for a moment further after you've finished your business?"

"Mistress," said Zettin, "it's your business that brings me here. I was furious when I learned that my staff had turned you away! Is there some place we can get privacy?"

He looked around. Faces ranging from infants' to that of the aged charwoman ducked away from his angry glance. The building served not only as the foundation's office but as a temporary barracks for orphans who hadn't yet been assigned to a pair of nurses in the community. A high nobleman like Lord Zettin would've been an object of wonder even if he hadn't been wearing a dazzling parcel-gilt cuirass.

"My business doesn't require secrecy," Ilna said, feeling her lips pinch over the words. It offended her that anybody might even think she was trying to hide something. "But we can sit in the garden, and I'm sure—"

She looked at—glared at, she supposed—Gilla.

"—that Mistress Gilla will see that we're not disturbed."

"Yes, mistress!" Gilla said. "Whatever mistress says! Ah, would mistress and her guest like some refreshment while you confer?"

"That won't be necessary," Ilna said firmly, leading her visitor through a reception hall in which six female clerks now worked on the foundation's accounts. In truth her mouth was dry from anger at Heismat, but she didn't want servants interrupting her with carafes and tumblers. This wouldn't take long.

She didn't bother asking what Zettin wanted. If *he* was thirsty, he could wait the length of a brief discussion also.

Lord Zettin was thirty-one or two, quite young for someone in so senior a position. Before the Change, he'd commanded the fleet and the phalanx of pikemen which the oarsmen formed after their ships were drawn up on the beach. He'd gotten the job not only because he was keen and clever—which he was—but because Ornifal's wealthy nobility considered the position a lowly one.

It *had* been lowly when Dukes of Ornifal claimed to be Kings of the Isles but had little control beyond the shores of their island. When Garric became Prince Garric and the real ruler, the fleet and phalanx became important—and Admiral Zettin showed himself to be skilled as well as clever.

The Inner Sea became a continent at the Change and grounded the fleet. Zettin now commanded the kingdom's new scouting forces, another job that established officers didn't want. The scouts were a mixture of hunters, shepherds, and cat men; they moved fast in small units which didn't bother with the baggage train of the regular army. From the scraps of conversation Ilna had heard from Garric, Liane, and Sharina, Zettin was again doing very well.

The house Ilna had taken for her foundation came with a courtyard garden. It had been not only ill-tended but awash in garbage—its most recent occupants had been renegade Coerli, and their immediate predecessors were bands of human pirates.

So far as Ilna was concerned the courtyard could've stayed a wasteland, though of course the garbage had to go. Members of the new staff had made it a priority, though, and the orphans seemed to have thrown themselves into the work. In less than a month the apple trees and the cypress had been pruned, and the planting beds were bright with zinnias, tiny blue asters, and even a late-blooming cardoon. The flowers must've been transplanted; they certainly couldn't have grown so fast from seeds.

Ilna sat on one of the two stone benches framing a small round table. She deliberately chose the seat in the sunlight rather than that shaded by the cypress. Her fingers were picking out and re-forming the pattern they'd knotted for Heismat. She didn't need to be able to strike Zettin with despair or paralyzing fear, but she could. So long as she was in the sunlight, he was certain to see whatever she lifted before his eyes.

"I apologize for my staff, Mistress Ilna," Zettin said, sitting straight up on the opposite bench. *A good thing he isn't in the sun; that breastplate would be blinding.* "They didn't realize who you were and mistakenly thought that they shouldn't interrupt the morning briefing."

Ilna opened her mouth. Before she could get a word out, he continued, "Mistress, I know I've seemed to be arrogant and not to, well, show the courtesy I should. But please believe me, I've always had the kingdom's interests at heart. If I push hard and don't always listen as well as I might, that's the cause. Believe me, I never would've allowed you to be turned away!"

Ilna frowned, not at what the nobleman was saying but because he was saying it to her. *He thinks he's offended me.* That was reasonable; he must by now be used to his pushiness offending people. What *wasn't* reasonable was Zettin bothering to apologize, as though she was powerful enough to hurt him.

"I stopped by on my way here," Ilna said. "I asked for you personally because you're the only person I know in the scouts. I have a favor to ask—"

"Anything, mistress!" Zettin said. "Anything in my power. Just ask!"

"I was trying to," Ilna said, glaring at Zettin. He was a slim, good-looking man who was careful of his appearance; his dark-blond hair and mustache were neatly trimmed, and there were no smudges on his armor.

Zettin's mouth worked on a sour thought. He brushed his left hand over his face and said, "Mistress, my apologies. Again."

She paused, suddenly struck by a vision of the Ilna os-Kenset which this nobleman saw. She *was* powerful. A word to her childhood friends Garric or Sharina would send Lord Zettin off to command a garrison regiment or as envoy to a distant, minor court.

Ilna wouldn't do that, of course; she hadn't been angry, and politics disgusted her anyway. If she *had* felt a need to punish the man, she'd have done it directly as she'd done to others in the past. Quite a few others, now that she considered the matter.

"Yes," Ilna said. "During my travels immediately after the Change, a pair of former hunters named Asion and

Karpos helped me. They're here in Pandah, but they're uncomfortable in cities."

She smiled wryly at herself.

"They're even more uncomfortable than I am," she said. "They'll take reasonable orders. They wouldn't make good soldiers—"

That was a mild a way of putting it; Ilna grimaced. In fact it was mild enough to be a lie if you looked at it closely, and Ilna hated lies.

"—but I think they'd be useful as scouts for you. They . . ."

She paused again and swallowed. She suddenly found herself choking on emotion, an unexpected circumstance and a very uncommon one besides.

"Asion and Karpos," she resumed forcefully, "earned my respect and gratitude. I suppose you take courage for granted, but they also showed cool heads and great skill many times. I'd like them to be in a good situation."

Zettin nodded crisply. "Yes, of course," he said. His eyes drifted toward bees buzzing about the calendula, then met hers again. In a sharper tone he went on, "Can they work with Coerli?"

"Yes, that won't be a problem," Ilna said. "I'll tell them to dispose of the cat-scalp capes they made while they were with me."

Zettin barked a laugh, then looked shocked. He muttered, "Sorry, mistress, I didn't mean to laugh. . . ."

He stopped.

"I *intended* it as a joke," Ilna said tartly. "It's true, of course, but Asion and Karpos have too much judgment for me to need to tell them that."

"It would've been all right," Zettin said, the cool professional again. "The Scouting Corps has all-human units—and all-Coerli units too, for that matter. But the mixed units get better results, and it's one less thing to worry about when assigning billets."

He cleared his throat. "Ah, mistress?" he went on. "You

won't be needing the men's services again yourself? Because I can see to it that they're stationed near Pandah if you'd like."

Ilna shook her head. "I don't know how long I'll be here," she said. "I've already stayed much longer than I cared to."

She heard the bitterness in her voice and scowled; she was showing weakness.

"I don't know what I'll be doing in the future," she said, keeping her tone neutral. "Dying, I suppose, but before then . . ."

She spread her hands, palms up.

"Well, no doubt something will appear."

Zettin appeared for a moment to be glaring at the cardoon's purple face. He drummed the fingers of his left hand on the bench beside him, then turned to Ilna with a look of resolution.

"Mistress," he said firmly. "I'm about to bring up a personal problem, nothing whatever to do with the business of the kingdom. The only reason I dare to mention it is that you implied that you want to get out of Pandah?"

"Go on," Ilna said. Her fingers were taking apart the pattern they'd knotted; when she'd reduced it to loose yarn, she'd again recast it. Weaving gave her something to do while she listened. . . .

"My sister Zussa has married into a wealthy family, but they're in trade," Zettin said. "I want to be very clear about that."

Ilna sniffed. "I suppose my family was in trade also," she said, "before my father, mine and Cashel's, drank up his share of the family mill. Please get to the point, Master Zettin."

She *would* not call him or any man "Lord."

"When her father-in-law died last year," Zettin said, smiling faintly, "her husband Hervir took over the family's spice-importing business. The firm was based in

Valles, but after the Change Hervir put in motion plans
to move it to Pandah. He's, ah, quite a forward-looking
young man."

*Also, he's smart enough to take advice from a well con-
nected brother-in-law,* Ilna thought.

Zettin had noticed the deliberate slight of "Master,"
and had been amused by it. Before this conversation she
would've said she didn't care for Zettin particularly, putting him in the same category as all but a handful of the
people she knew. To Ilna's surprise, the fellow was edging toward that select handful.

"Hervir heard that a source of saffron had appeared
on the north coast of Blaise since the Change," Zettin
said. "As you probably know, in the past saffron came
only from two or three valleys in the mountains of Seres.
Saffron from Blaise could come up the New River almost directly to Pandah."

"Go on," Ilna said. It was simpler to be politely non-
committal than to snarl that *of course* a peasant from
Barca's Hamlet knew nothing about a spice so expensive
that it was weighed out with carob seeds, just like jewels.

"Hervir had been planning to set up the new headquarters in Pandah himself, but when he heard about this
opportunity, well . . ." Zettin shrugged. "Hervir and I
haven't always seen eye-to-eye."

He flashed Ilna a wan smile that made him look unexpectedly human. Zettin usually had points sticking out
in all directions; everything he said or did seemed to be
a way of getting advantage. For the first time in the two
years since Ilna met him, that wasn't the case.

"Or perhaps," he said, "we do see eye-to-eye—we're
too much alike to be friends. Regardless, I respect Hervir whether or not I like him. He sent Zussa here to prepare the new headquarters and set off himself to Blaise
with his secretary, six guards, and a belt of money. He
planned to buy a riverboat on Blaise and sail down to
Pandah with the saffron."

Zettin paused, looking across the table. Because something was obviously expected of her, Ilna said, "Go on," again.

This time the pattern her fingers were knotting wasn't a weapon. The lines in yarn were a reflection of the universe, though Ilna herself was never conscious of their meaning until she concentrated on what her fingers had woven without her conscious mind's control.

"Two days ago the secretary and guards arrived in Pandah," Zettin said. "Hervir wasn't with them, nor the money either. The secretary—his name's Ingens and he's been seven years with the house, a perfectly reliable man Zussa says—Ingens says that Hervir went off alone at night with the chest. He was meeting a man with the saffron, supposedly. He never came back."

Zettin spread his hands with a grimace. "Now," he said, "I don't want you to think that I believe in fortune-tellers, but Madame Raciana, Hervir's mother, does. She went to a fellow, a charlatan I'm sure, who swears that Hervir was spirited off by wizardry. She's prodding Zussa to get one of my wizard friends in the court—"

He grimaced apologetically. "I'm sorry," he said, "but that's what they think. One of my wizard friends to rescue her son. And Zussa, I'm sorry to say, is making my life a misery until I act. Mistress, I know you're not a wizard, but, well, you have that reputation."

He paused with a cautious look on his face. *To see how I'm taking that,* Ilna realized. The statement was true, so she certainly wasn't going to snarl at Zettin for what he'd said. And it was possible that the belief that Ilna os-Kenset was a wizard also was true. Not the way Tenoctris was, or the cat woman Rasile; but there were things Ilna did that only wizards could do, and she did some things that even wizards could not.

"Go on," she said aloud.

"If you could come with me and tell Raciana that there's no wizard's work involved, that Hervir was knocked on

the head and robbed," Zettin said earnestly, "then she'll
let me take care of the business the way it should be. I'll
send a troop of my scouts under a good officer up to
where Hervir disappeared. They'll get to the bottom of
the trouble, I'll warrant."

"I'll certainly go with you," Ilna said, rising. She began to reduce the oracle to short lengths of twine again.
"I'd like to talk to this secretary."

She smiled coldly at the nobleman as he rose with her.
She could see her reflection in the breastplate, distorted
across the gilded images of sea gods cavorting.

"But I won't tell Madame Raciana that her fortune-
teller is wrong," Ilna said, "because to my surprise that
doesn't seem to be true. Master Hervir really was taken
by wizardry . . . and I think I may have found a sufficient
reason to leave Pandah."

LIANE SAT IN the roof garden, her back to the west so
that the sun fell over her shoulder onto the *Books of
Changes* from which she was reading to Garric. She
turned a page.

" 'Piety lies conquered,' " she continued. Her voice was
like polished amber, smooth and soft and golden. " 'Starry
Justice leaves the bloody earth for the far reaches of the
heavens.' "

She paused and grinned at Garric. "If Pendill's to be
believed," she said, "things were as bad by the end of the
First Age as they are now. Perhaps we should feel en-
couraged that they haven't gotten even worse?"

Garric laughed. He sat in the tiny grape arbor; Liane
had moved a wicker bench for better light, but they were
both out of the direct sight of everyone else in—well, in
the whole world. That was unusual for anyone who lived
in society, and almost unheard of for a prince and his
consort in a palace full of servants, office-holders, and
courtiers.

"I think we've improved from that," he said, luxuriating in the fact that he wasn't for these few moments being ruler of a kingdom under threat. "Piety hasn't given up the fight yet, and as for Justice—I was a peasant, and a peasant'll choose the king's law any day over the local squire's justice. I think the kingdom's moving pretty well in the direction of having a rule of law, though I don't pretend to've convinced everybody."

"If you're dealing with human beings," said King Carus, the ghost in Garric's mind, *"you won't convince everybody that the sun rises in the east. And there's no few of 'em who'll try to brain you if you won't agree that it really rises in the west."*

Garric chuckled in unison with his ancient ancestor. Carus had been the last ruler of the Old Kingdom; he'd spent his reign battling usurpers as well the monsters which entered the waking world as wizardry rose to its thousand-year peak. In the end a wizard had destroyed both Carus and himself, had destroyed the Old Kingdom as well, and had very nearly destroyed mankind.

"The thing is, lad . . . ," Carus said. Garric saw the ancient king as a man of forty or so, leaning on the battlements of a half-glimpsed tower. He wore a bright blue tunic and red breeches more vivid than the roses clinging to the masonry. *"I was as quick to knock heads as the next fellow. Quicker, I dare say, and certainly better at it. I'd have brought the kingdom down myself without any wizard's help. None of which I understood until I saw you ruling the right way, of course."*

Garric's lips pursed as he considered the matter. Liane knew about the ghost in his mind, but she wasn't party to their silent conversations. Therefore he said aloud, "You can't rule with a sword alone. But until the Golden Age returns, you can't rule without a sword either. I'm very fortunate in having an ancestor who was the greatest warrior of . . ."

He paused again for thought. Carus grinned, and

Garric's grin echoed the ghost's. "The greatest warrior ever, I think," he said aloud.

"It does seem," said Liane, closing the book, "that there's more peace if everyone's convinced that Prince Garric and the royal army will destroy anybody who breaks that peace."

She reached down for the portable desk in which she kept current files but straightened again without touching it; the details of government could wait for the time being. "That's particularly true of the Coerli. I'm frankly amazed that the integration of them into the kingdom has been so smooth."

"The Coerli aren't comfortable unless they're in a hierarchy, but once they've got one they'll live with it even if they're not on top," Garric said, smiling faintly. "There's a lot of human beings the same way. Just about every professional soldier in this army, for example."

Liane set Pendill down, though she didn't open the traveling desk to put the book away properly. "I'm still glad it worked this way," she said. "If it hadn't, we would've had to wipe the Coerli out."

She stepped into the arbor and settled beside Garric. It was a muggy day, but her soft warmth was welcome.

"You said something about a sea serpent in the south?" Garric said. It disturbed him to realize that he couldn't completely relax anymore, not when there was still work to be done. There was always work for a prince to do. . . .

"In Telut," Liane said. She would've risen to get the report covering the matter from her desk; Garric tightened his arm slightly to keep her where she was; she relaxed against him again.

Liane used her notebooks as props, but she normally didn't bother to open them while discussing the matters they contained. Though the archives of the kingdom's intelligence service were well indexed and staffed by skilled clerks, Liane really ran it out of her head.

Her father had been, among other things, a successful

merchant. She'd used his contacts and business training to weave a web of spies through the Isles. That was now as necessary as the royal army, but it worked only because Liane, demure and cultured and beautiful, sat like a spider at its center.

"Refugees from the city of Ombis on Telut," she said slowly, wriggling against him, "said an army, an armed rabble under a chief calling himself Captain Archas, summoned the city to surrender. They closed the gates."

Garric gently rubbed the back of Liane's neck, massaging the sudden tension from it. Her voice softer again, she continued, "Two of the refugees swore they saw Archas call a huge serpent out of the sea. But Ombis hasn't been within ten miles of the coast since the Change."

"What do your own agents say?" Garric said, more to show he'd been listening than because he didn't think Liane would get to that question on her own.

"They haven't reported," she said. "A Serian who crossed the Seaway says that Ombis was completely destroyed, however."

"We'll take care of it," Garric said calmly. He'd learned in childhood that keeping his tone calm was more important than what you said. That insight was even more valuable when dealing with humans than it had been with sheep. "I don't know how yet but we will, whether it's real or a hallucination. We have Tenoctris and the army and anything else it might take. We have the whole kingdom's resources. Evil *won't* win."

"No, Garric," Liane whispered. "It won't."

After a moment she said, "When we were studying Old Kingdom epics at Mistress Gudea's Academy, I thought they were terribly boring. I didn't want to *read* about adventure, I wanted to be off with my father visiting distant places and sailing even beyond the Isles themselves. Now . . . sometimes I think I'd like to be a scholar and never see anything wonderful except after it'd been written down in a book."

"You wouldn't like it, dear," Garric said.

"For a little while, I think I might like it," Liane said, smiling. "But it doesn't matter. I'm glad I can be useful to the kingdom, and to you."

A discussion, low-voiced but heated, broke out on the third-story terrace. The outside staircase there was the only way up to the roof garden, and the platoon of Blood Eagles on guard was making certain that Prince Garric wasn't disturbed until he told them different.

"That fellow arguing," King Carus said with the grin of a man who'd learned to find humor in places that civilians generally didn't, *"is going to be lucky if he doesn't wind up back in the street without needing to take the stairs."*

"Starshine!" an unfamiliar voice shouted. "Starshine!"

Liane jumped to her feet. "Garric, he's one of mine! I'm sorry, I have to see him!"

It was good that she'd moved, because otherwise Garric would've flung her aside on his way to the parapet of plaster over wickerwork. A man wearing a light cloak struggled in the arms of two Blood Eagles. He'd lost his broad leather hat, and the disarranged cloak let the bloodstain on his dull blue tunic show.

"Send him up!" Garric called to the guards. He was already belting on the sword that he'd leaned against a pot holding a forsythia. Liane had unlatched her traveling desk and was setting it up.

"You got a good one there, lad," Carus said. *"She'll have to change her emergency password now, though."*

Chapter

2

WHEN THEY REALIZED how bad the agent's condition was, Garric went down to the terrace and sent a Blood Eagle off to fetch a surgeon. By the time he returned to the roof, Liane had settled the man on the bench with his head and torso lifted. She was bathing the wound with wine from the carafe set to cool in a water pot, dark with evaporation through the coarse earthenware.

"His name's Aberus," she said quietly. "He's from District Three, the South."

"Palomir," Aberus muttered. His eyes were closed. When Garric looked closely he could see the fellow was in his mid-twenties, but he seemed thirty years older from any distance.

"That's the pain," Carus said with the dispassionate precision of a man who'd been in pain many times and who'd learned to function no matter how bad it was. *"He'll lose the arm, I shouldn't wonder."*

"The Empire of Palomir, they call it," Aberus said, his voice stronger though he kept his eyes closed. "But Palomir's a ruin. There's acres and acres of crystal buildings, but they're falling to pieces and there aren't many people left. A few hundred. There's tenements in Erdin with more people than the whole city has."

The carafe had been wrapped in napkins. Liane had used one to mop the wound; now she pulled the other out of the throat of the carafe and squeezed wine from the cloth into the corner of the agent's upturned mouth. He slurped greedily.

"Bless you, milady," he said. "Oh, may the Lady bless you."

His breath caught. "Those bloody *rats*," he squealed. "Oh, by the Lady. But I got away. I got away, didn't I?"

"You're safe in Pandah, Aberus," Liane said. "Tell us about Palomir. Tell us what happened to you."

"They were praying in the main temple every night, all the citizens of Palomir," Aberus said. He spoke in a light, quick patter like a moth's wings beating against the inside of a lamp chimney. "And I thought, nothing surprising, lots of people praying since the Change, you know. And they didn't let strangers into the ceremonies, but I never spent a farthing on incense for the gods anyhow, what do I care about what they do in the temple? And I was coming back to report, only . . . only . . ."

He paused, breathing deeply. His face had gone pale under the tan; the resulting color was dirty yellow like that of a cheese rind. Liane sponged more wine between his lips. His throat worked spasmodically, then managed to swallow.

"I was coming back," Aberus said, "but I thought instead of coming straight back to Pandah, I'd see if the road was open to Cordin. I used to know a girl in Ragos and she'd married, you know, but that was before. A lot could've happened, and anyway . . . So I went out the west road, and I went out at night while they were all at the temple because they said there were monsters in the jungle west of the city and they wouldn't let anybody go that way for their own safety."

Feet banged up the wooden steps from the terrace. A Blood Eagle peeked over the parapet and said with a worried expression, "Your Highness, there's a doctor here. Do you want . . . ?"

"Yes, by the Shepherd, send him up!" Garric said. Everybody was afraid of offending Prince Garric by doing the wrong thing. They constantly asked for his approval instead of simply doing what he'd said to do in the first place.

He couldn't remember a single epic in which the king or city-founding hero had that problem. *Maybe I should retire and write an epic of my own in seclusion. . . .*

The thought was so close to what Liane had said a moment ago that Garric barked a laugh. Neither of them were going to retire while the kingdom needed them, though; or anyway, needed somebody to do the jobs they were doing well at present.

"I kept off the main road for the first half mile or so," Aberus said. He hadn't opened his eyes since he collapsed on the bench. "I cut through the orchards mostly. I thought there might be guard posts, but there wasn't any so I got back on the road. Funny not to have guards if they were really worried about monsters in the jungle, but I hadn't believed about the monsters anyway."

Daciano, the staff surgeon of the Blood Eagles, entered the garden with his pair of young female assistants. "Are you all right, Your Highness?" he asked.

"This is the man you were called for," said Garric peevishly. He gestured toward Aberus, though the surgeon should've been able to see the fellow's condition already.

"And I'll get to him," Daciano said, smiling pleasantly at Garric as he stepped into the arbor, "now that I know Your Highness is all right."

The ghost of Carus chuckled. *"He's gotten more from serving with the Blood Eagles than just experience stitching up holes in people,"* he said.

That was quite true. Lord Attaper commanded the bodyguard regiment. He'd made it clear to his troops that if they kept safe the people they were guarding, he'd stand between them and anybody who complained about the way they went about their job—most certainly including Prince Garric himself.

The Blood Eagles' rigid priorities frequently exasperated Garric, but he'd finally decided that a real craftsman was always going to put his task first. He couldn't very well object to that when he was pretty much the same way himself.

"I wasn't far along the road before I heard a lot of people coming the other way," Aberus said. Daciano had eased Liane aside, but he knelt to look at the agent before touching him. "I thought people, anyhow. Only some of them were, but I didn't know that. So I got off the road again and watched."

Daciano murmured to his assistants. One began to dab the wound with a sponge soaked in sour wine, while the other handed the surgeon a pair of tweezers. They were bronze with silver inlays, and the knob at the end was a finely modeled sheep's head. Despite the tweezers' decoration, they were a fully functional instrument with which Daciano began to clear threads, vegetable debris, and clots of dried blood.

Aberus whimpered deep in his throat, but then he resumed, "They came by, about a hundred of them. They didn't carry lanterns but there was a half-moon. Where trees didn't shade the road, I could see them clear. Mostly they were prisoners, neck-roped to poles by tens. They were all ages, grouped just by how tall they were because of the poles. Two coffles were kids but with a short woman in front to set the pace. Which was a shuffle, that's all it could be."

Garric could see bone now that the cut was clear. Aberus was a brave man beyond question, but even so it seemed remarkable he hadn't screamed and fainted; perhaps there was more than vinegar in the assistant's sponge.

"The guards were rats," Aberus said. "I couldn't mistake it, I was so close. I could smell them. I don't know why they didn't smell me; I could see their noses twitching, twitch twitch twitch all the time. Maybe because of the prisoners. There were plenty humans around. They were rats, only they were as tall as men. Tall as women anyway, and they had swords."

Daciano began trimming the edges of the wound with

a pair of shears. Like the tweezers, they were bronze instead of steel. The assistant with the satchel of tools held another pair ready, and a third was laid out with a range of scalpels and probes on the leather pad at her side.

"Alongside there was a man who wasn't tied," Aberus said. "He was riding, but he was on an ox instead of a horse or mule. Slow as the prisoners could go, it didn't matter; an ox was fast enough to keep up. A sheep could've kept—*oh!*"

The surgeon growled at the woman with the sponge; she immediately reversed it and squeezed so that fluid dripped along the blade of the shears. When Daciano resumed his careful cutting, the assistant traded the sponge she'd been using for another of those soaking in a shallow bowl.

"I knew the fellow, I'd talked to him when I arrived," Aberus said. His voice was thin; he wasn't whispering, but he didn't have enough breath to give power to the words. "He was a junior priest named Salmson. The high priest was Nivers, but him I only saw on a balcony of his palace. It was all falling to pieces and he didn't seem in much better shape. And Salmson was talking to the prisoners. He had a skin of wine with him, and I think he'd drunk a lot from it already."

Daciano set down his shears and took the needle his assistant held out in her left hand. It was strung with a glistening strand of gut. The wound looked horrible, worse than it would've done when it was curtained by a wash of blood.

"Salmson was shouting, 'The gods have returned,'" Aberus said. "I told you, he sounded drunk. He said, 'You are honored to be among the first subjects of Franca and His siblings Fallin and Hili. You will help prepare the way for them to rule the whole world. Praise Franca whom your blood serves!'"

The surgeon began sewing, starting deep in the muscle instead of at the lips. The assistant continued to dab with her sponge, but now she held a linen cord ready to place where it could drain the wound.

"The prisoners didn't seem to be listening," Aberus said. "They were walking dead; I don't know how far they'd come already. They're really dead now, I suppose. Well, everybody dies, don't we, Lady?"

Garric wasn't sure whether the agent was praying or speaking to Liane. Of course he might be delirious and think that Liane *was* the Lady. It didn't prevent him from reporting, however.

"One of them saw me," Aberus said. "Or scented me, maybe it was that finally. It squealed just like a rat and jumped. I wasn't expecting it but I was ready, I'm always ready. I put my dagger through its throat and ran, but others came after me. I don't know how many, but there were two more I killed; maybe the rest turned back. They cut me, I couldn't help that, but I kept on going. All the way here, I kept going. All the way."

Daciano was on the upper layer of stitches now, closing the wound. Aberus' forehead was beaded with sweat, but he didn't flinch from the needle. The surgeon was impassive, but his assistants' faces were warm with compassion.

"Franca and His siblings will rule the world!" the agent shouted. Was he quoting or had he come to believe that himself?

"I'm calling an immediate council meeting," Garric said to Liane. "I'll need you."

"Of course," she said. To Daciano she added, "Do whatever's possible for him, regardless of cost. I'll pay for it."

"No," said Garric. He took the handle of the traveling desk in his left hand rather than leave it for Liane to carry. "The kingdom will pay."

"The Gods of Palomir rule all!" Aberus cried.

"Not while *I* live!" muttered Garric, stepping onto the staircase.

Which of course didn't, he knew, mean that it wouldn't happen.

* * *

CASHEL HAD NOTICED long since that the actual words a wizard chanted didn't seem to matter. It was the rhythms they got into that told you what they were doing.

Rasile had laid a pattern of yarrow stalks around the floor of the tower. She sat in the center of it, making sounds that were nothing like the words of power Tenoctris used. They weren't anything like the cat men's ordinary speech, either. Even so, Cashel would've known what was going on even if he hadn't been able to watch her.

The air flickered. It looked a bit like heat lightning, but the only clouds today were horsetails in the high heavens. It must've been the sky itself, twisted by Rasile's power so that sunlight didn't slip through it the way it ought to.

A deafening crackle spread outward from the star pattern. Cashel wasn't sure it was really a sound. It wasn't his ears or even the soles of his feet that noticed; it was more something that prickled inside his head. *The whole world's breaking apart around us!* Spreading his legs a little wider on the tower's floor and gripping his staff midway to either side of the balance, he waited to deal with whatever happened next.

Cashel's feet didn't move. The air cleared. He hadn't known that he and the wizard were in a smoky gleam until it was gone again. They were right where they had been, but the tower was gone and the city was gone. He and Rasile were in the midst of armed civilians and a few soldiers, looking from stone battlements toward a ragtag army on the plains below.

"Begone, you thieves and vagabonds!" cried a man not far from Cashel. He was using a megaphone. The three fellows next to him were older, fatter, and wore gold chains for ornament, so the herald was probably speaking their words. "If you're not gone in three minutes by the sand glass, we'll shoot you all down like the dogs you are!"

They were on top of a gatehouse. There was a socket where a catapult was probably meant to pivot, but there wasn't one in place now. Several soldiers had bows, though, and the folks below were only a furlong away. That was in range of a good bowman.

Rasile was getting to her feet. Cashel put out his arm for her to grab. A man wearing a molded breastplate meant for somebody much thinner strode through them on his way to the group around the herald. Cashel didn't feel the contact, and it didn't seem like the local fellow had either.

"I think we're seeing something that occurred recently," Rasile said. Her tongue clucked against the side of her long jaw in a Corl equivalent of a grin. "Or perhaps something that will occur shortly. I do not know *where* it is, however."

Cashel thought about the way the people around couldn't see or touch him and Rasile, but there wasn't any point in talking about something that the wizard knew a lot better than he did. He said, "We're on Ombis on Telut, I think. I've never been here, but the colors the servants of the envoys from there wore in Valles are the same as—"

He pointed to the cloth hanging down from the herald's megaphone. It was orange around the edges and slashed green on black inside the border.

"—that is."

Cashel noticed shapes and patterns without having to think about them. Sheep might all look alike to city folk, but a shepherd knows each of his flock by name even if he can't count above ten without a tally stick. Heraldry was nothing at all to somebody tuned to little differences in the brown/black/gray/white markings of Haft sheep.

"The fellow in the green robe there," he said as the tallest of the three men in fancy dress turned so Cashel could see his face, "he's the one who was the envoy himself last spring."

There were folks on the wall as far around as Cashel could see from the gate tower. The city wall was only twice his height—the tower was half that again—but that was still a huge advantage.

The defenders weren't well armed. Besides the soldiers, some of the better-dressed civilians had swords and maybe even metal armor, but the rest carried spears of a simple pattern that'd probably come from the city armory. They were in leather caps and breastplates.

That was probably good enough, though, because the attackers outside the walls were just what the herald had called them: vagabonds and thieves. Some were armed with swords as good as those of Ornifal nobles. The gold inlays and ivory hilts didn't mean much in a fight, but Cashel knew that fancy touches like those were often put on the best steel by the best craftsmen.

But there weren't many with swords, and even those few didn't go in much for armor. Some carried boat pikes, long-shafted weapons with a hook below the point to catch rigging or the rail of a ship trying to keep clear. Cashel guessed they were pirates. Even without better weapons, it would've looked hard for the city if the whole army had been that sort.

But all beyond a couple double handsful of pirates were escaped slaves, farm laborers, and the sort of thing you'd find if you emptied out prisons. Some had been branded or were missing hands. They had clubs, pitchforks, and poles with a knife tied to the end.

And there were women. Cashel knew women could fight: he'd seen Sharina joint enemies with her Pewle knife, and even Garric's delicate Lady Liane carried a blade that could—and had—cut deep enough to open the big blood vessels. Some of the slatterns below would be dangerous in an alley or a crowded taproom.

But they weren't going to batter through stone walls. There were plenty of women on the walls too, ready to throw cobblestones and pour down boiling water. Ombis shouldn't have had anything to fear from its attackers—

But Cashel knew that Rasile wouldn't be here unless there was more going on than they'd seen thus far. His hands polished his quarterstaff. He guessed that if the city folk passed through him without touching, so would a pirate sword; but just in case.

"That's funny," Cashel said to Rasile. He pointed. "Those people down there don't have any more ranks than a flock of sheep would, but they're making sure to leave a big space back from the chief."

The leader of the pirates was a tall man who'd braided scraps of cloth-of-gold into his blond beard. He was husky too, though not as big as Cashel; there weren't many people who were as big as Cashel. He had two long swords and many daggers dangling from his crossbelts, but they were all in their scabbards while he lifted something small and shiny in his left hand.

A city elder turned to a soldier with a bow. When he moved, his gold chains clanked. "Shoot him!" he ordered imperiously.

"I'd waste an arrow from here," the soldier said. He was frowning toward the pirates instead of meeting the eyes of the elder.

"I'm ordering you to shoot, Sister take you!" the elder shouted. "I want him to stop what he's doing!"

"I got twelve arrows," the soldier said. "I'm going to keep them for better targets than that. It's our asses too, remember."

Another soldier turned and said loudly, "If you want to cashier us now because we don't jump through silly hoops for you, Master Comian, you do that and we'll be out the back gate before you finish the words. Otherwise, pipe down and let us get on with the business of keeping these pirates on the other side of the walls."

The pirate chief was talking, or anyway his lips were

moving. He wasn't shouting to the city, though. It didn't seem to Cashel that the fellow was talking loud enough that anybody at all could hear him. His men gave him a wide berth; maybe they had more confidence in the defenders' archery than the soldiers themselves did.

"There!" said Rasile. Disconcertingly, she balanced on her right foot and scratched herself in the middle of the back with her left; she'd become a great deal more limber than she'd been when Sharina brought her to her first council meeting. "*That* must be why I was drawn here."

"That" was the shimmer of light beside the pirate chief. It reminded Cashel of the way the sun glanced off the face of an iceberg, bright and cold and as thin as the surface of a mirror.

A curved hugeness the color of layered shale squirmed out of the air. "A Worm," Rasile said. Her nose wrinkled. "Perhaps *the* Worm which devoured all its siblings after they had scoured clean their world."

Sometimes Cashel could see beyond the creature to a waste of shingle and sluggish gray water. Violet cracklings in that background suggested momentary shapes, but they were the shapes of nightmare. The Worm shifted forward.

Cashel pursed his lips. He had trouble at first figuring how big the creature was; it was out of scale with everything. Its gray body was banded the way an earthworm is, but the mouth was nothing like. It didn't squirm like a snake. The front of the body stretched forward, stopped, and then the back hitched up to join it.

The creature loomed higher in the air than Cashel could've reached with his staff from where he stood on top of the gatehouse. He couldn't guess how long it was; the second time it hunched forward brought its head to spitting distance of the wall, but the body still trailed back to the window in the air beside where the pirate chief was standing.

Cashel stepped in front of the wizard by reflex: there was danger, so he put himself between it and who he was looking out for. Normally he'd have started his quarter-staff spinning but there was too many people around, he didn't have *space*. He said, "Rasile, ought we to—"

Rasile squalled something, a word rather than a full incantation. It was enough to shift her and Cashel up to the height of a tall tree in a dazzle of scarlet wizardlight. Most of the civilians were scattering from the walls and the gatehouse in front of the creature, but the soldiers didn't run and the city elders didn't either.

The fellow in the too-small breastplate drew a sword from which rust had recently been polished. He screamed, "Shoot it! Shoot it!" to the soldiers. That wasn't very useful, Cashel guessed, but neither would anything else have been.

The archers were already shooting as fast as they could. The arrows were too small to do real harm to something the size of the Worm, and they sparkled off the sides anyway. The creature might've been a gray granite tower sliding toward Ombis on its side.

Was it really alive? It moved, but so would a flow of lava.

The Worm's mouth opened in a circle rimmed with teeth all around. The man in the undersized breastplate slashed toward it, though the tip of his sword passed through empty air. Cashel wondered if the fellow had his eyes closed.

Black smoke belched from the Worm's throat, coating men and stones alike. The elder's flesh shriveled and he dropped his sword. The silvered quillons had turned black and the blade glowed cherry red.

The Worm extended a long, ivory tusk and shoved forward the way water fills a millrace. The gatehouse burst inward. The jaws folded closed, swallowing masonry and the doors of iron-bound oak alike. Powdered rock puffed skyward.

The citizens of Ombis ran in shrieking terror, all but a few who stood transfixed on the battlements. The Worm hunched again, but this time its foreparts lifted high enough that Cashel brought his staff into a posture of defense again. The creature twisted and slammed down, flattening a section of the wall.

The Worm writhed sideways, grinding a swath of buildings into dust and splinters. Cashel thought he heard screams, but his mind might've been inventing them. People had run into those doorways when the Worm lurched toward the walls, some of them women clutching infants, but he doubted he could really hear their despair over the crashing ruin of the houses where they'd tried to shelter.

The Worm gathered itself to drive deeper into the city. Ombis had no citadel; it had trusted to the strength of its outer walls. Because the city was built up to three and four stories rather than sprawling, the circuit was modest in comparison with the population available to defend it. All order and discipline had vanished when the Worm engulfed the gateway, and with them was gone any hope of defense.

The pirate chief lowered the object in his hand; he shouted something also. Cashel couldn't hear sound, let alone the word itself, over the ripping destruction.

The creature's massive curves froze. Purple radiance gathered over its body, covering it the way fungus might cocoon a dead caterpillar. The Worm twitched once more and, twitching, vanished.

Only rubble remained of half a furlong of the walls, and not much of that. The creature's weight and iron-hard hide had crushed to powder ashlars which would've resisted battering rams for a week.

Shrieking in savage triumph, the pirates swept toward the breach in the walls. The Worm's progress had plowed a trench in the soil. Looking down, Cashel saw that the city walls had extended some distance beneath the surface, but the massive foundation courses had gone down the creature's maw as surely as the lighter masonry of the visible portion.

A soldier lay in the street where the Worm's impact had flung him. He'd been killed by the black smoke; his clothes were rotting and his upturned face had been eaten away to the bone.

Female pirates were entering with the men. A bare-breasted redhead knelt to lift the hand of a citizen whose lower legs had been trapped by the collapse of a building. For a moment Cashel thought she was helping the fellow; then light flashed on her knife as she cut off his fingers to get the rings.

Instead of rushing into the city immediately, the pirate chief stood with his head bowed, then put his talisman away in a silk neck pouch. Finally he drew his swords and went through the breach. Even now he was sauntering instead of running.

Cashel looked at Rasile. He didn't say anything. The wizard yowled a phrase and swept her right hand like she was wiping something out of the air. She and Cashel were back in brilliant sunlight on top of the watchtower in Pandah.

The yarrow stalks were scattered where Rasile's gesture had flung them. The cat woman sprawled on the flagstones. She'd been keenly alert while they stood where she'd transported them, but now her body demanded to be paid for that effort.

Cashel didn't have a pillow or a rolled cloak to put down, so he cradled her head with his left hand. She shuddered, then opened her eyes and looked at him. She didn't try to get up yet.

"I've seen that sort of thing happen to cities before," Cashel said. "I'll watch it again if I have to, but *only* if I have to. And I figured we'd pretty much seen all we needed to see this time."

"Yes, we've seen enough," Rasile said, rubbing her ear against Cashel's palm. "We've seen things I never imagined to see, though he seems to have the Worm under control. He's not a wizard, you know, but he has a wizard aiding him. A wizard or worse."

"Master Cashel?" called an unfamiliar voice from the stairwell. Cashel hadn't barred the trapdoor giving onto the parapet, but the person speaking from the stairs didn't presume to lift the panel. "Prince Garric sends you his compliments and hopes you and Lady Rasile can join him for a council meeting at your earliest convenience."

Rasile gathered her limbs under her with a smooth motion, but she didn't try to stand. Cashel glanced at her, then shifted to open the door with the left hand which the wizard no longer needed. The quarterstaff was in his right, and he wasn't in any mood to put it down after the scene he'd just watched.

"We'll come as quick as we can," he said to the messenger.

"Cashel, I will not be able to walk for a time, I'm afraid," Rasile said; she gave a little growl of frustration deep in her throat. She still hadn't tried to get up.

"Shall I call for a carriage, master?" the messenger said. He was one of the fellows Liane kept around her, not exactly palace staff.

"It wouldn't do any good, but thanks," Cashel said. "Horses don't, ah, like the smell of cat men. I'll carry her myself when she's ready to go."

Rasile started to rise. Cashel had been squatting. He set his left arm under her thighs and scooped her up instead of simply helping her.

"Can you do that, master?" the messenger said. "It's a mile to the palace, you know."

"It's no trouble," said Cashel, grinning in a mixture of confidence and quiet pride.

It wouldn't be hard at all. The Coerli were lighter built than people, and Rasile was frail even of her own kind.

Besides, it made him feel good. Cashel or-Kenset didn't

have any proper place in the council of smart, educated people, but he could look out for things. Since there weren't any sheep around, he'd look out for a Corl wizard.

SHARINA HEARD A clash of hobnails. The guards lounging outside the door to Tenoctris' burrow were bringing themselves upright to receive visitors. She was already turning when Captain Ascor called, "All right, Colemno, what's your hurry this time? The princess or Lady Tenoctris?"

Blood Eagle officers were generally recruited from the minor nobility, so they were capable of ceremonial formality when they thought it was necessary. On the other hand, even the officers—the enlisted men entered the regiment solely because of proven skill and courage in battle; they were *not* going to use proper forms of address—were likely to be informal on most occasions. Ascor obviously knew the courier.

"Both, Ascor," Colemno said. Sharina, stepping out the door, recognized the fellow as a member of Liane's staff. Seeing her, he bowed and continued, "Your Highness, Prince Garric has requested that you and Lady Tenoctris—"

Sharina felt the wizard beside her now in the doorway.

"—join him in his suite for an emergency council meeting."

"What's the emergency, Master Colemno?" Tenoctris said. She wasn't unpleasant about it, but she didn't sugarcoat the demand with flourishes like "if you please" or "if I may ask."

The courier glanced at Ascor and his squad, but that was reflex. Like the Blood Eagles, Liane's entourage took official rules as things you obeyed if they didn't get in the way of doing your job.

"Milady," Colemno said, "all I know is there's something happening in Palomir, the Empire of Palomir. One of the outside men named Aberus came in cut up pretty bad. I don't know what he said, but the prince heard it and didn't waste any time sending us to find you all."

"We're close to the palace here," Tenoctris said, to Sharina but without trying to prevent Colemno and the guards from overhearing. "Let me take a moment to learn more now. I think that'll be more useful than waiting for others to arrive from the ends of the city."

"Yes," Sharina said. She nodded to Colemno and the guards, saying, "We'll be with you shortly," before following Tenoctris into her room.

Sharina shut the door out of courtesy rather than because she was concerned about what the men might see. Wizardry made most people uncomfortable, even men as brave as those in the corridor. It was easier for them to ignore what was going on if a door panel stood between them and the incantations.

A slab of rock leaned against the room's back wall. Until Tenoctris stepped to it, Sharina had assumed it *was* the back wall. She looked carefully, shifting to the side to see the edge, and found that it was patterned chalcedony. The individual layers were hair-fine, and the whole assemblage was no more than an inch thick.

It'd make a very delicate cameo, Sharina thought, *though what it's doing here—*

"*Torial boichua knophi!*" Tenoctris said, and snapped the fingers of her left hand. Her now-youthful face wore a broad smile. Greater power hadn't made Tenoctris boastful or a show-off, but she took obvious delight in now being able to do things which most wizards could not.

Given that greater power hadn't cost Tenoctris the understanding and subtlety of touch that had set her above other wizards in the past, Sharina was delighted as well. The forces of good needed the most powerful allies they could get.

At the pop of the wizard's fingers, the brown outer layer of chalcedony eroded as though it were being carved by demons. What had been undifferentiated rock was suddenly a relief map on which threads of rivers twisted in all directions toward the surrounding sea.

Before Sharina could take it in, Tenoctris called *"Zonchar!"* with another snap of her fingers; the map of a continent became the chart of a city's streets. The city shown was huge, but its ragged edges seemed to be dissolving in the mass of encroaching vegetation.

"Ouk merioth!" Tenoctris said. Blue wizardlight, as brilliant as lightning in the darkened room, sizzled across the cameo like a stage curtain. When it passed, Sharina was looking down at a city from the angle of the sun an hour before setting. Crystal towers, halls, and bridges leaping from structure to structure gleamed in orange light.

Sharina's breath caught. It was splendid, but it was a splendid ruin. Jagged streaks traced their way to the ground from lightning-shattered pinnacles, roofs and walls were reduced to a carpet of jeweled dust where wind had toppled a tree toward the buildings, and saplings sprouted from cracks in the crystal streets.

"Is this Palomir?" Sharina asked.

"It's Palomir as it was three months ago," Tenoctris said. Her tone was distracted and she didn't take her eyes from the cameo for several silent moments.

She turned. "Sharina?" she said. "I, well, I want to try some other techniques to get a better grasp of the situation. This—"

Tenoctris gestured toward the cameo and its scene of ruin.

"—should be sufficient. I've prepared the sheet of quartz to create a very powerful tool, but it appears—"

She smiled with humor of a sort.

"—that it isn't a powerful *enough* tool. I have others, but they'll take a little time to bring to bear. If you wouldn't mind making my excuses to your brother, I'd like to remain here until I have something useful to offer to the council."

"Of course," Sharina said. "You've saved the kingdom repeatedly by demonstrating good judgment. It's still your judgment that we depend on, even if you're able to—"

She grinned to make it a joke, though it wasn't.

"—turn demons inside out with a snap of your fingers. I'll tell Garric that you're doing the things you ought to be doing, as you always have."

Moved by sudden impulse, Sharina hugged the other woman before throwing open the door. Tenoctris was small, but her youthful body was a solid surprise to someone who'd known her in the past. As a woman in her seventies, she'd been as delicate as a sparrow in the palm of your hand.

"Ascor, leave two men to accompany Lady Tenoctris when she's ready to come," Sharina said to the waiting eyes of the soldiers on guard. "I'll leave for the palace now."

As the Blood Eagles fell in ahead and behind her, Sharina reached through a slit in the side of her outer tunic and touched the horn hilt of the knife she wore out of sight between the layers of her costume. Generally the Pewle knife was just a good-luck charm, a reminder of the hermit who'd protected Sharina as long as he lived— and protected her now, she was convinced.

"Lady, aid us in carrying out Your will," she prayed under her breath.

Sometimes even a princess and a worshipper of the Lady of Peace could use a sharp blade. If that were the case again—

Well, then the Pewle knife was more than a charm.

LORD ZETTIN WAS an extremely neat man, so it surprised Ilna that the premises of Halgran Mercantile on the northern edge of the expanding city were a jumble of tents and tarpaulins within a fence of palings. Of course it was wrong to assume that Zettin's in-laws had the same priorities as he did.

"I apologize for this disorder," Zettin said with a look of disgust. "We just moved to Pandah, as I said, and proper quarters weren't to be had. We decided it was best to build a compound of sufficient size rather than buy a structure in the Old City that can't be expanded without knocking down walls like a siege."

"I'd forgotten that you'd—the company had—moved," Ilna said, an apology at least in her mind. "Regardless, I'm not concerned with the spice trade."

A group of Coerli were weaving withies into mats of wattle between heavy posts, the start of more permanent structures. She nodded approvingly. The cat men worked quickly, and they did a better job than most humans would have.

Ilna's lip quirked: the cat men did a better job that *she* would have, at least until her fingers adapted to the stiff material. Mistress Zussa was clever to have thought of going outside her own species to find workmen. Very likely the cat men were cheaper as well, especially in Pandah where so many buildings were being constructed at the same time. Human workmen, even bad workmen as most of them were, commanded high wages.

"No, of course not," Zettin said, but his lips were grimly tight as he stepped between piles of spice boxes. The heavy crates were probably weatherproof, but each stack was also covered with canvas pegged on the sides.

Laborers and clerks, two of them women, looked at Zettin and Ilna but lowered their eyes quickly when she glanced in their direction. The watchman had passed them through the gate with no more comment than a low bow. Whether or not Lord Zettin had a formal part in the business, the staff certainly treated him with deference.

"You there!" he said, gesturing to a clerk taking inventory of a stack of boxes. "Gradus, isn't it? Where's Ingens?"

The clerk turned, lowering the brush with which he'd been writing figures on the pale inner surface of an earthenware potsherd. "He's quartered in Tent Five, milord," he said, lowering his eyes in a show of humility. "He's been living in the compound since he returned from Blaise, I believe."

Zettin nodded curt acknowledgment and strode toward the rank of tents across the back of the deep property. His high-laced boots splashed; human traffic had turned a boggy plain into a sea of mud, as was true everywhere beyond the original shore of the Island of Pandah. Ilna had known what to expect, so she'd slung her wood-soled clogs over her arm as soon as they left the cobblestone street. She was barefoot, just as she'd have been at home in Barca's Hamlet.

"We're cutting a canal to the North River," Zettin said, again suggesting that he was more than just an observer of Halgran Mercantile's activities. "Zussa looked at a waterfront tract, but I don't trust the river to keep its banks when the fall storms come. The canal's a moderate expense compared to having the river swallow the whole compound when it changes its course."

They'd reached the line of tents. There were more than Ilna could count on both hands. Some of them were being used as offices; the sides were rolled up and clerks glanced briefly toward Zettin. Ilna doubted any of them noticed her, nor was there any reason they should have.

"Master Ingens!" said Zettin, who apparently didn't have any better idea which tent was number five than Ilna did. "Show yourself!"

The flap of a tent to the right flew open. The man holding it back was stocky and fit-looking, though Ilna noticed immediately that his hands weren't callused like those of a peasant or soldier.

"Milord?" he said. He wasn't many years older than Ilna's twenty, but the frown that seemed to be his normal expression made him look older. "I've made all the arrangements and expect to leave tomorrow morning. That is, if you were concerned that I might dawdle in returning to search for Master Hervir."

"Not at all, Ingens," said Zettin, who seemed to have been taken aback by the secretary's defensiveness. "Indeed, I hadn't expected you'd be ready to leave for several days."

He cleared his throat. "I'm glad I caught you, then," he said. "This is Mistress Ilna os-Kenset, the wizard who'll be accompanying you."

"What?" said Ingens, throwing his arms up as though Zettin had suddenly drawn his sword. "That's unnecessary, milord, quite unnecessary! I assure you, having a wizard along will just complicate matters. No, no. I'll take care of the business myself."

"Master Ingens," said Zettin, his face hardening into coldly aristocratic lines, "you appear to think that I asked your opinion. I am not interested in the opinion of such folk as yourself. Do you understand me?"

Instead of backing away as he started to, Ingens knelt in the muck; the tent flap fell closed behind him. "Milord, your will shall be done, of course, of course," he said with his eyes downcast. "I only meant that because there's no wizardry involved in Master Hervir's disappearance, a wizard's presence will only make the ordinary folk I'll be questioning nervous. As well as the difficulties caused by a woman on a riverboat crewed by the rougher sort of men."

Ilna stepped over to him. Ingens made a quick decision and rose to his feet, watching her warily.

She took a handful of his tunic front, rubbing her fingers into the wool. Ingens yelped, but Ilna was barely conscious of the present world.

The fabric filled her mind with a welter of images. They settled suddenly on a tall man in his thirties, standing beside gong of jade or verdigrised bronze. His tunics were plain but of very good workmanship.

"Does Master Hervir have black hair that's very thin on top?" Ilna asked.

Ingens twitched but didn't make a real effort to break her grip. Zettin said, "Why, yes he does."

He chuckled; there wasn't much love lost between brothers-in-law, Ilna could see. "Though he wouldn't thank you for that description, mistress."

Ilna took her hand away from the tunic. "And who is the woman, the girl with him, Master Ingens?" she said.

"How—" said Ingens, and stopped.

"What?" said Zettin. He probably didn't mean to raise his voice, but he was speaking louder than he had when he shouted to bring the secretary out of his tent. "Did you lie to us, you dog? You didn't say anything about a woman!"

"Milord, I didn't—" Ingens said. He gave Ilna a furious glare, but it melted to despair in the brief instant of safety he had before she reacted. "Milord, I wanted to avoid embarrassing Master Hervir. He met a young woman, Princess Perrine she called herself, when we were on Blaise. It seemed likely he'd gone off with her. With the money."

The secretary paused, breathing hard. He risked a side-long look at Ilna.

"Mistress?" said Lord Zettin. His face was as hard as Ilna had ever seen it; his right hand was on the hilt of his sword. Like most Ornifal nobles, Zettin carried a long horseman's blade rather than the shorter weapon of an infantryman.

"He isn't responsible for whatever happened to your brother-in-law," Ilna said. She shrugged. "If you want to punish him for not being completely forthcoming, that's your business, of course. But it seems to me that it'll leave you with an awful lot of people to punish."

Zettin relaxed slightly. The activities of the compound, construction and ordinary business alike, had stilled in a widening arc around him and Ingens. The staff of Halgran Mercantile was taking a break from work to be entertained by what might turn into a blood sport.

"Go on, Ingens," Zettin said. "But this time tell me *every*thing that happened."

"Yes," Ingens said and swallowed. "Yes, milord."

He closed his eyes, then opened them and resumed, "We reached the village of Caraman, which was supposed to be the source of the saffron. It turned out it was brought to Caraman from farther away."

"Farther how?" said Zettin, frowning. "From across the Outer Sea, you mean?"

"Milord, I truly don't know where they came from," Ingens said. "I didn't see a ship. The local people said to ring the gong in the grove on the east road out of Caraman. That's away from the sea and up on a hill besides. So we rang it, and a woman came out of the trees. That was Princess Perrine."

"And she had the spice with her?" Zettin said. He took his right hand away from the sword hilt, instead hooking the thumb under his belt.

"Just a sample, milord," the secretary said. "She talked with Hervir privately. He directed me and the guards to stay where we were while he walked with the young lady in the grove. She was quite attractive and richly dressed."

"How long had the gong been there?" Ilna said.

The men had forgotten her; their heads turned with expressions of surprise. "Mistress," said Ingens, "the villagers said it was just since the Change. A prince came from the grove with six apes who wore clothing and carried saffron in stoneware jars. He sold it and said there was more for anyone who called him with the gong."

"Sold for how much?" Ilna said. "In Barca's Hamlet the only people who had any amount of silver were merchants who came during the Sheep Fair. But this spice of yours sells for gold, doesn't it?"

"Yes, mistress," Ingens said with a look of respect. He'd shown fear when Ilna read his history in the cloth of his tunic, but this was something else again. "The prince took copper and silver, the villagers swore. If that's true, then he can't have gotten but a tenth of the saffron's real value. That's why Hervir was so excited at the prospect."

"Did Hervir make a deal with this princess?" Zettin asked. "You know, I can't understand why you concealed all this previously, Ingens. You needn't think that your behavior is going to be ignored, you know."

"Milord, you'll do what you do," Ingens muttered toward the ground. "I've been a loyal servant of Halgran Mercantile for seven years. I was simply trying to save . . . awkwardness for Master Hervir and for your noble sister."

"Well, I see your point, my man," Zettin said with a touch of embarrassment. "You should certainly have come to me privately, but I don't suppose anything would be gained by rubbing my sister's nose in a business that would be distasteful to her."

He cleared his throat. "Go on, then," he said. "Did Hervir continue to see this so-called princess?"

"I don't know that for certain, milord," Ingens said, "but that's what I believe, yes. Hervir had rented the chief's house for a few bronze pieces. He and I slept there, while the guards—we had six of them—slept in a drying shed for fish. There was little enough to choose between the lodgings, I must say."

Ingens licked his lips; fear dries them worse than a desert wind, and he'd had good reason to be afraid. Ilna was impressed by the way Ingens had deflected Lord Zettin's anger; but though she was sure that he hadn't made away with Hervir, she was also sure that he wasn't telling the whole truth. She decided not to pursue the matter, at least now. Zettin's temper was still balanced on a knife edge.

Ilna's lips quirked in a humorless smile. She'd once woven a pattern which caused everyone who saw it to tell the truth. She'd done it as punishment for the house it hung in, and even she had been shocked by how effective it had been.

"I woke up in the night," the secretary said. "I thought I'd heard the gong again. I looked in Master Hervir's room and found him gone with the money. I went to the grove but he wasn't there, either. Then I roused the guards and we made a full search, but we still didn't find anything."

"Did you ring the gong?" Ilna said. "That would seem to be the obvious next step."

"Ah . . . ," said Ingens, turning his face sideways and looking at the ground again. "I did, yes, mistress, for several days. It didn't seem to me . . . That is, it seemed to me that my first duty was to bring word back to Lady Zussa and Mistress Raciana as soon as possible. But of course I intend to pursue all avenues to a solution when I'm back in Caraman."

Ilna's face remained blank while her mind tried to unknot the truth of the secretary's tale. It'd be simple enough to assume that Ingens was a coward who'd run rather than endanger himself, but that wouldn't explain why he was going back to find his master of his own will.

"What do you expect to accomplish that you couldn't have done when you were in Caraman the first time?" Zettin said, putting his finger on the same point. His eyes were narrowed, but his hand hadn't returned to his sword.

"I'll hire a full troop of Blaise armsmen when I get to Piscine, twenty at least," Ingens said promptly. "I have a draft on our agent there for the money. The guards we had with us were fine as a normal escort, but I'll want real soldiers to back me if I *expect* trouble. The whole village may be in league with Princess Perrine, you know."

The explanation was perfectly reasonable. Another person might've proceeded in a different fashion, but Ilna couldn't fault the fellow's logic.

He was lying, though. She was as sure of that as she was of sunset.

"I really believe I'll be able to do a better job without . . . ," Ingens said earnestly. "That is, by myself."

"Don't be a fool, man," Zettin said irritably. He turned to Ilna and said, "Mistress, how long will it take you to prepare for the journey?"

Ilna shrugged. "I'll pack a spare tunic and I suppose a cloak," she said. "And I'll tell Mistress Winora that I'll be traveling. She really runs the Society; I'm just a boogeyman. I can serve that purpose from Blaise or wherever, so long as they're afraid that I might come back."

"Mistress?" said Zettin.

Isn't it obvious? Ilna snarled in her mind; but it hadn't been obvious to Zettin or he wouldn't have asked the question. Calmly she said, "The staff, and I include Winora in this, will sort out their own differences quickly and quietly in order to keep me from hearing about trouble."

"Ah!" said Zettin. "Because they respect you and don't want to disturb you."

"No, Master Zettin," Ilna said. "Because they're terrified of what I might do if I became angry. Since that concerns me also, I'll be just as glad to be away from Pandah while things are still being organized."

She looked at Ingens. From his expression, he'd understood what she was saying—better than Zettin had, at any rate. She'd frightened him badly by what she'd learned by touching his tunic.

That meant the secretary had something to hide, but almost everyone had things to hide. Ilna herself didn't. Ilna didn't have anything at all.

"I'll . . . ," Ingens said. "We'll leave at midmorning, from Krumlin's wharf on the river, then. The boat I've engaged is the *Bird of the River*. If that's all right with you, mistress."

"Yes," said Ilna, turning away. "Certainly."

A commotion approached from the direction of the

compound's gate. One of Lady Liane's attendants—Ilna didn't recall his face, but the collar of his outer tunic was embroidered with a pattern she'd seen only on Third Atara—was striding toward them, followed by a squawking bevy of clerks. The watchman hobbled along behind, cupping his groin with both hands.

"Lord Zettin," the courier said, "I'm sorry for the bother—"

He glanced over his shoulder. The clerks chirped in fear. The watchman glared, but he stopped also.

"—but it isn't for sweepers and the like to tell Prince Garric's messenger to wait."

Ilna eyed the man. He was younger than most of Liane's people, sure of himself—with reason—but not experienced enough to know that there were other people who were also rightly confident. He'd learn, probably sooner rather than later judging from his attitude. If he survived, he'd be better at his work in the future.

If he survived.

The courier bowed. "His Highness," he said, "requests your presence and that of Mistress Ilna—"

He dipped his head in further acknowledgment.

"—at an immediate council meeting in his suite."

"Yes, all right," Zettin said. His face blanked. Turning to Ilna, he said, "That is, *I'll* come at once—"

"Yes," said Ilna, "and so will I. Good day, Master Ingens. I'll expect to see you in the morning."

She and Zettin strode back through the compound side by side, as they'd come. The courier was already gone on ahead; neither of them needed a guide to the council room in the palace.

Zettin cleared his throat. "I wonder, mistress?" he said. "Perhaps rather than being enrolled in the Scout Corps, you'd like your hunters to accompany you to Caraman? Quite apart from what you might find there, I'll admit that I don't entirely trust this Ingens. Though Zussa says he's been perfectly satisfactory during his employment."

Ilna sniffed. "I don't trust Ingens at all," she said. "I'd still rather that Asion and Karpos join you."

"They'll be very welcome, mistress," Zettin said diplomatically. They'd reached the gate; it was standing open. "I thought you might want familiar companions on a long journey, is all."

That was the problem, of course: Asion and Karpos *were* familiar companions, men who'd willingly risked their lives for her and whom she'd come to like. Their deaths in her service wouldn't be as terrible a loss as that of Chalcus and Merota, but she didn't have much margin for further loss. And the hunters would certainly die, sooner or later, if they continued to travel with Ilna os-Kenset.

Life had been easier when Ilna didn't have any feelings beyond occasional flashes of anger, back when her emotions were shut down. Life without feeling was pointless, of course; but then, life was probably pointless in any case.

Ilna would go on until something stopped her, though. If it was this Princess Perrine who stopped her, then so be it.

But the princess would feel she had something to boast about.

Chapter

3

SHARINA'S ESCORT WAITED outside the council chamber with other guards and the lower-ranking aides of the bureau chiefs seated at the long table. The room had been a banquet hall: one of the pirate captains who'd

infested Pandah before the army arrived had eaten here
with the fifty-man crew of his galley. It was none too large
for the royal council in its present form, though.

An usher whisked Sharina through the murmur of aides
standing behind their principals, holding document cases
or preparing to take notes on tablets of waxed boards.
Princess Sharina's place was directly across from Garric;
he smiled to see her, but there was a shadow of frowning
concern on his forehead.

Half of the original dining tables had been removed.
The remainder had been covered with what was originally a wall hanging—a crudely woven hunting scene of
stags and horsemen in a mountain landscape. It was here
simply because it was the right size to hide the names
and smutty drawings a generation of pirates had carved
in the tabletop.

Courtiers filled the rest of the room. None of them
spoke loudly, but even whispers and the shuffle of feet—
hobnailed in the case of the soldiers—created a din that
echoed from the beams of the high ceiling.

The walls had been freshly plastered; the smell of
lime was sharp enough to make Sharina's nose wrinkle.
She supposed it'd been necessary to cover the graffiti—
the drawings were even more explicit than what brutes
could engrave with the points of their daggers—but the
chamberlain was turning necessity into a virtue: an artist
had already started drawing cartoons for a mural showing humans and Coerli together battling monsters.

She leaned across the table; Garric got up so he could
lean even farther, bringing their heads close together. It
probably wouldn't meet the standards of court etiquette,
but they'd been brother and sister for a long time before
they became prince and princess.

"Tenoctris will be delayed," she said. "She wants to
get information on the problem before she discusses it."

Garric nodded and smiled, then settled back on his
chair. Its high back—higher than the other chairs around

the table—was carved in a clumsy imitation of a grape arbor. Sharina suspected it was even more uncomfortable to sit on than hers, but presumably it met what the palace servants considered to be the requirements of royal dignity.

"We'll get started now," Garric said, speaking loudly enough that the room quieted instantly around him. "I've just been informed that the Empire of Palomir is allied with a race of rats the size of men. Presumably they're intelligent as well, since they use swords and armor. We're working to get a better understanding of the numbers involved—"

He winked across the table at Sharina.

"—but we know that the rulers of Palomir claim that they'll be able to conquer the kingdom. Conquer the world, in fact."

There was a dull explosion of sound—no individual part of it loud but in combination overwhelming. People whispered to their neighbors, sorted through documents, and shuffled their feet. Garric let it go on for a moment.

The present council was a larger body than Sharina had become used to. In the past there'd been a council in Valles, the capital. Garric took a smaller group of advisors with him when he led the fleet and army around the Isles, reminding the rulers of individual islands that they were part of the kingdom rather than independent principalities.

In the past few weeks, Chancellor Royhas had moved his entire establishment to Pandah. His great rival, Lord Tadai, had traveled with Garric and gained real power even if he lacked the title of chancellor. When Royhas saw Garric delaying at Pandah instead of returning to Valles, he'd acted and the other bureaus had followed him.

Lord Hauk, the minister of supply, had moved even earlier: he was a former commoner who took a very pragmatic view of things. In the Change the Isles had become a single continent, and Pandah was in the center of it. That made it the best location from which to communicate with all parts of the kingdom, and transport was the core of Hauk's duties.

"I'll direct the regional governors to begin raising reinforcements," said Lord Waldron. "If Palomir thinks it's strong enough to conquer the Isles, then we may need more troops than we have on hand at present."

Waldron, a stiff-backed former cavalryman, commanded the royal army. He'd never fully approved of Garric, who wasn't a noble from northern Ornifal like himself, but he couldn't have been tortured into breaking his oath. He'd repeatedly shown that at least one cavalryman knew more about war than how to lead a headlong charge.

Waldron would lead the charge also, of course. Much as Sharina disliked many of the assumptions of men of Waldron's class, she respected their bravery. Physical courage was as natural to them as breathing.

"I believe there's nothing but broken buildings left of Palomir," Lord Tadai said, tenting his hands in what was for him a familiar gesture. He was well fed, well groomed, and very intelligent. His formal title now was City Prefect; Pandah's explosive growth and the likelihood that Garric would make it the official capital provided both need for Tadai's skills and scope for his ambitions. "There aren't enough people to be a military threat—"

"*They* think they're a threat!" Waldron snapped. The two men were both Ornifal nobles, but Waldron was a northern landowner while Tadai's wealth came from trade carried on in Valles. They had as much in common with Garric, raised as a peasant on Haft, as they did with one another. "I'd be very pleased to learn that they're wrong, but I do *not* choose to ignore dangers."

"Nor do I, milord," Tadai said. His softness was entirely physical; he was just as focused and ruthless as Waldron, though they used different weapons. "I rather suggest that the danger is likely to be one whose solution needs a wizard more than it does a soldier. Since Lady Tenoctris isn't present—"

Sharina opened her mouth to speak. Before she could, her brother said, "Lady Tenoctris is looking into the matter already. She'll report to me when there's something *to* report."

"What about the cat, then?" said Waldron, nodding toward Rasile. "Lady Rasile, I mean."

Some of those present had been upset that a Corl was allowed to attend council meetings. Waldron, somewhat to Sharina's surprise, was perfectly willing to accept the Coerli as peers. The cat men were brave warriors, after all, which to him gave them higher status than city merchants like Tadai and Royhas.

All eyes turned to the Corl wizard. A chair, sturdier than most, had been set for Cashel at the end on Sharina's side of the table. Seating protocol at council meetings was a nightmare for the chamberlain and her staff. Fortunately everyone knew that the prince and princess didn't care, and that they'd tear a strip off anybody who made trouble about the business. Cashel was on the end because it was a great deal easier for so broad a man to sit down and get up than it would be beside Sharina in the middle.

Today Cashel had entered with the Corl wizard in the crook of his right arm and his quarterstaff upright in his left hand. He placed her in the chair—she crouched on the seat—and stood behind it like a servant.

In a sense Cashel was right: they were all servants, of mankind and of good in the struggle against evil. To the people who really knew him, however, he was the equal of anyone else in the hall.

"Just Rasile, Warrior Waldron," Rasile said. "I have been concerned with the Worm which infests Telut, Warrior Cashel informs me."

Liane uncapped her silver pen; it had an ink reservoir

in the barrel so that it didn't have to be dipped after each few strokes. She began jotting notes in a notebook made from thin sheets of elm wood, her eyes on the Corl wizard.

Rasile turned and tilted her long face up toward Cashel. He nodded solemnly and said, "She means the thing that attacked Ombis on Telut. It ate through the walls and then the pirates with it took the city."

"Yes," said Rasile. "But I know nothing about Palomir. If the wizard Tenoctris is giving that her attention, I would be a fool to interfere."

Liane, sitting to Garric's right but slightly behind him, leaned forward and whispered. He nodded twice, his eyes unfocused, then said to the gathering, "It appears that it will be necessary to march with the army shortly, since I don't intend to wait here for our enemy or enemies to attack us at their leisure."

Lord Waldron snorted.

"Such being the case," Garric continued, "and given that I expect to be leading the army myself—"

He looked at Waldron. Waldron nodded crisply. "Of course, Your Highness," he said.

"—I propose to leave Princess Sharina as regent as I've done in the past. Does anyone care to comment on my decision?"

"I don't think anybody in this room is such a fool," Lord Waldron said. He glanced to his right, toward Chancellor Royhas on Garric's other side, and added, "No soldier is, anyway."

"I've had the pleasure of working under the direction of Princess Sharina in the past, Your Highness," Royhas said mildly. "I couldn't imagine a better deputy in your absence."

He smiled. Though Royhas wasn't a morose man, Sharina had found him generally too reserved to smile in public. His expression seemed chosen as a polite counterpunch to Waldron's verbal sneer.

"Very good," said Garric. "Then all I have in addition is to direct that all bureaus and districts—"

He nodded toward the eastern gallery where stood the representatives of the kingdom's new districts. Most of them were based on the islands which existed before the Change. The representatives didn't have seats at the table, but they were present so that their reports would help outlying regions feel they were parts of the kingdom rather than merely sources of taxes.

"—to be prepared for possible invasion from the south."

Garric quirked a tired smile toward Rasile and Cashel. "And apparently from the east as well. I'll keep you informed as we get additional information, and I'll expect you all to pass on the information you and your subordinates come across."

The door latch rasped; Sharina turned to look over her shoulder. A Blood Eagle shoved the door open and sidled in. He and his partner were holding the ends of a spear between them, providing a makeshift sedan chair for Tenoctris. The wizard's face was drawn; she was so weary that she seemed barely able to grip the soldiers' forearms to balance herself on the shaft.

Sharina started to get up, but Cashel was already moving. Several aides who'd been in his way bounced to one side or the other with startled squawks. He scooped Tenoctris into the crook of his arm with a practiced motion.

Sharina thought of how alert and healthy Tenoctris had been an hour before. The spell she'd worked after Sharina left her must've been of enormous weight to have drained her so thoroughly.

Rasile hopped down from the chair. Cashel set Tenoctris on it with the delicacy of a cat with her kitten.

"Lady Tenoctris," Garric said. "Do you have information for us?"

"Yes," said the wizard. She was trying to sound bright, but exhaustion made her voice wobble. "I'm afraid that I do, Your Highness."

* * *

I'M OUT OF my depth here," Tenoctris said, but despite the words her familiar rueful smile lifted Garric's spirits. She always deprecated her abilities, but they'd always proven adequate to the kingdom's needs.

"I'm a wizard," she continued, "but while there's wizardry involved, there's theology also."

People whispered, one of them a junior officer leaning close to Lord Attaper's right ear. "Silence!" Garric said, pointing his left index finger at the two Blood Eagles. He knew he was taking out his nervous anger on people whose mildly improper actions didn't deserve that level of response, but that was better than Carus' urge to use the flat of his sword to quiet the room.

Carus grinned in his mind. Garric grinned back in response, feeling his mood lighten.

"The problem with lopping somebody's head off if they screw up," Carus said, still grinning, *"is that the victim isn't much good to you afterwards. As I learned the hard way a time or two."*

In the silence that followed Garric's shout, a slender man with the white robe and black stole of a senior priest said, "We of the Temple of the Lady of the Grove would be honored to assist you, Lady Tenoctris."

"I didn't say I needed priestcraft," Tenoctris snapped. She was regaining her animation and apparently her strength, as she was now sitting upright at the edge of the chair.

She cleared her throat against the back of her hand and resumed, "I've discussed my religious beliefs only in private, and even then rarely. To be brief, I *had* no religious beliefs. I'd never seen the Great Gods and I saw no reason to believe they existed."

The babble greeting the wizard's words was momentarily overwhelming. Even to Garric, the statement was disturbing. His family hadn't been particularly religious, but before each meal there'd always been a crumb and a drop for the little shrine on the wall of the dining room.

"Oh, I say!" cried Lord Hauk, shocked out of his normal deference toward born aristocrats. "Being a wizard doesn't justify blasphemy!"

Cashel banged the iron cap of his staff on the terrazzo floor. "That's all right!" he said. It wasn't like him to break in, especially not in a council meeting, but he obviously felt responsible for Tenoctris. "I figure she's wrong, but you leave her alone unless you want to discuss it with me, all right?"

"Continue, Lady Tenoctris," Garric said mildly. Because of the sudden silence, he didn't have to raise his voice. That was good, because shouting both sounded angry and made him *feel* angry when he did it.

"My friend Cashel is quite correct," Tenoctris said, cheerful and apparently herself again. "I was wrong about the Great Gods: they did exist, and there was sufficient evidence to have proved the fact to me if I'd been willing to consider it. Sharing my mind with a demon has—"

There was another chorus of gasps, though it stilled instantly of its own. The *crack!* of Cashel's ferrule on stone wasn't really necessary.

"I never learned to watch what I said around civilians either," said Carus wryly. *"At least she doesn't wear a sword."*

"—forced me to become more realistic," Tenoctris said. "Which is something of an embarrassment to someone who thought she *was* a realist."

Tenoctris looked around the table, touching everyone seated with her smile. Garric didn't understand where she was going with the discussion, and he was very doubtful that anyone else did either. He wanted to take Liane's hand, but that wasn't proper behavior for a council meeting.

"The problem, you see . . . ," Tenoctris said. Her voice became minutely thinner; the brightness remained, but it'd become a false gloss over her concern. "Is that the Great Gods of the Isles do *not* exist in this world which the Change brought. The Gods of Palomir-that-was are trying to climb the empty plinth, and they have power of a sort that I don't completely understand."

She shook her head, smiling. "In fact I don't understand it at all," she said. "It's working through principles that are nothing like those I do understand. But I can help deal with it. And Wizard Rasile can help, and everyone in the kingdom will help according to their skills. There will be enough work for men with swords to satisfy even a warrior like your ancient ancestor, Prince Garric."

The ghost in Garric's mind clapped his hands in glee. *"By the Lady!"* Carus said. *"If I was still in the flesh, I'd manage to forget that she's a wizard, I swear I would!"*

"Obviously we need to deal with whatever upstarts challenge the rule of Prince Garric," said Tadai. "But—"

He pursed his lips, his fingers extended before him. He was apparently studying his perfect manicure.

"—need we really be concerned about which statue is up in which temple?"

"What?" cried the priest of the Lady. "This is quite improper! I protest!"

"Lord Tilsit," Liane whispered.

"Lord Tilsit, be silent!" said Garric. He glared at the west where those outside the royal bureaucracy stood, then the east gallery for low-ranking palace personnel. "I remind you that those who aren't seated at the council table speak only when requested to."

The priest raised his hands and genuflected. His face had gone blank.

"Lady Tenoctris?" Garric continued mildly, grinning in his mind. "Does that suggestion ease our problems?"

He'd been using that tone since he was a tall thirteen-year-old and men in the common room started bothering the inn's pretty waitress—Sharina. Nowadays Garric didn't have to knock people down himself if they didn't take the hint, but there were times he wouldn't mind the chance.

"Lady Tenoctris the atheist," Tenoctris said, adding a self-deprecating laugh, "would be perfectly happy with no Gods or Gods she could ignore as she's done all her life till now. Unfortunately, while the Great Gods of your—our, I apologize—former world watched, the Gods of Palomir would rule. Their rule in former times was the rule of men over beasts."

" 'Boys throw stones at frogs in sport,' " whispered Liane, quoting the ancient poet Bion, " 'but the frogs die not in sport but in earnest.' "

Garric squeezed her hand. Propriety could hang for the moment.

"Franca the All Father, Fallin of the Waves," Tenoctris said, "and Hili, Queen of the Underworld. They're immanent now. If Palomir's rat armies succeed, widespread belief will make Them all-powerful and perhaps eternal."

"The solution appears to be to defeat the rats and anything else that allies with Palomir, then," said Garric. King Carus had come to that conclusion long since. While marching instantly with an army wasn't always the best choice—

"It got me and my army killed in the end, lad," the ghost agreed.

—acting fast was *almost* always a better choice than dithering.

"Lord Waldron," Garric continued, "prepare the army to move as soon as possible. We'll determine which troops to take based on the supply situation, which you'll coordinate with the proper bureaus."

"Done," said Waldron, and nodded. The young officer standing behind him started for the door at as fast a walk as the crowd permitted. Hauk, Tadai, and Royhas were muttering to aides also.

"Your Highness?" Liane said. She spoke in a polite

undertone to indicate she wanted to address the council instead of informing Garric in a private whisper.

"Go ahead, Lady Liane," Garric said, silencing the room again without really shouting. Well, not shouting as he'd have thought of it in the borough, calling to his friend Cashel on the crest of the next hill.

"Your Highness," Liane said, "we know that our enemies have been capturing humans on Cordin. They probably believed that because of Palomir's location, it would be some time before we in Pandah learned about the raids. On the other hand, they must know that their grace period will be over shortly."

Garric kept from frowning by conscious effort. Liane had remarkable skills, but she was too much a lady to project her voice to be heard beyond the ends of the table. He supposed he could repeat anything that had to be known more generally.

"Before you commit the army," Liane said, "it might be well to be sure that there isn't a large body of rats already marching toward Sandrakkan to strike fresh victims while they still have surprise. Or toward Haft."

Garric's body tensed as though he'd been dropped into ice water. *Toward home,* he thought.

"Yes," he said, marveling that his voice remained calm and businesslike. "Lord Zettin, I want you to put your companies across all the routes to the west and northwest of Palomir. If they meet small raiding parties, they're to attack after sending a courier back. If they find a larger body, they're to shadow it while waiting for reinforcements. And send messengers to the district that the enemy is threatening."

Duzi, may a rat army not already be attacking Barca's Hamlet.

Instead of simply acknowledging the order, Lord Zettin said, "Your Highness? Might I suggest that I send at least one troop to Telut to see what these pirates and their creature are doing?"

That's a good—

Cashel's quarterstaff rapped the stone floor again. "If you please?" he said. "Rasile has something to say about that."

CASHEL STOOD, HIS staff planted. He looked around the hall, not so much because there was anything in particular he wanted to see, but because it was reflex in him. Sheep wandered all different ways, and as soon as you let one out of your sight for a minute or two, you could be sure it was getting into trouble.

Rasile raised a tumbler of water. It was a pretty thing with a design in gold between two layers of clear glass, or mostly clear. A servant had fetched it from the sideboard next door in the private room where Garric could go off with one or two people to talk about things the whole council needn't hear.

Cashel had ordered it brought because the servant ignored Rasile asking. A lot of people didn't like the cat men, which wasn't hard to understand. It was just as well for the fellow that he hadn't said the wrong thing when Cashel stepped in, though.

"The one who controls the Worm," Rasile said, "is moving toward a particular place. I do not know where it is, but perhaps one of you will recognize it."

"What place is that?" asked a long-faced man who had something to do with transport. "I don't see—"

Rasile upended the tumbler. As the contents poured out, she said something that sounded more like a hinge binding than it did words.

Scarlet wizardlight flickered around the stream the way a potter's thumbs mold clay. Instead of splashing down, the water spread into a round temple with a domed roof; an instant later the roof vanished and the columns that'd held it up crumbled into a ring of stubs, some taller than others. Fallen barrels lay scattered roundabout.

The illusion ended; the water splashed onto the tapestry. Some of it sank in, but the cloth was tightly enough woven that beads and little rivulets quivered nervously in the surface.

"Why, I've seen that!" said Lord Attaper, leaning forward with a puzzled expression as though he were trying to make sense of the way the spilled water now lay. "That's the Temple of the Tree, they call it. In Dariada on Charax."

"There must be a hundred ruined temples like that, every one as likely as the next!" Lord Waldron protested. "Maybe more, since the Change."

The guard commander and army commander acted like two rams in a flock, though it never got out of hand. Cashel figured—and they figured—that Garric would end the trouble quick if that happened.

"I know that," Attaper said, grimacing. "And it was twenty years ago I was on Charax, I know that too. But I tell you, I saw what Rasile showed, and I was sure it was the Temple of the Tree."

"Yes," said Rasile, grinning with her tongue out. "The image I formed is not wholly to be seen with the eyes, Warrior Waldron."

Tenoctris turned to Rasile, standing beside her. The Corl was short even for her own species, so their heads were nearly on a level.

"Can you face the Worm?" Tenoctris said. "You were drawn to it, after all."

"You know what the Worm is?" Rasile said. "Of course you do; you are Tenoctris. So yes, I can face it."

Rasile grinned again. People around the table were straining to hear. Cashel didn't have a problem because he was standing right behind them, but it must be just a buzz to anybody more than arm's length away.

"But I do not see how I can possibly defeat it," the Corl said, "even if I have the help of your friend, the warrior Cashel."

"We're even, then," said Tenoctris. Her own smile, though human, made her look a bit like a dog getting ready for a fight. "Because I assure you, I have *no* idea how I'm going to deal with entities who—"

She shrugged expressively.

"—emotionally I can't even make myself believe in."

Garric was holding the room quiet by glaring at anybody who started to chatter while the wizards were talking. "Your Highness," Tenoctris said, "Rasile will go to Dariada with the aid of Master Cashel, if he . . . ?"

Tenoctris looked up at Cashel.

"Yes, ma'am," he said. He'd go wherever somebody who understood things told him to go. "That is, if . . . ?"

Sharina was already looking over at him; she nodded. She didn't look happy about it and Cashel wasn't happy himself, but it was good to be doing something useful.

He frowned and said, "But Garric? I don't mind fighting a pirate or even a couple pirates, but there was a herd of them at Ombis. There'll be more pretty quick, because tramps and no-goods will join in for the loot. I guess there's going to be a lot of ordinary fellows too, only they'd rather drink wine than sweat plowing somebody else's field."

"Right," said Waldron. "I'll send a regiment. Ah— one of the units from the Valles garrison would probably be sufficient, if we don't want to weaken the field army."

"Your Highness?" Liane said.

"Lady Liane, please move your stool forward and join the council," Garric said. "And state your opinion of Lord Waldron's proposal."

He'd been sharper than he usually was, and sharper for sure than he usually was with Liane. Cashel felt sorry for his friend with so many different things to keep track of all at once, but it was sure a wonder how well he did.

"Charax since the Change is a loose federation of cities, each with control of the region around it," Liane said. She held a gilt-edged scroll, but she didn't bother to open it. "They insist on their independence, and they won't allow foreign troops on their territories. That's particularly true of Dariada, because the Tree Oracle is located there."

"They've been turning away the envoys I've sent regarding tax assessments," Chancellor Royhas said in a growl. "I suggest we use enough troops that at the same time we deal with these pirates, we can convince the Dariadans and their fellows that they're parts of the kingdom, now."

Cashel could see Liane stiffen. A flash of anger touched her face—and vanished just as quickly.

"No, milord, we will not do that," said Garric. He didn't seem to have glanced to the other side to see Liane's expression, so the edge in his voice must mean that he felt the same way anyhow. "Cashel—and Lord Waldron? Bands of pirates have very rarely been a danger to walled cities. This gang would be no exception were it not for the Worm, and troops wouldn't help with that problem. Take whatever escort you want for the journey, but we won't upset the folk of Charax by marching into what they consider their independent territory."

"We will not be walking, Warrior Garric," Rasile said politely. "We will not need the escort you offer."

Cashel didn't say anything. He was happier than not that they wouldn't have soldiers around, though, even if he didn't have to command them. It wasn't exactly that he didn't like soldiers, but he didn't have anything in common with them.

"I don't know anything about a Tree Oracle," said Lord Tadai. "Though since the Charax I *did* know of before the Change was an island of fishing villages and goat farmers, I shouldn't be surprised."

Cashel liked Tadai because he didn't bluster even a

little bit, though he was tough as they came in his own way. A lot of people with power liked to show off, including big fellows with a mug or two of ale in them. Cashel wasn't like that himself, and it was good to know other folk who were the same way as him.

Liane cleared her throat; Garric nodded to her. "The whole island of Charax," she said, "appears to be as it was in the past millennium, before the Isles were unified under the Old Kingdom. The Tree Oracle is just that, a tree which responds to petitioners through human priests. A very old tree. The oracle is administered by a federation of the whole island, though the states fight one another regularly."

"The historians of the Old Kingdom treat the struggle against the Confederation of Charax as a major step in the predestined rise to greatness of the Kings of the Isles," Garric said with an odd smile. "It didn't occur to me when I read the accounts that I'd someday be dealing with people who wouldn't view the sack and burning of Dariada as a splendid triumph."

"I suppose the oracle's a fraud," Waldron said. He snorted. "A way to make priests rich and keep everybody else in line."

"I wouldn't know, milord," Liane said, leaning forward to look past Garric at Waldron. "*I* don't have enough information."

Cashel couldn't help smiling. He knew Lord Waldron had been insulted, but he wasn't sure Waldron did. There were other smiles around the table, though. Waldron was curtly sure of himself, and it didn't help his popularity that he was generally right.

"It would appear that the pirates do not consider the oracle a fraud, Warrior Waldron," Rasile said. "I would not usually hope to learn wisdom from folk who have been cast out of their bands, but these outcasts have bent a Worm to their will. I could not do that, and I think that even Tenoctris would find the task difficult."

"I," said Tenoctris forcefully, "wouldn't dare to try. The Worm destroyed its own world. Should it get loose in ours, it would destroy a second."

Garric looked around the room again. Everybody kept their mouth shut. They'd learned not to waste Garric's time babbling when there was work to do, and there was plenty of work now.

But instead of the dismissal Cashel expected, Garric said, "Mistress Ilna? Do you have something to add before I close the meeting?"

Ilna stood on the west side of the room, knotting one of her designs. Lord Zettin was standing beside her, which surprised Cashel more than most things would. The soldier—who'd been a sailor not long back—had a seat at the table, but he was leaving it vacant.

Ilna caught Cashel's eye and smiled; not much but as much as she ever did. Then she said, "I don't have anything to say, no. I'll be going off shortly to deal with a problem that Master Zettin showed me."

ILNA HEARD WHAT was going on in the council meeting, but her attention was on the pathways opening as her fingers knotted lengths of yarn. The design was like a track through a forest, forking again and again. She saw nothing beyond the path itself, but she had a sense of the direction.

Aides jostled and whispered around her. Ilna knew she could've had a chair at the table. She didn't feel she had any business being at the council meeting in the first place, so she hadn't asked for that, today or ever in the past.

She wasn't sure why she'd even bothered to come. Common courtesy, she supposed: her friend Garric had asked her to attend, so here she was. She'd been surprised that Lord Zettin, who *did* belong and had a chair placed for him, had chosen to stand beside her. She hadn't asked him what he thought he was doing because that was none of her business. She'd certainly wondered, though.

Garric's direct question had taken Ilna by surprise, but she'd given the same answer as she'd have done with a week to prepare. That was one advantage to always telling the flat truth.

Not that she did it because it was advantageous.

"Say!" piped the young courtier standing behind Lord Waldron. His tunics were of the best quality and he wore them well. "What does she mean saying Master? He's a peer!"

Ilna dropped the pattern into her sleeve and reached for more yarn. The action was reflex: there wasn't a real threat, and hostility toward her was no new thing.

"Lord Halle!" Zettin said. "If you persist in discussing matters which touch my honor, I'll send you home to your father with your ears cropped!"

"Quite right, Halle!" Lord Waldron said. "Gentlemen don't need a pup like you to tell them their business."

Waldron turned. "I wonder, though, Your Highness," he continued with his eyes on Lord Zettin rather than Garric. "If Mistress Ilna should be bothering about private matters while the kingdom's got the enemies it does?"

Ilna wondered if the army commander really had any notion of what she'd done or could do. Perhaps he did, since she knew Waldron wasn't a stupid man.

She was quite sure that his comment had nothing to do with her and little at best with the kingdom, however. Zettin was Attaper's disciple and Attaper was Waldron's rival, so Waldron jabbed at Zettin. Children did the same thing—but animals didn't, not any animals that Ilna had seen during life in a peasant hamlet.

She'd done worse things herself, of course. That didn't make her like human beings better.

Aloud she said, "I've never met a kingdom, Master

Waldron, but I've got a good notion of what I myself ought to be doing. If you don't agree, you're welcome to your opinion."

Waldron glared fiercely, but not so much at her as in her direction. Until Ilna'd spoken, he hadn't really been thinking about her as a person; she'd been a stick to beat Zettin with.

Ilna smiled as broadly as she ever did. Sometimes what you thought was a stick turned out to be a snake.

"All right, I take your point," Waldron said. "I shouldn't have said anything. No offense meant."

"Ilna?" said Tenoctris unexpectedly twisting around in her chair to meet Ilna's eyes. "It might be useful for you to describe to the council how you came to your decision. There's obviously—"

Her glance spiked Waldron; he scowled even tighter.

"—a great deal of ignorance about the business."

Ilna shrugged. Discussing this sort of thing made her uncomfortable, but discomfort was so ordinary a part of her life that she felt foolish complaining about it—even to herself.

"I wove a pattern," she said, gesturing with the yarn in her hand, as yet unknotted. "Patterns, I suppose, more than one. They—"

How to describe it? It wasn't seeing or even feeling, it was knowing *a thing, a direction.*

"—indicated to me that I should—"

No, that's not the word!

"—that it would be *right* for me to go look into Hervir disappearing up in Blaise. And don't ask me what I mean by right—"

She was angry and it came out in her voice, but she was angry at herself. She didn't have the words to explain to educated people what she meant!

"—because I don't know. Looking for Hervir will take me in a direction that someone, something, thinks it's right for me to go, and that's all I know."

Perhaps she'd find death on Blaise. But she'd learned not to expect anything that she might want.

"I work in certain ways," Tenoctris said, addressing the whole council. "With an incantation I could display a future. Some of you have seen me do that, have you not?"

There were nods and murmurs around the room. One of the soldiers, an older man who'd gone bald to the middle of his scalp, forced his clenched fists together and muttered a prayer.

"But I couldn't show you *the* future, or the *best* future," Tenoctris said, "because I don't know what those things mean. They're results. They depend on the choices I make when I choose the words of power that I chant. Someone like—"

Pausing suddenly, Tenoctris got up from her chair and walked around it to where Ilna stood. She put her arm on Ilna's shoulder; her touch was as light as a hopping wren's.

"There isn't a 'like Ilna,'" she said. "Mistress Ilna, alone of all those I've met or heard of. Ilna can determine the best course for herself, which means the best course for mankind and for the good. I would no more argue Ilna's decision than I would tell King Carus how to fight a battle."

Garric chuckled, though Ilna wasn't sure that it was really her childhood friend laughing. "All right," he said. "The matter was decided when Ilna stated her preference, but now you all know *why* that's the case. The council is dismissed."

Feet shuffled and chairs scraped the floor of chipped stone in concrete; attendants threw open the double door. Cashel stood, waiting for the bustle to clear so that he could go to Sharina without knocking people out of the way.

Ilna stood; her fingers were knotting a pattern. She thought of the path she'd taken, the one whose varied turnings that led to the deaths of Chalcus and Merota. *If that was the right choice, then where would the other choices have led?*

Ilna's fingers moved, and her mind bubbled with anger at the person she was.

Interlude

B ARAY, EMPEROR OF Palomir and the World, stood at the entrance to the Temple of Franca. Beside him was Nivers, the high priest, with three of the girls from the harem Nivers had accumulated since the return of the Gods. The youngest of them couldn't have been more than ten, which disturbed Baray; but not as much as the scene in the courtyard twenty-seven crystal steps below, where Salmson chanted at the altar and rat men sacrificed the latest captives.

Baray took another drink from his flask. When he was young, he'd dreamed of someday drinking the finest vintages. Now he had his choice of hundreds of wines, but he found the greatest solace in that grown on the jungle terraces of Palomir itself. Baray drank it unmixed; he hadn't found a stronger wine anywhere in the world.

"Alba thanalba thalana!" Salmson chanted. He was getting hoarse; Nivers would have to take his assistant's place soon. But not yet, not quite yet.

The woman below screamed as two rat men forced her to bend over the altar backward. A third rat struck with a broad-bladed dagger and ripped upward; the screams gurgled to silence. More rat men led up the next victim, a man too stunned to struggle.

Baray drank again. The flask was empty. He flung it away and shouted, "Come!"

The servant waiting beside the storage jar at the base

of the stairs came shambling up with a full flask, this one silver instead of bronze. He'd find the one Baray had flung down in disgust, wipe it if necessary, and have it refilled for the next usage.

The steps were shallow and steeply pitched, but the servant didn't lose his balance. He was a recent prisoner, and he knew better than most the fate that lay in store for him if Nivers lost patience with him.

The man on the altar had been silent until the knife went in. Now he cried, "Ak! Ak!" and then gave a bubbling groan. The rat men holding him dragged the body away, dumping it with the rest in a pile before the Temple of Fallin on the right side of the courtyard which had Franca's temple at its head.

Rats, the ordinary vermin which had infested the ruins of Palomir for generations, swarmed over the corpses, chittering and squeaking as they gorged on warm flesh. The stench of rotting blood permeated the moist midday heat. Baray had gotten used to it, or almost used to it.

"Must we kill so . . . ?" he started to say. He turned to look at Nivers and found the high priest fondling the youngest girl. Her face mimed delight, but there was terror behind her half-closed eyes.

The emperor jerked his head straight. "Nivers!" he said. "This isn't right. We want more citizens for Palomir. The city's almost empty, and instead of repopulating it we turn it into a slaughterhouse!"

"We have no choice, Baray," Nivers said in a thick voice. "You know we have—"

The girl screamed.

"Hili take you!" Nivers said, slashing at her with his open hand. The girl ducked back and collapsed against the doorpost, blubbering. The priest's blow missed; he overbalanced and would've fallen down the cracked crystal steps if Baray hadn't put a hand out to steady him.

"We don't have any choice, Baray," the priest mumbled on his knees.

"Alba thanalba thalana!" Salmson chanted. The Temple of Hili faced that of Fallin across the courtyard. From its open door blew a wind with a red tinge. At each syllable that wind wrapped a rat on the pile of bodies—swelled it, molded it, and lifted it at the size of a human onto its hind legs.

For a moment, each new-made rat man squeaked in confusion. Some snapped their long incisors at whatever was closest, often their own forelimbs—now arms. After a few moments their new souls merged with their new bodies and they settled.

At the clicked and chattered orders of a subchief—the rats knew their leaders; Baray could tell no difference from one gray-and-dun body to the next—they moved off through the crumbling archway at the foot of the courtyard. In the colonnaded ruin that had been the city's vegetable market, the new rat warriors would be equipped with weapons looted from overrun human settlements or forged by human captives who, like the palace servants, made themselves as useful as they could to their masters.

The rats moved with springy steps, but when they halted they threw their hindquarters and stiff tails back; their heads and chests slanted forward. At rest they wobbled like birds balancing on a slender branch.

"We can't," Nivers repeated in a whisper. "You'll be leading the army when it marches on Haft, Emperor. You want it to be huge, do you not? Overwhelming. I've told you how strong the Kingdom of the Isles is. Franca showed me their forces sweeping through every enemy the kingdom faced . . . and now they will face you."

"Yes," said Baray. "Yes."

He closed his eyes. His hands were trembling, so he gripped the flask with both to lift it to his lips. The harsh red wine burned his mouth, but his throat continued working until he'd emptied the flask again.

"Alba thanalba thalana!" said Salmson, but he chanted

in a rasping singsong. Nivers would *have* to replace the man soon.

The man on the altar this time was young and strong; he lunged as the blade plunged downward. He couldn't free himself from the grip of the two rat men, but he twisted enough that the point gouged the side of his rib cage instead of splitting his breastbone as intended.

The rat conducting the sacrifices gave an angry squeal and stabbed repeatedly. The victim shouted for almost the entire time, though his voice lost strength by the end. The hot, red wind sparkled over the corpses and lifted vermin from them to chitter and mow.

"A huge army . . . ," Baray said. "Overwhelming. An overwhelming army."

Tears were running down his cheeks. He threw the empty flask at the attendant who waited below, his back to the slaughter and his head bowed down.

"Come!" said Baray. "More wine!"

The high priest was fumbling his women again, though the youngest still crouched sobbing in the doorway. Baray rubbed his temples, waiting for the servant to climb the stairs. The wine had spilled a bright haze over his senses, but he could still hear and smell; and he could see enough.

"I must have a huge army," the emperor whispered. But despite the smothering pillow of wine, he wondered what would happen when the rat armies had conquered the whole Land. Would there be any humans left by then?

And would there be any *need* for humans?

Chapter

4

Here's the relief petition from southern Atara," Liane said, sliding a document across the table to Garric beside her. It was on vellum, and each of the twelve petitioners had pressed their signet into a blob of wax beside their name. From the look of the signatures, though, half of them had no more experience of writing than Cashel did. "The priest regnant—the island's ruler is the high priest of the main temple of the Shepherd—is ordering that taxes continue to be paid in kind at the temple, which is on what was the north coast."

Garric frowned. He looked at the petition by reflex, but he'd learned by now that reading official documents was a waste of time. Liane or her clerks would've précised the attempts of a rural scribe to sound high-toned because he was writing to the prince.

"This is what they did in the past?" he asked, looking at Liane.

"Yes," said Liane, "but before the Change they could ship the grain—they grow wheat on Atara—by sea. Now they'd have to transport it by wagon and treble the cost to themselves."

She smiled faintly. "The petition says twelve times the cost, but an assayer of Lord Tadai's who knows the region says three. They want to have the tax paid locally—"

"That sounds reasonable," said Garric. This sort of business wearied him more than a day in the sun wearing armor.

"—but I suggest that commuting the in-kind payment

to money at the local values will give the treasury a considerable benefit," Liane continued calmly. "With the landowners behind us we can push the measure through, despite the temple's objection to losing the amount they were skimming during collection. Mind, the landowners would've fought us even harder than the priests if we'd tried to do it last year."

There was a quick *clink/clink!* on the door's latch plate. Liane met Garric's eyes; the office was the innermost of the three in her suite. When he nodded, she called, "Enter!"

Instead of Liane's doorman in civilian dress, the captain of the Blood Eagles guarding Garric opened the door; he'd knocked with one of the bronze finials of his double-tongued sword belt. "Lord Zettin's here to see you, Your Highness," he said to Garric. "He says it's important."

The ghost of King Carus grunted sourly. He didn't like Zettin, thinking him too clever by half. *"But he's not really a bad sort,"* he muttered in half-apology. *"And you need the clever ones too."*

Zettin waited for the captain to nod him through before he strode into the office. Garric smiled. Brash with everyone else, Zettin was always very punctilious regarding the Blood Eagles. He'd been an officer of the regiment himself before Attaper's support—and his own abilities—had gotten him promoted out of it.

Now he closed the door behind him and said, "Palomir's marching on Haft, Your Highness. And it's not a raiding party, it's an army of thousands of rats—all rats. Four of my troops are in contact with them, but they have to keep out farther than they would with humans because the rats move so quickly."

Nodding with excitement, Zettin resumed, "Headman Clarey's one of my best officers. He says he very nearly lost his whole troop because the rats sent out a flanking company that got behind him. The main body rushed

him, and they had to fight their way through the blocking company."

"We've gotten used to fighting wizards who don't have
any better notion of ordering an army than I have of flying," Garric said, echoing his ancestor's thought. "It
looks like there may be a general on the other side this
time. That could be worse than another thousand rats."

"I regret I can't tell you how many we *are* facing, Your
Highness," Zettin said. "Headman Clarey's troop got closest. He's the only one who could more than say, 'Many,'
and he says ten thousand men. Though they aren't men, of
course."

Garric shrugged. "Then we're in for a fight," he said,
"but I'm not concerned about winning it."

*"The day our troops can't handle half their number
of animals, even if they're clever animals with swords,"*
Carus said, *"then you'd best be off to a monastery. And
I'll be right there with you praying, because I won't be
good for anything else."*

"The problem with that estimate is that Chief Edril,
who commands the Coerli in Clarey's troop . . . ," Zettin
said. He was standing at parade rest, entirely a soldier
rather than an official reporting. "Insists that there're
many more rats than there are soldiers in the royal army.
Clarey disagrees, but he says that Edril's never been wrong
to his knowledge."

Garric frowned. "With all respect to Chief Edril," he
said, "counting above twenty is higher mathematics to
the Coerli. Their hunting parties weren't any bigger than
that, so they never needed to think in greater numbers
until they ran into us after the Change."

"Your Highness, I agree completely," Zettin said, his
face working uncomfortably because he *wasn't* agreeing
with his prince. "I only point out that Edril was giving a
relative measure rather than an absolute one; and, well,
as you said, the Coerli think in terms of hunting parties.
A hunting party doesn't have supply wagons or servants

or, ah, if I may say so, hired companions and other enter-
tainment for the soldiers. A hunting party is made up
solely of warriors . . . which appears to be the case with
this army of rat men as well."

"He is a clever fellow," Carus said. *"Didn't I say that
you need that sort too?"*

"Liane," Garric said, turning to the woman at his side.
She was writing on the last of three tablets with quick,
firm strokes of her stylus. "I need to inform Lord Waldron immediately. Now we've got a target to strike at."

"Yes," said Liane, closing the tablet and holding it
seam upward with the other two. "And I thought Lords
Royhas out of courtesy and Hauk for immediate planning."

With her free hand she lifted the tray of wax from the
frame that held it over an oil lamp, then splashed blobs
across the tablets. The red wax was still tacky when she
pressed the royal signet in the third time. She rose with
the grace of a flower opening and walked past Zettin to
the door.

"Yes, I agree," Garric said, smiling wryly. The ring
she'd sealed the notices with was in theory Prince Garric's; he didn't recall ever having used it. That was what
he had Liane for, he supposed. One of the things.

"From a supply standpoint," he said to Zettin in a conversational tone, "we're much better off with Palomir attacking Haft. Supplying Pandah is a problem even without
refugees flooding in ahead of an army of ratmen; the villages of Grass People in the district around here don't
have a great deal of surplus."

"Why do you suppose Palomir attacked us instead of
one of the southern islands where the royal army couldn't
intervene, Your Highness?" Zettin asked.

He glanced over his shoulder, then jerked his head
around in embarrassment for his instinctive curiosity. Liane was giving crisp orders to attendants in the hallway,
directing them to deliver the three notices at once.

Garric shrugged. "For all we know, there's other armies marching on Shengy or elsewhere, milord," he said. "Though I doubt it. Shengy at least is mountainous terrain and never seems to've had much of a population. It's pretty clear Palomir's out to capture people to rebuild the city."

"We can't march on Palomir if their army's behind us," Carus said. The ghost's expression was one of cheerful enthusiasm. *"By the Lady, if they did go haring off to Shengy or Seres, there wouldn't be anything left when they wanted to come home!"*

I don't think the Lady's the right one to invoke for destroying cities, Garric replied silently. Though blasphemy was pretty minor as the sins of soldiers went.

"If She's any kind of gardener," Carus said, *"then she kills the slugs on her vegetables. And Palomir's a nest of slugs if there ever was one!"*

Liane returned to the table. "I sent a messenger to Tenoctris also," she said. "Asking her to join us as soon as possible."

"Right," said Garric. "I should've thought of that."

He cleared his throat. "Lord Zettin," he said as he rose to his feet, "will you excuse us for a moment? I'll want you present again when the others arrive."

"Your Highness," Zettin said with an apologetic nod. He was out the door and closing it behind him in a single flowing motion.

"He moves like a swordsman," Carus noted approvingly. "And *clever.*"

Garric put his arms around Liane, drawing her close. "I'll be commanding the army," he said quietly into her hair. "We'll be moving fast, just the troops themselves and the supply column."

He cleared his throat. "The men won't be permitted to bring companions along. And therefore neither will I."

"Yes," said Liane. "Of course."

She didn't pull away from Garric, but she leaned back

so that she could look him in the face. She said, "Dear, we both have jobs to do. We'll do them, and if we're successful we'll be together again afterwards."

Garric bent to kiss her.

Liane was very smart, and beneath the surface she was as ruthless as an executioner. Garric had seen how she ran her spy network, directing—and doing—things that made him queasy to watch.

She wasn't arguing with his assessment of what was proper and therefore necessary to the good order of the kingdom. But he knew Liane bos-Benliman too well to think she was going to sit quietly in Pandah and wait for his return.

SHARINA HAD FIVE minutes to dress by the water clock in the courtyard, and getting into her formal robes had never taken fewer than ten to her knowledge. There was no real reason to change, but there was no real reason for Princess Sharina to be meeting the delegation of merchants from Valles. If she was going to meet them—and for political reasons she should—then she had to wear court robes. To do otherwise would be to insult the delegates, making the situation even worse.

"Raise your arms," said her maid Diora. Sharina obeyed promptly; the maid grunted and settled the plain inner robe over them.

Master Helcote, the chamberlain, would've been horrified to hear Diora speak to the princess in a tone of brusque practicality, but he was already horrified that the princess had dismissed the establishment of twenty servants who should in his opinion be waiting on her.

Sharina had been a servant. She didn't expect any more privacy in a palace than she'd had in her father's inn, but neither did want to have twenty tongues gossiping about what the princess did or about what made a better story than what she really did.

Diora was willing to dress Sharina, fix her hair, and tidy the suite to Sharina's satisfaction by herself. In exchange, the maid was paid double what she'd otherwise have earned, and she had leave to spend most nights with her fiancé, a Blood Eagle captain. They both thought they did well out of the arrangement.

Someone knocked on the suite's outer door. Sharina grimaced and said through the smothering folds of the robe, "Who is it?"

Could they even hear her? And why were the guards outside letting somebody bother her now in the first place?

"Her Highness says to wait," said Diora in her harsh Erdin accent. She was the daughter of a small shopkeeper, and could if she chose to strip plaster off the walls with her tongue. Not in front of Princess Sharina, of course.

"If you please, Sharina?" Liane called, pitching her voice to penetrate the door panel and the robe now sliding over Sharina's shoulders. "I won't take a moment and you can continue dressing."

"I'm so sorry, Liane!" Sharina called. Diora had let go of the robe and opened the door without being told to. "Come in!"

"I'm sorry to disturb you when you're so busy," Liane said, closing the door herself. "I have many things to take care of also, and there's not much time."

"Busy!" Sharina said and snorted. "I'm meeting Valles merchants who want Prince Garric—want the kingdom—to redirect the River Beltis to drain into the Southern Seaway instead of into the marshes between Charax and Bight as it has since the Change. Otherwise Valles will cease to be a major port."

"Yes, it will," said Liane. "And the sun will continue to rise also, but I don't blame someone who's to be executed at dawn from regretting that. The delegates deserve to be given the death sentence of their city with dignity."

She picked up one arm of the outer robe. "Here," she said to Diora. "I'll help you."

"When I've got these pleats tied, milady," said the maid, tugging at the laces running up the middle of the back. Every time Sharina was dressed in a court robe, she reminded herself to have Diora show her exactly how the arrangement of ribbons and plackets worked as soon as she next took it off. And every time she took it off, she forgot everything in the pleasure of getting out of such hot, heavy, confining garments.

Liane was from Sandrakkan; her father was a nobleman with an estate west of Erdin. Even so she'd spoken with real compassion for the residents of Valles, the capital city whose existence had twice in living memory brought Sandrakkan to rebellion. *My brother's very lucky to have found someone as able as Liane, and as compassionate.*

"Sharina," Liane said, "during my absence I'm leaving my special duties—"

The intelligence service.

"—in the hands of my deputy, Master Dysart. He's both organized and careful. I don't believe you'll notice any difference in the quality of the information that you receive."

Sharina kept from frowning only by an effort of will. After only an instant's reflection, she realized that Liane wasn't talking in front of Diora in the arrogant assumption that a servant wasn't a person and therefore couldn't hear. Liane *knew* Diora as a person—and trusted her, as Sharina herself trusted the maid.

"I don't question your personnel judgments, Liane," Sharina said. "I don't think anyone who knows you would do that."

She was still surprised to learn that Liane was accompanying Garric on campaign, but that was none of anybody else's business. The kingdom depended on Garric's decisions. If Liane's presence helped him perform better, then that was more important than anything Liane could do in Pandah, where her duties were in the hands of a trustworthy replacement.

"The only problem you might have with Dysart," Liane said, "is that his family had a small importing business in Erdin; he's not a noble."

"Pardon?" said Sharina. She was sure she'd misheard. "Liane, *I'm* not a noble. Nor, well, is my brother."

"Oh!" said Liane. She paused, holding her hands palm-out. "I didn't mean that the way it sounds. I didn't mean—"

"I'm ready for the outer robe now," said Diora. "If you're really willing to help."

"Thank you," said Liane, gratefully seizing the chance Diora had given her to organize her thoughts. "Yes, of course."

Liane and the maid lifted the outer robe between them and settled it over Sharina as she held herself very still. The garment was heavy brocade with embroidery and appliqués in metal thread. Uncomfortable didn't begin to describe it, but Liane was right: the delegates deserved courtesy when they were told that their city, the capital of the Isles for centuries, was doomed.

Sharina's head emerged from the heavy garment. She breathed deeply; she'd been holding her breath without being conscious of it while her head was covered in thick silk. As Liane stepped out of the maid's way, she and Sharina exchanged rueful smiles.

"I didn't mean noblemen had a monopoly on intelligence or honor," Liane said, no longer grasping for words. "You don't have to read much history to know that. But Dysart doesn't *think* like a noble. You do, and Garric does. You weren't raised to think that your village or your business is all the world."

"But Dysart runs day-to-day operations now?" Sharina said in puzzlement. "Which is the whole kingdom and beyond."

"Yes, and he runs them very well," Liane said. "But he

thinks in terms of agents and facts and incidents. He'll know everything that can be known, but there may be things he doesn't understand."

She smiled ruefully. "There've been times I thought that Dysart doesn't understand *any*thing," she said. "Which isn't fair. But please, when he gives you summaries, which he'll do every morning, remember that there may be a forest which Dysart isn't seeing for the trees."

"I see what you mean," Sharina said. She grinned, because she suddenly felt warm at the realization that she was a part of a family. They were all working for the common good, passing duties back and forth when the need arose, but all *working*. "It's bad enough to be my brother when he's gone. I guess being you as well means I won't sleep."

"I'm sorry," Liane said. Her lips were trembling. "But I . . ."

"A moment, Diora," Sharina said to the maid who was tying the myriad tucks and bows that were part of the outfit. She stepped forward and embraced her friend.

"Be safe, dear," she said. "Garric and the kingdom are very lucky to have you. And so am I."

Oh, Lady, I'm crying too!

In the background, Sharina heard Diora murmur, "I'll send Lancombe to tell the Valles merchants that you'll be a little late."

ILNA HAD NEVER cared much about the landscape. That didn't mean she was unaware of it, though, and the North River waterfront was ugly by any standard. The landings were rickety straggles standing over an expanse of sedges, reeds, and mud.

Especially mud. The riverbank was low, and storms upstream regularly spread water half a furlong back from the normal channel. Anything like organized business required a wharf, though Ilna watched small traders wading to and from their boats.

The river was lined with willows and alders when Ilna first saw it. For as far as she now could see through the haze, the trees had been cut down for building material.

Krumlin's wharf was more solid than most: it stood on piles, not a lattice of withies, and the floor was sawn lumber rather than a corduroy of thin poles. Ilna smiled minusculely. This was better than splashing through muck to midthigh, though she'd have done that too if it had been necessary. It might well be necessary when they landed downriver.

She started down the wharf, checking the vessels moored to either side. Those near the bank were aground, though they didn't seem the worse for it. Each sat in a glistening wreath of water, waiting for another freshet to lift them free.

Master Ingens popped his head up from a berth near the far end, just before Ilna reached that point. "Oh," he said. "You came after all."

"I came, of course," Ilna said. She considered whether to go on; then she said, "Master Ingens, we're going to be together for some time. This will be less unpleasant for both of us if you learn that I mean what I say. Do you understand?"

"It was getting late," the secretary said. He backed down the ladder to the boat below. "Still, you're here. It doesn't matter."

"We'll also do better if you stop telling lies when you make a fool of yourself," Ilna said, swinging her bindle—a few necessities wrapped in a middle-weight cloak, itself the bulkiest item—around to her back to follow him. "The sun's an hour short of midmorning, which is the time you set."

"Whatever you say," Ingens muttered.

The boat reminded Ilna of the dories that men in Barca's

Hamlet had used to fish the Inner Sea, though it had a flatter, shallower bottom. It was about as wide as Garric was tall and as long as five men that height. The mast was unstepped. It and the yard with the sail furled around it were lashed to yokes, keeping the belly of the vessel free for cargo. Since they carried only supplies for the journey, the "passengers' quarters" were as spacious as Ilna ever remembered on shipboard.

The crew of four Dalopans eyed her in flat-faced silence. They wore swatches of bark cloth around their waists and bone pins thrust through parts of their bodies. Mostly that meant nose and ears, but one of the squat, dark men had a triangle woven into each cheek. It'd been done long enough ago that knots of scar tissue swelled over the bone splinters.

The captain wasn't any more prepossessing, though he was from a northern island. The black zigzags slanting across his tunic were a Blaise style. The garment was of good quality, but worn and a little too small for this man to have bought it new.

"Well, girlie," he said, leering at Ilna. "I guess I don't mind having a woman aboard for the trip after all."

Ilna thought for a moment, then adjusted the pattern in her hands slightly. The fellow was necessary, she supposed.

"This is Captain Sairg," Ingens said. "His boat and crew brought me—"

Ilna stepped so that her back was to Ingens and the Dalopans were on the other side of Sairg; the boat shifted nervously. The captain apparently thought she was offering herself to him; he grinned broadly and reached for her. Several of his teeth were missing and the survivors were black.

Ilna spread the pattern. Sairg screamed and staggered backward, throwing his hands over his eyes. He'd have gone over the side if a crewman hadn't grabbed him.

"Captain Sairg," Ilna said. "You are a hireling and I am your employer. If you ever again forget that, you will spend eternity in the place you glimpsed a moment ago. Do you understand?"

"You bloody fool!" Ingens snarled at the captain. "I told you she was a wizard, didn't I?"

Sairg rose to a squat, looking out past the edges of his splayed fingers. Despite his terror, the boat didn't wobble when he moved. He was somewhat lower in Ilna's estimation than the carp browsing Pandah's sewage on the river bottom, but he remained a sailor.

"Sairg, now that Mistress Ilna's aboard, we should get under way," Ingens said, reverting to a brusquely businesslike tone. "There's nothing to gain by hanging around on this mudbank longer than we have to."

Sairg grimaced, spat over the side, and moved to the stern. He kept as far as he could from Ilna. When he'd taken the steering oar in hand, he squealed and clicked to the crew in a language Ilna didn't recognize. They were already lifting the sweeps into rowlocks made from deer antlers.

"The crew speaks only Dalopan," Ingens said. "He's telling them to push off."

Sairg cast off the stern line; the bow line was already coiled. Ilna looked at the secretary and said, "Do you speak Dalopan, Master Ingens?"

He looked at her, apparently surprised that she had noticed. "A little, yes," he said. "Master Hervir generally took me with him on his travels. But Sairg hired the crew; I don't interfere."

The two Dalopans on the left shoved against the pilings, sending the boat sideways into the channel. They leaned so far over that Ilna was sure they'd fall in. When they were almost parallel to the water, they twisted back aboard with motions Ilna couldn't have described even though she'd watched them do it. Their toes must grip like a skink's. The men settled onto their benches and began dragging the long sweeps, swinging the bow outward against the controlled strokes of their fellows on the right side.

Ilna chose a place and leaned her shoulders against the furled sail. She began knotting a pattern, an occupation rather than an end in itself. At one time in the past she'd have brought a small loom with her, but a hank of yarn would do her as much good as the frame and be much easier to carry. There was plenty of space now, but she had no way of knowing what she'd be getting into later on the journey.

"You've traveled a great deal, have you not, mistress?" said Ingens. He was seated on the bench between the fore and aft pairs of oarsmen, looking toward her with polite interest.

Ilna thought for a moment. "Yes, I suppose you could say that," she said. For a peasant who'd never expected—or wished—to leave the hamlet in which she'd grown up, she'd traveled very widely indeed.

In a slightly harder tone—she supposed her tone was never what you'd call gentle—she went on, "But why *do* you say that, Master Ingens?"

The secretary held a scroll in his left hand, his thumb marking his place. He used it to gesture mildly and said, "I guessed you'd traveled because you didn't come with a wagon train of luggage. And I spoke because, as you pointed out, we'll be together for some time. If you prefer, we can try to keep silent save for necessary business, but that isn't my preference."

Ilna considered, then smiled faintly. "Nor mine, I suppose," she said. "I gather you and Hervir traveled widely also?"

"Yes," Ingens said. "Hervir took over the prospecting, I suppose you could call it, six years ago when his father moved into the office. When he became head of the family at Halgran's death, he left the office work to his wife and mother and continued to handle contacts with suppliers all over the Isles. He kept me with him on all his journeys. He said my notebooks—"

The secretary gestured again with the scroll.

"—were invaluable. He was always very appreciative of my efforts for the company, in fact."

Ilna kept her face blank as she digested what she'd just heard. The words alone could've been bragging—very possibly truthful, but bragging nonetheless. Ingens' tone, however, was either bitter or sarcastic. Or both, she supposed; there was no reason it couldn't have been both.

She looked to her left—the boat's right; starboard to a sailor, she knew, but she wasn't a sailor. They were well into the channel, so she could see the far bank despite the blur of mist which the sun even now hadn't completely burned off. The trees and brush were gray-green, indistinguishable save by shades of color that she perhaps alone would note.

"You were a friend of Hervir?" Ilna asked. Her fingers started to knot a pattern that would give her the answer, but she paused to let the secretary speak. She supposed she was being polite.

"Master Hervir was my employer," Ingens said. "He was a considerate employer who paid me a fair wage and who was both in public and in private appreciative of my efforts for the company. As I said."

He considered Ilna for a moment, either choosing his words or choosing the words he was willing to speak to her. "We were not friends, no," he said. "The relationship was not a personal one."

"You didn't sail to Caraman with Sairg in the first place?" Ilna said.

"I hired Captain Sairg on Blaise when I reached the river," Ingens said. "He'd made the trip up the river twice already before. We sailed to Pandah on the prevailing wind; downstream we'll use the current. The sweeps are mostly for steering."

The river was a muddy brown picked out by patches of scum and flotsam. The debris was mostly vegetable, including a large tree whose roots, washed clean by a flood, wriggled in the air like an ammonite's tentacles. Ilna saw the corpse of a dog, though, and a sheep so bloated that it looked like a fleece mattress.

"We went overland from Valles," Ingens said. "Hervir's plan all along was to find a suitable ship for our return via the river. I simply followed his intentions. Though without the saffron, of course."

And without Hervir, which is all that concerns me, Ilna thought. She wondered if it concerned Ingens. There was nothing in his words or expression to suggest that it did, but on the other hand he *had* started back to find his employer immediately after delivering word of his disappearance.

"The channel is constantly changing, Sairg says," Ingens said. He pointed with his whole arm toward the near shore. "Even I can tell that. See that stand of cypress?"

"Yes," said Ilna, when she was sure that she did.

"There's only three trees left," the secretary explained. "I remember counting seven when we were coming upriver. Four were undercut and fell into the river. I don't think the others will survive much longer. The whole world is still in flux."

Ilna sniffed. "Trees have always fallen into rivers," she said. "Things have always died."

"Yes, but *everything* is new now," Ingens said. "This whole river is as new as the lands it drains."

He paused, then added, "Hervir was adamant about that. He said there was no end of what a bold man could achieve in this new world. Hervir was a very ambitious man. Marrying the sister of an Ornifal nobleman was barely the start of it."

"Are you a bold man looking to better yourself, Master Ingens?" Ilna said, watching the secretary's face.

How he chose to respond to the question would tell her more than the mere words he used.

He snorted. "Me?" he said. "Boldness isn't enough, mistress, if you don't have money to back it up with. I have my salary; which is adequate to my needs, but not the sort of stake I'd need to set up as a spice merchant on my own."

"Did you think of asking Hervir for a loan?" Ilna said. "You say that he valued you and respected your abilities."

"Hervir valued me as an employee," Ingens said. He didn't try to hide the bitterness, perhaps realizing that he wouldn't succeed anyway. "He saw no benefit to himself or to Halgran Mercantile in having me as a rival. He laughed, in fact. 'I haven't spent six years training you, Ingens my boy, in order to have you undercutting me with my suppliers.'"

The secretary's face worked; another man would've spit into the brown water. "Him training *me*," he said.

"I see," said Ilna.

She might've said more, but at that moment Sairg chittered an order to the crew. "He's telling them to move us farther out into the channel," Ingens translated. "We're over a flooded forest here, and brushing a treetop the wrong way could tip the boat over."

The oarsmen quickened their stroke. One started what was obviously a chantey even though Ilna didn't understand the words. Her mind flashed bright with an image of Chalcus bending over the stroke oar, his tenor voice floating, "To me, way, haul away—"

And Merota's clear soprano answering, "We'll haul and hang together!"

Ilna wasn't crying, she *didn't* cry; but she closed her eyes and rubbed her face in the sleeve of her tunic until the moment was past.

* * *

WHEN LIANE SAID she needed to meet with him and Rasile, Cashel asked her to do it sitting on the walls of Pandah. He was about as comfortable here as he would've been in any city: he could look out and see green. It wasn't the right pale green of the sheep-cropped meadows south of Barca's Hamlet, but it was close enough he could pretend.

There hadn't been a lot of building here on the west side because the ground was so boggy. There were tussocks of grass and sometimes willows, but the road to the North River had to be the next thing to a bridge for most of its length. Crews had laid tree boles for stringers and pinned cross-logs to them with treenails. Putting up houses would've taken pilings, or maybe boats.

"Dariada is the largest city-state in Charax," Liane said. She'd opened her little portable desk and had three unopened books and a scroll laid out on it. "It's not the capital, though—the island, the region it is now, doesn't have a capital. There're seventeen states, and for the most part they don't get along well. Usually some of them are at war with one another."

Pandah was growing so fast that if the army—there was a city watch, but they weren't up to the job yet and the army was here—hadn't kept the battlements clear, there'd have been folks camping on them and in the streets below, for that matter. Lord Tadai wasn't going to have that, which Cashel was glad of for as long as he had to be in the city. For right now, a squad of troops blocked the staircase to the tower Liane had picked.

Cashel smiled at a thought. Given half a chance, folks'd pack in as tight as sheep in a byre. Since sheep ate grass instead of meat, sheep manure didn't make near the problem human manure did. It was a good thing it rained a lot in Pandah, but that was another reason not to build in the bogs which storms washed the streets into.

"That is . . . ," Liane said, angry because she hadn't been as clear as she thought she ought to be, "that was true of Charax during the first three hundred years of the previous millennium. What we in our day call the Old Kingdom, though the cities of Charax were independent at the time. That's the situation since the Change, too."

Rasile watched Liane intently, which bothered Cashel a little to see: it reminded him of the way a vixen tenses toward a tuft of grass that she'd just seen move. As for Cashel himself, well, he was listening. He'd learned long since that not much of what folks as smart as Liane said made a lot of difference to him, though.

People didn't expect Cashel to talk politics or philosophy. The sorts of things they did take up with him, well, those weren't a problem. He knew how to deal with them, good or bad.

"Dariada is the most important city of the region, though, because the Tree is there," Liane said. "It's sacred to all Charax, but it's still in Dariada."

"Ma'am?" said Cashel, because trees were something he understood. "What kind of a tree, if you please?"

Liane scrunched her face up over an unhappy thought. "I don't know," she said. "The ancient descriptions—"

She lifted the scroll from the table and waggled it.

"—aren't clear, and my agents haven't been permitted within the separate enclosure within the city walls. From the accounts, the Tree Oracle is a pod with the face of a man, and it gives responses to questions. The priests choose who can address the Tree, but the petitioner him or herself puts the question."

Cashel frowned. "Rasile?" he said. "Do we need to talk to the oracle, or are we just going to the city to start out with? Because I don't guess they've seen a lot of your folk on Charax, Coerli I mean. And it seems like they may get, well, perturbed."

One thing Cashel learned the first time he came into a city is that people in cities talked a lot; *really* a lot. Also stuff took a long while, especially if there was a lot of people needing to agree before things happened. What with one thing and another, it seemed like the pirates might be up to the city walls before a shepherd and a Corl wizard got anybody to listen.

"I must speak to the oracle, Warrior Cashel," Rasile said. "I did not understand why I saw a tree on the path till you told me that."

Her smile didn't disturb Cashel now that he'd gotten used to it, but he hoped she wouldn't try it on suspicious strangers in Charax. They were going to have problems enough as it was.

"Cashel," Liane said, setting down the scroll she'd picked up as an illustration. "Wizard Rasile. I will be accompanying you on your journey. Neither of you—"

"Ma'am?" Cashel blurted. He blushed when he realized he'd broken in on a woman talking—and her a lady besides—but he'd just had to! "You shouldn't be doing that. It's not right."

"It's not only right, it's necessary," Liane said. She didn't snap the way Ilna would've done if somebody talked to her like Cashel just had, but he didn't hear any more give in Liane's voice than there'd have been from his sister. "To begin with, neither of you can read. It's more than probable that you'll need to read in the course of this business."

"Ma'am, I know you're right," Cashel said. "But a clerk could do that."

He wouldn't like it even if she wasn't Garric's girl, because she was nice and this wasn't going to be a nice business. He'd seen what happened to women in Ombis when the pirates got through the hole in the walls, and what the male pirates were doing wasn't the worst of it. "Or an officer, I didn't want soldiers but maybe that'd be a good idea."

Liane was Garric's girl. Cashel *wasn't* going to take her along!

"And as you've already understood, Cashel," Liane continued, her voice smooth as polished diamond and just as hard, "we'll have to negotiate with the priests of the Tree. Neither of you are suitable for that task. I am the best person for it in the government, with the possible exception of Prince Garric. Even Garric would have a great deal to learn in a short time, though, and I'm already familiar with the business."

"Ma'am . . . ," Cashel said. He felt awful, his guts twisting themself tighter every time he breathed in. He couldn't think of anything to say that would change her mind. *Nothing* he said: Lady Liane said she was coming, so she would come.

He sighed. "Yes, ma'am," he said.

"Female Liane," Rasile said. She'd never stopped looking at Liane, and Cashel hadn't seen the old wizard's expression change from beginning to end. "I will take Warrior Cashel and myself to Dariada by a shorter route than walking through the waking world. If you come with us, you will take the same route."

Liane looked at her coldly. "Thank you, mistress," she said, clipping the words in a way Cashel hadn't heard her do before. "I am familiar with wizardry. My late father was a wizard himself. I'm not concerned with the means by which you accomplish the task in which I assist you."

"Tomorrow morning," Rasile said quietly. She looked at Cashel. "I would like a wooded grove for my incantation. Can you lead us to such a grove, warrior?"

"There aren't real groves anywhere near the city," Cashel said, mulling the question in his mind. "There's been too much building going on, you see."

"The palace has a roof garden," said Liane. "Will that be adequate?"

"It will," said Rasile, wagging her tongue in agreement.

Liane rose to her feet. "I have more business to attend," she said. "I'll see you tomorrow morning at the palace."

Cashel offered Rasile a hand, mostly for courtesy. She was spry enough she didn't really need it. They didn't speak as they watched Liane disappearing down the stairs into the guard room below.

It was true that Liane knew about wizardry: her father had trussed her for a sacrifice. If she was willing to go where and however Rasile led, then she was even braver than Cashel had already thought.

Chapter

5

CASHEL HADN'T BEEN here in the garden before. There were three small trees in pots: a weeping willow which must've been a trial for the servants carrying water to it and a pair of silver birches. The grape arbor was nice, and there were terracotta planters with flowers.

Anyway, Rasile seemed satisfied as she placed the yarrow stalks she used to lay out her figures. Cashel was used to being around animals whose legs bent the wrong way so it didn't bother him when she hunched, the way it did some folk looking at the cat men. When Rasile stood up, though—well, a sheep never did that.

Liane stood like she figured to be hanged by midday. She wore sturdy tunics that must've been from Ilna; nobody else Cashel knew could weave cloth so practical and still have designs that seemed simple until you looked at them close. The sleeves and torsos mated perfectly.

"These myrtles seem full grown even with being so small," Cashel said quietly.

It took a moment for Liane to understand he was talking to her. When she did, she jumped like he'd poured ice water down her back.

She flashed a wide, embarrassed smile. "Yes," she said, "they're a dwarf variety from the mountains of Shengy. One of Mistress Gudea's tutors grew this kind. It's hard to imagine a pirate with the same tastes as Mistress Lassa, but I suppose it makes a change from drinking blood and cutting people's fingers off."

Cashel laughed. He had a notion of what it was like in Liane's head right now, and it wouldn't have been right to let her wallow there. If she'd been Sharina, Cashel would've put an arm around her—or more likely, Sharina would've put an arm around him. Cashel wasn't comfortable doing that, but sometimes it was the best thing there was.

"I guess," Cashel said. "I think I'd rather have peonies, though."

He kept on smiling, but mention of pirates made him think of Ilna's friend Chalcus. They'd never talked about the things Chalcus had done before he met Ilna, but you could read from the scars all over his body that he hadn't been the kind of sailor who took a tub from Shengy across the Inner Sea with a load of oranges ripening aboard.

Had Chalcus cut off fingers and drunk blood? Not without a reason for it, but Cashel guessed there wasn't much Chalcus *wouldn't* have done if he'd had to. Because Ilna wouldn't have been happy with a man who wasn't that way, since she surely was herself.

"Cashel?" Liane said, looking at his smile and maybe seeing what was behind it. She was smart, just as smart as Garric.

"I was thinking about my sister, ma'am," Cashel said. He didn't talk much, but he'd answer a question if somebody asked him. It was easy when you were willing just to tell the truth. "She's gotten a lot mellower since we left home—even after she lost Chalcus and Merota, I mean, though for a while there she was something else. But you still wouldn't want to be on the wrong side of her."

"No," said Liane, "I wouldn't. But I don't think anybody could be a better friend."

Cashel smiled. "Yes, ma'am," he said. "But she's not a good friend to herself."

Rasile got to her feet, looking like a toy unfolding. "Are you ready, Cashel?" she said.

"Yes, ma'am," he said.

Rasile's eyes were a little harder as she turned them on Liane. The expression reminded Cashel that the wizard's jaw was long and full of pointed teeth. "And you, female Liane?"

"Just Liane, please," she answered pleasantly. "Yes, I'm ready."

"Then join me in the heptagram, Cashel and Liane," the wizard said. "The star of power, we of the True People call it."

She waggled her tongue in the equivalent of a grin. "We will see if it has *enough* power," she said.

"The power . . . ," said Liane as she stepped over the jagged line of yarrow stalks. "Is in you, Rasile, not in your symbols. And you have power enough."

"The wizard Tenoctris trusts me more than I trust myself," said Rasile. "But in this, I think she is right."

There was room enough in the star for Cashel with the two women, but it was pretty tight. Since there was time, Cashel counted the points: there was a handful and two fingers. It'd seemed like more just to look at; it must be that the yellow stalks were tricking his eyes.

Rasile began to chant, wagging her slate athame side to side in front of her. She sounded like a catfight instead of wizardry unless you paid attention to the rhythms, but if you did that, you knew it was just the same as Tenoctris.

Liane was standing really stiff. Part of that might be how close they were together, but she relaxed a trifle when Cashel gave her a slow smile. She carried a bag of waxed linen with a broad strap over her shoulder. It wasn't big, but it looked heavy. Cashel would bet anything that there was books in it.

Garric generally carried a book with him, too. Sharina said that she read for pleasure, but her brother was the real scholar of them. That was another way he and Liane were well matched.

Cashel had his usual leather wallet, the one he'd used when he was watching sheep or doing any other job that would keep him away from the mill at lunchtime. In it was hard bread, whey cheese, a gourd of ale with a wooden stopper, and a couple onions. It would keep for a week and not be the worse for the wait. It wouldn't be any better either, of course, but that had been what he'd eaten for most of his life. Nobody could look at Cashel or-Kenset and say simple food wasn't enough to keep a man healthy.

Rasile yowled her incantation. The sky looked bright when Cashel glanced at it, but it didn't seem to throw as much light down on the roof slates as it had a moment before. The shadows of the flowerpots were blurring into general darkness.

Rasile shrieked something that ended with a spitting sound, *pft-pft-pft!* The yarrow stalks burned with red wizardlight, and a razor of ice shaved Cashel's marrow. The landscape beyond them changed.

Tufts of grass, yellow and dry, sprouted from gritty soil. The wind was harsh and cold and terribly thin. Cashel drew a deep breath, but it felt like he was being smothered with a feather pillow. In the distance was a great mountain, its slopes glittering with ancient snow. From its peak trailed steam with a sulfurous tinge.

Cashel had been holding the wizard's woven satchel in his left hand and his quarterstaff in his right at the balance. Now he slipped the looped handles up over his shoulder so that he could spread both hands on the staff. He didn't swing it horizontal, though, because the ferrules would've stuck out beyond the edges of the star.

Rasile called out again, rousing another pulse of

wizardlight. Liane stood with her eyes closed and her face set. Bone-chilling cold cut again.

They were on a shore. Basalt spikes, one of them hollowed into an archway by the surf, stood up from black sand; the landscape for as far as Cashel could see had no other features. The water was bright blue where it rolled onto the beach, but in the middle distance it changed sharply to the dusty green of olive leaves.

Something on the horizon curled up, then back into the depths. Cashel wondered how anything alive could be so big.

Rasile called, and ice carved deep again. The sea vanished and the sand they stood on was red. The air smelled wet. Soft-bodied plants sprouted around the margins of a pond near the figure of yarrow stalks. There wasn't any grass and the tallest plants were horsetails that Cashel could touch the tops of by stretching his arm up.

Rasile sank onto her haunches. Cashel and Liane both reached to grab her, but she hadn't collapsed; she was just settling.

"Our route is over these sands, companions," the wizard said, looking out over the waste. Sandstone ridges slanted across it; there were more plants in their lee. Cashel felt a breeze, but it didn't smell of anything in particular.

"Where is this place?" said Liane. Now that they'd arrived she sounded calm, the way she usually did. "That is, is it in our world?"

"Perhaps," said Rasile. "Not our time, though; your time or mine either one."

"Ma'am?" Cashel said. "Give me a moment, if you will."

He stepped out of the star so that he had room to limber up with his staff. He began to spin the iron-shod hickory in slow circles. Having the wizard's satchel over his shoulder cramped him, but it was all right if he kept his arms up a little more than usual.

He'd drop the gear if there was time, of course. But there might not be time.

Cashel brought the staff around in a figure eight, spinning faster. He wasn't surprised that the tips left sparkles of blue wizardlight behind them. The landscape looked simple enough, but something here was making the hair on the back of his arms and neck prickle.

He slowed to a halt and slanted the quarterstaff in front of him with his left hand high. Looking back to the women, he said, "I guess I'm ready now, Rasile."

The wizard rose from her crouch. "And I am ready to lead, Cashel," she said. "This is not a place to tarry."

Rasile started off to the southeast, her legs taking quick, steady strides. She seemed to have recovered from the wizardry, though she was still pretty old.

Liane glanced at Cashel. When he nodded, she followed Rasile by a double pace behind. She wore sturdy sandals that even had cleats; they weren't anything like her usual footgear. Cashel hoped they wouldn't blister her feet.

Liane usually kept an ivory-mounted case knife in her sash. The finger-long blade was etched and gold-filled, but both edges were sharp and the steel was the best Cashel had ever seen. She held it bare in her hand now.

Cashel brought up the rear, looking in all directions. Not looking for anything in particular, just for things that might be a problem. Which was anything at all in this world, he figured, from the way his skin tingled.

He smiled. And that was true where they were going as well. It made him feel good to know he might be useful.

DIORA PAUSED IN the bedroom doorway and looked back at Sharina in her nightdress. "Your Highness, are you really sure you wouldn't like me to stay tonight?" she said. "Hachon will understand."

The maid frowned, apparently thinking about what

she'd just said. "Well, it doesn't matter what he thinks anyway, does it?" she said. "You being the princess and him just a captain. But he would."

"Thank you, Diora," said Sharina as she stepped forward to close the door herself if the maid didn't do it. "I prefer to be alone."

Well, of course what she'd *really* prefer was for Cashel to be with her, but that wasn't possible. The needs of the kingdom came first. Sharina was too . . . flat, she supposed. She wasn't physically tired, not unusually so at any rate, but after watching Cashel vanish she had no mental energy left to protest.

She'd be all right again soon. She always was.

Sharina walked to the window looking down on the courtyard. It wasn't a real garden, but four stubby palm trees stood in pots to punctuate benches which were empty at this hour. The quarter-moon showed everything clearly, though without color.

She hadn't been with Cashel when he went off this time. Rasile had said that many passages would be opening. Those protected within her seven-pointed star could choose the path they wished to take, but others who stood too close would find themselves in some uncertain elsewhere.

There was a bird nest in the top of the palm nearest Sharina's window. A chick peeped and a muted cooing responded; it must be a dove.

Sharina had watched Rasile's incantation from the fire tower, two furlongs from the roof garden but tall enough to give a good view of what was happening. She'd been alone, though her escort of Blood Eagles had been below in the tower just as they stood outside the door of her suite now. Cashel and his companions hadn't moved, though the ruby wizardlight swelled and waned about them in response to the Corl's chant.

Sharina looked away from the window. The bed had curtains but it was far too warm to need them tonight.

Diora had turned down the sheet before she left, but for a moment Sharina considered throwing an extra rug from the storage chest onto the floor and sleeping there.

Well, she could do that later. She got into the bed.

She'd expected a flood of wizardlight to blaze around her friends at the climax of the incantation. Instead, the heptagram had grown fainter and the three figures had slowly dissolved as though they'd fallen into a vat of acid. For an instant Sharina thought she could see Cashel's skeleton holding his hickory staff upright. She knew that was an illusion, but even so she had to step away from the parapet in fear that she'd topple over in a sudden wash of blackness.

Cashel will be coming back. I have to keep things going here so that there'll be comfort and safety when he returns.

Sharina was sure she wouldn't be able to sleep. She knew that if she tried to work, though, she'd just stare at tasks without doing anything useful.

She might've been able to accomplish something if Liane were with her. They worked well together, better than either did alone—and that was better than most people, she'd learned by going over documents prepared by others, even experienced clerks.

She missed Liane, but she missed Cashel more. She missed Cashel so much that her chest hurt with longing. She wouldn't be able to sleep—

And Sharina was asleep.

She floated above an enormous city. She recognized it from drawings by the architects Lord Tadai had engaged to plan Pandah's rebirth as capital of the kingdom. The old quarter remained, though the city walls had been razed to form boulevards and the tenements of the poor had been replaced by splendid public buildings.

The greatest was a soaring black temple; the dream Sharina curved toward it. The colonnaded plaza was paved with the same polished granite as had been used for the structures. In the center of it stood a tall man in a hooded black robe.

"Your gods are dead, Sharina!" he called. His voice came from everywhere. Storm clouds began to pile up as suddenly as foam covers a mug of ale.

"Come to me and worship Lord Scorpion!" the man said. Sharina felt her dream self drawn toward him like a straw in a millrace; she struggled.

"Worship the One Which rules this world and will rule it for eternity!" the man said, lifting his arms toward her. Her dream self was so close now that she could see the scorpion on the shoulder of his velvet robe, perched there like a trained magpie.

"Worship Lord Scorpion!"

Sharina willed her arms to drag her away, but she had no form to fight the current dragging her. Nonetheless she felt the fabric of the dream tearing about her.

"Worship Lord Scorpion!"

The clouds were black as starless night, twisting and shaping into a monstrous scorpion.

"Worship!"

Sharina lurched out of her bed. The sky had begun to hint at false dawn.

The Pewle knife lay on the small bedside table. She gripped the sealskin sheath with her left hand and drew the long blade. There was no enemy to face with the weapon, but its presence settled her.

Her mind still echoed with, *"Worship!"*

LORD ATTAPER WAS an Ornifal noble and as good a horseman as anyone in the royal army. Places in the Blood Eagles he commanded, however, were filled by soldiers who'd proved their courage in *any* of the regiments, most of which were infantry. It didn't surprise Garric when a trooper in the squad trotting ahead of him and Tenoctris wobbled, grabbed his saddle horn, and fell off anyway.

He hit with more of a thud than a crash of armor, since the ground was soft.

"Get up and rejoin us, Mitchin!" Attaper snarled, furious that one of his men had embarrassed him. "And quickly!"

"That seems a little unjust," said Tenoctris, riding beside Garric with ladylike grace—she was sidesaddle—and perfect skill. "This may be the first time he's ridden a horse in his life."

The wizard's family hadn't been wealthy, but they *were* noble; Tenoctris had learned to ride and, for that matter, to drive a coach and four. That latter skill had proven useful in the past, because it certainly wasn't one people raised in a peasant village were going to have.

"I don't think 'justice' is one of the concepts Attaper dwells on when he's doing his job," Garric said.

"Which is every bloody minute he's awake," Carus said. *"And I'd bet half his dreams are about guarding you, too. You don't make his life easy, lad."*

Then, in what was for the warrior king a reflective tone, he added, *"I don't think he's ever been as happy before."*

The cornicene of the cavalry troop they were riding with blew an attention note on the horn coiled about his body. The captain wigwagged his arms in a field semaphore, signaling the ten troopers of his lead section. They spread to left and right as they disappeared over the next rise.

Lord Zettin's scouts ranged far and wide across the continent, but the army's own cavalry was responsible for its close-in reconnaissance. Garric needed to see the terrain himself if he were to dispose his troops properly in event of a battle, and there wasn't likely to be margin to cover any mistakes he made.

Trooper Mitchin thundered past on his way to rejoin his squad. His shield, a section of cylinder, banged against him every time the horse gathered its legs. The Blood Eagles were equipped as infantry. Attaper had mounted this platoon only to allow them to keep up with the prince. If they had to fight, they'd dismount.

Lord Waldron hadn't liked Garric riding off with a troop of cavalry and a platoon of Blood Eagles, but he understood the logic of the plan. More to the point, he understood that it was his duty to obey when his prince ordered. Attaper wasn't nearly as clear on the latter point. He simply would have ignored Garric telling him to stay behind, so Garric hadn't bothered.

"Tenoctris?" Garric said. "I'm here to get a feel for the country."

"So that you and I get a feel for the country, lad," Carus reminded him. The ghost smiled, but his words were true enough. Carus had been a formidable swordsman, but his armies wouldn't have won every battle they fought if he hadn't also been even more impressive as a tactician.

Grinning at the silent comment, Garric continued, "But what are you here for? Are you looking for particular places to use your art?"

Tenoctris laughed. "Not at all," she said. "In fact, this country is very peaceful. Pleasantly bland, I feel. It's unusual to be able to look from horizon to horizon and not see signs of mass slaughter or dreadful rites anywhere. Well, it's been unusual for me in the past, at any rate."

This country in general ranged from bog to marsh, though the leading section had thus far been able to find ground firm enough for horsemen. It'd be a bad place to meet an enemy, since the soft ground would channel the fighting along a series of parallel causeways.

"It'd be worse for the rats, though," Carus said judiciously. *"They've got narrow feet."*

"No," Tenoctris said, "I'm here because you are, Garric. I believe that whoever is ruling Palomir will sooner or later attack you personally. I want to be where the excitement is."

She laughed merrily, but Garric didn't imagine her light tone took anything away from its truth.

"I don't think I'm that important," he said carefully.

Tenoctris shrugged.

"I *think you are, lad*," said the ghost in Garric's mind. *"If a sword and an army could've held the Isles together, I'd have done it. But that's all I had, and it wasn't enough. Nobody I've seen in this age has even that much. Nobody but you."*

The main body—the Blood Eagles around Garric and Tenoctris, and the ten-man section with the cavalry commander—reached the crest of the ridge. Garric saw the troopers of the lead element halfway down the swale, proceeding very slowly. Two of the horses were in mud to their knees, and a third man was backtracking from a bog he'd decided was impenetrable. The troop commander was changing his advance section every few miles, because picking the trail required considerably more effort than following did.

"The supply wagons are going to have the Sister's own time getting through this," Carus noted grimly.

We're using oxen, not draft horses, Garric reminded him silently. *Their hooves are broader, and they spread with pressure so they won't sink in as badly.*

Even as Garric's mind formed the thought, a trio of spiral-horned antelope sprang out of a willow copse and bounded across what looked like choking swamp. They made great leaps that seemed to be higher than they were long, pausing briefly between one and the next. Their feet must be adapted to the environment, though just how Garric couldn't imagine.

A pity we can't saddle them, Garric thought. *That would give us an edge against the rats.*

Aloud he said, "Tenoctris, if the Gods have vanished—or anyway, if They don't exist in this present . . . what does that mean for us? I mean, in the future?"

Tenoctris shrugged again. "Well, possibly nothing," she said. "After all, that's the world I lived in all my life until very recently: a world in which the Great Gods didn't exist."

"But you said you were wrong?" Garric said, frowning.

"Yes, but it's what I believed at the time," she said with a wry smile. "Despite all the evidence to the contrary, I believed it. So I have no difficulty in imagining a world in which the Gods really *don't* exist, rather than them simply not existing in my mind."

Garric considered a world without the Great Gods. He'd never doubted Their existence—people in Barca's Hamlet *didn't* doubt the Gods—but neither had They been a major part of his life.

Reise offered a crumb and a drop of ale to the Lady at family meals, but any true worship Garric had done was to the rough stone carving of Duzi on the hill overlooking the south pasture. The Shepherd Who protected the world was far too grand to worry about real shepherds, but little Duzi *might* find a lost sheep or deflect the lightning from the elm which sheltered the shepherd against the sudden thunderstorm.

So perhaps it really wouldn't make much difference. Garric was uncomfortable with the thought, but there was no end of more serious problems facing the kingdom.

"The difficulty is that I'm not sure the throne, so to speak, will remain empty," Tenoctris continued. The Blood Eagles had gone through this section single-file, but there was room for two horses abreast, or almost so. Garric nodded and Tenoctris pulled ahead; he followed closely enough that his horse nuzzled her left thigh.

"Certainly the Gods of Palomir hope to fill the void," she said. "And we hope, of course, to disappoint them. I rather doubt that they're the only powers who wish to rule this age, however. And they may not be the worst of the possible choices."

"First things first," Garric muttered. The leading element was signaling back to his captain with what seemed cheerful enthusiasm; perhaps they'd gotten through the boggy stretch. If so, it was time to turn back and carry the intelligence to the main body of the army.

But there'd be another day, and another day; each with its own problems.

Garric rose in his stirrups to stretch his legs; his gelding whickered without enthusiasm. "First things first," he repeated.

He was just tired, he knew, but he was very tired; in body and now, thinking of the Great Gods, soul. *I wonder when it stops?*

"For folks like you and me, lad," Carus said, standing arms akimbo on the battlements of a dream castle, *"it stops when we're dead. And it seems that for some of us, it doesn't stop even then."*

The ghost of the ancient warrior-king threw his head back and laughed, but it was a moment before Garric was able to laugh also.

THREE LARGE ANTELOPES whose horns curved like the arms of a lyre stood on the bank and stared wide-eyed at the riverboat as the Dalopans rowed past. They seemed terrified.

"Captain Sairg?" Ilna said. "There's a chance for some fresh meat."

The captain's face was set in a rictus of anger; he pretended not to hear her. The crewmen might *really* not have heard. They'd been stroking with the regularity of a waterwheel ever since the land started to quiver a little after dawn.

The sky was pale and its tinge reminded Ilna of a frog's yellow throat. She disliked it, and she disliked the vibration even more, though she didn't suppose it hurt anything. Instead of being muddy and opaque, the river's surface had become as finely jagged as the blade of a file. It was still opaque, of course; not that she thought there was much reason to want to look at the bottom of a river.

Ilna didn't know where they were beyond that they'd come several days north of Pandah; she'd never had much concept of geography. That had puzzled some folk when she was growing up, because Ilna os-Kenset had the most connection with the outside world of anybody in Barca's Hamlet. Her fabrics were sold in Sandrakkan, Ornifal, and even to the Serians who spun silk from the nests of caterpillars and shipped it to nobles throughout the Isles.

Merchants told her the size and thickness of the cloth they wanted for the places they would sell it. The patterns were Ilna's own, and the names of the islands to which the cloth went were merely that, names, to her.

Ingens muttered numbers as he laid down the cross-staff with which he'd just taken a sight on the rocky hill to the northeast; it was the first real feature the landscape had displayed since they pulled away from Pandah. He extended the parallel lines he was drawing on a strip of paper and added a note in the margin.

"It's a map of the river," he muttered to Ilna. "For later voyages."

"I see," said Ilna, then frowned because she wasn't sure that was true. She understood that the markings on a map told people where things were in the world—but they didn't tell *her* anything. She was always aware of direction, but place—here rather than there—had never been part of her world.

Ingens pointed to the hill which seemed to Ilna to be in their general course, though the way the river twisted across this flat landscape kept anyone from being sure. "That's Ortran," he said. "The island of Ortran before the Change. It didn't have anything on it but fishermen then. I don't know what they do now that the sea's gone. Fish in the river, perhaps, since they're in a bend of it."

As he spoke, Ingens was unrolling the strip between two sticks like an ordinary reading scroll. The portion he'd already written on was an ell long, the width of the largest loom Ilna kept at home. Kept wherever she decided home was at the moment, that is.

"Is it going to be helpful?" Ilna said. "Because it appeared to me that the riverbed's changing constantly. Even in the center of the channel we've gone aground."

Underscoring what she'd just said, a section of the bank ahead of them toppled slowly into the river, carrying with it a pin oak of considerable size. Foaming water lifted and swelled outward, though it didn't seem that it'd be any danger to the vessel. The tree twisted and rolled as it moved downstream; mud was slumping off its roots and unbalancing it.

"I don't know!" the secretary said. Then he grimaced and continued more calmly, "It's something to do, mistress. This sound is, is very disturbing."

"Was it like this when you were coming upstream?" Ilna said. She'd never been on this stretch of the river before and she'd assumed the way everything shook was normal. It was unpleasant, of course, but that wasn't unusual.

"There was nothing like it!" Ingens said. "I thought, I wondered I mean . . ."

He composed his expression and met Ilna's cool gaze. "I wonder if it has anything to do with Master Hervir's disappearance, mistress?"

Why in the world should it? thought Ilna, but she decided it was a legitimate question. She began plaiting the cords already in her hands into an answer. Everything was connected with everything else, of course, but it didn't appear that Hervir had any more to do with the shaking than he did with the price of wool on Sandrak—

"I'm sorry, I shouldn't have pried into your affairs," snarled Ingens in a tone of embarrassed anger. He uncapped the brass inkwell pinned to his collar to resume writing on his map.

Ilna looked at him more in surprise than anger. *Oh, he thinks I ignored his question and started weaving instead even of telling him it was none of his business.*

"I'm sorry, Master Ingens," she said. She *was* sorry: she hadn't communicated adequately, which was a problem she regularly had when dealing with people. That was a good reason to avoid dealing with them, of course, but there was no excuse for doing a bad job of what she'd started. "I've been looking for an answer in the pattern here. It doesn't seem that—"

Ilna lifted the loose fabric which her fingers had continued knotting as she spoke. As she did so, she looked at it—

And looked again. The pattern which she'd seen initially had formed into something quite different because she'd continued it beyond what she'd normally have done.

"There *is* a connection," she said. She hoped she hid the anger she felt. It was entirely directed at herself for having seen a pattern merely by good luck. Her anger was usually directed at herself, of course, but other people didn't generally understand that. "But it's distant, and they're both parts of a whole that's very much larger. Two knots in a carpet, so to speak; but there *is* a carpet and—"

The vibration stopped. The river was as still as the pond which drove the mill in Barca's Hamlet. A dozen lightning bolts ripped across the southern horizon, brightening the yellow sky to the color of melting sulfur.

One of the Dalopans in the bow dropped the oar and jumped up, shouting in a language that sounded like the chattering of a magpie. Ilna looked over her shoulder at him. All four crewmen were yammering now, looking more than ever like birds as they hopped about. They didn't disturb the balance of the boat, though.

Sairg called to the Dalopans in their own language; they ignored him. He let go of the tiller and rose to his

feet, holding the short, broad-bladed spear which Ilna
must've missed among the spars and cordage of the
stowed rig.

Ingens started to get up also, but he paused when the
boat began to wobble. From a half crouch he cried, "Sairg,
what's going on?" Pointlessly, it seemed to Ilna, but most
of what people did seemed pointless to her.

As though the secretary had shouted an order, the Dalopans dived into the brown water as gracefully as so
many kingfishers. A violent tremor to the south sped
across the flat landscape, lifting land and water as high
as the waves of a winter storm. A line of alders, spared
by the eroding riverbanks, jumped skyward and toppled
flat.

Ilna tucked the yarn into her sleeve and tugged loose
the silken cord she wore in place of a sash. Sairg was
blind with terror: she'd seen the signs too often not to
recognize his condition. She rose to her feet unwillingly,
hoping she wouldn't upset them but certain that even for
her—she couldn't swim—a ducking wasn't the worst
present danger.

"Wizard!" the captain screamed. He raised his spear.
"You've done this!"

How he'd come to that conclusion was beyond Ilna's
imagination, but the fellow was mad now or the next
thing to it. She took the cord's running noose between her
right thumb and forefinger, holding the remainder of the
lasso looped against her palm.

"Sairg, put that—" Ingens said.

The captain cocked the spear back to throw. Ingens
lunged, grappling with him as the wave struck, lifting
the riverboat on its crest.

The first wave. What had been the flat plain to the
south now rippled like brown corduroy. It was sprinkled
with vegetation uprooted when the ground itself flowed.

Ingens and Sairg pitched over the side, their legs flailing in the air. Ilna spun her lasso out sidearm.

She drew back, tightening the loop around the secretary's right thigh, and threw herself into the belly of the ship. Though she braced her heels against the gunwale, for a moment she felt her buttocks lifting from the wet planks: she was fighting the weight of both men. She wouldn't let go while she still lived, but all the determination in the world couldn't prevent them from pulling her into the pitching river with them.

The boat slid off the back of the wave. The flat bottom slapped down with what might've been a deafening crash if it hadn't been for the overwhelming roar of the world shaking itself like a wet dog. Ilna bounced as if she'd been struck by a swinging door. Ingens' head and torso lifted over the gunwale; he'd shaken himself loose from Sairg. His face was white and empty.

The boat rose again on the next tremor. The lashings that held the rigging had loosened, so the mast was jerking about. Ilna grabbed Ingens' collar with her left hand and leaned back, bracing her feet again on the side of the boat.

Ingens' eyes had no more intelligence than those of a fish, but his muscles moved with an instinctive urge to survive. His right hand scrabbled blindly in the boat until it closed on a thwart; then, with a colossal lurch, he rolled over the gunwale and into the belly of the vessel.

Ilna toppled back, but her grip on the lasso kept her from falling over the other side. The humor of the thought struck her. She didn't laugh often, but she barked one out now.

The boat crashed down, bouncing Ilna upright again. Ingens had his arms and legs wrapped around the mast as though he was adrift in the waves.

The boat scudded forward more swiftly than any normal current could drive it, lifting on the next throbbing pulse. The landscape was brown and splashed to either side, mud-choked water merging imperceptibly with land shaken to a liquid.

The earthquake throbbed, mastering the land the way a winter storm rules the sky: harsh, merciless, overwhelming. Ilna gripped the thwart she'd been seated on and looked in the direction the cataclysm drove them. Ortran was a rocky wedge thrusting from a landscape that otherwise was no more solid than the sullen yellow sky.

A pulse lifted the *Bird of the River* again, rushing the vessel toward an end of the disaster's own choosing. Ilna thought of a squirrel being sucked slowly and inevitably down the gullet of a snake.

The dark mass of Ortran loomed close ahead. Ingens' eyes were closed as he prayed in a singsong; Ilna could hear his voice only as rhythm woven into the roar of the earth tearing itself apart and reknitting.

Her own face was calm. If this was death, well, then she'd die. She'd have regrets, but the thing she'd regret most was that she'd ever been born. When she was dead, she wouldn't have to remember Chalcus and Merota laughing, or Chalcus stabbed through a dozen times and falling beside the corpse of Merota.

The boat scraped and skidded up the slope of coarse gravel which had been Ortran's shoreline. The shock didn't break Ilna's grip, but it lifted her over the thwart and slammed her numbingly to the planking on the other side.

Like a squirrel going down a snake's gullet. . . .

Chapter

6

IT SEEMED TO Cashel that the moon was bigger than it ought to be, but this way it threw plenty of light on the sandy hills even though it was just in the first quarter. Liane's shadow stretched back toward him, and ahead of her Rasile's did also.

The moon phase bothered him more than its size did, because back home it was only two days past the full. He knew that was silly: he was in a completely different world from where he'd been last night. But a shepherd takes the moon and stars as certain when nothing else, not even the seasons, ever is.

Something croaked from line of horsetails in the low ground to the right. It might've been a frog, though Cashel didn't suppose it was. To see wild animals, all you really have to do is sit in one spot and not do anything at all. If you were moving, though, even somebody as sharp-eyed as Cashel was would be lucky to catch sight of more than a squirrel on a high branch or maybe a rabbit. Rabbits didn't have any more sense than sheep did.

Rasile's slender legs scissored along quicker than a human's, which made it seem like she was really striding out in the lead. She took short steps, though, so really they weren't moving any faster than Cashel would when he was following a flock of sheep.

Liane suited her pace to the wizard's. Cashel looked at the thick woolen socks she was wearing and tried again to understand why. He guessed it wasn't just being nosy since they were going to be together in any kind of condition, so he said, "Liane, are your legs cold here?"

She glanced over her shoulder and smiled. "No," she said, "but my feet aren't used to the kind of walking I thought we might be doing."

She smiled even wider. "Walking like this, in fact. I wore the socks so that the sandal straps wouldn't chafe my feet, especially in loose sand."

"Thank you," Cashel said. "I should've guessed that."

Though thinking about it, he wasn't sure that was true. There weren't a lot of people like Liane. She usually rode horses or even in a carriage, but she was willing to hike across a wasteland if she thought that might help other folks.

Cashel didn't doubt having Liane along was going to help.

He saw movement. At first he thought he'd seen a reflection from the surface of a bog a couple furlongs to the east, but the gleam shook itself together and paced along parallel with them.

"Rasile, we've got company on the left," he said, just loud enough to be sure the wizard heard him. He wasn't nervous. This wasn't a new situation to Cashel, and it might not even turn out to be a bad one.

Because it *wasn't* new to him or any shepherd, he turned and scanned the hills to the right instead of focusing on the thing that'd let him see it. Sure enough, another gleam was there behind a reverse slope. Just the top of it showed now and again as it followed along beside Cashel and his companions.

"And the other side too," he said. He began spinning his staff in slow circles. Blue sparkles spiraled off the iron butt caps, bright enough that they raised purple reflections from the sand.

"Wait," said Rasile quietly, pausing on a dune that something the size of a rabbit had crossed recently. Tracks like little hands marked the wind-scallops. To the thing moving on the east she called, "Come join us or take yourselves away. If you choose to follow us, we'll treat you as enemies."

The creature laughed and walked toward them. "We're not your enemies, wizard," it called. "We know our strength; we do not challenge such as you."

She called, Cashel thought. The voice was female and perhaps even human.

"And the other," said one of the figures who'd come out of concealment on the right. There were two of them, much closer than the first. They looked like women wrapped in shining gray silk, but they moved too smoothly to be walking on human feet.

"Yes . . . ," said her companion. "He's magnificent. Can you imagine . . . ?"

They both burst into laughter as shrill as the cries of screech owls.

"Stay where we can see you," Rasile said harshly. She resumed walking southward with quick, steady steps. Liane followed, tilting her head toward the figure who'd spoken to them first. Cashel kept his staff spinning and watched all directions as he brought up the rear. Every few circuits he fed in a figure eight just to keep his wrists supple and show whatever the figures were how quick he could make the heavy hickory change direction.

"What are you doing in this place, wizard?" asked the figure on the left. "Are you hunting? There's little to hunt here."

"So very little," said one of her fellows.

"We're hungry," said the other. "We starve, we always starve, and there's nothing here to hunt."

"They're empusae!" Liane said. Then, to the creature on the left, "You're an empusa."

"What do names matter, little one?" the empusa said. She'd come close enough to touch with the quarterstaff and was moving parallel with Rasile. Her passage didn't mark the sand.

"She would be our prey if she were alone," said one of her sisters.

"Easy prey . . . ," the third creature whispered.

"Not easy," Liane said. She flicked a hand toward the speaker, the point of her knife glittering like a jewel. "I have a charm against your like."

The empusae fell into shrieking laughter. Cashel noticed that they backed away, though.

"What do you hunt, wizard?" said the figure on the left. The empusae's voices were cool but sweet, like they were speaking through silver tubes—except when they laughed.

"We have business in another place," Rasile said. "And our business is none of yours."

The wizard didn't turn her head to either side when she spoke to the creatures, but Cashel didn't doubt she knew exactly where each of them was. If she wanted to, she'd finish the things. Just as Cashel would, though they'd use different ways to do it.

The empusae laughed, but they drifted outward by a half pace or so.

Rasile's course took her companions along the edge of standing water as broad as a millpond. The empusa on their left slid through the horsetails without making their stems waver or touching the surface.

When the moon shone on the creatures, they looked like human statues polished out of blocks of lead. In reflection from the water—

"Duzi!" Cashel said, turning to send the staff through where the empusa had been an instant before. There was a blaze of blue wizardlight but the creature swirled to the other side of the pool without evident motion, more like a puff of breeze than anything physical.

The reflection he'd seen was tall, twice as tall as Cashel and taller than anybody could be. It was dead, too: strips of skin were hanging down like bark from a sycamore tree, and some places he could see through gaps in its rib cage.

But it wasn't human anyway. The limbs had too many joints, the skull slanted up a high forehead to a point at the back, and the long fangs in the upper and lower jaws crossed like a crocodile's.

"You are not our prey, splendid one," called one of the pair of empusae in her clear, liquid voice. They'd dropped back only a pace when Cashel swiped at their fellow.

"We bow before you," echoed her companion. "You are our lovely master. . . ."

Cashel grimaced. "I'm not your master," he muttered. "But I shouldn't have done that. I'm sorry."

He'd swished his staff out without thinking, because what he'd seen was ugly beyond his mind's ability to grasp. He didn't think he was wrong, exactly, because he didn't have the least doubt that the empusae were evil; but Rasile didn't think they were worth the effort of killing, and he knew he'd struck because he was startled, not because of any better reason. That wasn't something people ought to do.

"Did the Gods of Palomir send you, wizard?" asked the creature that Cashel had swung at. It'd moved closer again now that they were past the pond, but it was drifting along with Rasile instead of staying beside Cashel at the end of the line. "They have returned, you know."

"They are great and powerful," another empusa said.

"The old Gods are dead," chorused the third. "They banished us to this hungry waste, but They are gone."

"The Lady is no more!" the empusae sang together in triumph. Their voices were beautiful. "Franca and His siblings rule the waking world, and we will return to feast on men!"

Rasile looked at the pair of empusae, then toward the single creature drifting along to their left. Her tongue lolled out in the Corl equivalent of laughter.

"Not yet, I think," she said. "Not quite yet."

Turning back to Liane and Cashel, she said, "This is where we will return to the waking world. I'll step forward, and you follow me."

Liane nodded. Her face was fixed like an ivory carving, and the little knife was steady in her hand.

"Yes, ma'am," Cashel said. He didn't see anything different about this place—a ridge of sand with a low outcrop a furlong to the right and a pool and dark vegetation about the same distance to the left. He didn't worry, though: Rasile knew what she was doing.

The wizard paced forward, blurred, and disappeared. Liane followed just as steady as could be—and blurred, and disappeared.

Cashel kept the staff spinning and his head swiveling from one side to the other. He didn't trust the empusae, not even a little bit, and if they tried to come close—

He stepped into fog. He couldn't feel the hickory in his hands for an instant. He was back with Liane and Rasile, and the stone walls of a city loomed before them.

The shrieking laughter of the empusae still rang in Cashel's ears.

THERE'S SOMETHING OUT there, lad," said Carus. The ghost's hand caressed the memory of his sword hilt. *"I can feel it."*

We know they're out there, Garric thought. *But we've got pickets out and a palisade. If the rats attack tonight, we'll be in better shape than any time in the past three days.*

"I don't like it," Carus said, then laughed and added, *"But maybe it's just that when I'm on campaign like this, I miss the flesh more than other times."*

"I wonder what kind of tree this is," Garric said aloud to Tenoctris, looking up in the moonlight as he kneaded the backs of his thighs with hard fingers. The grove of tall trees on this slope had branches that came out straight from the trunk, though some turned upward at a right angle; they were covered with needles for their whole length.

"There were a few in the garden of Duke Tedry," Tenoctris said. The moon silhouetted the strange branches, making them look hairy. "They weren't native to Yole, though; an ancestor had planted them. I heard a gardener call them monkey-puzzles, but I don't know if he'd heard the name or made it up."

Lights shone below, hundreds of yellow-orange campfires sprinkled across the darkness like dandelions in a meadow. The army was camped on what before the Change had been a nameless rocky islet in the Inner Sea.

Now it was a forested limestone ridge rising from rolling plains. The ground was better drained than that near
Pandah a few days previous, so the marching was vastly
easier.

The soldiers slept in their cloaks, but none of them
would've objected if Prince Garric had traveled with not
only a tent but a full entourage of servants. They knew
Garric led from the front. If he lived as well as a man
could on campaign, that was what a general *ought* to do.

"Servants are a Sister-cursed bother," Carus muttered
in Garric's mind. *"And a tent doesn't help a bloody bit
unless you're going to skulk in it all day, in which case
you may as well have stayed home!"*

Garric grinned and seated himself carefully. His back
was to the low limestone cliff that ran down the spine of
the former island. Blood Eagles were on guard ten feet
above him on top of the ridge, and there was another
detachment on the slope below with lanterns on poles.
Nonetheless, the solid rock behind Garric provided a
slight illusion of privacy.

Aloud he said, "I've been thinking about how nice it
would be to be home in Barca's Hamlet. I'd probably be
worrying about whether I need to drain the cesspool this
fall or if it can wait till spring. And thinking what a terrible job it'll be."

He, Tenoctris, and the ghost of his ancestor all laughed.

Garric ached in muscles which two years before he
hadn't known existed. Carus' reflexive skill made his
descendent as good a horseman as an experienced Ornifal noble, but Garric's muscles hadn't been hardened by
a lifetime of daily exercise. Sure, he was strong—but the
particular stresses of horsemanship were different from
those of walking, digging, or any of the other things that
a peasant did.

His mind slipped away from the simple physical problems that he'd been unconsciously trying to keep it to.

"Tenoctris?" he said. "We've—the kingdom has, but you and I have too . . . we've survived a lot of things."

"Yes, Garric?" Tenoctris said. The lanterns were twenty feet away, sufficient to see by but without the detail of bright sun. In the soft yellow glow, Garric could imagine that Tenoctris was the aged wizard she'd been when she washed up on the shore of Barca's Hamlet. Her new youth and vibrancy were positive advantages in all ways, and it was that rather than vanity which had impelled her to regain that youth. But—

Garric had grown used to the old woman. The additional change, even though it was for the better, was disturbing at a level well below his consciousness.

The thought was so foolish that he grinned. It was good to do that, but it didn't lead his mind away from the question.

"Every time we survive, something new comes at us," he said. "Eventually, we *won't* survive. You and I won't, and the kingdom won't. Isn't that so?"

Tenoctris laughed. She'd laughed often throughout the time Garric had known her, but this full-throated, youthful chortling was new. And a little embarrassing, truth to tell, because Garric had the strong impression that he was more the subject of her good humor than the person she was sharing it with. The guards didn't face around to watch, but he could see their heads turn slightly in hopes of learning why the pretty young woman was laughing so hard.

"I think, now that you've suggested it . . . ," Tenoctris said. She'd choked off a giggle and seemed contrite at her behavior. "I think that perhaps I *could* become immortal. That's certainly one of the things the wizard whose powers I've borrowed intended to do. But I don't believe I could remain human, or that anyone human would want what immortality entails if they understood it as well as I do."

She pressed three fingers of her left hand into the palm of her right while she considered how to proceed, then looked up with an affectionate smile. "The kingdom will be replaced, yes," she said. "Not necessarily fall, but no human creation lasts forever. Nor does anything else last forever, of course. Even cliffs—"

She patted the face of rock. Light reflected from the pale limestone softened her silhouette, thrown onto it by the moon.

"—will wear down to dust, then be squeezed up again in a different shape and place. Yes you'll die, Garric, though I hope it will be 'full of years and wisdom.' Certainly that's the result I'm striving for, for mankind's sake. But death's a natural part of life, not the triumph of evil."

"But that's what I mean," Garric said with more heat than he'd intended. "Chaos, evil, *will* eventually win, won't it? We have to win every time, but if chaos wins even once, the fight's over. Forever."

"Ah," said Tenoctris, nodding with a look of understanding. "Garric, these past few years have seen a great deal of disruption—a unique amount, even for the thousand year cycle, because this time it brought us to the Change. But the preferred state of the cosmos isn't chaos, it's stasis: things remaining more or less as they are. I think—"

She paused, apparently looking down past the scattering of strange trees to the encamped army. Garric doubted she was really focusing on her immediate surroundings, though. A trumpet blew, announcing a change in the guard detachments.

"—I *hope*, Garric," she said, "that when the Gods of Palomir have been returned to their rest, this world will rest also. Now, I don't mean there'll be perfect peace!"

Garric laughed. "Not unless people vanish too," he said. "Which I wouldn't regard as a good thing, though I suppose one could."

"Yes," Tenoctris said. "But if—"

She waved a hand in the air.

"—the priest-kings of Seres raise an army and conquer the Land, it doesn't matter in a cosmic sense. The Serians are human, and they'd be fighting for human reasons—the same kind of reasons that cause dogs to fight or boys when they're let out of school."

"The Serians!" Carus snorted. *"Not in this world or any world* I'm *in!"*

Which is missing the point, Garric thought, *or perhaps illustrating it perfectly.* Aloud he said, "I'll fight rat men or liches or demons, I suppose. I've fought them, and other men have fought them and won. But I hope if there're Gods to be fought, you'll handle the business, Tenoctris. I don't . . ."

He rubbed his cheekbones to give himself a moment to put into words the thought he was struggling with.

"Tenoctris," Garric said, "when I think about fighting with Gods, I feel like there's a wall of crystal stretching up to the sky. There's nothing I can grip, nothing I can even see."

"I'd like to say I know exactly how to deal with that problem," Tenoctris said with a wry smile, "but I don't think that lying to you would be helpful. I do hope that we can continue to gain information which will give me a better idea of what to do."

She chuckled, though this time Garric thought the cheeriness was a bit forced. "And I also hope we survive the process of getting the information."

"Yes," said Garric. "I—"

His face was turned toward Tenoctris. The shadow of her head in profile lay softly on the limestone behind her. Rippling over the pale stone was another shadow. It was faint as undulations in still water, but it was *there*.

"Hoy!" Garric shouted, leaping to his feet. He'd shifted his sword belt to the front of his body so that he could sit comfortably on the ground, but his ancestor's reflexes had the blade clear in a singing arc before he was fully upright. "Tenoctris, watch out!"

But there's nothing to see!

The slope down twenty feet to where the guards stood was bare. Something might've been hiding against the trunk of the monkey-puzzle tree, but the moon would surely have shown anything approaching close enough to throw its shadow on the wall.

It's clear!

Tenoctris had snapped a twig off a shrub growing at the base of the outcrop, ignoring the spines. Using it for a wand, she was murmuring words of power. A spiral of dust lifted from the gritty soil.

Garric slashed the air in front of him. His long sword cut higher than it would've done against a human enemy, judging from the moon's angle to where the extra shadow had hirpled on the stone. To his utter amazement, the blade met a faint resistance as though he'd cut a jellyfish floating in clear water.

Half the guard detachment ran toward Garric with weapons ready for use; the remainder of the platoon was faced out as before, though with their spears raised. Blood Eagles above on top of the ridge were standing to, their boots and equipment clashing.

"Your Highness!" said the commander. He must have thought the swipe of Garric's sword was directed at him and his men. "Friend! Friend!"

An overpowering stench flooded the night, thrusting Garric and the captain back in opposite directions. The next trooper got a long stride ahead his commander before he drew in a breath. He stopped, wobbled to his knees, and threw up on the inside of his shield.

"Neber saudry rish!" Tenoctris shouted. The tip of her makeshift wand flashed brilliantly red, turning the air a lingering rose color for a dozen double paces around. In its pale warmth, a bloody splotch dissipated into rags where Garric had cut at nothing.

Two dirty-looking creatures of serpentine horror swam through the air toward him; each was over ten feet long. Instead of fangs, their mouths were circular pits. In the wizardlight, the rows of teeth within gleamed like rusty iron.

"Duzi!" Garric cried, jumping sideways more in disgust than fear. He held his sword between him and the nearer creature.

A Blood Eagle stepped forward and hurled his javelin. The head was a four-sided pyramid, slender enough to punch through a bronze cuirass and the ribs it covered; it slid through one of the floating hagfish without slowing, then chipped rock from the cliff face twenty feet beyond. The creature began to deflate around the exit wound, spilling a brighter color out in tendrils.

"Sister!" Carus said. *"I've smelled mules that'd burst after a week in the sun and they weren't as bad!"*

The stink was something you could touch, worse than a tanyard at the height of summer. Even the worst smells quickly dull the ability of people to sense them, though. Garric had his equilibrium back.

The haze of wizardlight was fading, and the third creature was blurring back into the air through which it wriggled. Garric could still see it undulating toward him. He lunged to meet it with his sword point. The captain and two of his troopers struck at the same time.

The creature parted like gossamer at the touch of multiple weapons. It drifted away in pieces that dissolved as they sagged toward the ground. As they did so, the rosy glow vanished and with it Garric's ability to see the floating monsters. Only the smell remained, and even that was disappearing.

Garric sank down on one knee. The physical effort hadn't been excessive, but his blood was seething from the attack. Now that there was nothing left to fight, he was afraid he was going to throw up.

"What were they, Tenoctris?" he asked, his eyes on

the ground. He was taking deep breaths, trying to cool down. All his muscles were trembling. Men had come running, Lords Waldron and Attaper among them, but Garric wasn't ready to talk to them yet. "They were invisible!"

"They weren't invisible," said the wizard, "but they were the same color as air, at least in this light. How did you see them?"

Garric's body was beginning to settle again. There were soldiers all around them. "A rag!" he said. "Somebody find me a rag to wipe my sword blade!"

"Here, Your Highness!" someone said, handing Garric a cloth. It was the sleeve of his tunic; Garric could've torn his own sleeve off, but he hadn't thought of that because he was still reacting to what had happened.

"I saw the shadow on the wall beside you," he said. "Please, give us some room. Everybody! Back away if you please."

A moment before he must've sounded like the worst sort of nobleman ordering his servants about. He'd apologize later—not that anybody else would care that the prince had barked out orders.

"Carus knew something was wrong, though," he said, looking up to meet Tenoctris' quiet gaze. The ghost of his ancestor beamed from his mind. "I don't know how. Experience, I suppose."

"Your Highness!" Lord Attaper said forcefully. "Captain Willer says there were snakes in the air. Do we need to get you out of this place? Lady Tenoctris, do we?"

Garric raised an eyebrow toward the wizard. "No," she said. "There were only three and they're dead, thanks to His Highness. It must've taken weeks to prepare this attack and it would take even longer to prepare another one."

Her expression became unusually serious. "Garric, this wasn't precisely wizardry, because the creatures are natural. But they're not natural in this world and time, and there *certainly* was wizardry behind their presence here. I should have been ready. I'll not fail you in this fashion again."

"I don't think anybody failed," Garric said. "Except the wizard or whatever in Palomir who was behind this."

He got up. Lurched up, really, but he felt better with each movement.

He sheathed his sword and held up the borrowed sleeve. "Thank you, whoever gave this to me," he said. "But I think it'd better be burned immediately. I couldn't see what I was wiping with it, maybe nothing, but I'd burn it just in case."

"At once, Your Highness!" a Blood Eagle murmured, snatching the rag from him. *He'd say the same thing if I ordered him to jump off a cliff!*

"Just as you'd *jump off a cliff if the kingdom required it,"* Carus said with a hard grin. *"Duty is duty."*

Garric grimaced, but he knew that was true. Well, he'd work not to be the sort of leader who ordered men to jump off cliffs.

"We'll be meeting the first contingent of militia from Haft tomorrow, Your Highness," Lord Waldron said, putting up his sword also. "Before they arrive, I'd like to discuss with you my plan for how we'll use them, if you would."

"Yes, we'll do it now," Garric said, seating himself against the rock face again.

And how many boys from Haft would he have to order over cliffs? Because the kingdom required it. . . .

ILNA LURCHED TO her feet. The boat shifted with a scrunch of gravel, throwing her down again. This time her bruised right knee landed on the gunwale. The additional sharp pain on top of the battering she'd just taken made her dizzy, but she managed to catch herself before she tumbled onto the beach.

She closed her eyes and steadied herself. She supposed she should've gotten up more carefully, but if she'd been seriously injured she wanted to know about it *now*. Besides—

Ilna smiled, not widely but widely for her.

—while she wasn't rash, she generally acted on her initial impulse. Once that had taken her to Hell, but who was to say that she wouldn't have gotten there anyway? Anyway, that was in the past.

The beach was shingle like at Barca's Hamlet; here the fist-sized chunks of rock were red sandstone instead of the black basalt she was used to. Though by this time, Ilna supposed she was used to anything the world could put her into, as well as some things that had nothing to do with the waking world at all.

Ingens groaned. He was still holding onto the mast, so he hadn't been clubbed unconscious while the vessel was being thrown around.

Ilna leaned over the secretary and removed her lasso. She had to lift his right leg to get the silken noose clear.

"Ouch!" Ingens cried, twisting his head to look up at her. He'd bloodied his nose, though it wasn't broken or he'd been giving it more attention than he did the leg he was kneading with both hands. "What did you do to me?"

"Beyond saving your life?" Ilna said coldly as she looped the cord so that she could loop it around her waist again. "If I hadn't taken it off when I did, you'd have died of gangrene in a week or two. What you're feeling is the blood coming back into your leg."

"I'm sorry," the secretary muttered to his hands. "I wasn't . . . I didn't mean to complain. I wasn't thinking clearly. Wasn't thinking."

People were coming from huts to the right, above what would have been the shoreline before the Change. Ilna saw nets drying on racks; the men of Ortran must still fish, though now in the river rather than the Inner Sea.

Two men, then a third, began to trot when they saw Ilna was watching.

"Good day!" Ilna said as they approached. "We've been thrown here by the earthquake."

Her fingers were knotting a pattern that would sear anyone looking at it like a bath in boiling oil. That was her reflex when she met new people, but in this case there was more than the usual reason for it.

The whole village was coming, down to babes in their mothers' arms. The villagers didn't look hostile, precisely, but they certainly didn't seem friendly. The men wore the crude knives that were as much a part of peasant dress as a tunic.

"You're on Ortran, now!" called a burly man whose beard was lopped off square a hand's breadth beneath the point of his chin. He'd lost his right ear in the distant past; only a lump of gristle and scar tissue remained. "You're under our laws!"

The three leaders paused a double-pace short of the boat. Ingens got to his feet, but he seemed willing to let Ilna talk for both of them. He usually traveled with Hervir, of course.

"I don't see any sign of damage here," he murmured, nodding toward the village. "Those flimsy huts should've been thrown down. Can the earthquake just have followed the river?"

"We have no intention of breaking your laws," Ilna said coldly, letting bigger questions wait on immediate need. "We're only here because we were caught by the earthquake. We'll go on as soon as we're able to arrange a crew for our boat."

This place must be about the size of Barca's Hamlet, several double handfuls of huts. The villagers lacked the bits of ornamentation—a bracelet of carved wood, a ring mounted with a pretty piece of quartz—that some of them would've had back home, but they seemed well fed.

"I want enough cloth for a tunic!" said a woman with

a voice like stones rubbing. She glared at the woman beside her as she spoke; they both could've been any age from twenty to forty beneath the grease. "I want cloth for *two* tunics, because I got shorted last time. You know I was, Achir!"

"We don't take slaves here on Ortran," said a pale blond man, another of the three leaders, "but you're castaways and all you come with is salvage to us. You have the tunics you're wearing, no more."

"Aye, that's the law of Ortran," said the third leader, a fat old man who'd taken this long to catch his breath after scurrying to reach the vessel. He nodded solemnly. "The law of our fathers and their fathers before them."

"You're under royal law now," said Ingens sharply. "You can't rob travellers simply because your fathers used to rob them!"

A boy from the back of the crowd shied a stone. It missed Ingens' head, but he shouted and ducked away.

Ilna held up the pattern she'd knotted. The villagers staggered back screaming as if she'd flung live coals in their faces. The fool who'd been nattering about the laws of his fathers gasped twice, clutching his chest. His face flushed so red it was almost purple; he toppled forward onto the shingle.

Good, thought Ilna. *Maybe you'll have a chance to chat with your ancestors about why they should've come up with different laws.*

"I curse you!" she shouted to the departing crowd. The words didn't have any effect except to frighten the unpleasant fools further, but that was worthwhile. "May your limbs burn till they fall off!"

Not everybody had been looking when she'd displayed her loose pattern, and those at the edges of the mob hadn't gotten the full effect. They all joined the panic as their neighbors fled in screaming agony. The only remaining villagers were the red-faced fellow, now breathing in snorts like a hog, and a girl of eight or nine who'd been knocked down. She was bleeding from a cut on the forehead.

"What did you do?" Ingens said. "Have you killed them?"

"No," said Ilna, folding the pattern into her sleeve. There were more people coming, but these were on a path through the hills farther inland. "Well, not most of them. The effect wears off in an hour or two."

She climbed from the boat and knelt beside the trampled child. Pity that it couldn't have been the brat who'd thrown the rock, but he'd been glaring at Ilna when she spread the pattern. Being stepped on and hitting your head was minor by comparison with what the boy was feeling now.

The girl started crying. The fallen man wore a silk sash, probably stolen from some earlier castaway. Ilna jerked it off, then reached back to dampen it in a puddle nearer the river.

It wasn't clean—neither the cloth nor the water—but it would do for the purpose. She daubed blood away from the cut, then lifted the girl's hand and pressed it onto the bandage. "Just hold it here till you stop bleeding," she said. "And stop whimpering, girl! You and your fellows can expect worse if you don't stop trying to rob travellers."

"There are more people coming," Ingens said, apparently thinking Ilna wouldn't have noticed them herself. "Four men and a woman."

Ilna glanced up. The newcomers approached with a deliberate dignity which set them apart from the fisher folk even more sharply than the excellent quality of their garments. The men were in dark tunics with appliqués of indigo around the hems, while the woman's mantilla and white gown both had the sheen of silk.

"Girl?" Ilna said. She gripped the child's chin and turned her face toward the newcomers. "Who are those people?"

"*I* don't know!" the girl said shrilly. "They're from the new town! They don't belong here!"

"What do you mean 'new town'?" Ilna said. The girl tried to tug away; Ilna held her shoulder firmly. "When you've answered my questions, you can go back to your home, but not before."

"I don't *know*," the girl repeated, but this time she whined the words. She seemed to have given up struggling, which saved her from being bruised. "It wasn't there before the sea disappeared. It hasn't any business here!"

Ilna didn't speak for a moment. "Mistress?" Ingens said in a worried whisper. "I know that the Change mixed the eras widely, but where there's an enclave in a district which is generally of another period, it means . . . I mean, it seems to me to mean . . ."

"Wizardry?" said Ilna. "Yes, I've noticed that too."

She released the girl's shoulder and rose to her feet. "All right, child," she said. "Tell the people in your village that if I see them anywhere near this boat, they'll regret it. For a time. Now, go."

The girl was already running back the way she'd come. She was a dirty little thing whose eyes were set too close, like a pig's; but as she darted away, Ilna thought of Merota. Her mouth tightened.

"The grove where Hervir went to buy the spice was like that," Ingens said quietly. "Not Caraman itself, but that grove. That's why nobody from the town went there."

"Good day, Mistress Ilna os-Kenset," called the woman. Her voice was a cracking contralto which sounded as though the speaker was much older than the twenty-five or six that she appeared to be. "My name is Brincisa. I hope my servants and I can assist you in your present difficulties."

"How do you know my name, mistress?" Ilna said. She fished out the pattern she'd used on the villagers, but the part of her mind that fitted things together was quite sure it wouldn't be of any use against this woman. Though perhaps the four men with her . . .

"Like you, I have certain skills," Brincisa said. She walked to within a double pace of Ilna though her servants halted well back. "I saw that you were coming here and that you'd be in distress. Therefore I came to offer my assistance to a sister in the art."

Ilna grimaced. "Thank you for your offer," she said, "but we can pay our own way. Perhaps you can help us find a new crew, though? Ours were lost in the earthquake."

Brincisa wobbled and closed her eyes. A servant started toward her, but Ilna already had the other woman's arm; the servant stepped back.

"Are you all right?" Ilna asked. Brincisa was trembling as if she'd gotten up too quickly after a long illness.

"Yes, I'm sorry," Brincisa said. She opened her eyes again but put a hand on Ilna's shoulder to brace herself for a moment longer. "Just a spell of dizziness. It will pass."

She paused. Her eyes were a pale gray-blue, a startling color in a brunette with a dark complexion. Ilna wondered how she was able to keep her garments so shimmeringly white in this place.

"You said you would pay your way?" Brincisa said.

"Yes," said Ilna. "Of course."

She was aware that her tone had returned to its usual stiff reserve. For a moment she'd been reacting to Brincisa the way she would Tenoctris, weak after executing a major incantation.

Brincisa gave her a satisfied smile and took her hand away. "I'm all right now, thank you," she said. "In fact I was hoping that you could do me a service while you're here, Mistress Ilna. I have some ability in the art, but there is a thing I cannot do and I think you can. I would appreciate your help."

"What sort of help?" Ingens interrupted. "With respect,

mistress, we have our own business to attend. We can pay for lodging in the usual fashion."

Brincisa looked at the secretary, then laughed. "Your concern does you honor, Master Ingens," she said, "but I'm not an innkeeper. And this isn't your affair."

Returning her attention to Ilna, she continued, "The favor I ask will be a trivial one for you to grant, and I can help you in return. But we can discuss that later, after you've eaten."

She gestured to her servants. "Two of you carry my guests' belongings to the house," she said. "You others wait here to keep the vermin who live on the shore from rummaging through the boat. I'll send you relief at sundown."

Ilna glanced at Ingens, but the secretary returned her gaze without expression. He was obviously deferring to her.

"All right, thank you," Ilna said. "And we can talk about the favor later."

She walked at Brincisa's side toward the track through the hills. Ingens was giving the servants directions about what they should bring from the boat.

Brincisa seemed to have recovered from whatever had caused her weakness. Ilna looked at her, wondering if a pattern would tell her anything. She doubted it, and anyway it would be discourteous to weave one here in Brincisa's presence.

Sairg had hated wizards and blamed Ilna for the earthquake, because she was one. He was quite wrong about Ilna.

But he hadn't been wrong that a wizard was responsible for the boat being picked up and deposited here, where the wizard Brincisa waited for them.

BRAVO!" CRIED SHARINA as the trained rat spun end over end between the jugglers' wooden batons as they crossed. "Oh, marvelous!"

Lord Tadai, clapping with his usual polite languor, leaned closer and said, "Yes, they are good, aren't they? Though I suppose it's impolite of me to say so about the entertainers I hired."

The pair juggling were a youth of seventeen and a girl—his sister judging from her features—a year or two younger. At the open end of the U of tables, their parents played lutes while a ten-year-old boy piped on a treble recorder.

The family wore matching blue pantaloons and tight-fitting white jerkins—as did the rat. That a rat would wear a costume instead of ripping it off instantly was even more amazing than the way it danced and tumbled with the human performers.

"Everyone else agrees with you," Sharina said, looking around the cheering enthusiasm of the other guests. "And I *certainly* agree!"

Attending a banquet given by the city prefect was one of the duties expected of the regent, but Sharina was having a good time as well. She was probably as relaxed as she could be at any affair that required her to wear formal robes. Not only was Tadai a cultured, intelligent man, he had what he claimed was the finest kitchen staff in the kingdom.

The dishes seemed overly exotic to Sharina, but they tasted marvelous. She particularly liked the pike that'd been skinned, boned, and then molded back into its skin with a filling of rabbit sausage.

The jugglers bowed and somersaulted to where the musicians played. The rat pranced off with them, turning high cartwheels while holding its tail out straight behind it. How in goodness could you train a rat to do that?

This hall was perhaps the largest single room in Pandah, and its coffered ceiling was thirty feet high. One might've expected it to be part of the royal residence, though it wasn't unreasonable that it should be given to the city prefect who needed a courtroom at least as much as the prince needed a hall of audience.

Besides, Tadai cared—which neither Garric nor Sharina did. And Tadai gave *much* better banquets than anybody raised in Barca's Hamlet could've imagined.

The older woman began dancing, balancing a bottle on her head with a lighted candle stuck in the neck of it. Her feet darted a quick rhythm as she rotated, facing each of the three long tables in turn, while the flame remained remarkably steady.

Her husband accompanied her on his lute. Beside him, the rat played a miniature xylophone with six bars, syncopating the plucked strings in a plangent descant.

"There's a new religion appearing in the city, Your Highness," Tadai said, his voice covered by the music and his attention ostensibly on the dancer. "I didn't think it was worth mentioning to you at first, but it seems to be growing."

"People are worshipping the Gods of Palomir?" Sharina said, jerking her eyes onto the prefect. She wasn't nearly as good at dissembling as Tadai. He was not only older, he'd been a financier before becoming a member of Garric's council. Bankers had more occasion to lie than peasants did, except perhaps peasants who made much of their income in buying and selling cattle.

"No, Your Highness, or I would've said something immediately," Tadai said in a tone of mild reproof. "That would be high treason. This was something so absurd that I thought it must be a joke. It appears to be real, though."

"Go on," Sharina said, turning her eyes toward the dancer again. She already felt uneasy, but perhaps her fear wouldn't come true if she didn't say it out loud.

Thinking logically about her superstition made her grin at how silly she was being. That didn't make the fear itself false, of course.

"There are gatherings at night all over the city," Tadai said. "We've had reports of nearly a score of different locations. Well, seventeen. Some of them may be the same congregation moving to avoid patrols, but regardless it's a widespread business."

The dancer trotted out of the performance area, still balancing the bottle. The guests, council members with their spouses and so many more of the Great and Good as there were places available, stamped their feet and cheered in applause.

"Is it confined to Pandah?" Sharina asked. "Master Dysart hasn't said anything about it to me."

"I haven't discussed the matter yet with him," Tadai said, "because I couldn't bring myself to believe that it was real. I will of course, now that I've spoken to you."

He coughed slightly and added, "I regret that Lady Liane is absent, though I'm sure she's left her duties in capable hands."

"Yes," said Sharina. *And I regret that Cashel is absent, for better reasons yet.*

The mother and daughter entertainers picked up lutes; the older boy sat cross-legged holding a drum between his insteps. He beat a quick rhythm with his fingertips as his father did a series of backflips that brought him into the center of the hall. The tumbler flipped again, stood on his right hand alone, then his left, and finally bounced to his feet as his ten-year-old son backflipped out to join him.

"At least one of the leaders of the new cult is a priest of the Shepherd," Tadai said. "Very likely several are. I'm making inquiries, but discreetly of course. It's no proper business of the kingdom to tell people how to worship."

He coughed again. "Within reason."

The young entertainer gripped his father's outstretched hands. Acting in concert, they front-flipped him onto the older man's shoulders, facing the opposite direction. The audience shouted and stamped its delight.

Sharina touched her dry lips with her tongue. "You haven't said what they were worshipping," she said.

"That's the absurd thing," said Tadai. His mouth scrunched as though the words he was preparing were sour. "It's a scorpion. They claim their god is a scorpion!"

Sharina's mind was cold, as cold as the Ice Capes. She'd known what he was going to say. She'd known as soon as he mentioned a new religion.

The rat bounded out to join the human tumblers. It jumped to the father's right shoulder, then to the son's left. With a final delicate hop it reached the boy's head and perched there, standing on its hind legs.

"To be honest," Tadai said, "I was *hoping* that all this was a joke. It seems utterly insane."

"Men of Pandah, honor calls us!" the rat piped, throwing its little right foreleg out as though it were an orator declaiming. *"No proud foe can e'er appall us!"*

"By the Lady!" Tadai blurted. "Why, the rat's singing. They didn't tell me he could do that. Why, this *is* marvelous!"

"On we march, whate'er befall us," the rat sang. *"Never shall we fly!"*

"Bravo! Bravo!" bellowed Lord Quernan, who commanded the city garrison. He lurched to his feet. Foot, rather, because he'd lost his right leg at midthigh during the capture of Donelle a year earlier. The whole audience began to stand in irregular waves.

Lord Tadai started to rise, but he subsided when he saw Sharina remained frozen in her seat. "I must admit that I find this new cult disturbing," he said. "How could anyone worship something as disgusting as a scorpion?"

"How indeed?" Sharina whispered. The dream of the night before filled her mind with blackness and horror.

Chapter

7

$\mathcal{L}$ATER—

Sharina drifted toward the dream temple like a leaf nearing a mill flume. She didn't move swiftly, but she was locked into a certain course no matter what she wanted.

She was locked into certain doom.

"Sharina!" called the figure waiting for her on the black granite plaza. "It is time for you to bow to Lord Scorpion. Come and worship the greatest of gods, the only God!"

She tried to shout, "I will not!" but only a whisper came out.

"Worship!" the figure demanded. "Bow to Lord Scorpion willingly; but willing or not, you *will* bow. Worship!"

The force that gripped Sharina spun her lower, closer to the waiting figure. The Scorpion didn't lower from the clouds this time, but Its presence permeated the world; it was immanent in all things.

"You have no power over me!" she said. Her voice was a whine of desperation.

The figure laughed triumphantly. "Lord Scorpion has power over all things, Princess," it said. "Worship Lord Scorpion and rule this world at my side!"

"Who are you!" she shouted. She tried to reach the Pewle knife, but her arms didn't move. Perhaps she wasn't even wearing weapon; this was a *dream.*

But she knew it wasn't only a dream.

"You may call me Black," the laughing figure said. When she'd completed another full circle, he would be able to raise a hand and touch her. "You will be my consort. Together we will rule this world in the name of Lord Scorpion, Who rules all!"

Sharina remembered tearing the dream apart to escape the night before, but her fingers wouldn't close now. "Cashel," she said, but the name was so faint a whisper that even she couldn't be sure that she'd spoken.

"Cashel is dead!" said Black. "Cashel will never return, he *can* never return!"

"Lady, protect Thy servant!" Sharina prayed with frozen lips.

"The Lady is dead!" said Black. "Lord Scorpion rules all. Worship Lord Scorpion!"

He was reaching toward her. He would grasp her wrist and pull her to him. She felt the grip of long fingers, tugging her from this world into—

Sharina jerked bolt upright in her own bed. The moon shone through the slats of the jalousies. By its light she saw a rat wearing pantaloons and a white vest, sitting upright on her pillow.

"Ordinarily I would have waited for you to awaken normally," the rat said in a conversational voice. "From the way you were thrashing about, though, I didn't think you'd mind. My name is Burne, Princess."

GAUR HAD COBBLESTONE streets, which Ilna disliked intensely. The alleys to either side were so narrow that the three-story stone buildings overhung most of the pavement. Even here on the High Street, Ilna felt like she was walking up a canyon toward the gray limestone bluff lowering above the town.

She smiled slightly. She *had* walked up canyons, and into caves, when necessary. She didn't like stone, true, but there was very little she did like. She'd deal with Gaur the way she dealt with everything else.

"Lady Brincisa," said an ironmonger standing in his doorway. He extended his little bow to Ilna as well.

The shopkeepers they'd met were deferential, though they also seemed rather cautious. People going the other way in the street mostly bowed to Brincisa, but a few turned their heads toward the wall till she was past.

"How do the people here support themselves?" asked Ingens, walking a pace behind the two women. "Gaur seems prosperous."

Did it? The townsfolk were well enough dressed, so Ilna supposed that was true. She shouldn't let her dislike of a place color the facts.

"Rice farming and trade on the river," Brincisa said, apparently unconcerned by the question. "There was a special tax to pay for digging a canal after the river shifted its course during the Change."

She smiled with a kind of humor. "The town elders didn't assess us," she went on, "but my husband and I chose to make a payment without being asked. The money was of no significance, and we prefer to be on good terms with our neighbors—so long as they remain respectful."

"Is your husband expecting our arrival?" Ilna said. She was knotting patterns as she walked, but out of courtesy she didn't look at them. She too preferred to be on good—well, neutral, in her case—terms with those she had to deal with.

"My husband Hutton died three days ago, mistress," Brincisa said with a smile of cool amusement. "That's part of why I need your help. But our discussion can wait till we're at leisure in my workroom."

She paused and gestured to the house on her right. A servant in the familiar dark livery held open one panel of an ornate double door. It occurred to Ilna that she'd never heard Brincisa's servants speak, though they were perfectly ordinary to look at. Perhaps they were just well trained.

She entered and started up the stairs of dark wood. The staircase beside this one led down from the door's other panel toward a basement. Behind her Ingens said,

"Mistress Brincisa? This house—how were you able to build it?"

Ilna looked over her shoulder. Brincisa, also looking back, was following Ilna up the stairs, but Ingens was still in the street staring at the building's front.

"All the other houses are stone," he said, shifting his eyes to Brincisa on the staircase. "But yours is brick."

"My husband and I preferred brick," Brincisa said. "And not that it's any of your business, we didn't have it built here: we moved it from another place."

She paused. If her voice had been cool before, it was as stark as a winter storm when she continued, "Now—you may either come in or stay where you are, Master Ingens. What you may *not* do is trouble me again with your questions. Do you understand?"

"Mistress," Ingens murmured, lowering his head and keeping it down as he entered the house.

Brincisa turned to meet Ilna's gaze. In the same cold tone she said, "Do you have anything to add, mistress?"

Ilna smiled faintly. "I prefer brick also," she said. "Not that that's anyone else's business."

Brincisa waited for a heartbeat, then chuckled. "Yes, mistress," she said. "We can help one another. My workroom is on the top level, so go on there if you will."

Ilna counted the floors absently with quick knots in her fabric, one and one and one and finally one more; the fingers of one hand, four. Not only was Brincisa's house made of different material from the rest of Gaur, it was taller. The molded plaques set into the brickwork over windows were too ornate for Ilna's taste, but she had to admit that they *were* tasteful.

Each floor had a central hall with doors set around it. There was only one door on the uppermost hallway, closed like the others. Ilna stopped beside it and waited for the others to join her. Brincisa touched the panel; an unseen latch clicked and the door swung open.

"Enter, mistress," she said. "And you may enter as well, Master Ingens; but remember your place."

The secretary nodded. His face was tight, but he successfully hid whichever emotions were affecting him.

Save for the hall and staircase, the upper floor was a single high room lighted through a ceiling covered with slats of mica; it cast a faintly bluish shimmer over everything. The walls were frescoed with a base color of fresh cream. Roundels of green and gold framed the doorway and alcoves—there were no windows—and sea creatures swam in the upper registers.

Ilna stopped just inside the door when she felt sand scrunch under the soles of her bare feet. She looked down. What she'd thought was a gray pavement was instead a thin layer of ground pumice, brushed over tightly fitting slabs of pale marble. She looked at Brincisa.

"For my art, mistress," Brincisa said. "So that the incantations don't leave residues to interfere with later work. Don't worry—the grit won't follow you out of the room."

Ilna sniffed. "You're wrong that they don't leave traces," she said. "But it's no matter to me."

Ingens followed the women inside; the door closed behind him, though it hadn't been touched by anything Ilna saw. The secretary clasped his hands before him; he turned his head slowly to look around, but his body was as stiff and straight as if he'd been tied to a stake.

Brincisa's earlier spells *did* leave signs despite the care with which the sand had been raked, but the fact Ilna could see a pattern remaining didn't mean it was of significance even to the powers on which the universe turned. She'd really been slapping back at Brincisa for her assumption that Ilna was afraid to get her feet dirty. Brincisa obviously insulated herself from the realities of life even in this considerable town; she couldn't possibly imagine the muck of a farming hamlet.

Which raised another question. . . .

"Mistress?" Ilna said. "You came here from another place, did you not?"

"I will not discuss the place we came from!" Brincisa said. She was noticeably angry, but Ilna thought she also heard fear. "That has nothing to do with anyone but me and Hutton, and now with me alone!"

"Yes," said Ilna, silently pleased to have gotten through the other woman's reserve. "But the reason you came here concerns me, since I'm here as well. And—"

She smiled faintly to keep the next words from being a direct accusation.

"—I came here in a way that concerns me a great deal."

Brincisa made a sour face and nodded in apology. "Yes, of course," she said. "As I'm sure you've guessed, Ortran is a nexus of great power now, but the island of fishermen that existed in your former universe was just the reverse. It repelled the use of the arts. At the Change that, that *vacuum* so to speak, drew Gaur and its immediate surroundings into this present."

Ilna thought over what she'd just been told. She hadn't noticed any difficulty in seeing off the troublesome fishermen, but she hadn't knotted a very complicated pattern either. Regardless, Brincisa had answered her question in a direct, perfectly believable fashion.

"All right," she said. "What is it that you want from me?"

For the first time since she'd entered the room, Ilna took the time to look at its furnishings. A stuffed sea wolf hung from the ceiling, a young female no longer than an outstretched arm. Some of the beasts stretched as much as three double paces from jaws filled with conical teeth to the tip of the flat, oarlike tail.

Not far from the lizard was a series of silver rings around a common center, each with a gold bead somewhere on the circle. Ilna must've frowned in question, for Brincisa said, "An orrery. You can adjust it to show the relative positions of all the bodies in the firmament."

Ilna didn't know what "the firmament" was, let alone what "the bodies" were. She supposed it didn't matter.

Brick pillars projecting into the room to support the roof. On the lower floors the alcoves were probably pierced for windows, but in this workroom the walls were solid; the spaces were filled with bookshelves and racks for scrolls.

On one end of the long room was an earthenware sarcophagus molded in the shape of a plump woman who smiled in painted idiocy. On the other was a skeleton upright in a wooden cabinet—Ilna couldn't tell how it was fastened; it seemed to be standing normally—and a soapstone tub holding a corpse whose flesh lay brown and waxy over the bones.

The items were more impressive examples of the trappings of the charlatans who came through the borough periodically, their paraphernalia carried on the backs of wasted mules. Brincisa, whatever else she might be, was not a charlatan.

"My husband Hutton and I came to Gaur seventeen years ago," Brincisa said. "The town was very suitable for our researches, as you might expect. There's a peculiarity in the laws of the community, however, which has created a difficulty for me."

As she spoke, she toyed with a silver athame. The reflections on the flats of its blade didn't seem to show the room in which Ilna stood. "As I told you, my husband died three days ago."

Ilna nodded curtly. She expected there would be a point, and she'd learned that they wouldn't reach that point any more quickly if she said, "Why do you imagine I care about the death of someone I'd never met?" or even some more polite form of words to the same effect.

"In expectation of his death, Hutton placed his most valuable tool of art in a casket which he bound to his breast with a single hair," Brincisa said. "He then walked out of the house and died in front of the municipal assembly building. Even I couldn't prevent him from being buried with his casket."

She flung the athame at the stone floor. It rang musically away, its point bent. Ingens whimpered faintly.

"That was his," Brincisa said mildly.

She continued to smile, but the fury in her eyes was obvious to anyone. "My fellow townspeople fear me, as they should," she said. "But they are more afraid of violating their burial ordinances . . . and in that too they are wise. Nothing I could do or say would change their minds."

Ingens opened his mouth, then closed it again with a shocked expression. Ilna glanced at him, looked at Brincisa, and said, "Master Ingens, did you have a comment?"

Ingens licked his dry lips. His eyes shuttled quickly between the two women. He didn't speak.

"Master Ingens," Ilna snapped, "your place is whatever I say it is! If you have something to say, say it!"

She glared at Brincisa. Brincisa bowed politely.

"If Master Hutton knew he was going to die," Ingens said in a perfectly normal voice, "why did he choose to do it in a public place, Mistress Brincisa?"

"To spite me, of course," Brincisa said with an undertone of fury. "All those who die in Gaur are immediately interred in the clothes they die in, in the cave on Blue Hill. That's the bluff that you may have noticed at the head of High Street."

"Immediately?" Ilna said.

Brincisa shrugged. "Within four hours," she said. "Though I doubt that I could have untied the casket's bindings regardless of how much time I had."

Her gaze focused on Ilna. "*You* can untie them, mistress," she said. "And in exchange, I'll see to it that you and your companion—"

She nodded to Ingens.

"—reach your intended destination more quickly than you would've done had your vessel not been damaged in an earthquake."

"You want me to rob a grave for you," Ilna said.

Brincisa shrugged. "Yes," she said. "I'll help—the entrance to the cave is always guarded, but I'll put the whole town to sleep so that you aren't inconvenienced. But you'll go into the cave alone to remove the casket. After all—"

She smiled coldly.

"—you never met the man, so why should you care about him now that he's dead? I assure you, mistress, you would *not* have liked him in life."

Ingens gestured with one finger to call silent attention to himself. Ilna nodded to him.

"I'm sure Mistress Ilna can untie this hair," the secretary said, "but I'm perfectly willing to go into this tomb and cut the casket free without worrying about the knot. Wouldn't that be simpler?"

"Cutting this particular hair would not be simple, no, Master Ingens," Brincisa said with amusement. "Not though you used a sword of diamond. Untying the knot will not be simple either, but I think Mistress Ilna will find it possible."

Ilna shrugged. "It seems straightforward enough," she said. She felt her lips curl up in a kind of smile. "If it's a bit of a test, well, I don't mind a test."

"Then we'll go to the tomb tonight," Brincisa said with satisfaction. "For now, I had dinner prepared against your arrival. You'll have plenty of time to eat and prepare."

Ilna thought, but she said only, "Yes, I could use something to eat."

It wasn't a surprise that Brincisa had known to prepare for Ilna's arrival; but as the wizard had said, she and Ingens would reach Caraman more quickly this way. Ilna supposed it didn't matter.

BEFORE THE CHANGE, the Kolla River had flowed from Haft into the Inner Sea no more than thirty miles south of Barca's Hamlet, where Garric had lived for his first eighteen years. This was the first time he'd seen the Kolla, now a tributary of the North River. In the normal course of Garric's life as an innkeeper, he might never have gone thirty miles from Barca's Hamlet in any direction.

A similar thought must have occurred to Reise, standing beside him on the bank as they watched boatmen poling the grain barges downriver to the army. He gave Garric a twisted smile and said, "Everything has changed."

Reise plucked the sleeve of his silken inner tunic. "I've changed. But nothing has changed more than you have."

He cleared his throat; an ordinary man, not particularly impressive even now that he'd lost the stoop with which he'd stood all the years Garric was growing up. He said, "I hope it isn't presumptuous of me to say this, but I'm very proud of you, son."

Garric put his arm around his father's shoulders, hugged him quickly, and stepped aside again. "I don't know how I came to be . . . ," Garric said. "To be what I am now. But your teaching is the reason I've been able to handle it as well as I have."

"I didn't teach you how to be king, Garric," Reise said, his smile even more lopsided than before. He was now Lord Reise, advisor to the Viceroy of Haft—a hereditary nobleman whose only sign of ability lay in his willingness to do what his humbly born advisor said.

"And I certainly didn't teach you how to be a good *king,"* said the ghost of King Carus with a familiar chuckle. *"Though I suppose you could have used me as a bad example."*

"Let's say that I have a number of advisors," Garric said. "One of the things I got from my father was the ability to tell good advice from bad."

A herd of sheep was being driven eastward along the opposite bank of the river. Garric estimated the size with quick professionalism, flashing tens with his fingers and counting them out loud: "Yain, tain, eddero . . ."

He'd reached, ". . . eddero-dix, peddero-dix," before he completed the count: seven score sheep, and from two separate flocks. There were two rams, and the boys badgering the animals—rations on the hoof for the army—had their work cut out because of it.

Garric grimaced. "Duzi!" he said. "They'd have done better to leave one of the rams back in its district—or butcher it there, either one. If they had to combine the two herds to drive them, which I don't see that they did."

"I'll make inquiries, Your Highness," said Reise, jotting a memorandum to himself on a four-leaf notebook of waxed birchwood.

The company of Blood Eagles who'd escorted Garric were divided into sections standing ten double paces to east and west. Troopers of the cavalry squadron that had swept ahead were watering from the river by troop. Tenoctris sat on a rock nearby. She seemed to be observing the sky, though Garric found the high, streaky clouds unremarkable.

Lord Reise's camp was a village on a rise a quarter-mile back from the river. The knoll had been wooded before the accompanying regiment had stockaded the encampment.

Reise followed Garric's glance and said, "I brought a senior clerk from each department and from the twenty borough offices. I wanted to be ready to provide whatever information you need."

"Borough offices?" Garric said. He smiled and shook his head in amazement. "I didn't know there were borough offices on Haft."

"There weren't, Your Highness," said Reise. "But there are now. If you were wondering, Barca's Hamlet lies in Coutzee's Borough according to the last notation in the records in Carcosa. Your viceroy, Lord Worberg, has seen fit to change the name to Brick Inn Borough."

Garric laughed. "I wonder how Lord Worberg came up with that name?" he asked ironically.

The oldest building in Barca's Hamlet was the mill, built like the seawall of hard sandstone at the height of the Old Kingdom. The inn that Reise had bought and renovated when he moved from Carcosa to Barca's Hamlet was slightly more recent, dating from the years just before the Old Kingdom collapsed in blood and ruin. Uniquely for the east coast of Haft, the contractor had used brick. He'd fired the bricks on the site, using workmen he brought in from Sandrakkan.

"I believe one of his advisors suggested it," Reise said with a deadpan expression. "I can look into the matter if you'd like, Your Highness."

Shifting to a quietly serious tone he added, "Lara has been managing the inn for the past year and a half. I'm told that she was very pleased when she heard the pronouncement."

"Ah," said Garric with a nod. So that he didn't have to meet his father's eyes, he turned toward the men whom regular soldiers were marshaling on the bank just upriver of where he stood. He said, "Those are the Haft militia?"

"The first influx of militia, yes," said Reise. "The call-up was very successful, my military officials tell me. All Haft is proud that for the first time in a thousand years, one of their own sons is on the throne of the Isles."

He coughed slightly into his hand and added, "Pardon, Your Highness. I of course meant the viceroy's military officials."

Carus observed the recruits through Garric's eyes, though by now Garric himself had seen enough soldiers to come to the same conclusions. There were about three hundred all told, but they stood in many separate groups.

"They're all volunteers, you know," Reise said.

"Yes," said Garric with a cold smile. "That's fine so long as they don't think they'll be going home again till I release them."

A few men carried swords and had at least a helmet;

often there was a bronze cuirass besides. Those were prominent farmers, men with several hundred acres who owned their own plows and draft animals instead of sharing them with neighbors or renting them as required. Each had a retinue of up to a half-dozen of their farm-workers. The retainers had either a spear or a bow, but only one wore a metal cap. A scattering of others had plaques of horn sewn onto a leather backing.

The remainder, at least two-thirds of the total, were smallholders, tenants, and herdsmen carrying whatever they thought might be a weapon. Garric saw flails, scythes, quarterstaffs, and wooden sickles with flints set on the inner edge to cut grain. More useful were the bows, though few of the archers had a full quiver of arrows, the slings, and the men who had proper spears.

"Duzi!" Garric muttered, more in horror than disgust. To Reise he said, "I'd originally planned to assign the militia to Lord Zettin, since they're used to hard work and sleeping rough. I changed my mind, though, because they wouldn't like working with the Coerli as they'd have to in the scout companies. But now that I see them . . ."

"We can find javelins for a couple thousand, lad," Carus said. *"Our farriers can knock points together from spare horseshoes if we need to, and there's plenty of willow to make shafts. It's not much, but needs must when the Sister drives."*

"We still can't trust them anywhere that matters," Garric said. He muttered, a better choice than having his father wonder why he was glaring at the militia in angry silence. "If they break, they'll take real troops with them."

"Put them to guard the camp," Carus said, *"and to carry the wounded back out of the line."*

The ghost smiled broadly. *"Lad, what did you expect?"* he said. *"They're better than I expected, I'll tell you that."*

One of the recruits saw Garric watching. He took off his broad leather hat and waved it. "Halloo!" he called. "Prince Garric! Halloo!"

Two of the men standing closest grabbed the one calling by the arms, twisting him away and bending him over at the waist. A regular noncom rushed over and banged the fellow twice on the back, breaking the shaft of the javelin he'd used for the impromptu correction.

"That was Eyven!" Garric said in surprise. "From Northhill Farm. And Cobsen and Hiffer, aren't they?"

"At least half the men in the borough enlisted as soon as the call went out," said Reise. Though muted, his tone was proud. Garric couldn't be sure whether the pride was for the borough's response or because his son had aroused that response. "No few of the girls as well. Though the girls seemed largely to be hoping that Prince Garric would be swept away by the charm of an unspoiled village girl after tiring of the haughty falseness of noble-women."

Reise smiled. "They wouldn't have put it in those words, of course," he added.

Garric looked at the volunteers again and shook his head in dismay. "Well," he said, "our supply lines are short enough that we won't have a problem feeding them. And I guess at worst they can blunt the rat men's swords and make the real soldiers' jobs that much easier."

"Son?" blurted Reise in amazement. His face sobered instantly. He murmured, "Your pardon please, Your Highness."

"I'm sorry, Father," Garric said. He would've hugged him again, but Reise stepped back to forestall the gesture. "I . . . look, I'm used to . . . I mean, these are the boys I grew up with. I don't mean to sound as though I don't care about them."

"You have duties, Your Highness," Reise said softly. "You have the whole kingdom to consider. If you didn't think in terms of needs and resources, Barca's Hamlet and everything else would've been destroyed long since."

"Yes, but I shouldn't talk that way in front of you!" Garric said.

"The prince was talking in a perfectly appropriate fashion to Lord Reise, an official from the Haft bureaucracy," Reise said. "His Highness isn't the one who should apologize."

Garric reached out again. This time the older, smaller man stepped into his embrace.

"Are you going to see your mother?" Reise said as they eased apart again.

Garric felt his face harden. The grain barges were passing in a slow, constant rhythm. The Kolla was shallow here and the crews were poling to speed the slow current, walking bow to stern down the trackways on the sides of their vessels.

"Lara isn't my mother though, is she?" he said. The harshness in his voice surprised him. "I'm the son of the Countess of Haft."

"By blood, yes," said Reise, also looking toward the barges. "Lara was the only mother you had growing up, though. And she remains my wife, though we live apart."

He cleared his throat. "I'm not a soldier," he said. "But Barca's Hamlet seems to me to be well located to act as a base while you wait for Palomir to approach. While you wait for the rats."

"I'll think about it," Garric said. In his mind he was a child again, hearing Lara hector him in shrill anger. She'd thought Sharina was of royal blood and that Garric was her own offspring—and therefore negligible.

"I'll think about it, Father."

CASHEL SET HIS feet reflexively—the soil was hard with a lot of sand in it; it'd anchor him well in a fight— and glanced quickly about his surroundings. Rasile and Liane waited just ahead, the girl with her hand on the Corl's shoulder in case they had to duck away from a spinning quarterstaff.

They wouldn't, of course; Cashel was far too careful

to let that happen. But it made him feel better that he wasn't alone in thinking about how things might break in a fight.

Nobody else stood closer than the city gate half a furlong away, guards and loungers. They didn't look dangerous, just bored. One of the guards nudged the man next to him, who started to pick up the helmet on the ground at his feet. He changed his mind and straightened again without it.

"We can go on now, I guess," Cashel said, slanting the quarterstaff back over his left shoulder. It looked as harmless there as eight feet of iron-shod hickory could.

He glanced behind. They'd appeared off the road, so there was just sumac and lesser shrubs growing here on the slope. There was no sign of the sandy place they'd come from or of the empusae. He didn't expect there would be, but it seemed a good idea to check.

"Won't there be problems about us, well, just stepping out of the air?" Liane said quietly. She was in the middle, with Rasile on her right side and Cashel on the left. She'd put the little knife away, though Cashel didn't doubt she could have it in her hand quick enough if she had to.

"No ma'am," he said. Liane knew a lot of things, but she hadn't traveled with wizards as much as he had. "They didn't see it happen, they just saw us walking toward the gate. And if they *had* been looking right at us, they still wouldn't have seen it happen. They think we just came over the hill."

As they walked through the scrub toward the gateway, Cashel spread a big smile across his face like he was a bumpkin who didn't have a lick of sense and wasn't any kind of danger. He was a bumpkin, all right, but he had more sense than to make trouble with a group of soldiers unless he had to. If he really had to, well, they'd see how much danger he could be.

The guards were all looking at Rasile. They picked up the spears that'd been leaning against the wall and started cinching up breastplates of linen stiffened with glue. The fellow who'd decided not to put his helmet on now changed his mind again.

Cashel waved his right hand, grinning like a fool. This wasn't much different from his usual expression. The thought struck him as funny, so he grinned even wider.

"Not everybody thinks we're a threat," Liane said, not whispering but not speaking any louder than for her companions to hear. "The moneychangers look glad to see us."

She sniffed. "They'll be disappointed."

Some of the folk Cashel had taken for loungers had little tables in front of them. They whisked coverings of baize cloth off stacks of money and small scales.

"Best rates here!" one called.

"Best rates on all Charax coinage!" said another in a voice like a cracked trumpet. "All islands accepted and bullion by weight!"

The city wall was pretty impressive, though by now Cashel had seen better ones a number of times in the past. The stones in the courses were pretty small and seemed to have been reused from older buildings.

The gate itself was flat-topped, but it was set in a pointed archway rising a good three times Cashel's height. The top of the wall was that much again. Instead of simple square battlements for archers to shelter behind while they shot through the gaps, these went up in curvy steps like ornaments. Cashel guessed they'd still work, though.

There weren't guards on the wall, though people there were looking down at him and his friends. Looking at Rasile mostly, he didn't doubt. It was a hot day, and the walls were probably as good a place to catch a breeze as you'd find in Dariada.

"Where have you come from?" said the guard whose fancy bronze breastplate and sword made him the commander. From what Cashel had learned about soldiers since he left Barca's Hamlet, the other men did this for a living but the commander, middle-aged and not only well-groomed but *soft,* was a citizen. Probably one of the richer ones, too.

"I'm Lady Liane bos-Benliman," Liane said, putting on the voice that told anybody hearing it that they were so many crickets that she could step on if she felt like it. "Prince Garric has sent me from Pandah to view the Tree Oracle."

She nodded toward Cashel, then Rasile, as she took a ribbon-tied sheet of parchment from her scrip. "These are my assistants," she said, handing the parchment to the officer. "And here is my authorization from Prince Garric. Now sir, what is *your* name?"

He took the sheet doubtfully. "Ah," he said, "I'm Bessus or-Amud. Ah, Captain Bessus. But you can't enter the city, milady. Dariada is independent. We've sent envoys to Prince Garric to explain that to him."

Liane glared at the regular soldiers. "Master Bessus," she said, her voice even snootier than it'd been before, "will you please tell your men to stop pointing spears at Mistress Rasile? An old woman is scarcely a threat to Dariada."

"She's not a woman at all!" said one of the guards, his knuckles mottled on the shaft of his spear. Liane had said there weren't many cat men on Charax, but from the way this fellow sounded he might *never* have seen one before.

"As old as I am, you're probably right," Rasile said. The Coerli laughed by wagging their tongues out the side of their mouths; fortunately, she didn't do it this time. It didn't look like laughing to human beings the first time they saw it. "I was never a warrior, though, and I don't think you need worry about me tearing down walls like these."

She curled the back of her forepaw up to her mouth and puffed across it like she was trying to blow the walls down. One of the guards jumped away; another laughed at him. They tilted up their spears, though they didn't lean them against the wall.

"I'm not here to discuss Dariada's independence," Liane said with a dismissive flick of her hand. "And I very much doubt whether your City Assembly—"

Trust Liane to know just what to call the people who ran things in a place she'd never been before!

"—placed you here at the gate to precipitate the crisis which your envoys in Pandah are trying to avoid. Now, unless you really want to be responsible for bringing a royal army down on Dariada, please conduct me and my assistants to the priests of the Tree. I have business to discuss with them."

Bessus held the parchment gingerly between the fingertips of both hands. "I don't . . . ," he said and stopped. He probably didn't know where to go from there.

The regular soldiers were moving a bit away from him. They'd straightened and brought their spears upright, too. Folks who heard Liane using that voice didn't want her to turn it on them.

"Oh, all right," Bessus snapped. "You're scarcely an invading army, are you?"

To one of the spearmen he said, "Obert, I'm leaving you in charge while I take Lady Liane to the Priests' Office. I'll be back promptly."

He bowed to Liane. "Milady, if you'll come with me, I'll take you to the Enclosure. I believe only Amineus, the high priest, will be there at the moment, but he can make such further arrangements as are required."

"Yessir, we'll handle things," said the soldier, obviously relieved that the problem was going away.

Bessus strode down the street, with Liane beside him. He was talking to her. Cashel would've liked to be close enough to hear—he wouldn't have said anything, of course—but he figured it was best he follow at the back behind Rasile.

The streets of Dariada were mostly narrow and always

crooked as a sheep track. In lots of places, the street vendors and people walking the other way couldn't have kept clear if they'd wanted to.

Some of the men seemed to think they ought to grab Liane as she walked past them. Cashel held his staff by one end and kept the length of it stretched out alongside Liane like a railing. If somebody didn't take the hint, they learned that Cashel was strong enough to slam them back against the wall despite the awkward way he had to hold the staff.

Rasile made everybody stop and stare—that, or sometimes run the other way. Nobody did anything really hostile, though, not even spit. Maybe they just didn't have time to react. Because of the way the old wizard walked with two people in front and Cashel behind, people generally didn't see her until they were right alongside.

Bessus led them out into a plaza, sort of, though it straggled along a curving wall more than being square or any real shape. In Carcosa it wouldn't be much more than a wide street, but there hadn't been anything close to it in Dariada. It was the town market, with people selling ordinary goods and produce to either side. In the middle where Bessus took them, folks hawked souvenirs made of everything from pottery and embroidered cloth to silver and gold.

Dariada's houses had mostly three floors—stone on the bottom course, concrete mixed with broken chunks of brick to make it lighter as you went up. The walls were painted, but patches had flaked bare lots of places. Occasionally there was a top floor of plastered canes too. There were so few windows that Cashel thought they must have courtyards or most rooms wouldn't have any light at all.

The building Bessus was heading toward across the plaza was round and covered with a tall copper dome; it didn't look anything like others in the town. The tile-roofed porch on all sides was held up by pillars; the web

between them at the tops curved and stepped like the
battlements of the city wall.

It wasn't the building that really caught Cashel's attention, though. It was set in a old brick wall just a trifle too
high for a man to reach with his arm stretched up and
standing on tiptoes. That wasn't new to him either: it was
a lot like the wall around the royal palace in Valles, only
that one was half again as high.

The tree spreading over the wall in all directions,
though, *that* was nothing Cashel had seen before. At first
he thought it was a whole grove of trees, but occasionally
the branches—and some of them were as thick as his
waist—joined a different bole from the one they sprouted
from.

Tiny little leaves sprouted from long tendrils that dangled over the plaza in a ragged curtain. Some branches—
never ones with leaves—had what looked like pea pods
hanging from them instead. A few pods were as long and
thick as Cashel's forearm; those were beginning to turn
from green to brown.

Broad as the tree was—and if it filled the enclosure
the way it seemed to, it was at least a furlong across—it
wasn't especially tall. Cashel eyed it critically, the way
he'd have judged if he'd been hired to fell it and needed
to know what it would cover when he laid it down. None
of the tree's joined trunks would run to half the height of
a big white oak.

Bessus pushed his way through the hucksters and
their customers, a wide assortment of folk with the dress
and manners of every part of the Isles and beyond. A
servant—he wasn't a guard; he wore a bleached tunic
and a red vest with gold embroidery, but he didn't have a
weapon—stood in the doorway of the round building.
"Yes?" he called.

"Go fetch your master," Bessus ordered, skipping up
the three steps of the temple's base. Liane and Rasile followed just below him, but Cashel stayed down on the

ground for now. He turned sideways so that he could keep the building's doorway in the corner of his eye but still watch what was going on in the plaza. "Is Amineus on duty today? Fetch—ah, there you are, Master Amineus!"

A very large man—he was certainly fat, but he was so tall that he seemed more massive than plump—stepped onto the porch. He'd probably have cleared the transom, but he ducked as he passed under it nonetheless. He was holding a cylindrical loaf of bread in his right hand and a serrated knife in his right.

"What is it, Bessus?" he said. "And couldn't it wait till I've had my lunch?"

With Cashel in front of the round building was a slab of granite about as tall as he was. It was gray, though flecks of white sprinkled the darker crystals. The surface was as uniformly rough as that of a weathered boulder despite obviously being a worked stone.

"Amineus, I've brought you Lady Liane bos-Benliman, the envoy of Prince Garric," Bessus said, showing that he'd been paying more attention than Cashel'd thought when Liane introduced them. "She says her business is with you, so I'll leave her in your capable hands. I'm getting back to my duties, now."

The slab's edges on the side toward Cashel had been rounded over, but on the back they were sharp: it must've stood in a sandy place once, where the wind had worn off whatever'd been on the side toward it. He thought about the desert they'd crossed to get here. Had Dariada been there before the Change—or maybe been there much, much longer ago than that?

"Say there, what is this?" boomed the big priest. His voice had the rumble of a bull calling a challenge. "Bessus, if she's an envoy, then she needs to go before the assembly, not come to me!"

People in the plaza were listening to the argument, but that wasn't any danger. The same folk would gawk and laugh if an old woman slipped in sheep droppings. They wouldn't mean any harm by it. Cashel moved around to the sheltered side of the slab to see what was there.

"Master Amineus, my business is with you and your colleagues as priests of the Tree," Liane said crisply. "I believe we can take care of it without difficulty. However I strongly suggest that we go into your dwelling—"

She nodded to the doorway.

"—and discuss it there."

The other side of the slab showed a giant with a walled city between his spread legs. He was holding a snake by the neck with both hands; strangling it, like enough. The snake's coils writhed over the stone's curved upper edge. Around the bottom of the picture were the little spikes that stonecutters used to mean waves. Cashel wondered if the city was supposed to be Dariada, back before the Change when it was a port.

Amineus looked from his bread to the knife, then scrunched his face up in frustration. "All right, come in, milady," he said.

"I'll leave you to it," Bessus said, turning and striding back through the crowd.

"Bessus, you come back here!" the priest said, but he didn't sound like he thought the guard captain was going to pay any attention. He was right about that.

Amineus shook his head in disgust. "Come in to the Priests' House, milady," he repeated. "You'd best bring your servant and the animal with you or there might be trouble."

The priest gestured them to go ahead of him. Rasile dipped her head politely as she stepped into the building after Liane. Cashel had thought of saying something about how the fellow ought to talk to respectable old folk like Rasile, but that wasn't what they were here for.

He thought, *I wonder if Rasile could turn him into a pig?* And because that was a funny image, he was chuckling as he entered.

* * *

SHARINA REALIZED SHE was holding the Pewle knife bare in her hand. She slid it back in its sealskin sheath.

"Thank you," said the rat. "I thought that it was a little excessive. Though flattering, I suppose, to be considered so dangerous."

"It wasn't for you," Sharina muttered in embarrassment. "I was having a bad dream. Though—"

She grinned at the rat. He seemed quite ordinary, save for the little vest and pantaloons.

"—I don't suppose it was going to help much with a dream either. Ah—thank you for waking me up, Master Burne."

"Don't mention it, Princess," the rat said. "Now if you'll pardon me, I'll take off this absurd clothing. Nothing against clothing of course, but for human beings. And—"

He pulled off the vest and dangled it critically from the, well, toes of his left forepaw.

"Well, I must say, I can't imagine wearing something like that even when I was human. Could you?"

Sharina swung her legs over the side of the bed and tucked her feet into the sandals waiting there. She didn't stand because she was already looking down at the rat—at Burne. "You haven't always been a rat, then?" she said.

"No, no," said the rat, tossing the pantaloons on top of the vest and then beginning to groom himself. Between licks he said, "This was my mother's idea, I'm afraid. She thought it was time I took a wife. I wasn't interested in any wife, and as for the woman Mother had picked, well, I absolutely *would* not have anything to do with her. So Mother lost her temper and cursed me."

Sharina wondered if she was dreaming. The knife she still held had real weight, and out in the street she heard cartwheels clattering on the stone. The royal palace in

Valles constructed of many small buildings within a walled compound; it was well insulated from the great city beyond. The houses of the pirate lords of Pandah, though certainly luxurious, were built around courtyards with their outer walls on the public streets.

"Ah," she said. "Your mother is a wizard, then?"

"Oh, something like that," said Burne. He eyed his tail critically, straightening it and then curling it closely around him again. "Anyway, being a rat isn't such a bad life. Certainly it's better than being married to the very strong-willed lady Mother picked for me. A harridan in training, *I* called her."

He looked up at Sharina and chuckled. His eyes twinkled in the moonlight streaming through the jalousies.

"I'm afraid I have something of a temper too, you know," he said. "Maybe if I'd been a little more diplomatic, Mother wouldn't have become quite as angry. Still, what's done is done. And as I said, it isn't so bad. I quite like my fur, don't you?"

"It's, ah, very smooth," Sharina said. She wondered if she ought to pet him—and recoiled at the thought. Not because he was a rat, but because he *wasn't* a rat.

"I joined that family of mountebanks as a more comfortable environment than living with rats," Burne said. "Not that I couldn't have done so, but quite frankly the norms of rat society aren't much to my liking. And then there's the matter of the females. I'd have been the leading male, I assure you, but that entails duties which I would have found quite unpleasant. Even more unpleasant than my mother's blond termagant."

He wiped his whiskers in front of his muzzle and licked them also, right half and then left. "No," he said, "I preferred a cage and rather better food than the mountebanks themselves were eating. They valued me, you see. They'll be quite distraught to learn that I've escaped, as they'll view it."

"Ah," said Sharina. She seemed to be saying that a lot tonight. "You're leaving them? Leaving the show?"

"Now don't you go thinking that I'm treating them unfairly!" Burne squeaked sharply, sitting up straight on the pillow. "They didn't capture me, of course, and the fact they believe they did is an amazing insult. Surely it would be obvious to the meanest intellect that no lock a human could open would be beyond *my*—"

He raised a forepaw and spread the toes with their tiny claws.

"—delicacy and intelligence to open also."

"I think . . . ," said Sharina, answering the implied question instead of treating it as a rhetorical device. It settled her mind to deal with the business on an intellectual level. "That they weren't able to think of you as other than an animal. Even when you spoke and practiced the tumbling routines with them. They didn't let themselves believe what they really knew."

She pursed her lips. "I guess you practiced, I mean."

"Of *course* we practiced," Burne said waspishly. "No matter how skilled one might be—and I'll admit that the Serulli family was skilled; it wasn't by chance I picked them for my purposes, you know. But despite that, the timing can only come from practice."

He settled himself onto his belly, his limbs drawn up under him. "They treated me well—except for the lack of intellectual companionship, of course. But they more than got value from my association with them. I owe them nothing, Princess, so you needn't feel that you've harmed them because I've decided to associate with you instead."

"I beg your pardon?" Sharina said sharply. She got up, rocking the bed on its rope suspension.

Burne waited till the bed had stilled before sitting up on his haunches. "Yes, I'm joining you now," he said. "I won't pretend that I don't have my own reasons for doing so, just as I preferred the mountebanks to living with rats. Other rats. There's a difficult time coming for this world, and I suspect that there'll be more safety with you than there will be anywhere else."

He groomed his right whiskers again and added, "In the long run, of course. The immediate future is likely to become unpleasantly exciting."

On a silver tray by the bedside was an earthenware jar with a tumbler upended over its neck. Though the tumbler was glazed, the jar itself was not; water wept through the sides, cooling the remaining contents. Sharina filled the tumbler and drank.

"I'm rather thirsty myself," the rat said pointedly.

Sharina paused. *If I were home in Barca's Hamlet and found a rat in my bedroom, I'd have—*

But Barca's Hamlet wasn't home anymore, and even when Sharina was an inn-servant she'd probably have hesitated before trying to crush a *talking* rat. She grinned. *I hope I'd have had that much sense,* she thought.

She poured a little water into the tray. It wasn't perfectly flat, so a shallow pool formed along one raised edge. "All right," she said.

Burne hopped from the pillow to the table. He bent, his tongue lapping quickly but his bright black eyes still focused on Sharina.

"You'll find me good company," he said, raising his head again, "as well as being useful. For example—"

Burne shot up from the bedside table, rattling the tray with the suddenness of his leap. Sharina jerked back instinctively, but the rat struck the wall more than arm's length from her and dropped to the floor. Gripped in its forepaws was a finger-long scorpion.

The chisel teeth made a quick snap, shearing off the sting. His paws shifted their grip; the teeth clicked twice more, nipping the scorpion's pincers.

"One this size isn't really dangerous," Burne said conversationally, "but it can send information to places we'd prefer should remain ignorant."

He began eating the scorpion, starting at the head; bits

of black chitin sprinkled the marble floor around him. He paused, cleaning his muzzle with his long tongue. "Useful, as I told you," he said.

Sharina giggled. She supposed it was reaction. She sheathed the big knife for the second time tonight.

"All right, Master Burne," she said. "Though I *will* make a payment to your former, well, associates. A considerable payment."

She giggled again. The scorpion's tail fell from the rat's jaws. It was still twitching.

"I can see," Sharina said, "that you're not going to be expensive to feed."

Chapter

8

"*BARAK KNEPHI* . . . ," SAID Brincisa, kneeling before a basalt nodule originally the size of a child's skull but now split in half. The hollow interior was lined with amethyst crystals. She used it instead of drawing a figure like most of the wizards that Ilna had watched. "*Baricha!*"

Instead of a flash of wizardlight, a bluish haze spread from the nodule in all directions. It was as faint as the sheen of moonlight on nacre; Ilna saw only the boundary between light and nonlight, moving outward at the speed of a man running. It vanished through the walls of the workroom.

She felt only a faint tingle when the light passed through her body, and even that might have been the expectation that she *ought* to feel something. Ingens stood facing an alcove so that he wouldn't accidentally catch a glimpse of what Brincisa was doing. He didn't react at all to the haze; he probably didn't see it.

The wizard rose to her feet, then paused with her eyes closed and swayed. "No no," she said sharply when Ilna reached out to support her. "I'm all right. Come, the effect should last till dawn, but we don't know how long our business with the tomb will take. Master Ingens, bring the rope."

Ilna nodded curtly. She found Brincisa's manner brusque and unpleasant, which would amuse her former neighbors in Barca's Hamlet. On the other hand, Brincisa was commendably businesslike and obviously skilled in her arts. Perhaps Ilna's distaste was simply a matter of like being repelled by like. Though—

Ilna had eventually broken the link to the powers of Hell from which she'd gained her skills. Brincisa may well have had the same teachers; but if so, Ilna doubted that she'd turned her back on them.

Brincisa led the way down the stairs. Until she got to the first landing the wizard used the railing for half her support, but she had full control of her balance from then on.

A dark-clad servant waited in the entranceway. Ilna expected him to open the street door for them, but instead the man remained where he was. As they passed, she realized that the servant's eyes were open and staring: he'd been paralyzed by the incantation.

The full moon lighted the path up the bluff. Ilna wondered if the moon's phase had anything to do with the other business that was going on, but Brincisa was the only person who would know. Brincisa would say no more than what suited her—and would be pleased that Ilna was concerned.

Which she was, of course. She wasn't afraid to die, and she wasn't worried about meeting the test that waited for her in the tomb. Ilna didn't think she was arrogant, but she believed down to the marrow of her bones that she would succeed at any task having to do with fiber or fabric.

The night was silent except for the rustle of breezes through the needles of pine trees clinging to the rock. Their feet scraped on the path, and sometimes Ingens grunted from the burden of the coil of rope; those were the only animal sounds.

The *uncertainty* of what Ilna was facing—they were facing; she and the secretary were together in this at least—was what disturbed her. As they climbed, her fingers played with patterns: some that would guide her, and others that would deal with threats they might face.

As quickly as she'd tied one, she picked it out and started another; they only occupied her fingers. The answer would come, but it wouldn't come that way.

"Here," said Brincisa. They'd reached the top of the bluff. "We'll roll back the stone first. Ingens, set the rope by the post. You can tie it later."

Two guards sat by a fire which had sunk to a pile of white ash and the ends of billets smoldering around it. The men were as stiff and mute as Brincisa's servant. A spear, a wicker shield, and an iron cap sat on the ground behind either man, but their real purpose here was the large bronze bell hanging from a yoke nearby. A stroke on the bell with the mallet beside it or even a flailing hand would rouse the whole town to deal with tomb robbers.

The silence made Ilna uncomfortable. Unlike her brother she didn't think much about nature, but its chorus was a constant backdrop to night in a hamlet: birds calling and rattling their flight feathers, the varied trills of insects, and frogs making every sound from the boom of a bullfrog to narrow-mouthed toads bleating like a herd of miniature sheep.

Brincisa's wizardry had stilled all that. Though Ilna didn't particularly care for the sounds, she disliked being without them.

The stone closing the entrance wasn't a slab as Ilna had assumed. It was a roller as long as she was tall, a large version of the querns women used in villages that didn't have watermills to grind grain.

It was limestone like the hill beneath it, pierced through the center so that the thick hardwood pole sticking out on either end acted as a handle for the men moving it to and fro. A fist-sized rock waited on either side to chock the tomb open while bodies were being lowered into the cave.

"We have to move that by ourselves?" Ingens said doubtfully.

"We'll manage," said Ilna curtly as she eyed the situation. Ingens probably hoped that Brincisa would use an incantation to open the tomb. Very probably the wizard could've done that if necessary, but Ilna knew that wizardry was better left for matters which nothing else could accomplish. Physical effort was less draining for any task that you could do either way.

Brincisa turned to the stone roller. The pole extended far enough that two people could push on either side if they didn't mind rubbing shoulders.

"Mistress Ilna," the wizard said, "help me on the left side. Your secretary can take the right."

Ilna looked at her. Brincisa was still breathing hard. She hadn't stopped to rest on the climb up the hill, but she was far from having recovered her strength after the incantation.

"Ingens and I will move the stone," Ilna said. "You brought along a lantern for me? Light it now."

She squatted and braced both hands on the pole. It was smooth from long wear, fortunately. Even if it hadn't been, Ilna's palms weren't soft like a fine lady's who might be gored by a splinter.

"Ready?" she said to Ingens. He nodded. Behind them, metal clicked on stone; Brincisa was striking a spark with steel on a chip of pyrites instead of using wizardry to light the wick of the candle she'd taken from the lantern.

Ilna and the secretary shoved forward together. The roller moved more easily than she'd expected; though the track sloped very slightly upward, years—centuries?—of use had polished it. Ilna's only problem was that she was too small to easily extend to the stone's resting position, but by hunching forward from her squat she was able to get the chock in place on her side.

She stood and looked back at the hole they'd uncovered. There'd been gaps big enough to stick an arm through when the stone was in place, but now that it'd been removed the opening didn't look any too big. She could crawl through without difficulty, but she wondered how much trouble it would've been to bury her uncle Katchin—a pig in all senses.

She frowned. The air inside the cave was dank, like the interior of a well. She didn't smell rotting flesh, however. Three days even deep in rock should've been enough for Hutton to turn, quite apart from the reeking corruption of centuries of previous dead bodies.

"Mistress Brincisa," Ilna said, "I don't smell death." What she really meant was that she didn't smell corpses, but she was being polite since the woman's husband was one of them.

"There's a special property of this cave," Brincisa said with a flash of irritation, there and then gone. "It's of no consequence. Master Ingens, tie the rope around this post. And you, mistress, may want to tie the other end around your waist."

The "post" was a thick bollard. Ilna rang it with her knuckles and found what the moonlight had led her to expect: it was bronze, not wood or even iron. It was set too deeply in the rock to quiver when she threw her weight against it.

Lowering bodies into the cave was obviously so familiar a practice that considerable preparation had been made to make it easy and dignified. More dignified than simply tossing them down a hole in the rock as though they were so many turds falling into a close chest.

Ingens threw his rope around the post. He started to loop the free end around the main length, then paused.

"I'll take care of that," Ilna said, trying to keep the disgust out of her voice. Ingens could read and write, after all. She'd have to be out of her mind to trust a knot he'd tied, however. "Since I'm the one who'll be hanging from it."

Ingens stepped out of the way obediently. Brincisa rested on one knee, her face set; presumably she was still recruiting her strength. Ilna let her fingers run over the rope for a moment; it was linen, new and easily strong enough for Ilna's slight weight even though it was the diameter of her fourth finger. It would do.

She tied it with two half-hitches, simple and satisfactory, then rose. "I'm ready," she said. "Give me the lantern."

"Mistress, how will you carry it?" Ingens asked in concern.

Ilna glanced into the hole. The moonlight showed that it slanted slightly for about the length of her body before dropping away. She couldn't see beyond the initial slope. The rope would rub, but not badly; and anyway, it was new.

She wore a silken lasso around her waist in place of a sash. Now she uncoiled a two-ell length and tied it around the lantern's loop handle.

"I'll carry it in my hand till I'm over the drop," she said to the secretary. Brincisa remained silent, watching like a cat attending the actions of human beings but holding aloof from them. "Then I'll let it hang so that it lights the floor of the cave before I reach it."

"It's not far," the wizard said. The fact she spoke was by now a surprise. "Twenty feet, no more."

"Fine," said Ilna, "but I still want light."

She supposed she'd be dropping into putrid corpses, the remains of centuries. She wasn't squeamish, but if she could avoid putting her weight on a spike of rotting bone, she would.

"Shall I lower you, mistress?" Ingens said softly. He seemed genuinely concerned, which made no more sense to Ilna than the other parts of this puzzle. Well, her own task was simple enough.

"No," she said. "I'll climb down myself."

She turned and started down the rope backward. The linen filled her mind with memories of terraced fields rising from a broad brown current—not the North River, at least not the North River of the present. The sun was bright and hot, and little blue flowers nodded from long, kinked stalks.

It was good to have the rope to touch, because it insulated her from the narrow rock about her. Below, waiting for her, was ancient death.

But for now, flax flowers smiled at the sun.

SINCE YOU HAVE an oracle here . . . ," Liane said.

"Please sit down, milady," Amineus said, gesturing to the cushions along the left wall of the single round room. He must've been sitting on the other side, for the table there had a bowl of fruit, a wedge of deep-yellow cheese, and a lidded silver flagon with matching goblet. "Ah, would you like some refreshment?"

The door across the room had three lock plates in it, all set together in the middle. The panel looked heavy enough to be the street door in a city where folk had to worry about robbers smashing their way in.

"There's no need of that," Liane said, flicking the suggestion away with her left hand. "Nor time, I dare say. My colleagues and I need to question the Tree Oracle. And what I was saying—"

She froze the start of the priest's protest with a raised finger.

"—is that since you have an oracle, you are aware that the Worm is approaching Dariada. The city is doomed unless we stop the creature."

Other than the second door, the room didn't have much to see. Solidly joined storage chests sat along the walls, two and two, and above the cushioned seats the plaster'd been frescoed with pictures of fountains. Cashel liked paintings; they were the one thing he'd found in cities that he'd have regretted missing if he hadn't left Barca's Hamlet. There didn't seem much reason to paint a fountain when you might've had the real thing about as easy, though.

"You don't understand the difficulties in what you're saying," Amineus said, shaking his head in slow frustration. "The College of Priests—all three of us, not just me alone—has to consider the petition and—"

"I don't care about the difficulties," said Liane, slapping the words out. "I certainly don't care about your procedures—and neither should you, since you and your whole city will be destroyed unless my associate Lady Rasile—"

She gestured to Rasile, who grinned but kept her tongue inside her long jaws.

"—who is a wizard, is able to find a solution. To accomplish this, she believes she needs to see the Tree."

"A *wizard*?" Amineus said in amazement. He stared at Rasile, then back to Liane. "You mean this—"

"Stop!" said Liane. "If you use the word 'animal' again to refer to a friend of mine, Master Cashel will knock you down. You can do that, can you not, Cashel?"

"Yes ma'am," Cashel said. A cudgel would be handier, but short-gripping the quarterstaff would do the job too. He figured he could probably handle the big man without a weapon at all, but wrestling around inside chanced squashing the women like shoats when a brood sow rolls over.

"As to your question, yes," Liane continued more calmly. "Rasile is a wizard. Now, take us to see the oracle."

Amineus sighed and set the bread and knife down on the low table. "You may as well," he said. "It's improper, but what does that matter if the danger's as bad as we think? As bad as you say, milady. But I warn you—"

He looked around the three of them.

"—we've tried ourselves, following all the rituals. And the Tree has told us nothing. Nothing!"

"We'll go now, if you please, Master Amineus," Liane said. She wasn't near as harsh as she'd been a moment before, but she didn't expect an argument.

"Yes, yes," the priest said tiredly. He turned to his servant. "Ansco, go tell Masters Hilfe and Conwin that I'm taking a noblewoman and her retinue into the Enclosure. If they want to join us, they'd best hurry."

He paused, frowning. "Better see Conwin first," he said, correcting himself. "I can't imagine Hilfe will be willing to tear himself away from his counting house so early in the day."

The servant nodded and trotted off. From his look of disappointment, Cashel guessed the fellow wanted to watch whatever happened next.

Amineus lifted the key he wore chained to a heavy leather belt. Cashel expected him to go to the back door, but instead he knelt beside one of the storage chests.

"The priests of the Tree are elected to three-year terms, you know," he muttered as he fitted the key to chest's lock. Maybe Liane knew that; Cashel certainly didn't. "One a year, and the senior man is high priest. I took it for an honor and thought it worth the trouble, but this business now . . ."

He lifted the lid. There was nothing in the chest but three more keys.

"*I* don't know what to do, none of us do!" Amineus

said. "An army of ruffians coming toward us with a monster—everybody says they're coming for the Oracle! We've got refugees from Telut, they tell us what's going to happen. I'm responsible and I don't know what to do!"

He rose with the three keys in his hand. They were the kind that had thin pins sticking out from the end to fit and turn in arcs cut in the face of the latch plate.

"We're each supposed to keep our key with us at all times," he said, "but the gardeners have to go in and out at any hour. That's, well . . . There's always one priest in the office. That's inconvenience enough."

"You're doing what you needed to do, Master Amineus," Liane said firmly. "You're putting the problem of the Worm into the hands of those who may be able to solve it."

The priest sniffed. "Am I?" he said, fitting the three keys into the locks. "Well, I hope you're right, but it doesn't really matter. Since I don't know of anything else to do that would be better."

He turned and looked at Liane. From his expression, he might've just learned that his whole family had died.

"I don't know anything at all to do!" Amineus said. "Except run, and I won't do that."

Liane stepped past the big priest and turned the keys one after the other. Each bar withdrew with a solid *clack*.

She looked up at him. "We won't run either, Master Amineus," she said. "That's why we're here. Now, lead us to the Tree."

Instead of pushing the panel herself, Liane gestured and stepped aside. Amineus smiled crookedly and opened the door, leading them through. Beyond was what seemed like another room, only this one was as big as a stadium and the roof was the branches and leaves of trees growing around the inside of the wall.

The one tree. Each trunk was joined to the trunks on either side, just like it'd looked from outside the wall. The limbs arched overhead like the beams of an impossibly great hall, linking to one another in a wooden spiderweb.

"This way," the priest said, taking them to the left around the curve of the enclosure. "The Stone of Question is across the enclave."

The ground was bare, dry and packed from ages of exposure. The only undergrowth Cashel saw, if you wanted to call it that, was moss in places where rock had broken through the top of the dirt. The soil under these leaves and branches didn't get any more sunlight than it would on a thatched porch; that was why it was barren, not because the gardeners Amineus talked about had dug out everything but the Tree's own roots.

Though the roots were everywhere. Amineus kept wide of the boles by longer than Cashel could touch with his staff; even so it was like they were walking on a floor of ridged wood, the roots lay so thick. Cashel would've avoided stepping on them, but there wasn't any way he could; and the priest wearing leather-soled sandals—Cashel was barefoot—didn't seem concerned about it himself.

The reason for going around the side of the enclosure was to avoid what was left of a building in the center. It'd been a temple, Cashel guessed, but not a very fancy one even before it'd all fallen in.

A foundation course of rough limestone showed a rectangle three times a tall man's height on the long sides and not quite that wide on the front and back ends. There'd been two stone pillars framing the doorway at the front, but extensions of the side walls had carried the ends of the porch roof.

There wasn't any sign of a roof or the rest of the walls, either one. If there'd been a statue, it was gone too. All there was inside the base course was a litter of fallen leaves and husks from the Tree's seedpods.

"Sir?" Cashel asked. "The temple there in the middle? What is it?"

Amineus had been lost in his own thoughts. He gave Cashel a look that was peevish if not quite angry.

"That's no matter of ours," he said. "It's a temple, yes, but it's very old. Nobody knows who it was dedicated to."

He cleared his throat. "We avoid it," he added, "out of courtesy for those who worshipped here in former days."

"You're afraid of it, Master Amineus," Cashel said, as polite as he could be while calling another man a liar. It wasn't something he often did, but he couldn't take the chance that Liane and Rasile would mistake what was going on before they spoke to the oracle. "It sticks out all over you. I'm sorry, but it does."

Amineus stumbled but caught himself the next step. His face went red, then white. He didn't say anything or even look over his shoulder at Cashel.

"He is right to be afraid, warrior," said Rasile calmly. "There is much power focused here, power that could turn this universe. Power enough perhaps to put the very cosmos into a spin."

Her tongue lolled in laughter. Either she thought the priest was smart enough to understand she wasn't slavering for his blood, or maybe she didn't care.

"When we came beneath the walls of this great place made of stone," the wizard continued, "I thought the great power I saw was the oracle. It made me doubt our success, for power like that would make nothing of such as me. It was too great for any person, of the True People or of the Monkey People. Who are true in their own way, as I now see."

She cocked her head to look at Amineus. He must have felt her foxlike sharpness, but he didn't turn to meet it.

"But it is not your tree that has the power, elder," she said. "The tree has grown here because of the power of the temple in its center. And you fear it."

"The temple is very old," Amineus said softly. "Its walls were mud brick. They've been gone, crumbled to dirt, from long before records. And the records of the priesthood of the Tree, the questions and responses, go back to the age before the age before the Old Kingdom."

He stopped and turned to face the three of them. "I didn't lie to you, Master Cashel," he said. "We know nothing about the temple beyond what you yourself see. And if you prefer to think that I would not act respectfully to a site of ancient worship if I didn't fear it, then you go ahead and believe that. But you're wrong."

Cashel felt uncomfortable. He wasn't sorry for having brought the business out in the open, but it now seemed that the priest hadn't had any bad intention in not wanting to discuss it.

"I don't think that, sir," he said. "You've showed yourself polite to us, for which we thank you."

"Yes," said Amineus, "but perhaps less forthcoming than a man in fear of his life should be to his rescuers, eh? My pardon to all of you."

He turned again and gestured with his left hand. "Milady," he said. "This is the oracle itself."

Cashel hadn't known what to expect. There was an aspen grove in Cafardstown, three days north of Barca's Hamlet. Folk said that if you slept in it, the Lady would speak to your dreams in the rustling of the leaves. Cashel had never seen the grove or cared about it one way or another, but he knew folk who'd made the journey.

Some said they'd got their answer, too. Widow Bassera had asked the trees to pick between her suitors, then married young Parus or-Whin instead of a settled man her own age. The match had worked out well, but Bassera was a clever one who might've decided to get the Lady's support for the choice her own wits had made.

Here at Dariada. . . .

A flat stone was set into the ground. It was polished black granite an ell across, not local limestone like the foundation of the old temple. Though the stone had been cut to be round, the surface was etched with many fig-

ures inside each other, from a triangle up to something
with more sides than Cashel could count with both hands.

Describing the Tree would make it sound like the
stands of mangroves that Cashel had seen in his travels.
That was nothing like what it really looked like, though,
because these individual boles were as thick as the trunks
of live oaks.

Slanting up from the nearest trunk was a branch thicker
than Cashel could've spanned with both arms. From it a
seedpod hung almost to the ground in front of the granite slab. This pod was huge, bigger than Cashel in every
dimension. Its casing had turned a brown as dark as wal-
nut heartwood, and the seam running from tip to stem
was almost black.

That seam had started to split open at the top. Inside
the pod was the face of a man with his eyes shut. It was
the same deep brown as the casing around it.

"I've brought you to the oracle, milady," Amineus said,
turning his hand toward the pod. "The querent always
asks his—or her—own questions. We of the priesthood
merely make the administrative arrangements."

"Thank you, Master Amineus," Liane said. She seemed
a little taken aback. "Which . . . which of us is to do the
questioning?"

The priest shrugged. "That's up to you," he said. "I've
already explained that the oracle refused to tell us—the
priests of the Tree—anything beyond the fact that the
Worm will come to Dariada regardless of what we wish
or do."

"All right," said Liane with a crisp nod. "Rasile, this is
your business properly."

To the priest she added, "Master Amineus, is there a
form she's to use in addressing the oracle?"

Amineus shrugged again. "The Tree will speak if it
chooses to," he said.

Rasile stepped onto the slab, placing both feet carefully within the triangle that was the innermost of the

forms. Before she could speak, the eyes within the pod opened.

I thought it was a statue, Cashel thought. *A carved statue. . . .*

"What have I to do with a Corl?" said the wooden head. "Other than kill it as an affront to the world that is given to men, that is. Or do you think that because you are a wizard, you can force me to speak?"

"If you know my heart . . . ," said Rasile, standing as straight as the joint of her hips permitted. Cashel had seen the wizard's face when she confronted a wyvern that had just torn a muscular Corl chieftain to dollrags. Then too she'd shown a fierce certainty that though she would die, she would die fighting. "Then you know I claim no power over such as you."

The face—the Tree—laughed. "I will not harm you," it said. "But step away, Corl. You have no part in my world."

Rasile bowed, then hopped onto the bare ground without touching the slab again. Liane, delicately but without hesitation, stepped into her place.

The Tree laughed again. Its voice was a deep baritone. It reminded Cashel of stormwinds booming through a hollow log.

"Greetings, Lady Liane," the Tree said. "Another time I would speak with you, but now as the world of men nears its end I will talk to your champion instead. Cashel or-Mab, come face me."

"Sir," said Cashel, stepping onto the granite. He held the staff crossed before him at waist height. It wasn't a threat, but it showed he didn't intend to be pushed around.

Cashel knew the Tree's sort. He *was* the Tree's sort; which he guessed was why it'd called for him.

"My father's name is Kenset, sir," he said. "Not Mab."

The Tree's laughter boomed. The carven face was handsome, but its lines were just as hard as the wood it was shaped from.

"Your father was a weakling," the Tree said harshly.

"He made bad choices and drank because he regretted them. Your mother Mab, though . . . she is not weak. Nor is her son. Ask me what you want to know, Cashel son of Mab."

"Sir," said Cashel. Without really thinking about it, he pivoted the quarterstaff to stand straight up beside him, gripped in his right hand. "There's a Worm loose in the world, now. How do we kill it, please?"

"No man living can kill the Worm, Cashel," the Tree said. Its words were rumbling like distant thunder. "In times more ancient than you can imagine—"

The eyes looked from Cashel to the women beside him, just like they were in a human face instead of a wooden one.

"More ancient than even Lady Liane has read of in the oldest books. In those times lived a hero named Gorand. He was the champion of his people as you are of yours, Cashel. He vanquished the Worm when fools let it into the world of men."

"Yes sir," Cashel said. He was speaking like the wooden face was another man; but it talked like another man, and anyway that was the polite thing to do. "Can you teach me to do what Gorand did? To beat the Worm?"

The Tree boomed another peal of laughter. "No, Cashel, I cannot," it said. "That is a thing not even you can learn. You must rouse Gorand and convince him to banish the Worm for you. To banish it for mankind, as he did before."

Cashel didn't say anything for a moment, making sure that he understood what he'd just been told. He caught Liane out of the corner of his eye: her mouth opened like she was going to speak, but she closed it again. Rasile reached out and touched her arm. Both women were looking at him.

"Sir," said Cashel, "how do I find Gorand and rouse him? Please."

The Tree had said that Cashel couldn't learn to fight

the Worm. Cashel wasn't sure that was true, but that didn't matter if there was another way to get rid of the creature. If the Tree said to rouse Gorand, that meant it thought they could do it. All they needed now was to learn how.

There was no point saying that Gorand was long dead. The Tree knew that, had *told* them that.

"There is a stele in front of the Office of the Priests," the Tree said. "On the reverse of the stele are carved directions to reach Gorand. But I cannot tell you how to convince Gorand to return to help you, Cashel son of Mab. The people of this world repaid Gorand with evil for his good, and the people of Dariada worst of all. Gorand was a citizen of Dariada, and they treated him ill."

"I'm sorry for that, sir," Cashel said. "A man like you say Gorand is, though, he won't let that keep him from doing what he needs to do."

Sure, there were people who'd cheat and do all manner of low things to the folks who helped them; it'd happened to Cashel and he'd seen it happen to others. But you couldn't hold it against everybody.

"Do you think so, Cashel?" the Tree said. Cashel thought it might laugh again, but instead there was something else in the tone that he couldn't place. "That's for you to convince him, then."

The eyes of the wooden face closed; the mouth settled back into grim silence. Cashel stepped off the slab.

Liane's face worked with frustration and a touch of anger that she was trying to conceal. "The stele's worn smooth!" she said. "Any information there was lost ages ago. Perhaps—"

She looked from the pod to Amineus.

"—we can speak to the oracle again?"

"Milady," said the priest, "you're welcome to speak to the Tree as much as you wish. But as you saw, the Tree was unwilling to answer you even once."

"It's all right, Liane," Cashel said. He stretched with

the quarterstaff, but he didn't spin it as he might've done in another place. There was room here, but it didn't seem, well, respectful. "He knew what he was doing. The Tree did, I mean. We'll go look at this stele. You think he meant the slab out in front of the door here?"

"Yes, of course," said Liane sharply. That wasn't like her, but she wasn't used to being off on her own this way. By now, Cashel was. "That's a stele, *the* stele. And I did look at it. The image on the obverse is clear, but the legend on the reverse has been completely worn away."

The priest was watching. He seemed even more worried than before. He probably hoped the three of them were marvels who never doubted what to do next. Seeing that they were human after all put him right back where he'd been before they came, frightened and despairing.

"Warrior Cashel is correct," Rasile said calmly. "We must trust the oracle."

She dipped her head to Amineus. "Thank you, wise one," she said. "We will examine the stone outside your gate again. I think we will find that the stone is not as blank to a wizard as it might be to a layman—"

Her tongue wagged toward Liane.

"—no matter how wise that layman is."

Liane's face went hard for an instant; then she stepped forward with her arms spread, managing to sort-of hug both Cashel and Rasile. "Thank the Lady!" she said.

Cashel figured they could all agree with that.

AH, YOUR HIGHNESS . . . ," said Lord Tadai, looking around the room in which Sharina had told him to meet her. "Wouldn't we be more comfortable discussing this religious problem, ah, elsewhere?"

No, I wouldn't, Sharina thought grimly. Obviously.

They were in the little chamber off the bedroom of her suite, intended for the maid or manservant who'd normally be attending a noble at night. There was only room for a cot, a wash stand with a chest of ease beneath it, and ordinarily a rack holding additional sheets and blankets for the main bedroom.

Sharina'd had the rack replaced by the chair in which she now sat; a cloak hung over the back of it. She gestured Tadai to one end of the cot and said, "We won't be here long, milord," she said. "There'll be a one more—ah, here he is. Master Dysart, close the door behind you, if you will."

Liane's deputy seemed more like a coney than a mouse: plump, soft, and timid. That can't have been true—well, he was plump enough—but nonetheless Sharina felt a pang at Liane's absence. Even though Dysart had to be competent to hold his position, she still missed her friend's presence and advice.

"Before we proceed to the matter of Scorpion worship . . . ," Sharina said.

Dysart was still standing, though he'd pulled the door to. It was very quickly going to become close in this small chamber with three people and the flames of a two-wick oil lamp.

"Please sit, Master Dysart," Sharina snapped, gesturing to the other end of the bed. She had no right to be irritated with the man for being afraid to do the obvious without permission, but the night's business had disturbed her.

She cleared her throat. "There's another matter you need to know as my closest advisors," she said. "Master Burne, you may come out now. Master Burne helped me—"

The rat squirmed from behind a fold of the cloak. He rose to his hind legs, bowed, and hopped to Sharina's lap. Both men kept blank expressions, but Lord Tadai had stiffened to leap up before he caught himself.

"A new pet, Your Highness?" he said in a neutral voice.

"Not exactly, milord," said Burne. "Though it's probably better if most people think that's what I am. Otherwise they'll start whispering that the princess is a wizard herself, you know, and there's no telling where that will end."

"By the Lady," Tadai said quietly.

"Master Dysart, do you have any comment?" Sharina asked, raising one eyebrow.

"I defer to Your Highness' judgment," the spymaster said. He didn't shrug, but there was a shrug in his tone. "If I might suggest one thing?"

"Just speak, Master Dysart," Sharina said, her voice again sharper than she'd intended. "We all want to get out of this closet as soon as we can."

"Yes, Your Highness," Dysart said, making a seated bow. "A gold chain or the like around the . . . around Master Burne's neck might be useful to prevent an accident with your guards or the palace staff."

Sharina looked at the rat. "Oh, he's right, I know that," Burne said disgustedly. "You wouldn't believe the prejudice—"

He paused and wrinkled his whiskers. "Well, you probably would," he said. "And to tell the truth, *I* find my fellow rats a rather unsavory crew—though there are rough diamonds among them, I assure you, gentlemen. Still, I think a ribbon will be satisfactory, don't you? Because chains chafe my fur. Yes, a nice ribbon of bleached linen will do admirably."

"Now that we've seen Master Burne," said Tadai with a flick of his perfect manicure, "perhaps we can remove to more a comfortable meeting place, Your Highness?"

"We're here because I'm afraid of being overheard," Sharina said, "by scorpions. There are suddenly a lot of scorpions in Pandah—"

"Yes indeed," said Tadai. He might not have interrupted Princess Sharina at a formal council meeting, but she'd noticed that the prefect had a tendency, despite his formal politeness, to disregard things that a woman said.

"That's why I requested a meeting, Your Highness. The infestation of scorpions in concert with the new worship, that is."

"City Prefect Tadai," Sharina said in clipped syllables. "Will you please *listen* to me?"

Tadai's face became very still. "Your Highness," he murmured, dipping his head.

"Burne believes that the scorpions are communicating with one another," Sharina resumed. "Ordinarily if I wanted to speak to you without being overheard I'd go out in the middle of a park, but we couldn't possibly avoid such small eavesdroppers there. It should be possible to keep this room clear for the time we'll be here."

"I *know* they talk to each other," the rat said. "It's arm signals, a regular little semaphore with their pincers, and they can see each other in what's the dark to you or me. Now, though, they're saying more than the usual, 'This is my patch,' or 'I'm too big for you to eat.'"

He shook his head in disgust. "I'd say that scorpions didn't have any more society than a pile of rocks does," he said, "but at least rocks don't eat each other."

"Are you saying that scorpions are intelligent, Master Burne?" Dysart said. He carried a document file of heavy black leather, much like Liane's collapsible traveling desk. Unlike his mistress, he kept the case locked while he was in conference.

"Them?" Burne jeered. "You could have a more intellectual conversation with the lamp up there."

His muzzle twitched toward the simple pottery appliance hanging beside the door. Because the suite's wealthy occupant was never expected to look into this alcove, the lamp's only decoration was a leaf pattern impressed around the filler hole on top.

"But whoever's sending the beasts here must be pretty intelligent," he added.

"The same person who's behind the scorpion worship, presumably," Tadai said. He raised an eyebrow in question. "There've been hundreds of people stung by the creatures in the past few weeks. That's not serious—"

"Not serious?" Sharina said in amazement.

Tadai waved a hand. "Your Highness, we must keep the matter in proportion," he said. "There've been that many knifings in the dives that the drovers and rivermen frequent. And soldiers, I'm afraid. For the most part a scorpion sting is merely unpleasant."

"Yes, Your Highness," said Dysart. He stretched out his right leg and pointed to a welt the size of a thumbnail just above the inside of his ankle. The swelling was red, but the center was dead white. "It's numb, is all. Though I'd rather it hadn't happened."

For an instant Dysart's eyes rested on Burne, grooming the base of his tail. He continued, "We made a sweep of the offices after this happened and found seven more, but they keep creeping back in the nighttime."

"Is it possible that the priests of this new scorpion god control the scorpions themselves?" Tadai said, frowning in concentration. "That they have real power, in other words?"

"I think . . . ," Sharina said, pausing to consider how much to say. If Liane were here, she'd discuss her dreams fully; but though Sharina trusted these men's ability, she didn't care to disclose her secret fears to them. "I think that there's someone or something beyond the priests. I think if we question a priest, though, we'll get . . . closer to the source of the plague."

"Right," said Tadai, nodding agreement. "I'll give orders to the city patrols to report to their district headquarters immediately if they see signs of another gathering, and for the watch officers to report to me."

"If I may suggest, Your Highness and milord?" Dysart said, running the tips of his pudgy fingers over the document case.

"Speak," Sharina said, this time with icy calm.

"Rather than the uniformed patrols, let my department

locate the gathering," Dysart said. "If the prefect would keep a strong body of his patrolmen ready to respond at once, I think we may have better results."

"What about the city garrison?" Sharina said. "Milord, you have four regiments, do you not? Have one company ready to move instantly with the rest of the regiment to follow in ten minutes."

"Yes," said Tadai, nodding and frowning. "Yes, a very good idea. I'll have to talk with Lord Quernan, my military advisor, however. Though the city garrison is under my command, quite frankly I don't know very much about soldiers."

"If I may suggest—" Sharina said.

Burne, crouching on her right thigh, snickered. She realized that she'd just used the form that Dysart had irritated her with.

"Of course, Your Highness," said Lord Tadai—of course. But the matter really was in his department, and Sharina didn't want to seem to be acting arbitrarily.

"You might use Lord Baines' regiment for the purpose," she said.

"If you have confidence in Lord Baines, that's quite enough for me, Your Highness," Tadai said.

"I have nothing against Lord Baines," Sharina said with a wry smile, "but as I chance to know his camp marshals, men named Prester and Pont. They'd probably be in charge of a task like this, and I have a great *deal* of confidence in them."

"Then if we're agreed on a plan . . . ?" said Tadai.

Burne launched himself from Sharina's lap to her shoulder, then sprang to the top of the closed door. His long chisel teeth *click*ed as he bounced back onto the bed between the two men.

Tadai started sideways. Dysart thrust his arm out to protect the rat, then withdrew it when he saw that Tadai hadn't tried to strike.

Scorpion legs spurted from the edges of Burne's mouth. "Scarcely a mouthful," he said, "but it could have sent word to whatever wants to know. I heard it on the top edge of the door, but I had to wait till it came out enough for me to snatch it."

Sharina rose to her feet. "Thank you, Master Burne," she said. "I'm going to be very pleased when we've found the source of this problem."

YOU'VE BECOME AN exceptional horseman," Reise said in muted surprise as he and Garric trotted in the midst of the escort. They were within half a mile of Barca's Hamlet, but only the tall slate roof of the mill-house was visible. Since the Change a pine forest covered what had been the Inner Sea east of Haft.

"Thank you," said Garric. Carus was almost as skilled a rider as he was a swordsman, and there'd been no better swordsman in the kingdom while he ruled it. "You've learned to ride well too."

His father chuckled. "I've known how to ride since before you were born," he said. "I was part of the entourage which accompanied the countess. It wasn't a skill I needed in Barca's Hamlet."

"Ah," said Garric. In the borough where he grew up, plowmen followed oxen and the only horses were those on which a few drovers arrived during the Sheep Fair. He tended to forget that Reise's life extended beyond being a father and the keeper of a rural inn.

"The difficulty wasn't remembering *how* to ride," Reise said. He gave Garric a rueful smile. "It was in managing not to scream from the pain until my thighs got back in shape. Or as close to shape as is possible at my age."

Garric and Carus laughed together. "I'm familiar with the problem," Garric said. Carus provided a horseman's instincts and techniques, but the ghost could do nothing to train muscles which weren't used to gripping the flanks of a horse.

The leading troops of cavalry had ridden into the hamlet and were lining both sides of the only street. Attaper and the first section of Blood Eagles followed, their horseshoes clinking and sparkling on flagstones laid during the Old Kingdom.

"Duzi!" said Garric. He'd never seen the street when it wasn't covered by a layer of dirt, save for the doorsteps of the more fastidious householders. "They've swept it!"

"Mucked it out, rather," Reise said proudly. "The prince is visiting them, you know."

There'd been changes at the mill; indeed, clay soil heaped to either side of a new channel showed that work was still going on. A tall man whom Garric didn't recognize stood in front of the building at the head of his household: his wife holding an infant, three other children in ascending order of age, and a servant boy with the features of Arham or-Buss—a farmer from the north of the borough who raised more children than he did any other kind of crop.

The tall man took off his velvet cap—an Erdin style, like the short matching cape—and waved as he cheered. The whole household did the same, causing the startled infant to begin screaming.

"Mordrig or-Mostert," Reise murmured. "He's the Sandrakkan merchant who bought the mill from Katchin's widow. He had to convert it from tidal operation to a flume brought down from Pattern Creek now that Barca's Hamlet isn't on the sea anymore."

There were more people in Barca's Hamlet than Garric had ever seen before, even during Sheep Fairs and the Tithe Processions when priests from Carcosa dragged images of the Lady and the Shepherd on large carts through the hamlet. There were outsiders, the various sorts of entertainers who're drawn to large gatherings the way flies find a fresh corpse, but mostly they were people from the borough and neighboring boroughs.

He recognized many faces, though not always with a name attached; but mostly he recognized the sort of folk they were. They were the same as Garric or-Reise had been, but he didn't belong here anymore.

"I didn't expect all these people!" Garric said. It wasn't that the crowd was huge in absolute terms: Valles and now Pandah had larger populations than the whole eastern coastline of Haft, and an address by the prince brought out a good proportion of either city.

But it was too many for Barca's Hamlet. They were overwhelming the eighteen years of Garric's memories.

"You should have expected them," his father said quietly.

Garric wore his silvered breastplate, but the helmet with flaring gilt wings was miserably uncomfortable to ride in and unnecessary now, even though he was well ahead of the main body of the army. Instead he wore a lacquered straw hat with a wide brim—in the latest Valles style, he'd been told, but practical nonetheless. Hidden beneath the colorful straw, because he *was* the prince and Lord Attaper had insisted, was a leather-padded steel cap.

He didn't want to uncover the armor by waving the straw hat to the crowd, so he waggled his right arm high instead. The saddle raised him as much as a dais would in a more formal setting.

"Fellow citizens of the kingdom!" Garric called. He doubted anybody but Reise and the closest Blood Eagles could hear him, because the crowd was screaming its collective heart out. The sound seemed thin, though: open air didn't give the cheers the echoing majesty that he'd become used to in squares framed by high stone buildings.

Garric swept his arm down, hoping to cut off the shouting. "Fellow citizens of Haft!" he cried.

The gesture worked pretty well. When a few people

decided they were supposed to stop cheering, those around them had an excuse to quit also. He wondered if everybody in the borough would be speaking in raw whispers tomorrow morning.

"Friends!" Garric said. "Not only because I see the faces of many who have been my friends since childhood, but because all those who stand firm against evil and chaos are my friends. My duties will carry me away soon—but please, since you *are* my friends and neighbors, give me a chance to visit the inn where I grew up. I'm not here for reasons of state: I'm here because Barca's Hamlet was my home and is still the home of my heart!"

Garric thrust his arm skyward again; the cheers resumed as he'd hoped and expected. He clucked to his horse and gave it a touch of his left knee, turning it toward the gate arch of the inn.

He didn't have to worry about the crowd respecting his privacy: the troops of his escort would make sure of that. Making it a matter of courtesy which the soldiers were merely enforcing was better policy than giving the impression of being an aloof brute, however. And as for claiming that Barca's Hamlet was still home to him—

I lied to them, Garric thought bitterly.

The ghost of his ancestor shrugged. *"Sometimes kings have to lie,"* Carus said. *"I didn't mind that—or mind killing people, to tell the truth—nearly as much as I minded sitting through arguments on tax policy. But sometimes kings have to do that too."*

Laughing, Garric rode under the archway. There was room for two horsemen—or a coach, not that there'd been a coach in Barca's Hamlet since the fall of the Old Kingdom—but Reise held his mount back for a moment to follow rather than accompany the prince.

Bressa Kalran's-widow, who'd sold their poor farm when her husband died and supported herself—poorly—with spinning and whatever else she could find, and her son—he must be fifteen now; he'd gotten his growth since Garric left the hamlet—stood to either side of the well in the center of the yard. The boy bowed so deeply that his carrot-blond forelock almost brushed the ground. Bressa threw herself onto her knees and elbows gabbling, "Your Highness! Your Royal Highness!"

"Get up, for Duzi's sake!" Garric said. Shouted, rather; he was shocked and disgusted.

"Arise, Mistress Bressa," said Reise, swinging from his horse to lift the widow by the hands, politely but firmly. "You honor neither your prince nor your old neighbor Garric by this sort of antic. We're free citizens of Haft, you and I and Prince Garric."

Bressa got up with a stunned expression. She dabbed her face with the kerchief pinned over her bosom, a poor woman's alternative to an expensively embroidered outer tunic. "Begging your pardon, Your Highness, I'm sure," she said in a frightened whisper.

Of course Lara would need to hire help for the inn, Garric realized. *She couldn't run it by herself with Reise and both children gone. And where is—*

His eyes went to the door of the inn. His mother stepped out as though she'd been listening to his thoughts. She was wearing a light gray tunic over a white one. Both were so well made that they might have been Ilna's work were it not for the cloth-of-gold borders appliquéd at the throat, cuffs, and hems. Even so, they were excellent examples of peasant dress, not a peasant's garish idea of what the nobility wore.

Lara lifted her skirts and dipped in a perfect curtsy. She didn't raise her eyes or speak, because one didn't do either of those things when greeting royalty. Lara knew the correct etiquette because she'd been maid to the Countess of Haft.

Garric dismounted. He—Garric or-Reise, not Carus—had first ridden a horse here in the innyard, a guest's mount being exercised. He'd been bareback and used a rope halter. At the memory, he was eight years old again.

Lara was smaller than he remembered, a doll of a woman. Even after decades of work in a rural inn, her face and figure would allow her to pass for a beauty at any distance at all. When she was younger . . . Well, it wasn't a surprise that the Count of Haft had found his way into her arms.

"Mother," he said, stepping toward her. Could it really have been only three years?

Lara looked up with an expression of anger and pain. "Pardon me, Your Highness," she said, "but I'm not your mother. Your father, Lord Reise, has made that abundantly clear to me!"

Garric looked at her for a long moment. No one who'd known Lara for even as much as a day would deny that she was a shrew: utterly focused on appearances and in lashing others with her barbed tongue until they did her will. Garric and his sister had been under her control for their first eighteen years, so they knew her personality better than most.

Reise had educated the children. He'd given them a wider and more sophisticated understanding of the world than they would have gotten if they'd been raised as royalty in Valles. And yet, and yet . . .

The ghost of King Carus had taught Garric many things about war and fighting, but he hadn't had to give the boy a backbone. Garric had been a man before he became a prince, and he'd learned to be *that* from Lara, not Reise.

He stepped forward and put his arms around Lara. She was even smaller than she looked, as delicate as a bird.

"You're the only mother I ever had," Garric said.

Still holding her, he stepped back so that their eyes could meet and continued, "Listen to me! When I was a boy, merchants coming to Barca's Hamlet looked forward to the meals they'd have at the inn here. They were better than they'd get in Erdin or Carcosa or even Valles.

I hope you can find food for a pair of hungry men to-day."

Lara didn't move for a moment, her eyes glittering like sword points. At last she said, her voice wobbling with emotions Garric didn't care to speculate on, "I've never turned away a hungry man with the price of a meal in his purse; and for the sake of the relation, there'll be no charge to you."

"Right!" he said, kissing her on the cheek. He didn't remember ever doing that before.

"But!" Lara said. "You've grown to a husky young fellow, so you can draw me some water so that I can wash up later."

Laughing, Garric strode into the inn to get the cauldron. Chickens scattered from before his boots.

"Kalmor?" he called to the red-haired boy, hoping he remembered his name correctly. "Water our horses and give them each a peck of oats. But don't overfeed them, because we'll be riding to the camp after what I expect to be the best meal I've had in three years!"

ILNA BACKED TO the edge on her elbows and knees, then eased herself over carefully. She'd already dropped the free end into the cavern, so the rope wouldn't rub at all if she avoided swinging.

She smiled wryly. It made no practical difference: she could scrape the linen against the soft limestone for the next three days and it'd *still* be strong enough to hold her. She just didn't want to hurt a good rope more than she had to. She tried to be equally thoughtful toward her fellow human beings, but it didn't come naturally to her.

Ingens' worried face was the last thing Ilna saw before she let herself down into the open air. The lantern was dangling beneath her.

Ilna went down hand over hand rather than choosing a more complicated method that the short distance didn't

require. She could see the cave floor, a glitter of grave
goods, as the lantern twisted back and forth on the length
of silk. She didn't see bodies or the remains of bodies,
though, and the air smelled of mold but not corruption.

"Mistress, are you all right?" Ingens called.

"Yes, of course I am!" Ilna said, pausing her own height
above the ground to make a real assessment of what was
around her. "I see Hutton, I suppose. Is he wearing a gold
robe?"

"Yes, cloth-of-gold," Brincisa said. "Do you see the
box? It was tied to his chest."

The voices from above echoed off into the considerable distance. Ilna was certain she felt a current of air
and thought there was a tang of salt in it.

"Wait," Ilna said. She pulled up the lantern, hooking a
little finger over the loop, and handed herself down the
rest of the way. At the last she twisted sideways to drop
beside Hutton instead of on top of him.

She untied the lantern and turned slowly, surveying
the cave. "Mistress Brincisa?" she called. "I see the box,
but there are no more bodies here. This place hasn't been
used as a burial chamber."

"You're wrong," the wizard said, "but that doesn't matter. Untie the box and send it up as quickly as possible."

The corpse lay on its side. Hutton's face was that of a
sixty-year-old man; the features were cruel rather than
merely ruthless. He'd worn a skullcap of cloth-of-gold
like his robe and slippers, but it must've slipped off when
the ropes that'd lowered him were jerked away. His hair
was iron-gray and cut short.

As Brincisa had said, a box the size of a document
case was tight against his chest. Hutton's hands grasped
it, but beneath them a filament as thin as spider silk tied
it to his torso. Ilna moved the lantern carefully to every
angle, shifting the corpse with her left hand.

The knots were *amazingly* subtle. How had this Hutton, however great a wizard, been able to tie them? Why,

no human being could have reached behind himself to make some of—

Oh. Hutton hadn't created this fabric of knots himself. Ilna could have tied them, and so might the Power Who had taught her to weave in Hell. She doubted that there was a third possibility.

Brincisa's voice echoed down: "Are you going to be able to loose the casket?"

"Be silent!" Ilna said as her fingers began to undo the majestic detail.

Brincisa had said that Ilna wouldn't like Hutton if she'd known him in life. Now that she knew who Hutton's friends had been, she was more than ready to agree.

Brincisa must have been telling the truth about people being buried here. The bodies had vanished but all around were robes, jewelry, and weapons—the sorts of things people buried with the dead. The lantern glinted on a lavaliere of cloisonné and jewels; its thick gold chain had been raggedly cut.

The atmosphere had a silent chill, very different from the normal unpleasantness of rocks dripping lime water in a cave. Ilna supposed it was a result of Brincisa's spell. It didn't affect her, precisely, but she felt like she was moving in something thicker than air.

Ilna began to work. She smiled, remembering the secretary's blithe offer to cut the box free. These knots bound far, far more than merely a wooden box. Some of what they controlled was harmless or even beneficial when properly treated, but even those aspects were dangerous if they weren't respected.

And they were only part of the greater fabric with the box at its center. The remainder could blast the world and beyond the world if freed by the drag of a blade.

Mind, Ingens couldn't possibly have cut the filament. Uniquely, Ilna didn't know where the pale strand came from or what it was. All her fingers felt was sunlight, sweeping and dancing and flooding all things.

Nothing but pure light could have bound the powers gathered here; but the work had been done for an evil man, by a thing that was the soul of Evil.

Ilna was aware of that the same way she was aware that she was breathing in and out. None of it mattered now, because she had work to do.

Brincisa had been right to believe no one but Ilna herself could unknot this shimmering fabric. If she'd therefore arranged the earthquake that brought Ilna to Ortran, that too was a matter for another time.

The work came first. Nothing existed save the work. She was Ilna os-Kenset.

She undid the last knot and paused, breathing deeply. She felt a vast crackling: the universe, bound by the pattern she'd untied, had broken free like a creek at the spring thaw. The filament lay about her like the sun spilled on crystal. It shone brighter than the feeble lantern that should have been the only light down here.

"Mistress Ilna!" Brincisa called from above. "Have you succeeded? Tie the casket onto the end of the rope and I'll bring it up."

The candle was little more than a smudge of wax. It wouldn't have mattered if it had guttered out after Ilna began. Her eyes hadn't—couldn't have—guided her on a task like the one she'd just completed.

"Mistress Ilna!" the wizard repeated. "Answer me!"

Irritation brought Ilna out of the mood of soft accomplishment she'd been basking in. Well, softness was for other people.

"I'll be up shortly," Ilna said. She deliberately didn't raise her voice; that expressed her opinion of Brincisa daring to give her orders better than a shout would've done. "I assure you that I don't want to stay down here longer than I have to."

She wished she had something to wet her throat. A pitcher of the bitters Reise brewed in his inn would be the best. It was one of the few things Ilna remembered about Barca's Hamlet that had remained constant, utterly trustworthy. Even water would do, though.

Ilna smiled coldly. A moment to breathe would be sufficient. She was used to making do with what she had, rather than having the things she wanted.

"Just tie the casket onto the rope," Brincisa said. "You can do that, can't you? Then I'll let the rope down again. You can bring up some of the grave goods. There must be a king's ransom accumulated over the years in the cavern."

Ilna frowned. *Does Brincisa really think that I care about baubles?*

Aloud she said, "I'll bring the box up myself. It won't be long."

She smelled decay. To her surprise, Hutton's cheeks had fallen in and his eyes, gray and staring a moment ago, were covered by bluish fungus.

Something moved in the depths of the cave. Ilna heard a dull clicking, the sound stones made when weight made them slide against other stones. She'd loosed more than the box, it seemed.

"Send up the casket!" Brincisa said. "You mustn't try to carry it. Send it at once!"

Ilna had started to tie the box with her silken rope the way she'd carried the lantern when she came down. Something shifted slightly inside; it wasn't particularly heavy. She paused and looked up at the opening. "Master Ingens!" she called. "Ingens!"

"Mistress, I'm giving you a last chance!" Brincisa said. "Send up the casket alone. Otherwise you'll stay down there and I'll send one of my servants to fetch it at a later time."

"Nothing goes up until Master Ingens assures me that he's standing by the rope and that it's secure!" Ilna said. "I'll bring the box up or it won't come!"

Heavy footfalls thudded closer from the darkness. She wondered how deep the cave was and what lived in it.

The rope rustled down, flailing like an angry snake. Stone clacked above. Ilna didn't recognize the sound until there was a second clack and a moment later something massive crunched, then settled. Brincisa had knocked the chocks out so that the roller returned to its resting position over the entrance.

A massive shadow lurched toward the lantern's faint circle of light.

Interlude

HAIL, LORD ARCHAS!" the new recruits shouted raggedly. They were probably weak with relief not to have been executed. Or fed to the Worm, of course; they had to be thinking about that. "Hail, the Prince of the East!"

"By the Shepherd!" muttered Tam, Archas' deputy, as he watched the Worm writhe through the ruins of the fallen city. He rubbed his scalp with the knuckles of his right—and only—hand while gripping his helmet in his fingers. "I tell you, Archas, I wish you'd send it away."

"Members of the Army of the East!" Archas said. "You've sworn obedience to me on your lives and souls. Don't think those are just words! It won't be some lady or shepherd in Cloudcuckooland waggling a finger at you if you forswear me! Look and look well at what your oath means!"

He gestured toward the Worm with a curved sword. In his other hand was the talisman wrapped in golden hair, the tool by which he raised and—thus far—dismissed the monster on which his power rested.

A row of walls collapsed in powder. The Worm had destroyed the rear of those buildings as it squirmed through city previously, but Archas had learned it was best to let the creature completely raze the cities he loosed it on. Otherwise it resisted his efforts to send it back into the gray wasteland it had turned its home world into.

"Go with the captains I've given you!" Archas said. His voice boomed over the terrified recruits, about two hundred survivors from the ruin which was now being ground into the bedrock. "Obey their every command."

Women had been saved as well, the younger, prettier ones. No children, though.

"You'll have wealth and power beyond your dreams, all the best of everything," Archas said. "But—"

He waggled the sword again.

"—never dare disobey me!"

The cities here on Charax had walls of brick instead of using stone over a rubble core like those of Telut. A furlong of wall—what was this city's name? Archas wasn't sure he'd ever heard—still stood, including one square tower. The Worm, moved by some impulse of its own, bent suddenly in a hairpin and advanced on the remaining section. Its circular maw pulsed open and closed. The creature's body towered over the thirty-foot battlements.

"You *can* send it away, can't you?" Tam asked uneasily. "Archas! Are you listening to me?"

"Of course I'm listening to you, Tam," Archas said with false good humor. He bobbed the talisman in his left hand as if he were estimating its weight. "And of course I can send the Worm back. You've seen me do that a score of times already, haven't you?"

It was easy to underestimate his one-armed deputy. Tam wasn't smart, exactly; nobody would say that. But he was perceptive in a way few smart people ever were. In the old days he'd twice noticed plots against Captain Archas—and had quashed them with strokes of his axe before anybody else knew what was going on.

"I'm just giving a warning about what it means to try

to fight us," Archas said. "It'll be easier yet if they open their gates when we arrive, the way places had started to do by the end on Telut."

Tam sighed. "I suppose," he muttered. "I don't like it, though. I'm no saint, Archas, but . . ."

The last of the ramparts disappeared in a rumbling earthquake, partly crushed but also swallowed by the enormous mouth. Orange-red dust rose in a cloud that staggered forward like a line of cavalry advancing. It covered the foreparts of the creature that had worked the destruction, but hundreds of feet of gray horror continued to grind forward like an unending landslide.

"Even if they surrender, it's all the same for most of them," Tam said. "You give the city to your, your thing. And all the ones who don't join us. Who we don't let join."

"Well, what do you care?" Archas shouted. "What did cities ever do for you, Tam? Why, if we'd tried to get in here a year ago, they'd have arrested us at the gate and likely hung us just for what we looked like!"

And he and his men sure wouldn't have attacked a place like this, whatever its name was. Archas had never had more than six ships under his command—three hundred men, maybe; certainly not more. They'd have had as much chance trying to gnaw through these walls—the walls that the Worm had just finished destroying—as they would assaulting them.

Archas looked at the army he'd assembled in his march north, straggling across the landscape. There were several thousand men, now. Most were slaves and farm laborers who'd joined the band because the life was better than what they were used to. They weren't very different from the pirates he'd commanded before the Change.

The men Archas had taken from captured or surrendered cities were generally soldiers who came with their weapons and knew how to use them. Despite how they feared the Worm they might've been dangerous to him if there'd been more of them, but he saw to it there weren't.

The Army of the East had been attacked several times during its advance. Because it had proper scouts and flankers, only one of the ambushes had forced Archas to loose the Worm.

He hadn't been sure the creature was going back to its own world that time. Hill tribesmen had attacked in a rocky gorge. They were after loot, not trying to halt the column, though by luck they'd swept down on the carriage in which Archas rode in state. He'd *had* to bring out the Worm to save himself, but there hadn't been much for it to destroy once it'd devoured the mountaineers' meager village.

The Worm had taken his orders at last, but he hadn't been sure it would until the last moment. He'd allowed it to destroy the next city they reached, down to the last mouse and pebble. He hadn't given the populace even a chance to surrender.

"I know, Captain, I know," said Tam with a sigh. "I never thought I'd have all the wine and all the women I wanted, all the time. We've got it good, I know we have. Only . . ."

He'd turned his eyes toward the women. There were more of them than the men by now and almost entirely captives from the cities. Not all whores, either: there were councillors' wives and priests' daughters. They'd volunteered after they learned the alternative, too, because Archas' men didn't need to bother with the unwilling.

Except for the men who liked a struggle, of course. The Army of the East had no few of those, but they generally discarded the women after they'd used them, picking out fresh companions when the next city fell.

"Look, Tam," Archas said. He was cajoling his deputy, but it was really his own heart that he was trying to convince. "They're lucky we're here, that's the truth. If they waited for the rats to spread this far, you know what'd happen. They'd *all* be sacrificed, right? They'd ask us to capture them if they knew the truth."

There was nothing left of the walled city but a pall of dust which continued to churn as the Worm writhed through it. Archas held the talisman close. He'd use it shortly, but he needed to ready himself for what he knew would be a struggle.

"Have another drink," he said to Tam, offering the wineskin he'd slung over his left shoulder. It was almost empty, but there were others.

Tam tossed his helmet to the ground to free his hand. He took the skin and drank deeply. Gesturing toward the helmet with his toe, he said, "Wouldn't be much use against that thing, would it? And there's nothing else I'm worried about here."

"You!" Archas shouted to a man standing nearby, staring transfixed at the Worm's continued progress. "Find some wine and bring it here. Now!"

Tam hadn't needed to explain what "that thing" was.

"I just keep thinking . . . ," Tam said. He looked critically at the wineskin, then shook it; there was enough left to slosh. "Pretty soon the rats are going to swarm over the whole rest of the world, right? Everything's going to be Palomir, except us. What's going to happen then, Captain?"

"Don't worry about that, Tam," Archas said with a confidence he didn't feel. "As soon as we take Dariada, everything's going to change. Everything'll be all right as soon as we do that!"

He touched his tongue with his lips. He was sure that things would change.

But he wasn't sure that they'd be all right.

Chapter

9

CASHEL LOOKED AT the stele's carvings again. Rasile, Liane, and the priest were doing that too.

There must be half the city trying to watch Liane and the rest of them. If it hadn't been for the company of soldiers making a half-circle to give them space, Cashel would've been pushing the crowd back with his staff to keep it from trampling the two women. It seemed like the people here had heard stories about the thing that was eating its way north toward them.

Looking between him and Liane—Rasile was squatting on Cashel's other side—Amineus said, "That's the hero Gorand, Your Ladyship. He's shown strangling the Serpent, as we thought."

He coughed in embarrassment. "We, ah, thought," he continued in a lowered voice, "that the story was an allegory of a great military leader who defeated an attack of pirates from the Outer Sea. Because the sea encircles the Isles like a serpent swallowing its tail."

Liane looked at the priest. "It appears that before the Change, Archas and his men were pirates on the Outer Sea," she said. "But no, I don't believe the image is a serpent. Or an allegory."

"The face looks like the one in the tree," Cashel said. "I think."

"How can you tell?" Amineus said. He wasn't trying to sneer, but he wasn't exactly trying not to either. "This is so small. And ancient."

Cashel shrugged. He moved to the other side of the stele, stepping carefully around Liane.

"Master Amineus?" he said as he stared at the sand-smoothed stone. Kneeling, he began grubbing in the dirt at its base with his knife. "Was this always here? This stone?"

"Well, there are no records about it being erected, I can tell you that," the priest said. "Though that doesn't prove it wasn't set up or moved here from somewhere else without anybody bothering to mention it. Or the records could've been lost, of course."

"The reason I ask is . . . ," Cashel said. *Yes, it was there like he'd thought, a row of letters in the swirly Old Script and maybe another row beneath them.* "There's still some writing here where it got covered before the wind could smooth it away."

"Let me see!" Liane said, squatting beside him. "Ah—please, I mean. And ah—"

"Ma'am, would you like my knife?" Cashel said politely, offering her the haft of the simple tool. A blacksmith had forged the iron blade and pinned wooden scales to it. It could do everything from carving at meals to picking stones out of ox hooves. Or digging dirt away from the base of a stele.

"No, Cashel," Liane said with a laugh. "I'd like you to finish clearing the inscription, as you were doing before I interrupted you. My pardon, please."

"It's more my line of work," Cashel said mildly. He scraped the back of the blade through the gritty earth like a plow breaking unpromising soil. He had to be careful not to snap the iron, because it might be hard to replace. City folks here didn't wear knives any more than they did in Valles or Erdin, and he didn't guess Liane and Rasile would want to traipse about the countryside looking for a smith with a sideline in knives.

Liane rubbed the last of the dirt away with the hem of her cape. The letters were worn, especially on top.

But not so they couldn't be read, apparently. "When the priests have carried out these rites," Liane said in a clear voice, her finger tracing the line to keep her place along the faint letters, "they may summon Lord Gorand from his rest. Lord Gorand will defend the people of Dariada from the Devouring Danger—I think that's what it is—as he defended them in the past."

She rose to her feet and turned. "The rites would've been on the upper part of the stone," she said quietly to Rasile. "I think."

Rasile wagged her tongue in laughter. "Wait," she said. "And read when you see."

The wizard settled herself arms-length from the stone and tossed the yarrow stalks onto the pavement. They fell—just fell as best Cashel could see—into a star with a hand plus two fingers of points.

Rasile started to keen. Because Cashel had been around her, he knew the sounds were Coerli words of power instead of a bellyache.

A column of wizardlight lifted slowly from the center of the star. It was as pure as the sun through a ruby. Folks watching from the other side of the guards shouted, some thrilled but the rest sounding scared.

A soldier glanced back over his shoulder, saw the light, and dropped his spear. He fell to his knees crying. The crowd wasn't pushing in the way it had been, though, so that didn't matter except probably to him.

The rod of red light twisted over slowly like a pine tree in a high wind. When the tip of it touched the stele, it spread across the sand-scoured face the way water soaks into a cloth. Instead of coarse gray stone, the background was a pink shimmer on which burned letters as sharp and solid as if they'd been cut from carnelian.

"If the Devouring Danger threatens again," Liane read, swinging into the business just like she'd been waiting for it, "the priests will speak the following words of power: *'Abrio set alarpho . . . '*"

Rasile yowled something that didn't have a syllable in common with what Liane had said. Cashel didn't think a human throat could even have made the sound. The cadence of the chant was the same, though.

Liane read, *"Alar alarioth . . ."* She stood just as straight and calm as if she was talking to Sharina about how formal to dress for a meeting. As her words spilled out, Rasile sang them back in Corl fashion.

The air was turning red like the surface of the stone. The crowd and soldiers had all run off by now. Some had opened their mouths open to scream, but Cashel hadn't heard anything over a sound like the wind rushing through a stand of hemlocks.

Amineus was gone too; back into his office, Cashel supposed. If you hadn't seen it before, this sort of business was scary and no mistake.

"Orthio!" said Liane, and there were more Coerli screeches. It seemed to Cashel that Rasile was responding even before she heard Liane, though he hadn't any real way to tell. He couldn't understand the words either one of the women were using.

The air glowed brighter than a ruby, as bright as pure flame. Cashel stood behind Rasile and Liane, his quarterstaff crossed before him. He wondered if he ought to turn to watch their backs, but this seemed the right choice just for now.

A flash of intense light swept everything else away. Dry heat engulfed Cashel and his companions.

SHARINA COULD HEAR the click of tiny claws as Burne patrolled the mosaic floor. He was much more active at night, though he adapted to a human schedule as he had to.

She smiled against the pillow. A year ago—a week ago!—she'd never have believed that she'd feel soothed by the sound of a rat walking around her bed . . . but she did. Still smiling, she slept; and as she slept, she dreamed.

"Come to me, Princess," the voice called. She didn't see Black this time. Perhaps he was below her on the blue world rotating slowly. "You have nothing to fear. Lord Scorpion exalts you over all women: He has chosen you for His priestess."

Land turned into view from the edge of the sphere, set off by a white border of surf. Sharina recognized the outline of the Isles against the Outer Sea: they'd been etched on the crystal floor of a room in the palace. Around the map cut by a great wizard of the Old Kingdom was written a legend added in the blocky New Script by a Duke of Ornifal before he seized the throne of the Isles: THE NAVEL OF THE COSMOS.

That had been a lie, of course. It was doubly a lie now that the Isles no longer existed as an archipelago but had rather become the periphery of a great continent. Valles was becoming a ghost town, sinking into a swamp because the River Beltis had drained into an Inner Sea which no longer existed.

"You *will* submit, Princess," Black said, cajoling her in a voice of thunder. "And even if you could resist, you would be mad to attempt it. From Lord Scorpion you will receive power and unexampled riches, but if the Gods of Palomir should take this world under Their suzerainty—"

The new continent had rotated so that it was directly beneath Sharina's vantage point. For the first time since she'd begun to dream tonight, she realized that she had a body. Pandah swelled in her awareness; not the real Pandah of mud and wicker around a core of ancient palaces but Pandah as rebuilt in black granite to honor Lord Scorpion.

"If the Gods of Palomir came to rule this world, Princess," crooned Black as the great temple grew toward her, "then your best hope will be to be sacrificed quickly. Lord Scorpion alone can defend you against Palomir. You will have power second only to that of the God!"

Black stood in the middle of the plaza, his arms spread to receive Sharina. She rushed downward with no more control of her movement than water in a torrent has. The scorpion on Black's shoulder curved its barbed tail into the sky. Above, clouds swept together into a monster image of the God, as black and dense as the granite temple.

Sharina fought, but there was no escape and—

Black shouted and looked over his shoulder. Sharina sat bolt upright in her bed; shards of the dream shimmered down the sides of her consciousness.

Burne bounced back from the wall to the floor; he must've leaped while she was still asleep. His jaws clicked, scattering bits of chitin.

"Go back to sleep, Sharina," he said. "No scorpion is going to reach you."

"You can't do anything about my dreams," Sharina muttered, but she put her head down on the pillow anyway. To her surprise, she felt sleep returning as soon as she closed her eyes.

She slept soundly until her maid Diora woke her at dawn.

ILNA SET THE lantern on top of the box she'd just freed and backed slowly away. There might be a way out of the cave in the direction the hulking creature was coming from, but she wasn't going to try going past the monster until all else had failed. There might be an exit on the other end too. That didn't seem likely, but Ilna wasn't in a mood to pass up even slim chances.

She was reasonably confident that the pattern dangling from her right hand would hold the thing, whatever it was, but *she* wouldn't be able to do anything else while she held it. Eventually she'd fall asleep, or faint, or the candle would burn out. She'd rush the creature with her little bone-cased kitchen knife rather than use her strength up in delaying what would shortly become inevitable.

The creature walked on its hind legs, placing its feet

with obvious deliberation. The rock shook beneath each step. She couldn't be sure how tall it was since the shadows might be exaggerating, but it was at least half again her own height and much, much broader.

Ilna took the box with her because both Brincisa and Hutton had thought it was valuable. She took the lantern because without light the creature couldn't see her patterns, so they'd be useless.

There was always the possibility that it was friendly. She figured that was less likely than her walking through a solid wall, but she was willing to be pleasantly surprised for a change.

The creature suddenly lurched onto all fours, throwing its face into the lantern light. Its muzzle was as long as a baboon's; great tusks in the upper and lower jaws crossed one another. The deep-set eyes glittered a savage red. It snuffled Hutton's corpse, then lifted its head in a howl that made the cave shiver.

Ilna's shoulders hit rock. There was no way out in this direction—

And she no longer entertained the slightest hope that the creature was friendly.

It stepped forward like a beast, then rose onto its hind legs and shrieked in fury. Turning its head away, it clawed toward the lantern. Its arm, covered with coarse reddish hair, was longer than that of a man of the same impossible height.

It's afraid of the light. Ilna lifted the lantern to the height of her arm.

The creature howled and staggered back. Filth matted its long hair, and its breath stank like a tanyard. Ilna waggled the lantern overhead, then regretted it: the candle guttered, dimming the light for a moment.

Nothing in the cave would make a good blaze. The cloth was shot through with damp and mold; it would resist burning even if tossed on a fire, let alone be able to sustain one.

The creature turned its shaggy back on her and hunched. It didn't have a tail. It lifted Hutton's corpse, then snarled over its shoulder as if afraid Ilna would try to take away the prize.

She drew in deliberate breaths. The flame had steadied, for which she was thankful.

The creature bent and bit off the face of the corpse. Thin bones crackled like a fire in dry bracken. It swallowed, then took a bite from the base of the neck. The ghoul's great jaws must be as strong as a sea wolf's; Hutton's collarbone snapped loudly as the fangs sheared it.

Throwing the rest of the corpse over its shoulder, the creature returned to the darkness. It didn't look back at Ilna, but it paused before its shadow disappeared into the greater shadows. Lifting its head, it gave another shivering cry.

Surely they must hear those bellows in Gaur? But perhaps the townsfolk were still under the weight of Brincisa's spell.

Ilna set the lantern in a niche in the cave wall. The candle would burn out shortly. By what light remained, she examined the box.

It was wooden, which meant she could break it open with the hilt of one of the daggers rusting on the cave floor. Even better, it was unlocked so she wouldn't have to.

That pleased Ilna, because the craftsmanship of the box was good enough to impress her. She'd have regretted smashing the dovetailed joints and the panels fitted so that the grain was almost undistinguishable each from the next—though she *would* have broken it if she'd had to, of course. She wondered if Cashel would be able to identify the wood.

Ilna slid the simple catch and lifted the lid, tilting the box toward the light so that she could see the interior. Packed in raw wool—which was so white that first glance made her think it was bleached—was a human head no bigger than her clenched fist. The lips were sewn shut with knots easily as complex as those which had bound the box to Hutton's chest.

Ilna ran her fingers over the knots. They'd been tied by a different hand; a human hand, she suspected. Hutton's? She couldn't be sure because she hadn't seen his work, but she didn't think so.

She smiled to remember the sound of the ghoul chewing Hutton's corpse. That was a proper end for people who kept the sort of friends he did.

Ilna began to pick out the knots. She had no better reason than that it amused her to test herself, but that wasn't a bad reason. Very few things involving fibers *did* test her.

The head felt leathery; well, it was leather, she supposed. It was packed with something, but she didn't think it was bone. Had the skull been removed and the skin shrunken over an artificial core?

Ilna removed the last knot and lifted the fiber to the waning lantern light. She couldn't tell what the material was; it had no feel at all. She couldn't remember ever having had that experience before.

The miniature head moved.

Ilna's first instinct was to leap up and fling the thing off her lap. Instead she held still.

Worms—no, tiny *hands* wriggled from the severed neck. The skin there hadn't been tied, just folded and shrunken into a tight mass. The hands were on the ends of arms which jerked their way out by fits and starts; Ilna had the impression of somebody trying to find the neck and arm openings in a tunic that was too small.

And it *was* too small. The arms were miniatures also, but they were far too large to fit into the shrunken head.

When the arms were free, Ilna saw that the shoulders had appeared also. What had been a head was now a bust.

The arms pumped up and down. The hands squeezed into fists and opened, then reached back into the stump of the neck. After much struggling they tugged out the whole remainder of the legs and torso of a man. He was wizened and incredibly ugly, besides being no taller than Ilna's knee if they were both standing.

The little man hopped off her lap and looked up at her. "My name's Usun," he said. "Who are you?"

The candle guttered out. For a few heartbeats the wick remained as a blue glow; then that too vanished. The darkness was complete.

EVEN BEFORE A trumpeter signaled the squadron on watch to mount up, the commotion at the gate roused Garric from the table where he sat with Chancellor Royhas and Lord Hauk. He jumped to his feet, grabbing the sword belt hanging from the back of his chair. That was Carus' reflex, but it wasn't a bad one.

Their meeting on prices and sources of draft animals took place under a marquee set up beside the headquarters tent at the intersection of the camp's two principal streets, surrounded at a respectful distance by aides. Garric would've had a view to the gate if it hadn't been for the clerks, secretaries, and runners now goggling either at the prince who'd risen or at the gate to see what was happening.

"Duzi!" Garric shouted. "*Will* you get out of the way so that I can see?"

The flunkies who were staring at him looked stricken and mostly dodged to the side, though a pudgy youth from the chancellery simply flattened on the ground as if Garric's glare were a ballista about to release. Those who were looking in the opposite direction didn't make the connection between their behavior and their prince's frustration until he shoved through them to get onto the street.

Part of Garric winced at his impoliteness. On the other hand, the ghost in his mind was ready to move them out of the way with the flat of his sword and curses much more

colorful than Garric using the name of a friendly shepherd god.

The royal army had built a rampart around its every
marching camp since Garric—better, since Carus—
began leading it. Fortifications took a great deal of work
and meant shorter marching days besides, but Carus
firmly believed that no campsite was safe until you'd
made it safe.

Garric had read enough history to accept the truth of
that assumption. His ancestor's vivid memories reinforced his acceptance.

Waldron kept a cavalry squadron and an infantry regiment ready to move on five minutes' notice. That meant
the horses were saddled though their cinches weren't
tight, and the troops wore their body armor—though
again they'd have to do up the straps and laces.

At the trumpet, detachments stood to at the four gates.
The whole camp was a clanging bustle as the rest of the
army grabbed weapons and equipment in case the next
signal was a general alarm.

There were various ways Garric could respond to the
signal, but there was only one way that wouldn't lead to
the ghost of King Carus bellowing in fury inside his
mind. He took off running for the gate a hundred double
paces away, buckling the twin tongues of his sword belt
as he went. Six Blood Eagles ran in front of him, and Attaper at his side bellowed, "Gravis, horses at the gate for
the platoon soonest! Move!"

Garric arrived at the same moment as Lord Waldron,
who'd been inspecting the horse lines when the sum-
mons came. He'd ridden, which wasn't surprising: he'd
come from almost the far end of the camp. He was bareback and using a rope halter, though, which for a man in
his sixties was an impressive demonstration.

"Rats, milord!" shouted a trooper who'd just dismounted from his lathered gelding. He ignored Garric
to speak to Waldron—like him, an Ornifal cavalryman.

"Foraging parties, not an attack, but Lieutenant Monner thinks there's three hundred maybe. Five miles southeast. Monner's watching them, but he won't try to engage. Ah, unless you want him to?"

"Why in the Sister's name did he send back a whole squad?" Waldron barked. "Are the rest of them here to hold your hand, Bresca?"

"Milord?" the squad leader said. "The rats're scattered across the countryside from here to the Underworld. The l'tenant, he thought we might run into something on the way back and, you know, he wanted to make sure the message got through."

Lieutenant Monner's subordinates assumed he'd be willing to fight several hundred rats with twenty or so cavalrymen . . . *and* he had foresight enough not to entrust a critical message to a single courier. Garric didn't need the grim-faced approval of King Carus to know that Lieutenant Monner should be commanding something more than a troop of horse.

"Right!" said Waldron. Turning to Garric: "Your Highness, I'll take the ready squadron, they're my old command, and the regiment of javelin men from northern Cordin. You follow with five thousand infantry and all but one squadron of the horse as soon as they get organized, right?"

The ready squadron was divided with a troop at the west, south, and east gates; the north gate was guarded by cavalry from a Sandrakkan squadron. They could be pressed into immediate service if necessary. Waldron had apparently decided it was, because they and their blue and silver pennant was trotting down the cross street to join the Ornifal red and gold.

In Garric's mind, Carus was estimating how long it would be before the support element arrived. It'd be an hour before they marched. Besides, heavy infantry regiments wouldn't move as quickly as cavalry and skirmishers—Cordin shepherds turned soldier, carrying only light javelins and hatchets.

"We'll both accompany the alerted troops," he said. He surveyed the cavalrymen walking their horses through the gate to form in the trampled ground just outside. Carus picked a rangy chestnut.

"I'll take that horse," Garric said. "Trooper, get your remount and follow."

"Your Highness!" said Waldron, looking up from the waxed tablet on which he was scribbling an order. "I'm going, but *I* have a deputy."

"And I don't, milord," Garric said, "which is why *I'm* going. I need to see the rats in action as soon as possible so that I know what we're dealing with."

"Your Highness, that's pointlessly dangerous!" Attaper said. "Nobody doubts your courage, *nobody*. Unless you distrust your officers to bring you an accurate information, you'll gain nothing from this."

"I'm going, Attaper," Garric said, grasping the horn and crupper of the horse he'd appropriated. He mounted. By now he could probably have made a smooth business of it without his ancestor's reflexes.

A squad of Blood Eagles rode up, each trooper holding the reins of two or more additional horses. Carus, watching through Garric's eyes, said, *"Attaper knew he couldn't argue you out of it, so he made sure he'd have a platoon ready to go too."*

After a moment he added with a mixture of amusement and regret, *"I never had anybody who'd fight me as hard as Attaper does you, lad. I'd have taken their heads off if they tried. Which was all right as far as it went, but it meant people with good sense made sure to keep shy of me."*

A trooper had saddled Waldron's mount while he was scribbling out orders to his subordinates. Tossing the last tablet to a runner, the army commander swung into the saddle. Checking the four troops waiting in neat columns—and the skirmishers who weren't in the least neat but were certainly ready—Waldron snapped to his trumpeter, "Sound the advance!"

The trumpet call and the horns of the line troops—the Sandrakkan unit used a cow horn which sounded harsh and thin in comparison the brass instruments curling around the bodies of the Ornifal cornicenes—set the patrol into motion. Garric's borrowed horse stepped off even before he tapped its ribs with his right heel.

"A trained soldier obeys commands in his sleep," Carus said. *"Likewise a trooper's trained mount."*

He sounded wistful. Perhaps the ghost was remembering the time when he too needed sleep.

Lord Waldron rode with the leading troop; so did the squad which had brought the alarm. It'd been remounted, and at least one of the replacement horses was clearly unhappy with his present rider.

Garric smiled faintly. He was sorry for the trooper, but he was very glad that he hadn't borrowed a skittish mount himself. Prince Garric could've ordered somebody else to trade with him—but he wouldn't have.

They trotted into woodland, a mixture of sweet gum and pine that must've sprung up from land that'd been clear within the past generation. The edge of the woods had been a mass of cedars sown too thickly to be of any size. The returning scouts had ridden the trees down as they approached the camp, providing easy entry for the Waldron's troop and the rest of the column.

The forest proper was open enough that the cavalry had little difficulty beyond having to break ranks. The skirmishers hadn't seen any point in ranks to begin with. Here among the tree boles they were the equal of cavalry man for man, and the cheerful way they trotted among the troopers showed that they were well aware of the fact.

Waldron shouted something to a man riding with him,

a member of the squad that'd brought the warning. That fellow reined back slightly so that the Blood Eagles just ahead of Garric overtook him.

"Let him through, Attaper!" Garric shouted. "I want to learn about the terrain ahead!"

The Blood Eagles parted, but Attaper himself dropped back with the line trooper. The man was Bresca, the squad leader who'd delivered the message. He leaned toward Garric as they rode along together and said, "It's the next valley and it's mostly cow pasture, sir. There's apple orchards on the north slopes, though, so they won't bloom till it's full spring and they can't catch frost. We'll come out through the apples. The l'tenant, he said he'd keep this side of the crest and not push unless, you know, he had to."

There were challenges and less formal shouts from close ahead. The instinct of King Carus slapped Garric's hand to the hilt of his sword. He drew the long gray blade, forged either by wizardry or by a smith as skilled as Ilna was in her different craft. There didn't seem to be anything magical about the sword, but you couldn't dull its edge even by slashing rock.

"That's the l'tenant, sir!" said Bresca. He hadn't learned that "Your Highness" was the correct form of address when speaking to a prince. It wasn't something that line soldiers often had to worry about, of course. "We're up with the rest of the troop!"

"Hold up!" a cavalryman shouted. "Pass it back, hold up!" The call wobbled through the woods, each man turning in the saddle to send it on to those behind him.

"Waldron isn't using the horns because the rats are just over the hill," Carus noted with grim approval. *"They'll have spotted the scout troop unless rats are stone blind, but horn calls will tell them to expect more company."*

He paused, then added, *"I could've used more officers like Waldron."*

Garric joined Waldron and an officer he didn't think he'd met—

"You have," snapped Carus. History claimed Carus had known the name of every man in his army. From what Garric had experienced in the years that his mind had been haunted by his ancient ancestor, history hadn't exaggerated very much. *"Monner, of course."*

—along with the four troop leaders of the reaction force, and a grizzled fellow with a silk sash over his goat-wool tunic—the commander of the skirmishers. Though on foot and as old as Waldron, he'd kept up with the trotting horsemen.

"Your Highness," Waldron said with a bare nod to royal authority. "Monner's been keeping watch. The enemy's scattered through the valley, rounding up the livestock. The horse will charge the length of the valley in line so that the rats don't have a chance to form ranks, with Ainbor here's—"

He gestured with his left hand to the skirmishers' commander. There was no love lost between cavalry and light infantry, but Waldron had always used the latter intelligently.

"—men following to mop up those we don't kill in the first pass."

The ghost in Garric's mind gave a curt nod of approval.

"Carry on, milord," Garric said. He managed a smile to show that his approval was more than formal.

The troop leaders trotted toward their guidons, snarling orders as they tried to align their men despite the broken forest. Waldron spoke quietly to the trumpeter; he nodded, holding his instrument ready.

Garric's blood trembled with anticipation of the coming battle. He started to draw his long sword. Attaper touched his elbow.

"No, Your Highness," he said. "You're not wearing armor, and you'll see *nothing* beyond the point of your sword if you rush down into a melee. If you're an honorable man, you'll watch from the brow of the hill."

"The bloody man's right!" snarled Carus. *"But by the Lady! if it was me—"*

Which fortunately it wasn't, as Carus knew as well as his descendant did.

"Yes, of course, Attaper," Garric said mildly. "We'll find a suitable vantage point. Though I reserve the right to defend myself if the rats attack me."

Attaper looked startled, then nodded agreement and removed his hand from Garric's arm. He wasn't a man who could laugh about his duties as a bodyguard.

The trumpeter sounded Advance, followed instantly by the horns of the cornicenes; they'd been waiting for the signal. The reinforced squadron, about a hundred and fifty troopers, trotted up the last of the rise and over it.

"Not a man of them but thinks they could do the job themselves without any infantry," Carus said. *"I'd think the same. But speaking as a commander, I'm just as glad of those javelins. If the rats keep their heads and hamstring the horses . . . and who knows how good troops rats turn out to be?"*

You and I are going to know in a few minutes, thought Garric as he clucked his horse over the crest. *Which is why we're here.*

The trumpeter signaled Charge. Again, the horns echoed him—four deep, mellow calls and the blat on the cowhorn. The Ornifal cavalrymen had their long swords drawn; on the right of the line, the Sandrakkan troop couched short lances that were light enough to have thrown if they'd been facing a shield wall.

The troopers started downhill, disarrayed at first by the apple trees but not slowed. The javelin men whooped and began loping along after them.

Garric and his guards trotted through the orchard. Beyond spread a broad valley several miles long, with a right dogleg extending it unguessibly farther. Instead of individual homesteads, there'd been a hamlet straggling along both banks of the stream in the middle.

A neck-roped coffle of the human residents, fifty or sixty of them, was almost out of sight to the southeast. A score of rat men guarded the prisoners. Hundreds more of the creatures were scattered by tens and handfuls throughout the valley, rounding up brindled cattle.

The horn signals had drawn the narrow muzzles of all the rat men toward the northwest slope down which the cavalry charged. Lord Waldron was in the center of the line; Ornifal's golden lion on a red field flapped above the standard-bearer to his left.

The rats were the size of short humans and wore bronze caps and breastplates. They stopped what they'd been doing and drew short swords, then began to trot forward to meet the attack.

The nearest clot of rat men was only two furlongs south of the apple trees through which the cavalry rode. They were directly in front of Lieutenant Monner's troop, but the Sandrakkan unit on the far right of the line was edging over to snatch the kill. Lord Waldron stood in his stirrups screaming abuse at the lancers, and King Carus' hot rage snatched the sword from Garric's scabbard before intellect could restrain him.

Nobody seemed to notice. Garric grinned faintly. Drawing your sword while you watched a battle swirl wasn't the sort of thing that aroused comment.

Monner was on the right of his troop and slightly ahead of his men. He held his sword vertical, ready to slash down at the rats, but he was trusting his mount to find its own course as he bellowed at the lancers crowding him.

The horse suddenly planted its feet in the cropped turf. Monner went over its head—*nobody* could've kept his seat. The horse had stopped as abruptly as if it'd charged into a stone wall, then nearly somersaulted over its rider.

Other mounts were going wild also, pitching and bucking. A pair of Sandrakkan geldings collided as they turned toward one another while both trying to flee back uphill; one had already thrown off its rider.

Chittering in delight, the rats—there were six or eight of them—rushed the sudden chaos. They ran on their hind legs, but the way they bent forward suggested they were about to drop onto all fours. Their swords were short, deep-bladed, and almost square-tipped.

Several horsemen dismounted or regained their feet after being bucked off. They poised to meet the oncoming rats, but the rhythm of the battle had shifted to the beast-men.

A mare reared, then pitched forward; her rider managed to land on his feet though momentum flopped him on his face an instant later. Freed of her burden, the mare charged into the rat men, whinnying and kicking with all four hooves. A rat went down, its skull crushed, and another flew backward with a dent in the middle of its breastplate.

The surviving rats slashed at her, one carving a line of blood all the way down the mare's ribs. The saddle rolled off her back when the cinch was cut. She squealed and twisted back to clamp the rat's muzzle with square, strong teeth. With jerk of her head, she sent the rat flying. Its limbs twitched spastically, and its head lolled from a broken neck.

Rats and dismounted cavalrymen met in a clanging melee. One of the humans went down, but thanks to the mare's berserk attack the remaining rat men were easily dispatched. Bleeding from a dozen stabs and slices, that horse continued to stamp and pivot on what had once been a dangerous enemy.

"May the Sister suck my marrow!" Attaper said in furious amazement. "What's happening? It's wizardry! They're bewitching the horses!"

The first skirmish was the model for those to follow. Every time cavalrymen bore down on the rats, their horses went out of control, either panicking or—in a handful of instances—attacking the rat men in a foaming rage. Generally the dismounted cavalry were able to defend themselves until the infantry reached them, but sometimes the rats hacked down a horseman who'd been stunned in mind as well as body by the unexpected turn of events.

"It's not wizardry!" Carus said. The face of the ghost was sallow with cold anger. *"It's the smell! The stink of the beasts sets the horses off. I've seen it with camels, and it's the same with these* bloody *rats!"*

There'd been no wind in the forest. A fitful westerly blew on this side of the ridge, bringing not only the high-pitched chatter of the rat men but their rank odor.

Garric's mount shied. Carus' reflexes clamped his knees tight against the horse's barrel and sawed the reins savagely when the beast tried to pivot to its right.

The Blood Eagles around him were in similar straits. Attaper and some of the others were horsemen by birth or training, but half the detachment came from infantry regiments and rode by dint of single-minded determination. That wasn't enough when their mounts began to pirouette and buck.

Garric's horse made a sound that was more a scream than a neigh. It thrust its head forward like a battering ram despite Garric trying to haul back on the reins. They thundered downhill with the suddenness of an eagle stooping.

Duzi. This gelding's one of the handful that the smell drives into a killing rage instead of a panic.

"Jump, Your Highness!" Attaper shouted. "Sister take this Sister-raping horse! Jump!"

Some of that must be directed against his own mount, though he probably wasn't any more pleased with Garric's. . . .

The bubbling laughter of the ghost of King Carus was infectious. Garric too chortled as he hurtled toward the rat men. Carus had picked a horse that wanted to fight. Why would that surprise anybody who knew him?

The tall gelding galloped through clots of javelin men and dismounted cavalry. Some fighting was still going on, but the horse apparently didn't think it was worth his attention. Instead he rode straight at about twenty—

"Twenty-two," Carus corrected.

—twenty-two rats, several smaller groups which had merged and were advancing uphill in a shallow V.

Garric was too busy to be afraid. Oh, this was a disaster, no question, but there wouldn't be time to worry until it was over—and probably no opportunity then either, of course.

He couldn't jump from the galloping horse, not with a bare sword in his hand. Attaper would've known that if he'd been thinking instead of reacting. Nor could Garric sheath the sword: under these conditions, not even Carus' skill could guarantee the point would find the scabbard mouth instead of the flesh of his thigh.

Of course Garric could've hurled the sword away before jumping and taken his chances of being able to escape uphill unarmed while the rat men pursued. He didn't figure that was an option he'd choose in this lifetime—nor would Carus choose it in another thousand years.

He might as well laugh.

The gelding charged the center of the line of rat men. There was nothing wrong with the rats' courage: the one which the horse had marked for his own stood his ground. His sword was raised and his little round shield advanced, though nobody could imagine that the impact of a horse weighing a hundred stone plus rider was going to be survivable.

They crashed together. The gelding pivoted. Garric gripped the saddle horn with his left hand and cut down to his right at a rat man. His sword sheared the rat's helmet and into the narrow skull, but the beast stabbed deep into the horse's flank before thrashing away.

A rat slashed from the left, slicing the back of Garric's thigh. Time later to worry about how bad that was. The screaming horse reared, kicking with both forefeet.

Garric swung his left leg over the saddle and slid to the ground over the gelding's bleeding right haunch. Four rat men were coming at him. He thrust the first through the throat, notching the little shield the beast man tried to interpose.

Thank the Lady for this sword! Or better, thank the Yellow King.

The other three would've had him but the gelding, continuing to turn, crushed them down, bathing them in gouts of blood from a deep cut in his neck. Garric drew his dagger in his left hand and turned to his left to meet the rat men coming from that direction.

Carus was in full charge of his mind now. There was neither time nor need of anything but reflex, and the ancient warrior had honed his reflexes in a hundred battles like this one.

Five or six rat men were squirming toward him, getting in each other's way. Their shields were wicker with thin bronze facings. Garric thrust through the center of the nearest, deep into the forearm of the rat holding it, and flicked his sword sideways to drag the squealing creature into the path of its fellows.

Garric jerked back on the sword to clear it. The preternaturally sharp blade screeched free, but one of the rat men vaulted the struggling knot and cut at his head. He got the dagger up in time to catch the stroke, but the rat cannoned into him.

Garric stepped back with his left foot, tripped on a furry corpse, and fell over beneath his attacker. It struck at him with its shield, numbing his left arm. He twisted the sword around and pounded the pommel into the beast's ribs. He heard bone crack, but the rat tried to hit him again.

Garric shoved the rat away. It didn't weigh more than eighty pounds, but Duzi! it was strong. Three more of the creatures pushed close.

Garric was still on his back. He kicked a rat in the crotch. They weren't built like men and anyway this one was female, but his boot slammed the creature out of the way for the moment. The other two—

Half a dozen javelins zipped overhead. A rat turned one with his shield but another took him in the belly beneath the lower edge of his breastplate. Missiles spiked the standing rat through the eye and shoulder, while the female Garric had kicked was skewered from knee to hip bone.

That last javelin nicked the toe of Garric's raised boot and could as easily have taken off a toe. A toe would've been a cheap price to pay for the rest of the volley.

"Yee-*ha*!" shrilled a skirmisher leaping past with his hatchet raised.

The female with the spear through her leg cut at him. The skirmisher blocked the sword with his remaining javelin—they went into action with three apiece—and sank his hatchet into the side of the rat's skull. She'd lost her helmet, but thin bronze wouldn't have helped her anyway. As she spasmed into death, other skirmishers stabbed or hacked the bodies of rat men who were still quivering.

"Thanks for baiting 'em for us, buddy," said the first skirmisher on the scene. He stuck the butt spike of his javelin into the turf and helped Garric up with his left hand. "The furry bastards 're too quick to spear when they're paying attention."

"Yeah," said another cheerful skirmisher. "I always knew cavalry pukes must be good for something."

Garric's borrowed mount lay in a pile of furry bodies. The gelding had died with his teeth clamped on a rat man's shoulder. In his death throes he'd almost bitten the creature's arm off.

"Ought to put up a monument to that horse," Carus said. *"For valorous conduct in battle."*

I don't think Attaper would agree, Garric thought.

The skirmisher who'd finished the female rat wiped his hatchet clean and turned to Garric. "You ought to have that leg looked at, buddy," he said.

"Hey, if it'd got the artery, he wouldn't be standing, right?" said his fellow. He knelt and lifted the skirt of Garric's tunic. "Still, let me have a look at it."

"You bloody fools!" bellowed Attaper. "That's your prince!"

"Bugger me if it ain't!" said the man thrusting the hatchet away under his belt.

"Yes, milord," said Garric, turning with a smile. He'd have to wipe his sword before sheathing it, but from the way the gelding had sprayed blood it didn't seem any of this group of rats had enough clean fur for the long blade. "And they saved my life, not to put too fine a point on it."

He grinned at the skirmishers. "Even if they did think I was just another cavalry puke."

"Sorry if, ah . . . ," said the standing man. "Some of those javelins came a bit close."

"Not as close as the rats were going to come if you hadn't been around," Garric said.

The other skirmisher stood. "I think your leg's going to be fine, B-B-Prince," he said. "But the surgeon'll want to stitch it up when you get back to camp."

"Yes, he bloody well will," snarled Attaper. He was panting and red-faced from running a good half-mile, obviously expecting a worse result than he'd found when he reached his prince. "And we're going to get you back there as soon as somebody drags a horse down here for you, Your Highness."

Garric looked up the valley. The prisoners had disappeared with their guards, and the only rat men visible were the hundreds of furry corpses.

"All right, we'll head back," Garric said. Much as he hated it, he had to agree with King Carus' cold logic: he couldn't go after the prisoners with the troops he had available. Cavalry was obviously useless, and the skirmishers had taken casualties also. If there were a thousand rat men concealed around the dogleg, they'd massacre their pursuers.

He looked at the carnage, the bloody, stinking carnage, around him.

"Well," said Carus. *"I wouldn't call it a victory, but I'm glad to have learned this before we tried a cavalry charge in a major battle. Because odds are, we'd have been leading it ourself. Right, lad?"*

Right.

Chapter

10

WHILE SHARINA WAS in meetings, she had only the others present to deal with. In between, however, she had to run a gauntlet of clerks, courtiers, and petitioners as she moved through the halls and passages.

It was no different this time. The fact Sharina was leaving her final appointment of the day—on road improvements which were absolutely necessary but either a huge financial drain or a political disaster if forced labor was used—and hoping to have a light meal in her suite before getting some sleep, just meant that she was more tired and hungry than she'd have been at midmorning. Though she'd been hungry and very tired at midmorning, too.

"Your Highness, about the canal project/the new barracks/the position for my nephew?"

She strode past them in a cocoon of Blood Eagles. Her escort made sure nobody actually touched Princess Sharina, but they couldn't shut off the voices unless they simply clubbed everybody out of her way. History said tyrants like Hawley the Seneschal and King Morail One-Eye had done just that.

Sharina sighed. The reality of being princess gave her a different and altogether more positive appreciation of men whom she as a scholar had regarded as brutes.

There was usually a dense clot outside the door she would next enter. That was true this time also, but all but one of those waiting were fit, very sturdy-looking men in identical neat tunics and identical grim expressions. The exception was Master Dysart.

The agents parted when the Blood Eagles arrived; they weren't here to fight, just to hold a prime location and to keep everybody else at a discreet distance from their superior while he talked to the princess.

"Your Highness, if you could sign these tonight . . . ?" the spymaster said, waving a sheaf of documents on vellum. Sharina doubted whether there was anybody in the palace who didn't know that Dysart was Lady Liane's deputy, but the colorless little man kept up the pretense that he was a senior clerk in the chancellery.

"Yes, of course," said Sharina, narrowly avoiding another sigh. Secret intelligence was part of her present duties, but experience had already taught her that the details of road construction were likely to be more interesting. "We can take care of that inside, Master Dysart."

Sharina opened the door herself. Burne sat upright on a table in the reception area as Diora fed him a round of hard bread. The rat was perfectly capable of feeding himself, but Sharina had noticed that the maid was more comfortable thinking of Burne as a smart pet than she might've been if she'd appreciated what he really was.

Sharina grinned. Whatever that was, of course, but Burne was certainly more than a smart pet.

"A late night, Your Highness," Diora said as she turned to greet Sharina. "What—oh!"

Dysart closed the door firmly behind him, then shot the bolts. Diora hadn't realized her mistress wasn't alone when she greeted her with what many would consider scandalous informality from a maid. She was obviously embarrassed.

"I have some papers to go over with Master Dysart," Sharina said nonchalantly. "Set out my nightgown, Diora. And shut the door behind you, if you please."

The bedroom was already prepared—of course—but it was a quiet excuse to prevent awkwardness with the spymaster. Dysart probably *was* scandalized by Sharina's friendly relationship with her maid, but the chance of him talking to another living soul was less than that the huntsmen and stags painted on the sidewall would.

On the other hand, Dysart would refuse to speak in front of Diora however much Sharina said she trusted the maid. Perhaps he was right.

Burne jumped down from the table and padded over to them. "I'm coming up," he warned, then hopped to Sharina's sash for a foothold and finally to her shoulder.

"There haven't been any scorpions in the suite all day," he said in a conversational voice. "I'm not sure whether they're giving up or just planning something more subtle . . . but for now at least, I think we have privacy."

Dysart waited, watching Diora till the bedroom door thumped shut. He grimaced—whether at the maid or the rat, Sharina couldn't tell—and said, "We're going to raid a gathering of Scorpion worshippers at midnight, Your Highness. We'll be using men from my own department and a company of soldiers in civilian dress. You'd said you wanted to be kept informed of progress, so—"

He shrugged.

"—I came to tell you."

A servant watching the water clock in the square outside the palace rang the hour with a mallet and a set of chimes. It lacked a half hour of midnight, which was time enough.

"Right," Sharina said. "Master Dysart, send a messenger to Captain Ascor and tell him to report to me immediately. He's to be without equipment and wearing a blue cloak to cover his sword."

"Your Highness," Dysart said in concern, "Lord Tadai has already provided for soldiers. I don't believe adding Blood Eagles is advisable."

"I'm not adding Blood Eagles," Sharina said, tugging at her laces. "I'm—"

This wasn't doing any good! She needed help.

"Diora, come help me get out of this!" she called. "And bring the Pewle knife!"

"Your Highness?" said Dysart, his eyes widening.

"I'm coming with you, Master Dysart," Sharina said. "And while Captain Ascor won't like it, at least with Lord Attaper's deputy present, I won't have to sneak out of this room to prevent the whole squad on guard from tramping along with me in their full gear!"

GARRIC STOOD WITHIN a coarse brushwood fence, watching as Tenoctris examined the dead rat man that they'd brought back to the camp. All the screen did was permit the soldiers not to watch wizardry if it made them uncomfortable—as it did almost all laymen.

They'd strapped the corpse to a lance carried by pairs of skirmishers who traded off the burden. Lord Waldron had thought there'd be at least one horse that didn't mind the rats' smell, but he'd apparently been wrong.

Master Ainbor—who'd chuckled to be referred to as "Master"—had volunteered that his men wouldn't mind carrying one of the rats they'd killed. He'd been quite obviously twitting Waldron, but Garric—and Waldron, from his sour nod—figured Ainbor had a right to do that.

His skirmishers had saved the lives of scores of the cavalry, not to mention the life of Prince Garric.

"We might've fought our way clear, lad," Carus muttered.

Right, the way you swam to shore when a wizard drowned your fleet a thousand years ago, Garric thought. *No, I'm pretty clear on why I'm standing here, and it's not because I have a strong sword arm.*

As it was, Garric's left thigh throbbed as though a horsefly had bitten him. Master Daciano, the Blood Eagles' surgeon, had sewn shut the lips of the wound and then bandaged over it a poultice of lettuce which was supposed to numb the pain. Maybe that was true, but if so it would've been *very* uncomfortable without the drug.

Tenoctris had said she'd do something for him as soon as she had a chance. Right now, both she and Garric thought that the first priority was learning as much as possible about the rat army of Palomir.

"That's odd," Garric said. "The rat isn't as big as it was when it was alive. As any of them were. Can it be shrinking, Tenoctris?"

Instead of answering, Tenoctris murmured a spell of which Garric caught only a few snatches: *". . . sethri saba . . ."* Blue light sparkled over the corpse and around the edges of the pentagon the wizard had drawn on the ground with corn meal.

For a moment wizardlight drew an image of the rat man as it had been when a javelin took it through the throat: half again as tall as the present figure and several times the bulk. Garric said, "Yes, that's—"

The image became *different* instead of changing. The sparkling azure shell of a young man with big bones and a vacant expression swelled about the furry corpse. He looked ordinary, a farm laborer or a common soldier. Garric had never met him, but he'd met the type a thousand times.

The dusting of light dissolved into the air. Garric found himself blinking away orange afterimages: the blue shimmer had been brighter than he'd realized until it vanished.

Tenoctris rose and turned to face him. The spell she'd cast hadn't completely drained her the way it would've done the Tenoctris whom Garric had first met: an old woman with a great deal of wisdom but limited power. Nonetheless the tightness at the corners of her eyes hinted that what she'd just done had required effort, even for the demon her will had bound within her.

"They're not shrinking, exactly," she said. The weariness was evident in her voice also, though it gained strength with every syllable. "They're returning to what they'd been before the rite that turned them into warriors."

"An incantation, you mean?" Garric said. "A wizard enchanted ordinary rats and made them as big as men?"

"Not a wizard," Tenoctris said. "And not a priest either, except that as a priest he summoned the God. It was the God Franca who turned rats into rat men, Garric. A very evil God."

"Ah," said Garric. He started to speak further, then swallowed the words.

"Of course we can fight a God, lad," said the ghost, answering the unvoiced question. Carus smiled with grim insouciance. *"I don't see any way we can win, but that doesn't stop us trying."*

Garric looked at the corpse again; it was smaller yet. From the way it stank, the extra bulk was being lost in the form of noxious gases.

Garric grimaced. He said, "Tenoctris, do you need this further? Because if you don't . . . ?"

"What?" she said, looking over her shoulder with a critical expression. "Oh, yes, you can bury it. And I have no more incantations for the present, so I suppose we can go outside—"

She nodded to the screen of brush.

"—this."

It struck Garric that Tenoctris, though born to an aristocratic family, paid almost no attention to her surroundings except as they had bearing on something she wanted to accomplish. A peasant might have ignored the stench because he was used to worse; Tenoctris had simply been oblivious of the fact the corpse stank.

The fence curled past itself like the coils of a snail's shell. Garric stepped out the open end and said to his aide, "Lerdain, have a detail burn the offal outside the camp. They can use this—"

He patted the screen they no longer needed.

"—for fuel if they like."

The camp was crowded and though as sanitary as possible—by Carus' order through Garric's lips, the latrines were dug before the troops were released to build personal shelters—it was a trampled, barren waste. It would've been far worse if it'd been raining.

"A soldier lives in dust or mud," Carus said. *"Unless the winter's particularly cold and there's ice instead. Even then it's mud inside the tents and around cook fires. If he's got a tent and a cook fire."*

Garric laughed and said aloud, "Who'd be a soldier, eh?"

Tenoctris looked at him. "Who indeed?" she said. "But why do you mention it now?"

"Because . . . ," Garric said, answering both the rhetorical question and the real one. "A soldier is told where to go and who to fight. He doesn't have to think about anything, so he's without responsibility for the result. Even if he's killed, he's not responsible for it. Whereas—"

He looked into the wizard's eyes. "—I'm responsible for defeating an empire that turns rats into soldiers. And I know how fast rats breed."

"Your Highness, if I might have a moment with you," said Lord Acer, newly appointed to the command of an

Ornifal cavalry regiment. There was no question whatever in his tone. "The food—"

"Master Acer!" Garric said. He was angry and frustrated at the greater situation. It was probably a good thing that this young fop was providing a legitimate outlet, though Garric wouldn't release his feelings—

King Carus laughed at the thought.

—with a sweep of his sword, the way his ancestor had been known to do.

"I am in conference with Lady Tenoctris, on whom the survival of mankind depends. Report to Lord Waldron, if you will, and inform him that you're to be reassigned to an infantry regiment at Pandah as of this moment!"

Acer's mouth dropped open. Other aides, waiting to talk to the prince when he was free, stifled laughs—or didn't, in the case of Lord Lerdain, a husky youth and the son of the Count of Blaise. If Acer wanted a duel, Lerdain was very much the boy to give him one.

Acer went pale and stumbled blindly away. He'd have tripped over a tent rope if another officer hadn't guided him around it.

"That was excessive," Garric muttered.

Tenoctris shrugged. "My mother always told me that high birth doesn't exempt one from basic courtesy," she said. "I'm inclined to agree with her, though it's not something I worry about a great deal."

She cleared her throat and resumed, "You're right that we can't attack the problem by preventing Palomir from finding rats. That's only one aspect of what's going on, though. The rats provide a physical core around which the priest and his God can form a warrior. He also needs human souls to animate the forms. Otherwise they'd still be rats—large ones, but no more dangerous or disciplined than so many wolves."

"We've heard that the priests are sacrificing everyone they capture," Garric said. His lips moved as though he were sucking on a lemon. "That's why, then? To make an army of rats?"

They were standing in the middle of the camp, close to the headquarters tent. The location was about as private—and comfortable—as anything available. The guards kept everyone else out of earshot, which a tent's canvas walls would not. Not that it seemed to matter whether anybody overheard them. . . .

"Not in the way you mean it," Tenoctris said. "The blood sacrifice increases Franca's ability to affect events in the waking world, but the souls themselves are those of the dead."

She grinned. Tenoctris had always had a bright smile and a whimsical sense of humor. "The innocent dead, I suppose you might say," she said. "Though I don't know that any human being is completely innocent. The dead weren't worshippers of Franca and His siblings, at any rate."

She nodded back to where they'd been. Lord Lerdain watched proprietarily as a Blaise file-closer and a squad of armsmen under his command tramped toward the main gate, carrying the remains of the rat man on the mat of brush that had concealed it.

"Any more than the rats who supplied the physical form were Franca worshippers, you see," she concluded.

Garric nodded. "All right," he said. "I understand the situation. What can we do to change it?"

"We need to prevent the priest behind this," Tenoctris said, "from haling souls out of the Underworld. We need to close the Gate of Ivory. And that will require a very particular hero."

Garric lifted his sword slightly and let it slide back, unconsciously checking to be sure that it wouldn't bind in the scabbard if he needed to draw it quickly. "Well, I don't know that I'm particular enough," he said. "But I'll try."

The wizard laughed merrily, making those waiting beyond the line of Blood Eagles look up eagerly.

"Garric, in most respects you'd be ideal for the task," she said. "You lack one necessary attribute, however: you're not dead. The late Lord Munn is therefore a better choice."

"I, ah . . . ," said Garric. "Can I help you reach Lord Munn, then?"

"If you mean, 'Can I help you go to the place where Lord Munn's body rests,' " Tenoctris said, "no; I'll get us there. But Lord Munn won't accept orders from a woman, not even a woman who's a wizard—"

She smiled, but the harshness of her expression was very unusual for Tenoctris.

"—and who has the power to plunge his soul beneath the deepest Hell. Of course, if Lord Munn did not have such a strong, ah, will, he wouldn't be any good to us. That will require the presence of a warrior-king."

Garric grinned and stretched. "Then take me to him, milady," he said.

Tenoctris nodded. "There's a sacred grove within a mile," she said. "It focuses a useful amount of power. We'll go now, if you're ready."

"Lord Attaper!" Garric called. "Lady Tenoctris and I are leaving the camp immediately, and I suspect you'll want us to have an escort."

Not even chalcus could climb a smooth rock wall and shove that roller out of the way, thought Ilna as she looked at the roof of the cave. It was solid black; only memory told her where the opening might be. *But I wish he was here.*

She lowered her eyes to where Usun probably was, though she couldn't see him either. "My name is Ilna os-Kenset," she said. "A wizard named Brincisa lowered me into this cave to fetch the box you were in. She left me here when I wouldn't send the box up ahead of me."

She sniffed and added, "She'd have left me anyway,

obviously. Well, this way I have company. Besides the ghoul."

The wizened little man laughed like an angry squirrel. "Oh, you have much more than mere company, Ilna!" he said. "You have Usun! And as for that Brincisa—"

He snapped his fingers.

"—she fancies herself a wizard, true, but Hutton could stand her on her head when he wanted to. He did that! Hutton had me, you see."

Ilna thought of the last time she'd seen Hutton; probably the last time anybody would see Hutton. Smiling faintly she said, "It doesn't seem to have done him a great deal of good. Unless his final wish was to become dinner for a ghoul."

As Ilna's eyes adapted, she became aware of a faint blue glow in the direction the ghoul had disappeared. She heard or at least felt a low hum. She couldn't tell where it came from or even be sure it really existed.

Usun cackled again. "Oh, no, Hutton had great plans!" he said in his harsh, high-pitched voice. "He didn't really die, you know."

"He certainly seemed to be dead, Master Usun," Ilna said tartly. "Even before the ghoul began to eat him."

"Ilna, I'll burst with laughing!" Usun said, chortling loudly enough to make it seem a possibility. "You're right, you're right, but Hutton didn't imagine you. Well, who could, eh?"

He paused. Ilna could now see a hint of the little man, squatting on his haunches at her feet. He was doing something with his hands—coiling the thin filament that'd bound the box to Hutton's corpse, she suddenly realized.

"He really did stand his wife on her head, you know," Usun said confidentially. "Stood her there, dropped her, and warned her that he'd do it again if she annoyed him. But maybe Brincisa wasn't so very thick, eh? She was sharp enough to fetch you and turn the tables on Hutton once and for all. He thought he was so clever, but now where is he?"

"He was dead when I met him," Ilna said irritably. "When I first saw him, that is. The ghoul started eating the corpse, but it didn't kill him."

Usun looked up. "Not really dead, no," he said. Familiarity didn't make his voice more attractive. "Hutton froze time in all this cavern. He sent his soul into the Underworld to gain knowledge that he called wisdom."

He laughed again. "Wisdom!" he said. "But Hutton knows better now, eh? He thought he'd return to his body in three days. He'd rule the waking world, *he* thought. Rule the waking world indeed! But you broke the spell and freed the ghoul when you cut Hutton's soul away from his body."

Ilna held strands of yarn in her left hand. She could plait a pattern that would direct her next action. She wouldn't be able to see it, but she didn't need to see fabric to understand it more clearly than an educated person like Garric would gain from a long written description.

On the other hand, there was another way which might provide more information still. "Master Usun," she said, "I want to get out of this cave before the ghoul or something worse comes back."

She coughed. "And if there's water that's safe to drink here," she added, "I'd like to find that even sooner."

"We'll have to dispose of the ghoul in order to get out, but we'd want to do that anyway," said the little man with an enthusiasm Ilna didn't share. "The first thing we'll do is scout the territory. You say that he carried off Hutton's body?"

"Yes," said Ilna, frowning as she considered the matter. "I don't think the light here is good enough for him to see my patterns clearly. If we can build a fire, though, I can hold him while you hamstring him with a dagger or whatever from the floor here."

"A bold plan and a clever one, Ilna," Usun said, "but you're wrong about being able to hold the ghoul. You think he's a beast, do you not?"

"Of course he's a beast," Ilna snapped. "I just watched him bite a man's face off. The fellow deserved to have his face eaten, but that doesn't make the thing that did it any less of an animal. And I've held other creatures, bigger ones, while Ch-Ch . . . while my companions killed them."

"The ghoul, as he now is . . . ," Usun said quietly. He was standing upright with the long filament a shimmering coil in his right hand. "Was a wizard in a former age, Ilna. A very powerful wizard, and that age was longer ago than even I can count. He tried to defeat death through his art and thought he had, but . . ."

He laughed. His glee had a cruel undertone, though Ilna didn't suppose she was one to complain about someone taking pleasure in the ill fortune of an enemy. And the ghoul was certainly no friend of hers.

"By trying to cheat death, he made himself a thing of death," Usun went on. "I wonder if he still thinks he won, eh? For thousands of years he's eaten the dead that are given to him, so that he won't come to the surface to hunt the living. He's not to be held by wizardry, Ilna. Not even by such great wizards as ourselves."

Ilna scowled in disgust. "He's human, then?" she said, just to be sure. Usun hadn't said that in so many words, and it might make a difference.

"He's as human as I am," Usun replied. He cackled again. "Oh, that's a fine joke, eh? But—"

He looked up at Ilna. She didn't need to see his expression to be able to imagine it clearly.

"The past doesn't matter, eh?" he said. "What matters is now, and we're going to hunt him down and end his little games, yes? Because he's in our way, and because we're great hunters, you and me."

Ilna sniffed. She looked upward again. Though her eyes were adapting to the blue glow, she still couldn't see the roof of the cave. Nor would it have helped if she could.

"Well, Ilna?" the little man said. "There are swords here. You can take one."

"I don't have any use for a sword," Ilna said. She reached into the darkness and found the loose tangle of the rope she'd been lowered by. She coiled it in quick loops, each one precisely the size of all the others.

"All right," she said. "I don't think we'd gain by waiting here and hoping that the stone rolls itself back, so we may as well hunt this ghoul."

"Oh, yes, the *greatest* hunters!" said Usun. He trotted toward the source of the glow. Ilna followed taking one stride for three of his.

CASHEL BLINKED. THEY'D stepped from Dariada into a rocky canyon suffused with smoky yellow light. The air was hotter than what they'd left in the sunlit square, and sulfur bit the back of Cashel's throat with each breath.

He stepped clear of the two women and spun the quarterstaff as he checked all directions. His butt caps trailed blue wizardlight, piercingly bright in this yellow dusk. The hairs on his arms and the back of his neck were already prickling at the presence of wizardry.

There were goats, which didn't matter. They were herded by things that weren't goats and *sure* weren't human.

"Are those demons, Rasile?" Liane asked calmly. She'd slung her satchel behind her and held the knife ready in her hand.

Cashel hawked up phlegm and spat toward a bristly growth that might be grass. Anything wet must be welcome in this place. Besides the maybe-grass, there were bushes that looked a little like the century plants he'd seen on Pandah before the Change, and there were full-sized trees farther up the cliffs. Those last were tall but spindly, and instead of leaves they had clumps of spines.

"They think of themselves as human beings, Liane," the wizard said. "They would be as bad as demons if we could not protect ourselves, but the same is true of many of those you consider human beings. Or I do."

The creatures had four legs with sharp hoofs, and the hands on their two arms had as many fingers as a sea anemone. Their bodies seemed to be covered with horn-like insects, but when Cashel stared at the nearest one, it flattened against the rock wall. It was light gray when he first saw it, but squeezed onto the rock it took on a mottled yellowish pattern that made it hard to see even though he knew it was there.

Hooting in high-pitched voices, a handful of the creatures came toward Cashel and his friends. They leaped over the rocks and bobbed their necks up and down. Each of them probably weighed as much as Liane, but their heads were small for the bodies and sort of wedge-shaped the way a possum's is.

They didn't seem to have weapons; but there was a lot of them, if they knew what they were doing.

"Tell me if something comes from the back!" he shouted to the women as he stepped between them and the little demons.

Funny. The goats seemed normal enough, but Cashel had never seen anything that looked like the creatures tending them.

He kept the quarterstaff spinning, but he was picking which of the creatures to strike first and who to pop next and next. You didn't go into a fight swinging wildly, and not expect to win; and Cashel always expected to win.

The demons clacked to a halt well out of the quarter-staff's reach; their hooves on the rocks sounded like gravel spilling down the sloping face of the seawall at Barca's Hamlet. They even stopped hooting, though they whispered to each other and sometimes waved their hands. Had they just been bluffing when the charged?

"We come as friends, People of the Valley," Rasile called. "We come as allies."

"You come to prey on us!" shrilled the midmost of the group that'd rushed Cashel a moment ago.

"The Lord preys on us daily!" another demon said. "You will join him and eat us all up!"

Cashel could hear the words clear enough, though it sounded like the demons were whistling instead of speaking. They didn't have lips that he could see.

The goats, white-faced with dirty gray hides from the neck back, went on with their business of scraping a meal from this rocky waste. Cashel didn't like goats, but they seemed to make a living here and he'd never known a sheep that'd could've done it.

He hacked again, though he didn't spit; he might need the moisture soon. The back of his throat felt like somebody'd taken a wood rasp to it.

"We've come to free you from the Lord," Rasile said. "In exchange you will guide us to the tomb of the hero Gorand."

Cashel took a quick glance and saw that Liane was keeping an eye on what was happening behind them. Nothing was, but he was glad for her doing that. *He* really wanted to keep his eyes on the nearest group.

"You are lying to us, demon," the leader of the, well, demons said.

"They are lying," said the other four in chorus. "They come to prey on us, like the Lord does."

"Our race is at an end," the leader said. "No one can defeat the Lord."

A descant of high voices keened, echoing faintly. All of the demons in the valley were howling like their children had died. There were more of them than Cashel had imagined at first; it was only when they moved that he could tell them from the rocks.

"No one can defeat the Lord!" the leader repeated. "We will all be eaten by the Lord and these new demons come to plague us."

"No one can defeat the Lord!" said his companions.

"And yet," said Rasile, "we shall."

She turned to smile at Cashel. "Are you ready, Warrior Cashel?" she asked.

"Yes ma'am," Cashel said. "Where do we find this Lord, please?"

"I think he's found us," Liane said, pointing with her left hand toward a blotch of light the color of rust. It was half a furlong distant, near a pair of the little demons flattened against the wall of the canyon.

"Yes," agreed Rasile. Cashel nodded and started toward the light as it flickered, swelling rapidly.

SHARINA WORE A pair of simple tunics and a nondescript gray cloak—borrowed from Diora—over them to conceal not only the Pewle knife but Burne. The rat rode in a fold of her outer tunic, his little nose wrinkling excitedly at smells that passed Sharina unremarked.

"Oh, my!" he'd murmur, and, "Now, who'd have imagined that?" Sharina thought of asking the rat what was of such interest in this grubby city, but she figured he'd tell her if there were something he thought she should know. She had enough on her mind already.

Sharina was in the middle of a group of twenty men, all of them soldiers except for Dysart and three attendants. She'd been wrong to expect that at least a few of the troops would still be wearing the hobnailed sandals which on these stone pavers would send a ringing warning several blocks ahead: they'd donned either soft boots or clogs. Prester and Pont, the regiment's camp marshals, weren't with this detachment, but Sharina suspected the

way the troops were prepared for their assignment had a
lot to do with those old veterans.

The clop of wooden soles—Sharina wore clogs
herself—could be heard at a distance also, but noise
alone wasn't a problem. The clang of many hobnails together cried "Army!" to everyone in earshot.

Captain Ascor was at her side. He wore a grim expression and she didn't need to be a soothsayer to know that
the hand he kept under his cloak was clutching a bare
sword.

Ascor had winced, but he hadn't argued when Sharina told him what she was going to do. She'd offered
him a plan which, though he probably thought was in-
sanely dangerous for Princess Sharina, showed a willing to compromise with a bodyguard's sensibilities. The
Blood Eagles had learned that guarding Garric and his
sister was a different business from the days when Valence III hunched in his room and drank morosely with
friends.

Dysart glanced over his shoulder to check where Sharina was, then paused for a moment so that she came
alongside him. "The graveyard where they're meeting is
to our right at the next intersection," he said. "Less than
a half block. There are three other teams approaching at
the same time."

Or so we hope, Sharina thought. They weren't concerned with the individual worshippers, who had nothing to tell. She was hoping to catch the man preaching,
though. According to Dysart, he was a former priest of
the Shepherd named Platt. Where Dysart or Tadai could
identify particular leaders, they'd been priests of the
Shepherd before being won over to the new heresy.

Aloud she said, "I'm surprised that there's a graveyard
within the city. They've been outside the walls everywhere I've been in the past. I guess the pirates who ruled
here weren't so superstitious."

"They were *more* superstitious than honest folk," Burne

said unexpectedly. "Well, what passes for honest folk. This graveyard's newer than the rest of Pandah."

"Master Burne," Dysart said quietly. If he felt any emotion about what he was saying, he certainly kept it concealed. "The Sultans of Pandah back for seven generations are buried on this particular site."

"Yes, but it *had* been outside the walls before the Change, when the sultans of your age ruled a sleepy trading port," Burne said sharply. "You know how graveyards concentrate power, though. This burial ground and several others ripped through the fabric of the past. That's why they're in the middle of an ancient pirate fortress now."

The rat laughed. "If you found human teeth in a hog's stomach, Master Dysart," he said, "would you claim that they'd grown there?"

"That's enough," Sharina said as the party reached an irregularly shaped plaza with a dry fountain in the middle. She spoke to end the squabble, but as soon as she did she heard the preacher they were hoping to arrest.

"Brothers and sisters in the one God, in the true Lord of Existence," Platt whined in a nasal voice. "The gods of the past are dead. The future is Lord Scorpion's!"

There must be a hundred or more listeners crowded close to the preacher. Low altars were built out from the fronts of the large tombs in the middle of the graveyard. The family of each deceased was expected to use them for offerings of wine and on the anniversary of his death. Platt stood on one of them, wearing a bleached wool robe that seemed to glow in the moonlight.

The soldiers carried truncheons for this raid, though they wore their short infantry swords as well. From all reports, the Scorpion worshippers were planning the violent overthrow of the kingdom. Sharina wasn't going to order a massacre of frightened, deluded people—but neither was she going to disarm soldiers who might be facing deadly weapons themselves on the kingdom's behalf.

"Only those who serve Lord Scorpion will be spared agonizing stings in this world and eternal torment in the world to come," Platt cried. He seemed to be looking upward, not toward the crowd beneath him. "You are the chosen, brothers and sisters! You are the wise ones who see the truth already."

The ashes of the common people of Pandah—those wealthy enough to have memorials at all—were buried in loculi, stone boxes three feet long and a foot in width and depth. They were clustered as near as possible to the row of sultans' tombs, but after generations they covered most of the field set off for burial.

The boxes were carved from Pandah's soft yellow limestone and weathered quickly. Within a few generations most had crumbled to shards and loose gravel that Sharina couldn't tell in the moonlight from the calcined bones of those interred.

Burne leaped from the fold in Sharina's tunic. She caught a flash of him darting among the boxes; then he vanished among the legs of the crowd. She grimaced in surprise, then drew the Pewle knife. She probably should have done that sooner.

"Sons and daughters of Lord Scorpion!" Platt called in a cracked, wavering voice. He sounded insane . . . and perhaps he was, but his shrill periods cut through the normal layers of doubt and common sense. "Our Lord's day is coming. On that day we will rise to glory with our God!"

The spectators were staring at the preacher with rapt attention. Dimly Sharina could see movement converging on Platt from the other directions. She stumbled and stumbled again. Around her soldiers cursed under their breath as they turned ankles or barked shins.

"The enemies of God are around us!" Platt cried. "Flee, my brethren!"

"Get him, boys!" bellowed a soldier in the group approaching from the opposite end of the cemetery. Everybody was lunging and crying out.

As the preacher shouted his warning, he'd turned and jumped off the side of the altar. Sharina lost sight of him, but she ran toward where he had to be. The stone boxes and terrified spectators made it an obstacle course rather than a normal race, but as expected she saw Platt an instant later; the bleached robe stood out like a flame.

"There!" shouted one of Dysart's men, snaking between two soldiers and grasping the preacher by the arm.

"Don't hit him!" cried another of the civilian agents, grabbing the other shoulder and tucking Platt's head under his own arm to keep the soldiers from clubbing the fellow.

"We want him able to talk!" Dysart said, his hands raised to prevent more soldiers from piling on enthusiastically. "We've got him! Stay back out of the way!"

"We've got him!" called someone from the other side of the large tombs. "Master Dysart, we've got him!"

"*Here* he is, by the Shepherd!" shouted a soldier well along to the east end of the cemetery. "Tell Marshal Prester we got him!"

Sharina jerked the captive's white hood back. A soldier clacked open the shutter of the dark lantern he carried, throwing yellow candlelight over the prisoner's face. He was an unremarkable man with a weak chin and high forehead.

"Is this Platt?" Sharina demanded.

"I'm Platt!" said the prisoner. "I'm the voice of Lord Scorpion!"

"Well, I don't know, Your Highness," Dysart said, wringing his hands. "He matches the suspect's description, but I've never seen Platt myself."

He obviously hated to make the admission, but he hadn't hesitated. As Liane had said, he was a good man.

"We got the man, Your Ladyship!" said Prester, patting a hardwood marshal's baton into his left palm. The veteran looked like a section of oak root himself, old and supple and *very* tough. "We'll need to carry him, I guess, but we didn't mark the face any."

The man two soldiers were carrying behind Prester was shorter than the captive Sharina's group had caught, but his face—allowing for the spasms of agony that transfixed it at intervals—would've fit the same verbal description. At least one of his knees had been broken.

"No, I'm Platt!" said the man at Sharina's feet.

"Your Ladyship," chirped Burne in a thin voice that nonetheless pierced the night's confusion. The rat must've learned to project when he was with the troupe of mountebanks. "I have the real Platt here, but I can't very well bring him to you."

"Who's that?" said Prester, turning his head. "Did we grab the wrong one, then?"

"If you did, you weren't alone in your mistake," said Sharina, clambering over a solid rank of loculi, many of them with broken lids or no lids at all. Dysart and Ascor were at her either side.

A man in a dark blue cape had fallen between two of the sultans' tombs. He was trying to crawl away. His right foot flopped loosely behind him: he'd been hamstrung.

"He threw off the white robe," said Burne, perched in an alcove of the dome-topped tomb, "and had the dark one on under it. He couldn't change his smell, though."

The rat licked blood off his whiskers with apparent relish. Sharina suspected that was partly an act, but it was a very good one. The fallen man certainly thought so, because he twisted to snatch at Burne. The rat hopped away, then leaped to Sharina's shoulder.

"I think we've found the real priest," Sharina said.

"Tie his hands," Dysart said brusquely to the squad of his men now gathered around him. "We'll take him to my office in the palace."

Men quickly stepped to pinion the captive. Frowning, Dysart added, "And check his foot. We don't want him bleeding out from a nicked artery before we question him."

"Lord Scorpion will infallibly smite you!" Platt cried. "The true God will avenge His prophets!"

Burne laughed. "I quite like scorpions, Master Platt," he said. "They taste even better than shrimp."

Chapter

11

THE BLUISH LIGHT in the burial cavern wasn't good, but Ilna found it was good enough as her eyes fully adapted to it. Indeed, it seemed to be getting brighter as Usun found a route for them. She wasn't willing to call it a track, let alone a path, but the fact the massive ghoul obviously came this way meant it was possible for a young woman in good health to do so as well.

The little man paused to bend over a litter of fallen stalactites. "There's been an earthquake recently," he said. "Well, tremors anyway. It could be that even without us, our ghoul would have to make other arrangements than living in a cave."

"An earthquake brought the riverboat I was on to the shore of this island," Ilna said. "What had been an island before the Change, anyway. I suppose there must've been some effect in Gaur and here in the cave, though I believe the quake itself was Brincisa's work."

"Hutton always underrated her," said Usun as he paced on ahead. "Still, she doesn't have the power to cause solid rock to crack. There had to have been a weakness already. Or indeed, maybe it was the Change that smashed it all like this."

He laughed, though Ilna noticed that now that they were on the track of the ghoul the little man's speech and laughter were muted. He had the trick of projecting his voice without raising it. It was barely a whisper, yet she could hear each word distinctly over the rustle and deep, directionless thrumming that filled the cavern.

"And one landslip will bring more, like as not," Usun said cheerfully. "Well, with luck we'll be out of here before it matters. And the ghoul, he'll be beyond worrying about anything now that we're going after him."

Ilna's lips tightened in distaste. The little man was bragging, and he was bragging on her behalf as well. Many people saw nothing wrong with that.

The scowl became a wry smile. In this as in so many other things, the many were wrong and Ilna os-Kenset was right. But she didn't think she was going to change their minds.

Beyond the narrow throat leading to the burial cave, the cavern rose to heights that Ilna wouldn't have been able to see by the light of a torch. The rocks' own blue glow alone made them visible.

Unnumbered broken stumps projected from the ceiling of smooth flow rock; some were again dripping the lime-charged water which had ages ago frozen into the huge stalactites whose shattered remains littered the floor of the cave. Many chunks were the size of tree trunks, fluted and ridged by the ages of their creation.

The closest Ilna came to believing in the supernatural was to feel that stone had consciousness and that it hated her. Certainly her undoubted clumsiness in dealing with stone showed that if nothing else, its presence affected her mind. Usun could squirm under some of the columns that Ilna would've had to clamber over with difficulty, but instead the little man led by a circuitous route that required her to do nothing more difficult than stepping high or bending at the waist.

It might've been wiser to have kept her hands free to

grab or catch herself if her foot slipped on the slimy rocks, but Ilna instead knotted patterns. They weren't weapons—there wasn't light enough here for them to be effective—nor was she trying to predict the outcome of this or any endeavor.

She tied a pattern that would bring a smile to the face of whoever saw it, then picked out the knots and worked one that would dull hunger pangs. Then a pattern which would leach away soul-searing pain but leave the injured person's mind as sharp as it had been before they'd been hurt.

Peaceful designs couldn't be seen any better in this dim glow than patterns to freeze or terrify or madden; and anyway, Ilna turned each back into raw yarn for a moment before starting the next. Regardless, they were what her instincts told her to create, and she'd learned to trust her instincts.

Ahead of them was a great chasm, visible as a black ribbon through the omnipresent blue glow. A waterfall plunged into it from the other side, and a tumbling stream at the bottom filled the cavern with its echoes.

A natural bridge crossed the split in the cave floor. Flow rock blobbed on the upper surface of the arch like wax that had cooled, and from the underside hung a beard of stalactites.

Instead of starting across, Usun hopped onto a broken stalactite which stuck slightly out over the gorge. It looked like a barrel from a column of a fallen temple, larger in diameter than Ilna's body and thus much smaller than many relicts of the earthquake. Ilna knelt, putting her head on a level with his.

"So, we've found our prey's den or I miss my guess," the little man said. "There, behind the waterfall. There's a cave, and you can see the wear on the rock going up to it."

"I cannot," Ilna said, primly careful not to claim more than her due even by silence. "But I take your word for it."

She had no idea how Usun saw a cave behind the thin sheet of water. Perhaps he heard a different echo? That seemed absurd, but she did things with fabric that others thought were impossible. The little man was a hunter beyond question.

"Well, the cave's there," Usun said blithely, "and he's there in it. We can't get behind him, and I wouldn't care to try the cave in hope that he's asleep. I'm not sure that he does sleep any more; wizardry and his diet have changed him, I think."

"I don't think we should walk straight into the creature's lair," Ilna agreed dryly. *Though if Chalcus was here, he with his sword as sure as the sting of a hunting wasp and me with a silken lasso to tangle even a creature as big as this ghoul—*

Chalcus was dead. And Ilna wasn't dead, not yet, so she had duties.

"There's another way, I think," said Usun. "I know you're a wizard, mistress, but wizardry won't work on him. How are your nerves?"

Ilna sniffed. He wasn't trying to insult her. "Adequate," she said. Saying more would be bragging.

The little man giggled. "So I thought!" he said. "So I thought! Well then, Ilna, this is what we'll do. . . ."

THE MOST IMPORTANT thing in the world I'll tell you freely," Platt said, sitting upright on the couch in Dysart's office. The desks at which several clerks would during the day transcribe documents had been moved into the hall, so there was room for the unusual number of people present. "Lord Scorpion is God. Worship Him or infallibly be destroyed!"

"When did you leave your former position as priest of the Shepherd, Master Platt?" Dysart asked. He was quiet and polite, a clerk from the tips of his toes to his thinning hair. Sharina had directed—over the protests of Lords

Ascor, Tadai, and Quernan of the Pandah garrison—that Dysart should handle the interrogation. She'd accept Liane's judgment on most matters, and Liane had put Dysart in charge in her absence.

"I didn't leave the Shepherd," Platt snapped. "The Shepherd is dead! *All* the old gods are dead. Lord Scorpion is Lord of the cosmos!"

"Why, you puppy!" said Lord Quernan. He raised his hand and stepped forward. Two of Dysart's agents grabbed him by the elbows and thrust him back.

"Out," said Sharina with a flick of her left index finger toward the door.

"But that's blasphemy!" Quernan protested. Other spectators made way for him; one of Tadai's clerks even opened the door.

"As well worship a dead donkey as your Lady!" Platt cried.

Sharina had been afraid that other soldiers would protest, but instead of equally clueless aides, Quernan had brought Prester and Pont. They remained at attention, as if nothing important was happening.

Knowing the two old soldiers, they might have brought themselves. They'd met Sharina in a hard place years ago. Because she'd performed to their approval, they seemed to have adopted her. She suspected that a number of junior officers over the years had had similarly good luck.

Platt let out a broken laugh. "Do you think to frighten me?" he said. "The disciples of Lord Scorpion need fear nothing. I am assured of my salvation!"

"But you were trying to escape us in the graveyard, weren't you?" Dysart said. "Your Scorpion didn't save you then, Master Platt. You're obviously a clever man. You know in your heart that he's not as powerful as what you preach to the rabble."

"Salvation is of the soul, not the body," Platt muttered. He was sweating profusely. His thin hair was plastered down so that his pink scalp showed through.

"Is your ankle comfortable?" Dysart asked. "I'm sorry about the injury, but we had no choice. For as long as you're in my charge I'll see to it that you receive medical care, though my department's facilities are too limited for any but the most important prisoners. I can only hope that the city prefect will be able to manage something if you have to be transferred to the jail."

"Are you out of your mind, Dysart?" Tadai said in a deliberately affected voice as he inspected the curve of his fingernails. "*My* budget doesn't stretch to doctors for a lot of drunks and vagabonds."

"How often to you meet with your fellow priests, Master Platt?" Dysart said as though the previous exchange hadn't occurred. He sat in the chair behind his desk; the prisoner was in the couch beside him. Everyone else stood along the inside wall. Burne padded from door to window ledge and back, his whiskers twitching.

"I don't," said Platt, squirming uneasily. He'd lost his bravado. "We don't have to meet, I mean. We, ah . . . I do at least, I suppose the others. God speaks to me in dreams, through his acolyte Black. I've never met another priest, though I know there's many of us. Preparing for the day!"

"You claim to get detailed instructions from your dreams, Master Platt?" Dysart said. He didn't raise his voice, but Sharina could hear the hint of a frown in it.

"Yes, that's true," the prisoner said. He'd lost the defiance that'd begun to creep back into his tone. "Black tells me where to preach and when. But I know there are many of us, throughout the world."

As far as information reaching Sharina went—both from Liane's clandestine service and the reports of regional governors—Pandah was the only center of Scorpion worship. It gave her a feeling of comfort to know that Black lied to his own acolytes—but he was real enough in her own dreams, and she was responsible for Pandah besides.

"Do you send messengers to chalk notices on walls to let the worshippers know where you'll be preaching?" Dysart said. "Or does somebody else do that? We've found the notices, you see."

"I . . . ," Platt said. He frowned in surprise. "I don't know, I never wondered. Lord Scorpion speaks to me, that's all. I suppose He speaks to others. People bring me food and hide me during the day, but I don't know who they are. I'm not from Pandah, you see. I came here from Valles when Lord Scorpion called me in the night."

"We'll need the names and lodgings of those who help you," Dysart said. His hands were tented on his lap, but clerks in opposite corners of the room were making notes on waxed tablets. "They'll already be in our records, but now they'll be cross-referenced with you."

"I don't know any of them!" Platt said in agitation. "It wouldn't matter if I told you—Lord Scorpion rules the world. You can't harm Him with your foolish opposition. Join Him!"

He raised his eyes from Dysart and swept them across the faces of those watching the interrogation. Sharina had never before seen such terror in a gaze.

"All of you!" Platt cried. "Worship Lord Scorpion! Worship the living God!"

Burne leaped to the top of the window casement and came down with something squirming between his forepaws. His chisel teeth clicked efficiently.

Platt screamed and fainted.

Dysart grimaced and used two fingers to check the pulse in the prisoner's throat. "He'll be all right when he comes around," he said. "It can't be helped, I suppose."

"No," said Sharina, "it couldn't be—unless we were willing to let Black's agents hear the rest of the interrogation. I don't think we were going to get any more of real value from him regardless."

"Surely he's lying about how he communicates with the rest of his cult?" said Lord Tadai.

"About Black and the dreams, you mean?" Sharina said. "I suspect that's true."

"How does Your Highness wish to proceed?" Dysart said. His agents were tying Platt's hands and feet again; he'd been loosed for comfort during the interrogation, but Sharina had seen how quickly Liane's men could move when they had to.

"I'm going to send him to Tenoctris," she said, crystallizing murky thoughts into a plan of action. "I doubt that Platt knows any more than he's told us, but I think Tenoctris can use him as a focus from which she can learn a great deal more. I hope she can help us."

She looked down at the unconscious prisoner. "The Lady knows we could use some help," she said.

Burne sat upright, cleaning his muzzle. Scraps of black chitin lay scattered about him.

"Oh, I don't know, Sharina," the rat said. "We're not doing so badly ourselves."

GARRIC WAITED WHILE Tenoctris dropped chips of white marble inside the ring of trees. They were bald cypress, their bases swollen. The roots which thrust knees up to breathe in the wet season crawled over dry ground, now; the waters which must sometimes turn this place into a marsh had receded.

The regiment that'd escorted them the mile from the main camp murmured in the surrounding darkness. The troops weren't within twenty double paces of the trees, but nothing could pass through the scores of encircling watch fires without being seen. Tenoctris and Garric had the privacy they wanted, and the laymen weren't compelled to witness wizardry.

Tenoctris straightened. She'd placed only five pebbles, one between each pair of trees to mark the inner angles of a pentacle. The points were the trees themselves. "It's the Grove of Biltis," she said.

"Who's Biltis?" Garric said. He was fighting his instinct to lay his hand on the pommel of his sword. He knew—not because Tenoctris had told him, but because of the feeling of quiet sadness he felt in this grove—that it wasn't a place for weapons. His disquiet—and King Carus' universal response to anything unusual—kept drawing him to the blade, though.

"A very long time ago . . . ," Tenoctris said, taking items out of her satchel. Besides a codex and two scrolls, she began to unwrap what turned out to be the silver statuette of a wasp-slim woman. "Biltis was a God. Biltis was *the* God, in fact. Later she was revered as an oracle whose answers were given in the ripples of her sacred fountain. By the time this grove was planted—and that was before the dawn of the Old Kingdom—Biltis was a spirit of the night who eased childbirth. The cypress as a tree of the waters was thought to be a proper attribute for such a spirit."

Tenoctris let her fingertips drift over the curve of the figurine's molded hair. She met Garric's eyes again and smiled sadly. "It's a place of power," she said. "And it suited my sense of whimsy, if you will, to use a site created by ordinary women who had ordinary female concerns. Since both those things are utterly divorced from my own life."

Garric cleared his throat. "I had a pretty ordinary life myself before you arrived in Barca's Hamlet, Tenoctris," he said. "If you hadn't changed that, I guess I'd be dead by now. Along with all the other pretty ordinary people in the world. I'm glad you came."

Tenoctris chuckled. "I might as well complain that I was born a wizard instead of being a mighty warrior, I suppose," she said. "No doubt I'd have been far happier then."

"Maybe until she drowned," Carus said. *"Because she*

didn't have a clever wizard and the other fellow did. No, I'm getting used to things being the way they are now."

Tenoctris looked at the books she'd taken out, then returned them unopened to her satchel. "They were crutches," she said apologetically. She seemed to be speaking to the figurine, not to Garric. "I don't need crutches anymore."

Without further preamble she chanted, *"Basuma bassa . . . "*

The statuette bobbed in her right hand, a dip to each syllable. A wisp of violet flame shimmered from the center of the hinted pentacle, as pale as moonlight. Garric thought the first flickers were reflections thrown from the silver, but it mounted as quickly as real fire in dried vines. It was silent and gave off no heat.

"Ashara phouma naxarama . . . ," Tenoctris said.

"Can the troops see the light or only us?" said Carus. His expression was as bleak as a granite headland, concealing the discomfort he felt even as a ghost to be a part of wizardry.

Garric shrugged. The tempo of the guards' murmurs didn't change, nor did the sprightly galliard a musician among them picked out on a three-string lyre. If they'd noticed the flame, there'd have been silence or perhaps shouting.

Tenoctris was facing Garric across the fire. Her lips continued to move but he no longer heard the words of power.

The grove vanished. Instead of a fire, Garric and Tenoctris stood a pool of violet light. The statuette in her hand rose and fell to the rhythm of the unheard syllables.

The charged atmosphere shattered into planes. Garric felt a rush of vertigo: there was no up or down, but there were infinite numbers of universes from which he and Tenoctris stood apart.

A speck in one of the planes swelled. Everything shifted *again*. A blur of darker violet coalesced into a boat—a perfectly ordinary vessel, different from the dories fishermen had used in Barca's Hamlet but of similar size and utility. It had one mast, a tall triangular sail, and a single boatman in the stern.

The boatman brought the tiller sharply over and at the same time loosed a halyard, dropping the sail as the bluff bow grazed to rest on the shore. The beach beneath Garric's boots was sand, not the black volcanic shingle of Barca's Hamlet and certainly not the expanse of roots, leaves and sedges of the grove they'd been standing in.

The boatman stepped out, gripping the sides of his vessel to keep it from drifting away when his weight no longer held it onto the bottom. He was a slight man with thinning hair and ink-stained fingers; though he was obviously strong enough, he seemed incongruous in this job. He reminded Garric of his own father rather than the fishermen who drank in the inn of an evening.

Tenoctris curtsied. "Thank you for coming so promptly," she said.

The boatman smiled faintly. "You have the right to command me, Your Ladyship," he said in a quiet, cultured voice. "Where is it you wish me to take you?"

"To the Gate of Ivory," she said. "Can you do this?"

"I can take you to the edge of the lake," said the boatman. "But no farther. Is that sufficient?"

Tenoctris sighed and lifted her chin in assent. "I feared as much," she said. "But yes, if that's the reality, it has to be sufficient. We'll find our own way across, then. Are we free to board?"

"Yes, Your Ladyship," said the boatman, offering the wizard a hand over the gunwale. She seated herself primly on a forward thwart.

"Ah," said Garric. "Sir, would you like help shoving off? I've done that, well, often enough."

"That's won't be necessary, Your Highness," said the boatman. Neither Tenoctris nor Garric himself had told the man who his passengers were, but he clearly knew.

"Though if you'll sit on the thwart just ahead of me, the boat will ride better. Whatever you please, of course."

Garric stepped aboard, placing his foot on the keelson so as not to rock the vessel any more than necessary. The hull settled slightly into the sand. He sat, facing the stern and the tiller rather than the mast.

The boatman strode forward, leaning into the vessel and bringing the bow around. Even on sand, that required great strength as well as skill.

Garric felt the hull bob free. The boatman took two more strides and clambered in over the transom. Keeping the tiller between his left arm and his body, he raised the sail of linen, tarred to hold the wind better. It filled with the breeze and drove the vessel into the seeming twilight.

Garric looked to port, then to starboard. The beach was vanishing into the horizon; he hadn't seen anything above the strip of sand.

The sea lifted with the slow, powerful motions of a brood sow shifting in her sty. The water was gray with a hint of green where foam bubbled in the vessel's wake, but when Garric bent to look straight down over the side he thought he saw twinkles of the violet flame which Tenoctris had kindled.

"I always liked the sea," Carus said. *"Of course, that didn't keep it from killing me in the end."*

He chuckled. *"If it hadn't been the sea,"* he added, *"it might well have been a woman. And I liked them too, lad."*

The boatman eyed the sail, then let out the sheet he'd snubbed to a starboard stanchion. Garric couldn't imagine how the fellow navigated; the sky was the featureless gray of a high overcast.

"Sir?" he said. They faced one another, so closely that Garric could have touched the boatman's knees just by stretching out his hand. "I'm Garric or-Reise. May I ask your name, please?"

" 'The boatman' will do," the man said, smiling again. "I don't have a name anymore, only a task."

Garric cleared his throat in embarrassment, though the fellow hadn't been deliberately insulting. Mainly to break eye contact, he looked to starboard as they crested a swell.

Midway to the horizon, an enormous back humped out of the water. It continued for over a minute to drive forward in a shimmer of droplets, like the paddles of a millwheel. Neither the head nor the tail broke the surface before the whole dripping mass sank into the depths again.

"Sir?" Garric said. "What was that?"

The boatman adjusted the sail again, this time taking it in slightly. "What you see," he said, "isn't the reality, Your Highness. It's the shape your eyes—your mind, really—gives reality."

"Sir?" said Garric. "Are you what you seem to be?"

The boatman laughed without reservation. Sobering, he said, "Nothing is what it seems, Your Highness. Much as you or I might regret the fact."

As the boatman spoke, he fitted a pair of looped ropes around the tiller to lock it centered. His hands freed, he worked the lid from the enameled tin box beside him and took from it a scroll made of split reeds. The fore-edge was vermilion, and the winding sticks had gilt knobs. Garric couldn't have been more surprised if the fellow had pulled out a hissing viper.

"Why!" he said. "That is, ah; you're a reader, sir?"

The boatman looked at him with an expression of disdain. "Yes, I'm a reader, Your Highness," he said. "At the moment I'm reading Timarion, if the name means anything to you. Perhaps Her Ladyship can inform you of who Timarion was, since like her he was of the Old Kingdom."

Tenoctris had been staring over the bow when Garric last checked. She twisted to look around the mast to the men, caroling a laugh.

"I assure you both," she said, "that unless he happened to be wizard or write about wizardry, I wouldn't know anything about this Timarion. He could be the greatest poet of my day, and it wouldn't have mattered to me."

"I know who Timarion is, sir," Garric said formally. "Though I've read him only as excerpted by Poleinis."

He cleared his throat and added, "Even in Lady Tenoctris' day, there can't have been many copies of Timarion's work. It was written nearly a thousand years before."

Garric knew he shouldn't have been so surprised that the fellow owned a book of such high quality. It was nothing you'd expect of an ordinary boatman, but there was nothing ordinary about this vessel. Still—neither was Garric an illiterate peasant who'd stumbled into kingship.

The boatman laughed again. "I was raised to believe that the sort of work I'm doing now was beneath a gentleman, Your Highness," he said in mild apology. "There are obviously compensations, but I *am* a menial when those who have authority require the services of this vessel. I'm afraid I sometimes allow myself to resent the assumptions that arise from my duties, however."

"I apologize, sir," Garric said. "You had the right of it."

After a pause he went on, "Poleinis judges Timarion harshly, as I recall?"

"Yes," said the boatman with a wry smile. "He would, wouldn't he? Since otherwise someone might notice that almost all his geographical information about the eastern portion of the Isles and the lands to the northeast of the archipelago was drawn directly from Timarion. What I've been doing for the . . ."

His voice trailed off; his expression became briefly melancholy, then returned to its normal quiet resignation. "Time isn't important anymore, is it?" he said. He faced Garric, but he was apparently speaking to himself. "The problem is—"

Now his gaze did meet Garric's.

"—that when I think that way, I'm apt to think that nothing is important anymore, not even the knowledge which I accepted these duties to gain. That leads into troubled waters, Your Highness. Even for a philosopher like myself."

"Sir," said Garric, "I know some philosophers deny there's any difference between good and evil, but I don't agree with them. I don't think anyone who really lives in the world could. By helping Lady Tenoctris, you're helping good against evil. Which is purpose enough for me."

The boatman smiled. "I was never a man of action," he said, "but I'll bathe in your purity of purpose for the time being. Thank you."

He handed Garric the scroll. "What I'm doing now," he said, "is annotating obscure portions of Timarion. For example, he speaks of permanent settlements far to the north, where fishermen not only winter over and salt their catches but also plant barley and onions."

Garric adjusted the winding sticks to open the full width of a page. The writing was in an oddly narrow form of the Old Script, making it hard for a moment to determine which were loops and which were vertical strokes.

"These capes are far to the north of the islands of the Ostimioi," he read aloud, "but nevertheless they have been settled by men from Wexisame who first followed the currents hither. The Wexisamians do not allow men of other tribes to fish in these waters, though they meet them on rocky islets midway and trade there."

Garric looked up. "Surely that's the Ice Capes?" he said, handing back the book with the reverence it deserved.

"I have never visited the Ice Capes when the glaciers didn't cover them down to the shore," the boatman said. "If you're right, Your Highness, then Timarion was using sources from a very long time before even his own age."

He chuckled. "Or of course Timarion may have made the settlements up, as Poleinis predictably claims," he said. "With no evidence whatever. I will continue to search for a solution."

"And then?" said Garric.

"There are other cruxes, Your Highness," the boatman said. He closed the scroll and placed it back in its protective container. "I'm sure a scholar like me will never exhaust the possibilities of increasing his knowledge."

He fitted the tin lid, then leaned out to look beyond the bow. Straightening, he unlashed the rudder.

"We're approaching your destination, Your Highness," the boatman said. "I wish you and Her Ladyship good fortune in your activities there. I hope to return you to the waking world in good health."

He loosed the half-hitches holding the sheet but held the sail in place with his hand. Looking at Garric again, he said, "I don't feel a lack of company, Prince Garric. Nonetheless your presence has not been a burden on me."

He threw the tiller to starboard and released several feet of sheet, though he didn't let the yard swing into Tenoctris. "I have brought you to your destination, Your Ladyship," he said; and as he spoke, the hull grounded on what this time appeared to be a muddy riverbank.

CASHEL SPUN HIS quarterstaff before him at a leisurely pace as he walked toward the blob of light. The vivid blue sparks crackling from his ferrules would've drawn the eyes of almost anybody, but the two little demons stared at the red blur between them instead.

They didn't move, though the demons at even a short distance were clopping away as quick as their little hooves could move. They ran stiffly, bouncing like their legs didn't have any knees.

The goats, the only other things in this landscape, didn't pay much attention. One blatted a nasal warning when another, smaller, goat moved toward the bush it was methodically stripping the small gray leaves from.

A monster stood where the blotch of light had been, just as sudden as the flash when a mirror shifts to catch the sun. It was taller than Cashel, twice as broad as he was, and looked like a toad on two legs.

Really like a toad. It had a broad mouth, goggling eyes, and a nobbly hide colored like bricks that had weathered to a pale, scabby red. Cashel kept walking toward it.

The toad didn't move for a moment. The demons standing on either side of it tried to stay frozen, but the one on the right started trembling. The toad turned its head slightly; it didn't have a real neck. That demon shrieked, "The Lord!" and sprang away in a tremendous leap.

The toad's black tongue shot out like a javelin. The barbed tip spiked the demon two double paces away. The tongue didn't look any thicker than a night crawler, but to drill into the demon's bony chest like that it must be hard as steel.

The demon's arms shot up into the air and its legs splayed like they'd been stuck on by a child who wanted his dolly to stand up. It was as stiff as a dried starfish. The demon on the other side took off running—well, bouncing—as soon as it saw that the toad was busy with its friend.

"That's over now," Cashel said. It wasn't exactly a challenge, but he thought there ought to be something beyond him just smashing the toad's skull. That's what he'd do to an animal, but he didn't think this "Lord" was an animal even if it acted like one.

The toad drew its tongue back, hauling the demon with it. The spitted body was starting to deflate: the slender legs drew together and the torso slumped slowly down over the abdomen; the arms hung slackly.

Cashel stepped off on his right foot, bringing the staff

around in a horizontal stroke aimed at the toad's head. The toad vanished. The demon flopped on the ground, empty as a split bladder. The hole at the base of the torso where the tongue had gone in oozed what looked like thin red jelly.

Cashel stepped forward to recover from the blow. His foot brushed the demon's corpse; it rustled. The skin had gone pale gray with a yellow underlayer.

"Behind you!" Rasile shouted.

He spun, leading with his right hand this time and punching the staff out like a battering ram. There was nothing when he started the blow save the wizard at a distance with Liane beside her, but the toad appeared a fraction of a second later—and vanished untouched by the driving iron butt cap as before. This time it gave a "Whuff!" of startled anger.

"Your right!" said Rasile.

Cashel turned, pivoting on the ball of his right foot. He swept the staff around with his left hand leading, stepping into the blow. The toad *was not/was/was not* standing before him, goggle eyes sparking with hate. Iron-shod hickory swished through where its head had been.

"Your right!"

That was awkward, but you couldn't expect the other guy in a fight to do the things that made it easy for you. Cashel punched the staff again, not a clean blow but he'd learned by now that the toad wouldn't be sticking around long enough to take advantage of him being off-balance. The creature was dodging the quarterstaff, but he didn't have time to think about it. As soon as his eyes caught movement, he vanished.

Like this time. The toad's size had been, well, a consideration—Cashel didn't *worry* exactly in a fight—at the start, but it wasn't willing to use its bulk and likely strength. Its blotched mass swelled out of nothing and then disappeared in a flicker, making it seem more like a cloud than an enemy. That was a dangerous way to think, so Cashel made sure he carried through on every stroke.

The last spin meant he was facing the canyon wall again, yellow-red sandstone with a surface that pretended to be crumbly. The corpse, really just the hide, of the dead demon was scrunched up against the rock where he must've kicked it. Or maybe the toad had? Did it really touch the ground when it flashed in and out of the air?

"Behind you!"

Cashel pivoted on his left foot; it meant a hair's breadth longer of an arc but it got him planted solider and moved him a little out from the side of the canyon. Hitting rock with the back of his stroke would end this fight right quick. . . .

Liane and Rasile were where they'd been. The wizard had spilled a figure of yarrow stalks on the ground in front of her. Where had she gotten the time?

Cashel swung with his right hand leading. At the same time Rasile chopped down her athame of black stone.

The toad *was not/was*—

Red wizardlight flickered over the huge body. It was barely a color, like dust lying on the bare blade of a sword. The toad didn't vanish.

The quarterstaff banged the left side of the toad's flat head. Cashel grunted; the heel of his right hand tingled as though he'd hit a full-grown oak tree.

His blow would've dented the bole of an oak tree, and it was strong enough to crunch bones in the toad's skull too. The creature staggered, throwing up arms so small that they looked silly on such a big body. Black blood dribbled from where the staff struck and also from the toad's left nostril.

Cashel spun the staff sunwise, pulling the stroke just a hair so that the ferrule would miss short if the toad jumped back. It did, just like Cashel figured it would. Instead of following through with the arc, he drove forward. His whole weight rammed the staff toward the creature like he was thrusting a spear. His leading butt cap slammed the base of the toad's broad neck, crushing bones this time too.

The toad was too big for the shock to throw it down, but it wobbled back a step and another step. Its tiny arms windmilled; the hands had sharp nails and only four fingers.

Cashel gasped in another breath. He swept the quarterstaff widdershins, trying to break the toad's left knee. The creature lurched toward him so the blow rapped its thigh instead. It had legs like an ox, so nothing happened aside from pain jetting through Cashel's tingling palm.

The toad's broad mouth opened, but the tongue which had speared the little demon now tumbled out like a loosely coiled rope. The tip had a spike from which trailed three hollow bones, each about the size of a finger. It twisted along the ground toward Cashel. He stamped on it—his calluses were hard as hooves—and drove the staff into the toad's face. He didn't think the blow had landed squarely and maybe it hadn't, but the toad went over on its back and started to thrash.

Cashel was still standing on the tongue; he felt it squirming like a snake's body. He took a full stride back so that the barbed end wouldn't cut him if it flailed around as the creature died. He didn't figure the toad was going to suck him dry like it'd done to the little demon, but Cashel had got banged and cut often enough in his life that he avoided it if there was a cheap way to.

There wasn't much thrashing, though. The toad's arms and legs quivered and kept quivering, but it wasn't in any kind of a pattern like when you took a chicken's head off and it ran around.

He guessed that straight jab to the throat must've crushed its windpipe. That wasn't a good way to die; but if it was going to happen, he didn't mind it happening to this creature. He didn't look like anybody's Lord, lying there on the gritty soil and trembling.

Cashel kept his eyes on the dying toad, but he wouldn't have been much of a shepherd if he hadn't felt Liane and Rasile coming over to join him. By now he figured it was safe, but he still backed a double pace so there wasn't any chance of the toad bouncing up and grabbing the women before he could stop it.

"Thanks, Rasile," he said, turning his head just a little bit to show he wasn't being disrespectful. "For holding him like that. I don't know how long I could've kept it up if he kept bobbing like he was doing."

"I think longer than he could have continued attacking, warrior," Rasile said. "Tenoctris spoke of your strength. I did not doubt the judgment of so great a wizard as she, but . . . she did not exaggerate."

The demons were showing themselves, moving a bit out from the sandstone walls or just letting their hides change to the light blue-gray color that seemed to be what they were when they weren't trying to hide. A few came closer, picking their way along like lambs who weren't sure their legs would hold them up.

"You have overcome the Lord?" piped the nearest. There was two on each side of him, a little behind. Cashel wondered if they were the same ones as before. Likely, he thought, but he couldn't be sure. Sheep didn't change color the way these demons did.

"Lord Cashel has killed the monster you allowed to prey upon you!" Liane said in a voice that rang from the rocks. The sulfur in this air had roughened it, but she still sounded like a queen. "Lord Cashel has freed you!"

She swept her right arm back toward where the toad lay. Cashel obligingly stepped to the side so that the demons could all get a look at their Lord twitching there on the ground.

"He is dead?" said the leader.

"He is dead?" the four behind him said all together. It was like watching mummers playing when they came through the district.

The five demons trotted toward the toad. Others were coming closer too, though they weren't running. There was a lot of them, a ten of tens at least; more than Cashel had seen when they first arrived here.

He moved farther out of the way. Stretching, he perched on his right leg to examine his left instep.

He'd cut himself pretty good above the callus. There'd been something sharp in the soil, a shard of quartz he supposed, that he hadn't noticed while he was moving fast. Squatting, he took out the little gourd of lanolin ointment out of his wallet and daubed it on the cut.

"He is dead!" the demons shrieked. They started jumping up and down on the toad's corpse, chopping with their little sharp hooves. "He is dead-d-d!"

The whole herd of them came bouncing to the spot. Cashel rose quickly and stepped between the women and the oncoming demons.

Rasile had been crouching on all fours, recruiting her strength after the work she'd done. Figuring where the toad was going to be next had taken wizardry. Holding the thing for Cashel to hit, well . . . The toad had obviously been strong. Cashel didn't doubt that the strength went beyond the muscles under that coarse warty skin, but Rasile had held it.

The demons swept past, to trample the corpse or anyway to try to. There were too many all to fit. It was like tossing meal into a pond and watching carp boil to the surface after it.

"They could have done that when the wizard was alive," Liane said. Her face was hard, which wasn't the usual thing with her. "But they were afraid."

"Wizard?" Cashel repeated.

"Yes," Rasile said. She raised her voice a bit to be heard over the demons shrieking and hooting. "The Lord, as they called him, was a wizard. Here in the place he'd made his own, I couldn't have defeated him."

The Corl let her tongue loll toward Cashel in a smile. "Tenoctris might have been powerful enough," she said, "but I think she too would've been glad of your presence, warrior."

Cashel looked at the scrum again, then turned away. "I'm not sorry to've put paid to that toad," he said. "But I can't say I much like the folk he was eating, either."

Rasile stood upright; she seemed to be recovered from the work she'd done. She turned toward the milling demons and called, "Teliday!"

Her voice was something between a shout and a screech. Cashel didn't know what she meant by it.

"Teliday!" she repeated.

A demon pushed his way out of the tramping herd. Maybe he'd been trying to do that since the first time he was called; it wouldn't have been easy. He limped a little as he hopped over to Cashel and the women. There was a long double cut on his foreleg, plowed there in the brawl by the hoof of one of his friends.

"Lady?" the demon said. Cashel was pretty sure he was the one who'd been doing the talking since they arrived in this brimstone-stinking hell. He didn't sound more than barely respectful now, though these folks' narrow, deerlike jaws and shrill voices meant Cashel might be misunderstanding.

"We've freed your people from the wizard who preyed on you," Rasile said briskly. "Now it's time for you to give us a goat and to lead us to the tomb of the hero Gorand."

The demon made a curt bow. "I will take you to the place of Gorand," he said. "Our goats are valuable. It will not be possible to give you a goat."

Rasile's equivalent of a shrug was to fluff the fur on top of her shoulders. "Very well," she said. "We don't need a goat. One of you folk will do for the sacrifice."

She pointed her athame at the middle of Teliday's narrow chest.

"No!" the demon cried, throwing his arms up in the air. "There will be a goat provided!"

"See to it," said Rasile, lowering the stone knife. Her tongue's wagging was just a smile, but from the way Teliday hobbled off he hadn't taken the expression as friendly.

Cashel cleared his throat. "Ma'am?" he said to Rasile. "I don't hold with sacrificing people. I don't like Teliday and his friends, but they're people. *I* think."

"Yes," said Liane, and you could've cracked walnuts on her tone. "They are."

"I agree, friends," the wizard said, looking from one to the other and wagging fiercer. "Warrior Cashel, could you catch a goat yourself?"

Cashel thought about it, eying a trio of goats on the cliff wall not far away. They weren't used to him, and just the fact he was human would likely spook them some. He figured he could work close enough to get a halter—his sash would do—on one, though.

"Yes, ma'am," he said. "It might take a while, is all."

"So I believed," said Rasile. "Therefore I spoke to Teliday in a fashion that would convince him to help us of his own free will."

"Oh," said Cashel, embarrassed not to have seen she was bluffing. Liane sucked her lower lip in and nodded. She still didn't look happy.

Teliday minced back, leading a half-sized demon who in turn led a goat by a strand of coarsely braided vegetable fibers. The goat was scrawny, but even so it was bigger than the runt tugging it along.

"The youth will guide you to the cave," Teliday said. He turned on his hind legs to leave.

Cashel laid his staff on the adult demon's shoulder. It wasn't a blow, just a tap, but it got Teliday's attention just like it was supposed to do.

"Sir?" said Cashel. "I think you better take us like you said. The boy can bring the goat, if you like."

"This way," said Teliday, turning again without argument or even hesitation. "Lord."

Cashel didn't have any special reason for saying what he did. He'd worked for a lot of crabbed, grudging farmers when he was a boy in the borough, though, and learned that you didn't ever let them out of a hair of what they'd promised. If you gave them the least break, then before it was over they'd leave you without two coppers' pay for a month's hard work.

Some people were just that way. And like he'd said to Rasile, these demons were people.

The valley Rasile had brought them to had branches off it, though the pattern was more like jagged spears of hoarfrost than like anything water had carved. Teliday took them up one of the angles, then into a third that was narrower yet. There weren't any demons or goats in that last branching, though there was more of the skimpy vegetation than there'd been till then.

Cashel couldn't figure what *had* made the valleys. There wasn't any sight of a river or even a dry streambed so far as he could tell. The rocks weren't worn, either, except by windblown sand.

"The cave is just ahead," Teliday said, pointing with both arms together.

"Lead us," Cashel said, shifting the quarterstaff slightly. The canyon here was narrow enough that he could've touched either wall with a ferrule if he'd wanted to stretch the staff out at arm's length.

The demon bobbed his torso. "Lord," he said obediently as he walked on ahead. His hooves made slow click/click/clicks on the rocky soil.

Cashel glanced over his shoulder. Rasile was close behind him, while Liane walked at the back. She still had her knife out, but with her free hand she clasped the little demon leading the goat.

Cashel smiled at her and went back to watching what was ahead of them. Garric had found a good one, and Sharina had a good friend.

"Lord," said Teliday, bowing again and pointing his arms toward a jagged opening in the canyon wall. "This is the entrance."

Unexpectedly the demon splayed his four legs and sprawled flat on the ground. "Please, Lord!" he said. "I have brought you to this place at your request. Release me now."

Cashel felt uncomfortable. "Ma'am?" he said to Rasile.

"This is the entrance," she said. "The entrance to the entrance, I should say. I know of no reason why Teliday and this boy shouldn't go back to where they'll be more comfortable. Though we'll need the goat with us."

"Lord?" Teliday begged.

"I have the goat's lead," Liane said in a clear voice. "Because Rasile says we must."

"All right," said Cashel, turning to speak to the little demon. "You two can go. Thank you—"

Teliday went bounding past. The little fellow unexpectedly hugged Liane's knee before trotting off himself.

"—for your help."

Cashel cleared his throat again. The air in this place was fierce with sulfur, but he guessed he could stand anything a goat could. "Rasile, do you want me to lead?"

"No," she said, "I will. It shouldn't be far."

So speaking, the old wizard stepped into the cave. It was big enough for Cashel to walk upright, though he had to be careful how he slanted the staff so it didn't knock the walls. He wondered if he should've brought a torch, and wondered what he'd make one out of if he went back outside.

Rasile paused; Cashel moved up beside her. The cave had opened out, though how far he couldn't be sure in the dim glow from the entrance. Liane joined them, holding the goat's harsh twine halter.

"Together, now," Rasile said. She stepped forward. Cashel waited just an eyeblink to make sure Liane was coming, but of course she was.

Quarterstaff braced before him, Cashel strode into a forest of unfamiliar dark trees. Insects trilled in a night smelling of damp loam.

In the moonlit clearing before him, sprites no taller than his ankle danced.

ILNA WALKED DELIBERATELY onto the natural bridge. It wasn't as slippery as it looked from a distance, because the ghoul's great feet had worn a path through the flow rock which the drips of a thousand years had deposited in a thin, glassy layer. Though wet and fine-grained, the limestone beneath wasn't quite as dangerous a surface.

Still, it was stone and she—Ilna smiled minusculely—was stone's enemy, at least in her own head. Regardless of whether or not stone really had an opinion.

Ilna trailed the climbing rope behind her. It was only long enough to stretch a double pace onto the upward curve of the arch. For choice she'd have been able to pass the centerpoint of the bridge, but for choice she'd have been home in Barca's Hamlet, weaving at her big loom on the porch while Chalcus and Merota chatted beside her.

She didn't have to like the reality of the world—she didn't remember a time she had, save for the brief period when Chalcus and Merota were with her. No one had ever claimed that Ilna didn't accept reality, however.

She didn't look over her shoulder at Usun. If things went as planned, he'd be out of sight anyway.

Ilna smiled again. If things didn't go as planned, she'd be dead very shortly and probably buried in the belly of a ghoul. She supposed she could throw herself over the edge of the chasm to prevent that, but if suicide had had any attraction for her, she wouldn't have survived this long.

If things went wrong, she'd attack the ghoul with the bone-cased paring knife she carried in one sleeve of her tunic. From what Usun had said, its hide was so thick with bony nodules that the little blade probably wouldn't be able to nick him. Still, it was something to do while the creature bit her face off.

Ilna placed the loop precisely on the pathway and straightened. She rather liked the rope. It was of good quality linen, and it'd been wound tight and smoothly. A pity to dispose of it in this fashion, but all things end. The rope presumably didn't care.

She walked on, past the center of the span. The ghoul might be watching her through the falls, though there wasn't any obvious reason why it would keep its attention a secret instead of rushing out to rend and devour her.

"Ghoul!" Ilna shouted. How good was the creature's hearing, anyway? This close, the water snarled as it tumbled down into the gorge. "Come out!"

She had only Usun's word that the ghoul was there. An almost-smile lifted the left corner of her lips. Indeed, she had only Usun's word that there was really a cave behind the waterfall. Well, she'd done far more foolish things in the past than shouting insults at a solid stone wall.

"You visited me!" Ilna said. She took another cautious step. Her eyes were on the waterfall, and to slip here would be more than embarrassing: the chasm was many furlongs deep. "Now I've come to see you, filth-eater!"

The curtain of water shivered aside. The ghoul stepped out, a hulking blackness against the blue shimmer.

"Are you afraid of me, ghoul?" Ilna said. Could the creature even understand speech? It was hard to believe that something so huge and misshapen had ever been human. Usun had been right on everything else he'd said, though.

The ghoul raised its bull-like head and roared, setting the waterfall atremble. Ilna stood where she was. She'd have to retreat shortly, but not just yet.

The ghoul stamped down the path toward his side of the bridge. Its steps were deliberate but as certain as the approach of dawn.

She wondered if she *could* outrun the ghoul. Probably not, since its size would be an advantage in this waste of stone jackstraws. Besides, there was nowhere to run, save to the pocket where Gaur deposited its dead. She wouldn't have a candle to drive the creature away a second time.

Not that it mattered. Ilna wasn't going to run.

The ghoul started across the stone arch. It was walking upright, but it hunched forward slightly.

Ilna began backing. She hadn't thought about how she was going to retreat. If a vicious dog was advancing on her, turning her back would draw a charge. She didn't know whether this ghoul would react like a dog, but it was certainly no less a beast.

On the other hand, if Ilna slipped—or tripped over a mound of flow rock—and fell, the ghoul would also rush her. Unless it was laughing too hard. Or unless she simply went over the edge into the chasm, in which case it didn't matter.

The ghoul crossed the centerpoint of the bridge. It seemed even larger than it had when it was close enough to grab her with its long arm.

She wondered if Usun would finish the creature if she was killed. She rather thought he would. The little man projected a sense of single-minded determination that Ilna found comforting.

Ilna stepped into the loop she'd laid in the path, then out of it. She was very close to her side of the chasm.

A stalactite grated over the rim of the gorge. White anger flared across Ilna's mind. She was going to die in a moment or two, but that didn't bother her.

Too soon, you fool! You should have waited!

Instead of uncasing her knife, Ilna knotted a pattern that would ease a troubled mind into sleep. Nothing she did would have any practical effect, so she did what gave her the most pleasure at the moment.

The ghoul dropped onto all fours and sprang like terrier on a vole. It smashed down before her, stinking of a meal that had been rotten before it started to eat, and reached out.

The weight of the stalactite Usun had levered into the gorge with his dagger snatched the rope taut. The loop closed with both the ghoul's feet in it, yanking the creature with it. The bestial face was expressionless, but Ilna thought she saw fury glint in the great eyes.

The ghoul grabbed at the arch as it went over. It was amazingly strong: the clawed forepaws actually plowed furrows in the rock as the stalactite dragged it to its doom.

Ilna crossed her arms and leaned over the edge of the chasm. She couldn't see the bottom. It seemed a very long time before she heard an echoing crunch, followed by a barely audible splash. She smiled in satisfaction.

The little man walked up beside her. The dagger's point was bent up at a sharp angle. He shook his head and tossed the weapon over the sheer cliff.

"With all the gold chasing on the blade," he said, "you'd think they'd have used better steel."

"I'm never surprised to find that people want something flashy rather than something useful," said Ilna. "Though, given that the man who wore that dagger probably never used it for anything in his life, I suppose I shouldn't fault his choice."

She cleared her throat. "Master Usun," she said, "I thought you'd sprung the trap too soon. I apologize."

The little man chuckled. It was probably meant for a laugh, but because he was so small it sounded disquietingly like a titter.

"He was tensing to pounce, mistress," he said. "And

there was a good deal of slack in the rope, which I had to allow for. I could have waited some seconds longer and still caught him, of course, but he would've started to eat you."

"Yes," said Ilna. "That's what I think also."

She looked about her. This was as bleak a landscape, so to speak, as she could remember seeing. Not even fungus grew here, and the rocks' odd blue haze added to the feeling of death and ruin.

"We're no closer to getting out of here," she said, "but disposing of that creature was worthwhile. Someone should have done it long since."

"Let's see what we find in the ghoul's lair, Ilna," said Usun, starting across the bridge. His short legs moved so smoothly that he seemed to glide rather than walk. "He wasn't always an animal, you know."

"I'll take your word for it," Ilna said, following him with less deliberate care than she'd needed to use when she was calling out the ghoul. Then she had a task to complete. Now, well . . . Despite Usun's cheerfulness, it didn't seem to matter whether she starved to death over a matter of weeks or plunged to her death in the gorge considerably sooner.

The track up the rock face on the other side was surprisingly narrow, given that the ghoul had come down it with careless unconcern. Perhaps its claws had gotten purchase on the rock; there were gouges that could have come from that. They roughened the path for Ilna's feet too, so in justice she should feel grateful to the beast. That'd be difficult, but if she lived long enough she might manage.

The waterfall sprang far enough out from the cliff face that only its margin cut the path, splashing away in all directions. The cavern's dead blue light didn't wake a rainbow the way the sun in open air would've done.

Usun paused just short of the spray. The water's impact could sweep somebody his size into the chasm, however strong and skilled they were.

"Here," said Ilna. She tossed him one end of the silk rope she wore in place of a sash. The little man flashed her a grin, then stepped through the curtain without accident.

Ilna followed, feeling the spray plaster her hair to her forehead and neck. It didn't soak through her tightly woven tunics immediately, though it would before long.

She expected the alcove behind the falls to be pitch dark. The cold, blue light was instead more intense than it had been in the main cavern. Its source seemed to be the convex circular lens which leaned against the sidewall. Shadows moved in its depths.

"It's a cyclop's eye," Usun said, looking at the crystal also. Even tilted, it was as tall as Ilna. "There are other things here as well, though I suppose a lot of them have moldered to dust."

He glanced deeper into the alcove. It wormed back deeper than Ilna could follow, narrowing visibly as it twisted away. The floor was deep in slime from which partial rib cages and skulls projected; there seemed to be other artifacts as well.

"He was a great wizard, you know," Usun said. He tittered. "He had to be great to destroy himself so thoroughly."

Ilna stepped over to the crystal. The squelching reminded her that she was walking in filth, but this wasn't the first time. It wasn't deep enough to drag the hem of her tunic, though that wouldn't have stopped her either.

The shadows looked almost . . . She bent closer.

"No," said Usun. "Stay at arm's length, but look squarely into the center. That's where it focuses."

Ilna straightened, then leaned back slightly. "That *is* Brincisa!" she said. "In her workroom. And there's Ingens, but he's not moving. Is he alive?"

"Alive, yes," the little man said; on him the slime rose to mid thigh. "But he won't move until a wizard releases him."

He gestured proudly toward the crystal and said, "The Eye doesn't only show images, you know. The ghoul used it as a portal in the days before he succeeded in making himself a deathless thing of death. I could do the same."

"You could walk through this crystal?" Ilna said. Her fingers paused in the pattern they were knotting.

"*We* could walk through the Eye," Usun said. "We could walk straight into Brincisa's sanctum. The ghoul wasn't the only wizard in this cavern, you see."

"Then," said Ilna, "let us do that, if you please. I have business with Mistress Brincisa."

Chapter

12

Usun's chant was a high-pitched warble, more like a chorus frog than anything human. Of course Ilna had only the little man's own word for it that he was human.

He continued to trill. Human or not, he didn't look much like a chorus frog. The surface of the lens rippled like light falling on the dimples that a water-strider's feet make in a pond's surface.

Ilna's fingertips played lightly over the knots in the pattern she held doubled between her hands. She was ready to act as soon as there was something to do. Till then she'd wait.

Usun hadn't marked the cavern floor before commencing to chant. The slime wouldn't hold lines, but he could've floated fabric or wood shavings on the surface if he'd thought he needed something.

Ilna smiled wryly. Normally she'd occupy the time by making and picking out patterns, but she couldn't do that now and still be prepared to face Brincisa. It served her right for using her fingers to control her nervousness.

Instead of an athame or a wand, Usun spun a doubled length of sinew in time with his chant. It had been coiled around his waist, the way Ilna carried her lasso. She wondered how the little man had come to be trapped in the box with his lips sewn shut.

If he really *had* been trapped, of course. Usun wasn't a person to underestimate, though Ilna was confident that they were on the same side. As distressing as she found most of the world and her life, she didn't recall ever having misjudged a person who she had to deal with. Mostly she judged people to be weak, treacherous, and stupid, of course, but Usun was an exception.

The little man gave a muted screech and fell silent, though he continued to spin the loop of sinew. Shadows swelled across the crystal, blotting out first the background and then Brincisa herself in the center.

"Now, Ilna," Usun said. He was drawing in deep breaths. "It's prepared. Step through the Eye."

It looks like a slab of polished stone. . . .

Ilna strode into the crystal. Many handfuls of candles made Brincisa's workroom a flood of light to eyes adapted to the blue dimness of the cave.

Ilna raised her pattern. Brincisa threw her left arm in front of her face; her baggy lace sleeve distorted the knotted fabric that was meant to paralyze her.

Something swished behind Ilna.

Snap!/thunk!

A pebble bounced from Brincisa's scalp. She flung her arms wide and toppled backward. The stone that'd felled her ricocheted off the far wall, breaking a divot from the fresco. It left a spot of blood against the sudden whiteness.

Ilna tucked the pattern into her sleeve and bent over Brincisa, jerking off her belt of braided leather. The strands were dyed black and each had a separate golden nib; despite the ornamentation, it seemed sturdy enough. Ilna flopped the wizard on her belly and tied her wrists securely behind her back with the belt.

Usun hopped onto a table with a top of polished cedar, carried on three bronze legs cast into the form of elongated demons. "My, look at the artifacts of power," he said, surveying the room. "She and Hutton had ages to gather them, of course. Though there's nothing—"

He tittered as he wrapped the sinew he'd used as a sling around his waist again. It didn't have a pocket, so he must balance each missile on the heart of the loop.

"—nearly as wonderful as I myself am. Which is why Brincisa sent you to fetch me, you see."

Ilna grimaced at the boasting, though it might well be true. Certainly she would've had a more difficult—and probably fatal—time in the cave if it weren't for the little man's help and guidance.

Ingens stood between an upright mummy case and a black stone carved to look like a leering human with breasts and a prominent male member. It had once been a pillar, but it wasn't supporting anything here.

Ilna's lip curled in disgust as she walked over to Ingens. His eyes were open but lifeless, and his cheek felt cold to her fingertips.

Usun hopped down from the table. He grabbed Brincisa's big toe through her openwork sandals and twisted hard. She yelped in surprise and jerked her foot away. By throwing her torso forward, she managed to sit upright and curl her feet under her.

The little man put his hands on his hips. His posturing should've looked silly, but Ilna got the impression of a much larger figure standing in Usun's place.

"You thought you'd use me like you do that statue of

Thrasaidon, did you, Mistress Brincisa?" he said, nodding to the black pillar. "Because Hutton used me, you thought you could?"

He laughed like an angry wren. "Hutton would've made a mistake one day too, you know," he said. "He's meat in the belly of a dead ghoul now, but he's better off than he would've been if it'd been me who repaid him. And you thought to use Mistress Ilna as well!"

"What do you want from me?" Brincisa asked. Ilna couldn't hear any emotion in the words—not even resignation. It was like hearing the statue speak.

"I'd as lief have put that stone through your head, you know," the little man said. "If I'd had a proper lead bullet, that's what I'd have done. You're lucky it was only a pebble from a stream."

"What do you want?" Brincisa repeated in the same calm, empty voice.

"Release Ingens," Ilna said. She was reducing the pattern to lengths of yarn, now that she had leisure to do so. "You can do that, can't you?"

"Yes," said Brincisa, glancing toward Usun. "But you'll have to untie my hands. I won't make trouble for you."

"No," said Ilna, squatting behind the other woman. Her fingers pulled and twisted, a deceptively simple movement which loosed the knot that a strong man couldn't have broken. "You certainly won't."

Brincisa stood up carefully, then touched fingertips to her head. Her hair was matted with blood, but it'd begun to clot into a mass that was probably as good as a lint bandage.

Either the wizard agreed with Ilna's dismissive judgment on the injury or she rightly assumed that her wishes didn't matter, because she turned to Ingens without commenting about her head. She touched the secretary's forehead with the fingers which had explored her scalp and said, *"Cmouch arou rou!"*

Ingens cried, "Wah!" and threw up his hands to ward

off something that only existed in his memory. Brincisa folded her arms and turned to Ilna.

"Are you all right, Master Ingens?" Ilna said. He certainly looked all right.

Ingens patted his cheeks in wonder. The wizard's touch had left two dabs of blood on his forehead.

"How did I get back here?" he said. "I was—weren't we on top of the mountain? Or did I dream that?"

"Mistress Ilna," Brincisa said calmly. "I told you I would send you and your companion here—"

She nodded toward Ingens with a look of distaste.

"—to the place where the man you're seeking disappeared. Let me do that now."

"I don't trust you, mistress," Ilna said. She stared at Brincisa. The wizard's lips tightened but she didn't flinch. "I didn't trust you even before you betrayed me."

"All I want now," Brincisa said, "is to send you on your way. I'll help you go anywhere you wish, just to have you away from here. I'll save you weeks in your search for Master Hervir."

"There's a way," Usun said. He twirled the coil of fine hair that had bound the box to Hutton's torso.

They looked at him. "Now, I wouldn't mind stretching my legs," the little man said. "I've spent a long time in that casket, a very long time. Cutting Brincisa's throat and hiking north to this village would be fine with me. But—"

He caught the coil and held it up. The candles waked not only gold but rainbows from the heart of each strand.

"—if you tie one end of this around Brincisa's neck and hold the other, then you'll be able to pull her into the place she's sent us. And if that's a bad place, so much the worse for her."

Ingens frowned. "Can't she just untie it herself?" he said.

Ilna gave him a cold glance. "No," she said. "Not if I've tied it."

Brincisa shrugged; her face was still as wax. "I'm in your power," she said. "If getting free of you means wearing a hair of the Lady around my neck for the rest of my life, then I'll do that."

A flash of fiercer emotion transformed her face, but only for an instant. "I'm not trying to bargain," she said. "I know I have nothing to bargain with. I'll help you in any way you wish. To keep you from killing me, which would gain you nothing."

"Nothing?" said Usun. He cocked a tiny eyebrow. "Well, there'd be satisfaction in killing you, mistress."

"I don't take any particular satisfaction in killing things," Ilna said, making up her mind as she spoke. "Give me the line, Master Usun."

The little man tossed her the coil. "No satisfaction?" he said. "Perhaps. But you've never hesitated to kill when you needed to, have you?"

Brincisa lifted her chin for Ilna to loop the shining filament around her neck. Ilna's fingers danced in a pattern that dazzled her even as she created it.

"I've never hesitated to do anything that I needed to," she said quietly. "Anything at all."

SHARINA SHOT UPRIGHT in bed. She'd been sleeping dreamlessly, as she had every night since Burne took up his patrolling, but these screams—

Another scream ripped the heart out of the night. It reminded her of the day a rabbit had leapt onto a sharp stake and spitted itself in the kitchen garden of the inn, but this was much louder.

—would wake the dead.

She drew the Pewle knife and started for the door. She didn't bother to put on slippers—in Barca's Hamlet she'd gone barefoot every year till the ground froze—nor with any garment beyond her sleeping tunic. It was modest enough in cut, and propriety didn't count for much when someone was being disemboweled nearby.

Diora stood by the door, holding the lamp that burned in her sleeping alcove through the night. "Mistress?" she said, her voice rising.

"Stay here," Sharina said, taking the lamp out of the maid's hand. "I'll be back."

Burne was perched on an unlighted sconce. He dropped onto her shoulder, saying, "Some clod will trample me if I'm running about on the floor."

"Let's go," Sharina snapped to the under-captain commanding the guards in the corridor. "And Burne, a little warning before you jump on me might help us both live longer lives."

"Your Highness?" said the officer as Sharina trotted down the corridor in the middle of a cocoon of black-armored guards. "Do you know what's going on? Ah, just so that we can be prepared for, ah, whatever it is."

"I don't," said Sharina. "I think it's on the floor below."

They started down the west staircase. It was narrow and unembellished, meant for servants. The Blood Eagles wore plain soles instead of hobnails while they were on duty in the palace, but their boots slapped and banged on the wooden treads.

"The cells are in the cellars on this end," said one of the troopers. "The ones Lady Liane's people use. They're convincing somebody who didn't want to talk, I'll wager."

"They'd better not be!" said Sharina. She wasn't squeamish, but she'd given orders that Platt was to be transported to Tenoctris. It'd been obvious to her—and she thought to Master Dysart as well—that the priest had nothing more to give to ordinary questioning. Crippling Platt—or worse—before the wizard could use him as a focus of her art would be both cruel and counterproductive.

The screams had ended, but servants standing agog in the hallways pointed them toward the basement. As the trooper had said, they were headed toward Master Dysart's suite.

The spymaster and four of his agents reached the barred door to his domain at the same time Sharina and her guards did. "Get out of the way!" the under-captain snarled, but someone inside was already pushing the door open for Dysart. It had been remounted to swing into the hallway, so smashing the latch out wouldn't be enough to move the panel.

"I haven't opened the cell in case it's a trick!" said the agent inside.

"Open it now!" said Dysart. He carried what looked like a short ivory baton-of-office. The *cling* when it touched the stone jamb told Sharina that it was painted metal.

The small cell was off the other end of the suite from Dysart's private office. Two of the agents who'd arrived with Dysart positioned themselves on either side of the door. Each held a cudgel in one hand and raised an oil lamp in the other. The man who'd been on night duty lifted out the heavy bar, then turned his key in the separate lock.

He jerked the door open. A trooper shouted.

The interior of the cell seethed with scorpions, ranging from tiny ones to monsters bigger than Sharina's spread hand. Still more of the creatures were crawling in through the barred window that slanted up to street level.

Platt's corpse was hidden beneath the writhing blanket. When the door swung, the chitinous mass surged toward the opening like a single entity.

Sharina smashed her lamp in the doorway. The olive oil splashed, then bloomed into pale yellow flames spreading from the wick across the surface.

"Burn them!" she shouted. "Quickly, fire!"

One of the agents hurled his lamp toward Platt and

jumped away. The other man threw his weight against the door and slammed it closed. Firelight flickered across the thin crack under the edge of the panel.

Burne leaped from Sharina's shoulder to the jamb and came down with a scorpion which had scuttled out before the door closed. The snicking of the rat's teeth mimicked the muffled crackle of oil flames within the cell.

"We may have to evacuate the palace," Sharina said, suddenly sick with horror. She hadn't liked the renegade priest, but *nobody* should die from the stings of a thousand scorpions. "The fire may spread."

"I think not, Your Highness," said Dysart. "The walls are stone, and the floor and ceiling are concrete."

"I have the fire watch coming," said Lord Tadai, who'd appeared unexpectedly. "Though I think Master Dysart's correct about there not being a serious danger."

Burne dropped the remains of the scorpion he'd caught. It had been a big one; the tail, still twitching on the floor, was longer than Sharina's middle finger.

"You seem to have been right, Princess," the rat said. "The priest would've been useful to Tenoctris. At any rate, the priest's master thought he would."

CASHEL STEPPED IN front of the women with his quarterstaff ready to strike. The woodsprites, more than a double handful of them, paused their dance in the middle of the clearing to stare at him and his companions. There were about as many men as women, slender and perfectly made. They wore garments woven from gossamer, bark fibers, and the down of small birds.

"Oh, look at them!" said a sprite who wore an acorn cap on his head. "He's a big one, isn't he?"

"And the girl's lovely. Could we bring her to join us, do you think?"

"The other one looks like a cat. Is she dangerous, do you think? She seems old."

"We won't harm you," Cashel said. "We've come to find Gorand, is all."

The sprites trilled like a dovecote when a snake squirms in. Some ducked into clumps of grass; others stood with their hands squeezed to their cheeks.

He can see us! How can he see us? Oh, what will we do?

The trees of this forest were like nothing Cashel had seen before. They weren't especially tall, but some had snaky boles, and the leaves of all were outsized.

The black bark of the nearest was as smooth as a palace floor; its simple oval leaves were the length of Cashel's leg, and the varied foliage of some of those across the clearing were even larger. One huge tree had a trunk bigger than two men could've spanned with spread arms, but its grassy leaves reminded him of bamboo.

"We'll not hurt you!" Cashel said. It made him uncomfortable to scare innocent, harmless people. "Please, can you show us to the hero Gorand?"

"Cashel, who are you talking to?" Liane said, trying not to sound frightened. The goat was nervously trying to pull the lead out of her hands. It wasn't used to breathing air that didn't have the poisonous bite of brimstone.

"The little people can't help us," Rasile said dismissively. She looked without affection at the dancers. "They know nothing and do nothing; they merely exist."

"We dance, cat woman," said a tiny female with quiet dignity. "We are very lovely."

"Go dance somewhere else, drones," Rasile said. "I don't want to listen to your twittering."

She rubbed her muzzle with the side of a paw, then added in a softer tone, "You won't want to watch this, little ones. Dance in another clearing tonight."

The sprites gathered, their heads together. They whispered for a moment, sounding like crickets behind a wall hanging.

The female turned and faced Rasile again. "We will

go," she said. "But you would do better to watch us dance. We are very beautiful."

The troupe faded off through the strange trees. The little man in the acorn cap paused for a moment in a patch of moonlight, staring at Cashel; then he too was gone.

"They were sprites, Liane," Cashel said. "Woodsprites."

To Rasile he added, "I like their dancing. It's like watching my sister Ilna weave."

The wizard's lips drew back in a grin of sorts. "Perhaps it is," she said, "but our sacrifice would disgust them."

She lolled her long tongue. "Either they don't belong in the universe," she said, "or I don't. And it disturbs me to think that they may be the ones who belong."

An animal screeched. It was hard to tell distance in woods so thick, but Cashel didn't think it was very close. He gave his quarterstaff a trial spin. The cry sounded like a cat, a big one, though it could just as easy be a night bird.

Rasile scratched at the loam with her long toe. "Cashel," she said, "can you cut through this to the clay underneath? We need a trough that will hold liquid for a time."

Cashel prodded the soil with his knife. He'd thought there might be tree roots, but it seemed just to be just leaf litter and grass as soft as a kitten's fur. He scraped the dirt carefully away. His knife would do the job, but cutting too thick a slice of the heavy clay would snap the crude iron blade.

The goat bleated peevishly. Liane said, "Rasile? Do we have to do this? I don't . . ."

Cashel had met Liane's father, Benlo. He'd been so powerful a wizard that he didn't let even his own death stand in the way of bringing his wife back from the grave. Liane was as brave as you could ask for, but she wasn't going to forget that her father had tried to sacrifice her.

"Yes, we do," the wizard said. She squatted, taking her yarrow stalks and black athame from the basket which held her gear. "We were fortunate that the folk of the anteroom kept goats, though no doubt Warrior Cashel and I would've been able to find something suitable here."

"Not a sprite," said Cashel, concentrating on his shallow trench.

"Not a sprite," Rasile agreed. "But there are apes here who wouldn't disturb you to use for the purpose, not if you got to know them."

She looked sidelong at Cashel. "Don't let the little drones mislead you," she said. "There's more darkness than light in this land, whatever they may pretend."

Cashel stood. The trench was as long as his forearm. He'd dug it a hand's breadth wide and about a finger deep in the clay beneath the leaf mold. "Is that enough, Rasile?" he said. "Or should I go deeper?"

"That will do well," Rasile said. She placed the yarrow stalks around the trough, seeming just to throw them down. They formed a neat figure against the black loam, however.

"Hold the goat and keep your knife out, warrior," she added. "By the horns, I think. When I begin to chant, it will try to break loose. The cord may not hold."

"Yes, ma'am," Cashel said. He took the goat by the right horn and drew it toward him, lifting the animal slightly so that its forehooves didn't have purchase as it tried to resist. It gave another whistling blat, but a peasant doesn't worry about the feelings of farm animals.

He wiped the knife on his bare thigh. Liane backed away, her face set in silent misery.

"The True People . . . ," said Rasile, looking into the dark distance. "My people. We very rarely use blood magic. Blood is too likely to madden us."

She turned to Cashel again and dipped her head to acknowledge him. Her tongue wagged a moment, then withdrew. She said, "I'm past that by now, I trust."

Rasile faced the trench and tightened like a lute string

being tuned. "Cut its throat when I give the order," she said; then without pausing she began to wail her incantation.

Shadows rippled in the night air. Cashel sensed movement across the clearing, but the patches of moonlight were empty when he looked squarely at them. Only with his head cocked to the side did he see the long-necked buzzards stalking and croaking among the debris of a battlefield. There were no trees, only half-grown oats that'd been largely trampled into the furrows. There were oats, and swollen corpses, and the buzzards.

"Now, Warrior Cashel!" said Rasile.

Cashel twisted the goat's chin up, then stabbed it in the throat. The goat kicked violently. The wizard resumed chanting, though at a higher pitch.

Cashel sawed the blade down. It was dull, but he was very strong and he knew the work. He forced the goat's head forward so that the blood splashed and spilled into the trough. Back in the borough, the woman of the house would hold a pan of cooked grain under the beast's throat to make a pudding.

The goat spasmed, then spasmed again and went limp. Cashel lifted its hind legs so that the last of the blood could drip downward. He wiped the blade, then tossed the drained carcass aside.

Standing, he looked about him for the first time since he'd taken charge of the goat. He could barely see the trees. A deep fog had gathered about him and the wizard. It eddied and thickened in harmony with the chant.

Rasile gave a final cry and plunged her athame into the trough of blood. The grayness shattered into terrible figures, all fangs and grasping claws and hunger. Cashel snatched up the staff he'd had to lay behind him.

"Let us drink!" the figures said, their combined voices whistling like wind through a cave of ice. *"We must drink! You have called us back, so we must drink!"*

"Guide us to Gorand and you may drink," said Rasile, sounding just as cold as these things of elemental hunger. "Until then, I bar you."

"We have no power over Gorand," the voices wailed. Their forms were smoke and fog, but as they writhed Cashel caught the hint of something human or once human beneath them. *"You must let us drink!"*

"Guide us to Gorand," said Rasile. "Until you do, there is nothing for you but want and longing. Guide us!"

"We cannot speak-k-k . . . ," the voices cried. *"We can not-t-t. . . ."*

Rasile twisted her athame in the clay. The figures shrieked, shrieked like damned souls; and so they were.

"We cannot-t-t!"

The figures blurred and melded, like sand statues slumping to repose when a wave washes the shore. *". . . not-t-t . . ."* echoed in Cashel's mind, though perhaps it wasn't a sound.

"Guide us to Gorand!" said Rasile.

The gray figures congealed. *"Gorand rules all!"* they cried. *"We cannot speak against Gorand-d-d. . . ."*

One of Liane's sandals lay on the grass beyond the ghastly circle. The girl herself was nowhere to be seen.

"Liane!" Cashel said. He lunged through the creatures, his staff spinning. Screaming in frustrated terror, they surged away like dust motes before an ox. "Liane!"

The animal screeched from the darkness again. It sounded closer than it had before. Other than that, the night was silent.

GARRIC EYED THE path and touched his sword hilt. Straight-trunked tulip poplars and spreading chestnuts that rose to a hundred and fifty feet dominated the forest; redbud and white dogwood, both in gorgeous bloom, formed the understory.

"You won't need that here," said Tenoctris. "The dangers are of a different sort."

"I'd feel better with it in my hand," Carus muttered in Garric's mind. *"Needed or not."*

Garric grinned and dropped his right arm to his side again. *Ah, but you don't have a hand anymore,* he thought. "Yes, ma'am," he said.

Though if it'd been him alone, he'd have drawn the blade. Garric wouldn't be here now if he were alone, of course, and Tenoctris had just told him what she wanted as clearly as if she'd given him a direct order.

He looked over his shoulder. The boat that brought them had vanished, and even the gray sea was fading into a forest like the one stretching before them. "What would you like me to do?"

"We'll follow the trail," she said, nodding. "It won't be far."

The path wasn't wide enough for them to walk side by side, so Garric strode ahead. He grinned wryly. There wasn't any reason to believe that danger waited in ambush ahead of them instead of creeping up behind, but at least he could pretend he was doing the bold and manly thing.

Tenoctris' feet and his own scuffed the leaf litter, but that was the only sound. There should've been the patter of dead twigs dislodged by a squirrel, or the rustle of a brown thrasher searching for grubs and beetles. This forest was as silent as a painting.

Garric reached the mossy edge of a lake so smoothly rounded that he was sure it had a stone coping. Instead the bank was black loam, crumbling slightly under his weight into the clear water.

"We need to get to the island in the center," Tenoctris said.

Garric shaded his eyes. Though the sun was bright, the mist over the water's surface obscured the other side.

He hadn't realized the dimly glimpsed temple was on an island rather than simply across the lake.

"I can swim it," Garric said. "Ah—"

Tenoctris had become young and active when she decided that her aged body couldn't carry out the duties required to save mankind. That didn't necessarily mean that she could swim.

"Or I could build us a raft, Tenoctris," he said. It would make him wince to cut trees with his sword, but in fact the keen, never dulling sword would do a better job than any axe.

"Not just yet," Tenoctris said, making a tiny movement with an index finger.

Garric's eyes followed the gesture: a perfectly formed youth with green skin was swimming toward them. To his either side swam a long-eared eel wearing a golden collar.

King Carus' instinct gripped the sword hilt. By an effort of will, and despite his ancestor's fierce scowl, Garric drew his hand away. He stood with his thumbs tucked in his broad leather belt.

"We have business at the Gate of Ivory," Tenoctris said in a cold voice. She'd taken an athame carved from amber out of her satchel. When the light struck it at the correct angle, Garric saw that not only a spider but its web were frozen in the honey-colored blade. "Let us cross."

The youth laughed and twisted onto his back with his head raised. Garric wondered how he managed to float; the slimly muscular body beneath his green skin should've sunk like a bronze statue.

"I'm not preventing you, Tenoctris," the youth said, his voice holding a silvery reflection of an Ornifal accent. "I don't imagine it's up to me to let or hinder so great a wizard as yourself."

Tenoctris dipped the athame very precisely, lifted it, and dipped it again. The amber point was never directed at the youth, but it described an arc around him. His hands spread as though they were pressing against the side of a boulder. There was translucent webbing between the fingers.

The eels had been writhing in complex knots to the youth's either side, like the supporters of a coat of arms. As the athame moved, they drove downward like rippling arrows. Their collars winked even after the sinuous bodies were out of sight in the clear depths.

"*Show me,*" Tenoctris said. She didn't raise her voice, but its timbre was that of a hawk's shriek. "I won't ask you again."

"You have no right," the youth muttered, but his hands clapped.

The surface of the lake shuddered. It took on a yellow cast, as though Garric were viewing it through the blade of the athame. Where the youth had floated, a muscular man kicked off from the bank. He was nude, but he pushed before him a float of reed stems. On it was a bundle of his clothing and equipment, including arrows and a short, stiff bow.

"*I'd do the same,*" Carus said, his attention fixed on the saffron-filtered image. "*Only I'd have a dagger in my teeth, because the water's deep enough to hold things I wouldn't want to fight with my bare hands.*"

The man swam with firm, effective kicks like a frog. He'd reached midpoint of the channel when his legs lost their rhythm. For a moment, Garric couldn't see what was wrong.

"*His pontoon's sinking,*" Carus said. "*The canes must've gotten waterlogged. He's going to lose his gear.*"

No, thought Garric. *Everything's sinking. His head's barely out of the water now, even though he's started thrashing like a lizard in a pond.*

The float and its burden slipped beneath the surface. The balled clothing should've floated for some minutes at least, but it drifted straight down alongside the reeds and the bronze-pointed arrows.

The swimmer tried to turn back, though by now it was no closer to return than to go on. He sank inexorably, his flailing limbs seeming to have no more effect than they would have done in air. His face wore an expression of tortured anguish as he sank into the depths.

"Enough," said Tenoctris.

Her voice recalled Garric to the present; he'd been lost in the yellow memory of the past. He took a deep breath. The youth and his attendants were no longer present, but the island and its temple were still visible through the haze.

"Very well," said Tenoctris, seating herself cross-legged on the lake's margin. The grass seemed normal, though Garric would've expected a coarser growth on ground so well watered. "We had to know what the dangers were before we could determine how to overcome them."

She opened her satchel and took from it a cord of red silk which she examined critically. In direct sun it resembled a wire because no stray fibers escaped the tightly woven strands to catch the light.

"Here," Tenoctris said, handing one end to Garric. "Tie this around your wrist. Don't cut your circulation, but it mustn't slip off."

She looped the other end about her own left wrist and bent to the task of tying it. Garric looked at the cord, then said, "Ah, Tenoctris? Could it be *my* left wrist?"

Tenoctris raised her head with a frown of surprise, then smiled brightly. "Ah," she said. "Yes, of course. Since it will apparently make you and your royal ancestor more comfortable."

Garric grinned as he tied a bowline which he then slipped over his left fist and tightened. In this mind the ghost of Carus guffawed and said, *"She's bloody well told it'll make me more comfortable. And I suspect she's happier too whatever she says, knowing that you can get to your sword when you need it."*

Tenoctris had set down her athame in order to tie the cord. She took it in her left hand again and stood, picking up the satchel in her right. The silk connecting her and Garric was an ell long, or almost.

"When I walk forward," she said, "walk with me. Just step normally, but don't lose the cord."

"Yes, ma'am," Garric said. He realized he was treating the wizard as the aged woman he'd found on the shore of Barca's Hamlet rather than as she now appeared, an attractive girl only a year or two older than he was. "Which direction will we go, if you please?"

"To the temple, Garric," Tenoctris said with a grin that seemed impish on her youthful face. "Across the water. Well, *over* the water."

"Yes, ma'am," Garric said, eyeing the lake again as the wizard began to chant. The water was so clear that he could imagine he was seeing the bottom, but he remembered the stricken face of the swimmer as he sank ever deeper. By the end he'd been antlike and his limbs had ceased to struggle.

"*. . . io mermeri abua . . . ,*" Tenoctris was saying. Instead of merely bobbing up and down, her athame moved in a sequence as complex as the dance of knitting needles. The spider in the amber blade seemed to be weaving.

"*. . . abrasax buthi . . .*"

Light quivered in the depths, mimicking solidity. It was only a distortion of the irregularities in the glassy surface, though. "*. . . mermeri . . .*"

Tenoctris stepped off on her left foot. Garric moved with her, his eyes on the temple rather than the glassy water underneath. The surface was as firm as stone.

"*. . . rasax buthi. . . .*"

Side by side they strode toward the island. Garric hadn't meant to look into the water, but at the midpoint instinct drew his eyes downward. He could see to the bottom with impossible clarity, as though the water were a magnifying lens. There were more bodies than he could count, uncorrupt but glaring upward in the final horror of their deaths.

With them were all manner of floats and buoys. There was even a boat of shining metal in which three young women lay with expressions of furious disbelief. Their long, blond hair framed their heads in sunbursts. Garric thought of Sharina and grimaced.

He was still thinking of his sister and of Liane when his boot came down on sod instead of water with the consistency of granite. He and Tenoctris had reached the island. Before them was a round temple with a gold caryatid on either side of the entrance. Inside the structure was a catafalque on which lay the skeleton of a tall man, clasping a long iron sword.

"That is Lord Munn," Tenoctris said as she began to take the cord off her wrist. "Our business is him. *Your* business, Garric."

Chapter

13

A TRUMPET CALLING Assembly awakened Sharina. The weeks she'd spent with the army on campaign made the sound familiar, but hearing it in Pandah threw her tired mind into deeper confusion. She had the odd feeling besides that it was an echo.

She got out of bed, wondering what time it was. She hadn't been sure she'd be able to get to sleep again after they'd found Platt's body, but she'd dropped off as soon as her head hit the pillow. Having both her previous responsibilities and Garric's left her exhausted. Besides, she no longer found sudden, horrible death an unfamiliar experience.

Another trumpet sounded. There was smoke in the air, drifting through the slatted jalousies. What was going on? *Lady, aid us in our time of need.*

"Your Highness?" said Diora, stumbling from her alcove with a bleary expression. She held the lamp she'd borrowed from a hall bracket to replace the one Sharina had smashed into the mass of scorpions.

"I just heard a second regiment called to arms," Sharina said. The maid didn't understand military signals; why should she? "That's half the capital garrison. I'm going to check on what's happening."

"That's the fourth trumpet, Sharina," said Burne from the floor. "And there've been horns."

"Hop up," said Sharina, curving her left arm into a cradle for the rat. She jerked the hall door open. To the waiting guards as well as Burne she said, "We're going to the city prefect's office at once."

Tadai's suite was at the far end of the same corridor. Its outer door was open, spilling light from the interior. A courier tried to exit as the leading Blood Eagles arrived; they pushed him aside without ceremony. Sharina winced, but the courier knew better than to resent it—and in fairness to the soldiers, there wasn't a lot of time for politeness.

The waiting room of the large office was already crowded. Tadai sat behind a clerk's desk instead of in his well appointed private chamber. "Lord Quernan," he was saying, "Put three regiments at the disposal of the city watch. They're to be under the command of the district captains, not their own officers, and they're to use only the butts of their spears. They're not to use the points, and they're not to carry swords."

"Look here, Tadai!" Quernan said. The military advisor's back was to the door; he didn't see Sharina enter, though Lord Tadai struggled to his feet to greet her. "First, you're wrong about putting real soldiers under the watch, and second, you can't disarm them in the middle of riots like this. It's not safe!"

"Your Highness," said Tadai, bowing. He was as close to being disheveled as Sharina had seen since earthquakes and an army of monsters had destroyed Erdin while he was present.

"What?" said Quernan, turning. "Oh!"

"Lord Quernan," Sharina said, "follow the prefect's direction as to command. The troops are not to use points and edges unless their own lives are endangered, but they'll carry their full equipment including swords. And if you will, don't waste time. It's obvious that things are in a serious state."

"Your Highness," Quernan muttered as he stumped out of the office with a train of aides following.

Lord Tadai grimaced. "Your Highness," he said, "if you leave it to the soldiers themselves—"

"They'll be making that decision regardless of what their orders are," Sharina said. She realized her mind was the same place it would've been if she'd been discussing how to deal with rats in the inn: weighing alternatives in terms of cost and effectiveness and ignoring all other considerations. "This way they don't go into action thinking they're under the command of fools."

She cleared her throat and added, "Besides, I'm more concerned about the safety of men putting their lives on the line for me than I am of people intent on burning down Pandah. That is what's happening, isn't it?"

"Some of them are," Tadai said, sighing. He'd aged noticeably since their recent conversation in Dysart's office. "There are riots in all parts of the city, and some involve fires. I have twelve separate reports, and there may be more."

Sharina gestured Tadai back into his chair. He probably hadn't been to bed tonight, and his duties as prefect required more physical activity than had ordinarily been a part of his life. She said, "What caused the riots? Do we know?"

Tadai settled with another sigh. "According to prisoners from all four districts of the city," he said, "they've heard that you tortured to death a priest named Platt because he refused to recant his belief in Lord Scorpion, the true God."

"May the Sister bite me!" blurted Trooper Lires. "*Nobody* could think the princess would do that!"

Lires had been part of Sharina's guard in several hard places, and they'd saved one another's life on occasion. That familiarity made him even less concerned about formal courtesy than most Blood Eagles, and propriety was well down Lord Attaper's list when he was choosing men to replace those who'd fallen.

"Of course they could, Lires," Sharina said, jumping in quickly so that nobody'd try to discipline an uppity guard. "Even in Pandah, not one in a hundred people have seen me closer than on the dais at an assembly. How difficult would *you* find it to believe a noble you didn't know would torture prisoners?"

"Well, even those I do know, Princess," Lires said in embarrassment. "But not *you*."

Sharina quirked a smile at him. To Tadai she said, "Milord, what do you want of me?"

Tadai shrugged. "The trouble's widespread, but I don't think it's very deep," he said. "With the help of the garrison, we should have it under control shortly. By dawn, at any rate. I suggest that you get some rest, if you can."

"Thank you, milord," Sharina said, "but I tried that and wound up here. I think I'll take a look from the roof."

"I'll accompany you if I may, Your Highness," said Master Dysart. He must've entered behind her.

She nodded, already moving. Tadai needed his office.

The guards swept them through the crowd the way the hull cuts the water around a ship's passengers. Captain Ascor allowed Dysart to walk beside Sharina, though she wasn't certain that Lord Attaper would've approved had he known.

"The riots must've been planned at the same time as the murder of the captured priest, Your Highness," Dysart murmured as they mounted the stairs. "They broke out in all parts of the city simultaneously."

"Yes," said Sharina. She considered options silently. There were really only two choices: to quit or to go on. She would go on, no matter how tired and frustrated she was. They all would.

Aloud she said, "The next time we capture a priest of the Scorpion, we'll know we have to guard against his former master murdering him."

How *could* they protect the prisoner? If they even managed to get another one. Their enemy and its minions were sophisticated and learned quickly.

Sharina looked out over the city. The moon had set, but several plumes of smoke rose into the starlit sky. Lanterns winked in the streets, but at least the fires weren't burning out of control.

"Ah . . . ," Dysart said. "I've directed my agents to look for the headquarters of the cult, rather than to spend their efforts in capturing another functionary."

"There may not be a headquarters!" Sharina said, more sharply than she'd intended. "All the Scorpion's worshippers may get their instructions in dreams and never see one another."

"Yes, Your Highness," Dysart said quietly. "In that case, nothing we do here will be of any real value. I prefer to assume that my actions have meaning."

We're all trying, Sharina thought. *We're all doing the best we can.*

She noticed something. "Master Dysart?" she said. "Ascor, any of you? Have you seen Burne? He's not with me."

"Your rat, Princess?" said Trooper Lires. "He went out through the window down in the prefect's office."

"Oh," said Sharina. "Well, I suppose he knows what he's doing."

Silently she added, *I only wish that the rest of us did.*

BRINCISA TOOK A deep breath as she finished her second set of chants, then moved to the final side of the triangle in which Ilna and Ingens stood. Space was tight, so Usun sat on Ilna's left arm.

The secretary was restive. Wizardry made most people uncomfortable, but the fact that they'd been standing in the symbol for long minutes without anything happening might bother him as well. It certainly bothered Ilna.

"Erek rechthi—" Brincisa said, gesturing with the athame she'd chosen for this work. It had been carved from jade with a faint greenish cast.

The words of power broke off in mid syllable. The world outside Ilna's eyes went black—shapeless and opaque. Her grip on the coil of fine blond hair tightened. If it was as strong as she suspected, a hard tug would slice the loop on the other end through the wizard's neck.

There was light. They stood in a grove of mature hardwoods: a pair of shagbark hickories, a white oak, and directly before them a huge red oak. Dogwoods and white birches grew outside the large trees, but the area within the stand was covered by knee-high fern.

The red oak stretched out a limb thicker than most tree boles. It grew from a point on the trunk that was a little higher than Ilna could reach by stretching to her full height. From it hung a stone gong supported by two bronze chains.

Usun hopped from the crook of Ilna's arm but climbed onto a fallen limb to see over the fern. He sniffed deeply.

"Rabbits, squirrels, and a fox," he said. He giggled and added, "Mistress Brincisa hasn't put us in a tiger's den, at least. Or found another ghoul for us to dispose of."

"This is the grove where Princess Perrine came to us," Ingens said in a dull voice. He walked away, keeping his back to Ilna. The ferns he brushed through gave off a faint odor of fresh hay. "The gong there . . ."

He gestured.

"Master Hervir tapped the center of it with his knuckles, and she came through the woods with four servants. The servants were apes but they wore clothes."

"Apes, now?" said Usun. He tested the air again. "Well, they haven't been here recently."

Ilna looked about. There was no sign of the way Brincisa had sent them to this place. The hair stretching from the coil in her hand vanished somewhere in the air behind her, but she couldn't be sure exactly what that point was.

"Do we agree that Brincisa has taken us where we asked her to?" she said to her companions. "And that there's no immediate danger?"

Ingens nodded, his back still turned. "Yes," he mumbled.

"No danger, certainly," Usun agreed. "But if you want to pull on the hair and take Brincisa's head off, then there won't be many mourners. Not even those servants of hers, I'll wager."

"What I want to do," said Ilna, "is to keep my word. Of course."

She gave the coil an underhanded toss in the direction the strand tended. It vanished in midair, a golden flash in the leaf-filtered grove.

"All right," Ilna said. "I'll ring the gong, then. You said that I can ring it with a finger?"

"Before you do that, mistress," Usun said, "there's one thing we might check. There, midway between the two hickory trees. The ground's been disturbed."

"Has it?" Ilna said. She'd been walking toward the gong, but out of politeness she glanced where the little man pointed. So far as she could tell, the ferns grew in a feathery, unbroken surface across the floor of the glade. Cashel might've been able to tell more, but neither them had been a forester.

Oh.

Ilna stopped. "Master Ingens," she said. "Face me."

The secretary buried his face in his hands. He didn't speak or look at her.

Ilna had taken yarn from her sleeve and was knotting it. That was more reflex than a conscious act, the way she'd have grabbed her weaver's sword if it slipped from her hand.

"Master Ingens," she repeated, "*face* me!"

The secretary turned slowly and lowered his hands. Tears streaked his cheeks, but his expression now was defiant.

"Hervir was completely healthy when I last saw him," he said. "I didn't kill him!"

Usun cackled. He stood arms akimbo on his low perch.

"Very well," said Ilna. She was coldly furious. She'd regarded Ingens as . . . not a friend, of course, but an ally who'd help to the limited degree he was able. It now appeared that—

Well, better to ask than to speculate. "Tell us what really happened to Hervir," she said. Her voice was calm. "Tell us everything. Or I will not only tear the information out of you, I will tear your eyes from their sockets."

"Yes, mistress," said Ingens. He sounded like a dead man. "I buried the money there."

He gestured.

"I was going to bury it beside a tree, but I couldn't because of the roots. I had only my stylus to break the ground and a wax tablet to scoop it away. I didn't plan to do this! It just happened."

"What happened to Hervir?" Ilna repeated, though this time without her previous anger. Ingens was weak, but almost everyone was weak. Ilna os-Kenset was weak at times, which she hated as she hated few other things.

"It was just as I told you," said Ingens, getting control of himself better. "Hervir met the princess and her apes. They talked. He told me he was going with her but that he'd be back in the evening. I was holding the money he'd brought to buy the saffron."

He took a deep, shuddering breath. He was looking at Ilna's feet, not her eyes, but he didn't try to turn away.

"The guards didn't know that," he explained. "Hervir always had me carry the money in a belt between my tunics. He didn't like the weight, and it chafed his hip-bones."

"He trusted you?" said Usun, laughter not far beneath the surface of the words.

"He was right to trust me!" Ingens said. "I'd no more steal than I would have killed and eaten him!"

He licked his lips and grimaced, trying to wet them. "He went with Perrine, just walked out of the grove—"

He pointed with his full arm, toward the gong. "They were out of sight behind this big tree," he said, "so I walked around it to see where they were going. I couldn't see them. I couldn't see anything, and neither could the guards. Just as I told Lady Zussa. They were gone!"

"And then?" said Ilna. She could hold her pattern in front of the secretary's eyes and drag his very soul out, just as she'd said, but he seemed to be talking freely.

Ingens licked his lips again. "We waited till evening," he said. "Hervir didn't come back. Nobody did. We had a room in Caraman—rooms, one for the guards and I slept on a truckle bed in Hervir's room. In the night I came back to this grove—alone. I didn't plan to . . . I just came to see if Hervir had returned. It was moonlight."

He turned away. Ilna didn't jerk his head toward her. Ingens was talking; forcing him to meet her eyes would merely be punishment. That wasn't her business.

"Hervir wasn't here," Ingens said. "He might have been! But I thought . . . And I buried the money belt here between the trees. I still had the traveling expenses, the guards' pay and food and lodging. But I hid the gold we'd brought to buy saffron."

"Why didn't you just carry it with you to Pandah?" Ilna said. "Or back to Valles, for that matter? Since you were stealing it anyway."

Ingens winced but looked up. "I thought if I had the gold with me on the journey back, the guards might have suspected. We'd have had a different relationship without Hervir."

He gave her a crooked smile.

"I was Hervir's dog, you see," he explained. "The guards believed that I thought I was better than a group of illiterate thugs with a modicum of skill at injuring people. If they decided to kick the dog in the absence of its master, they'd find the gold. Rather than lose both the gold and my life, I buried it here and planned to come back for it alone."

He started to cry. "I'm glad you caught me," he said. "I'm not a thief. I should never have thought I could get away with this, this . . ."

Ilna shrugged. "It sounds to me," she said, "as if your main concern was saving your own life. And while I don't put a high value on that—your life or mine either one—it's not unreasonable that you'd disagree."

She took the remaining few steps to the gong. She studied it critically. It was made of greenish stone with gray veins crawling through it; at first glance, she'd thought it was corroded bronze.

Looking back at Ingens, she said, "Did you try ringing it yourself after your master disappeared?"

"Yes, mistress," Ingens said. "We came back on the next three days, the guards and I. I struck the gong in the morning when we arrived, then in the evening before we left. No one responded, so we hired Captain Sairg to carry us to Pandah to report."

"They may not come for me either," Ilna said, eyeing the stone disk. It was about three handspans across and as thick as her index finger. "Still, we'll try this first."

She raised her right hand.

"Mistress?" the secretary said in a desperate voice.

Ilna turned in irritation. She held strands of yarn in her left hand; before she caught herself, she'd started to knot them in a fashion that *would* silence the fool while she had work to do. "Yes?" she said.

"What are you going to do to me?" Ingens said. "About the money?"

"I have nothing to do with money!" Ilna snapped. Her mouth worked sourly. In a milder tone she added, "And I have nothing to do with Halgran Mercantile, either. If we find Hervir, you can give the money back to him. If we don't, I suppose you can take it back to Mistress Zussa. If you survive, of course."

"Thank you, mistress," Ingens said. "That's what I'd decided to do anyway."

He gave her the broken smile again. "I'm not cut out to be a thief, you see," he said.

"No," said Ilna, "you're not. Now, if you're done with your questions, I'll get on with the business that brought us here."

"Before you bring Princess Perrine and her little beasties . . . ," said Usun. His voice managed to sound mocking even when he didn't mean it to be. If there *were* times he didn't mean it to be. "Why don't you roll me up in your cloak so that they won't see me?"

Ilna looked at him, then knelt to open her slung cloak on the bed of ferns. "Yes," she said. "That's a good idea."

The wizened little man arranged himself on the densely woven wool. He'd somewhere found a hollow reed which he thrust toward the open edge, just as though he planned to hide under water.

"What do you expect to happen?" the secretary asked as he watched in puzzlement.

"I don't *know* what's going to happen," said Ilna, rolling the cloak again. "That's why Master Usun's idea is such a good one.

She hung the garment's strap over her shoulder. Usun was so scrawny that, even knowing he was there, she saw no change in its lines.

Adjusting her tunics, Ilna faced the gong again. Taking a deep breath, she tapped the center with her knuckles. Though she disliked stone, she had to admit that the gong's note was cool and melodious.

Before the tone had died away, she heard the rustle of feet approaching through the dogwood and birch leaves.

GARRIC WALKED DELIBERATELY toward the circular temple. He wasn't gripping his sword hilt, but his right hand was closer to it than it would've been during a meeting with his council.

The sky had a pearly radiance like nothing in his experience. The scattered clouds he'd seen through the trees while walking to the lake margin has been completely normal.

Tenoctris walked alongside him, looking somewhat worn. Now in a youthful body, she worked to conceal the effort she expended in her art just as she'd done when she wore all her seventy years. That didn't mean the effort wasn't real.

The temple had solid walls instead of a colonnade, set on a three-step base. It had been built from unblemished white marble, save for the gilded dome and the pair of golden caryatids supporting the simple transom over the entrance.

Garric walked into the lighted interior. The dome didn't have an oculus in its center: the light, the same soft rainbow majesty as the sky, streamed from the circle of wall opposite the entrance. It swirled and diffused and seemed to seep through the stone.

Garric frowned for a moment, then turned his attention to the marble bier in the middle of the room. It must have had velvet coverings once, but time had reduced them to greenish dust on the surrounding floor.

Lord Munn was a skeleton, but the skeleton of a man with bones as dense as a deer's. In life he must've been seven feet tall. His two-handed sword was the most massive weapon Garric had ever seen.

"I've never seen anything like it either, lad," said the ghost in his mind. *"I'd use it if I had to, but I'll tell the world I'd find it awkward."*

Garric grinned. If Carus had to—*when* he'd had to—he'd tear out throats with his teeth. The warrior king's standards for what constituted a practical weapon were broader than most people could imagine.

"Garric, come out here if you will," Tenoctris said. The request was polite in form but peremptory in tone. And why not? They were here by Tenoctris' skill and in furtherance of her plan; if she thought he ought to be doing something, she didn't need put frills on her direction.

"Yes, ma'am," Garric said, walking out to where the wizard stood examining the caryatids.

The women who'd modeled for the golden statues were similar but not twins. The one on Garric's left had fuller lips and a broader nose; her companion was taller by an inch or two, though their hair, bound with silver fillets, was piled to level the transom which they supported.

Each held a codex open to the viewer. The book on the left read ASK in the fluid Old Script, while the other read AND IT WILL BE GIVEN.

"What do you think of them?" Tenoctris said, gesturing.

The words or the statues? Garric wondered. The caryatids were smiling; smiling mockingly, one might reasonably think. Aloud he said, "Is it a code, perhaps?"

"Perhaps," said Tenoctris, her tone meaning, "No." She looked from one statue to the other, then went on, "But I think . . ."

She stepped back, motioning Garric with her. He was already following her lead. She bowed to each statue in turn, then said, "Mistresses, please help us in our trial."

With throaty chuckles that certainly sounded golden, the caryatids shut their books and stepped out from under the transom. The stiff marble beam remained where it was, bound in place by the weight of the roof resting on the walls.

"Oh, it feels good, doesn't it, Calixta?" said one. She executed a complex dance step on her toes, then pirouetted away. Reaching up, she removed the fillet so that her hair swirled as she moved. Her tunic was still gold, but it belled out like diaphanous silk.

"I missed the grass between my toes, Lalage," said Calixta, executing a mirror image of the same dance. Her loosened hair was noticeably longer than her partner's. Each woman—each nymph? they certainly weren't statues anymore—held her silver fillet in one hand to balance the closed codex in the other. "But I knew it would be waiting for me."

Tenoctris waited with her arms folded in front of her. Garric stood at her side. He noticed with wry amusement that he stood straighter than usual and sucked his belly in. The nymphs had golden skin and eyes, but they were very attractively female.

"Come, Lalage," Calixta said after a final delicate swirl. She transferred her book to the same hand as the fillet so that she could touch her partner's wrist. "Our visitors asked us for help, after all."

Obediently Lalage walked with Calixta to face Garric and Tenoctris. "How can we help you, friends?" they asked in pure, melodious voices.

"Our enemies . . . ," Tenoctris said. "Enemies of life, really, have opened the Gate of Ivory. They're calling out the spirits of the dead to animate the bodies of monsters which they create. We have come here to ask Lord Munn to close the gate again."

"He won't listen to you, lady," said Calixta. "Not a woman."

"He won't listen to any woman," Lalage agreed. "No matter what you threaten him with."

"With your help, I will raise him," Tenoctris said firmly. "And then we will see who he obeys."

Lalage gave her deep chuckle again and handed her fillet to Tenoctris. "Put this on his right arm, then," she said. "And wake him."

"And this on his left," Calixta said, offering her fillet also. "We'll see, just as you say."

Tenoctris bowed to the nymphs, then stepped into the temple with Garric at her side. The golden women were whispering, and in Garric's mind King Carus watched with the grin he wore in battle.

LIANE!" CASHEL SHOUTED. "Ma'am, where are you?"

Something called, "Whoo! Whoo! Whoo!" in the distance. Cashel didn't suppose it had anything to do with Liane's wandering off, but he looked that way into the darkness anyhow.

"Liane!" he called.

With his staff crossways before him, Cashel shoved through a clump of plants whose sword-shaped leaves stuck up from a common center. He didn't think they were grass, though they might be. The edges of the leaves were light against a dark core; yellow and green, he supposed, but he couldn't tell by moonlight.

He stopped. He hadn't gone far from the trough he'd dug for Rasile, but already the forest was different. Here, instead of trees with boles like snakes, there were waist-high trunks with scaly bark supporting flower heads a full arm's length across. Some of the petals were darker than others, but again he couldn't tell the real color.

"Liane?" Cashel called again, but this wasn't doing any good. He turned to go back to Rasile.

He wasn't worried about getting lost himself—he didn't get lost outdoors, not even when the trees were strange and the stars were like none he'd ever seen before. He'd lost Liane, though, by not paying attention. He was responsible for Rasile too, and he'd best get back to her before something else happened.

The foliage rustled. Cashel cocked the quarterstaff to slam it forward like a battering ram, but he said quietly, "Rasile?"

"Yes, Cashel," the wizard said, slipping between the standing leaves instead of pushing through them the way he'd just done. "I let the elementals have the sacrifice."

Cashel grimaced. "Ma'am, I'm sorry," he said. "I shouldn't have run off like I did. I . . ."

He'd made one mistake, and then he'd made another right on top of it. There wasn't anything he could do now except go on and try to make things right in good time.

"Ma'am?" he said. "Do we need to go back and fetch another goat?"

The Corl's tongue wagged her laughter. "That wouldn't do any good, I'm afraid," she said. "Had I thought that I could force the answer out of them, I would not have left the work to find you. Desperate as they were for the blood, they would not speak against Gorand. I do not think that even Tenoctris could have dragged that from them."

Cashel nodded. He was sorry that Rasile hadn't gotten the information they'd come here for, but part of him was glad that he wasn't the reason it hadn't worked.

"Well," he said. "Before we go look for Gorand some more, we need to find Liane. Or I do, anyhow, because I should've been watching her while you were busy."

"She left one of her shoes in the clearing," Rasile said. If she had any opinion about whether going after Liane was a good idea, she kept it to herself. "With that to work from, I believe that I can determine a direction. Or better."

They went back through the glade. Cashel had intended

to lead and clear the way, but Rasile didn't need help and didn't give him the chance, either one.

The clearing was the same as it'd been when they arrived, except for the scar Cashel had dug in the sod. The gray hungry things were gone, the elementals; he was glad of that.

Blood no longer glistened in the moonlight. He guessed that if he'd touched the bottom of the trough, he'd have found it dry as a skull in a desert. Not that he cared, or that he had any intention of checking.

Rasile picked up the sandal and examined it critically, uppers and sole. She looked at Cashel and said, "I could probably get a clearer image if I placed this where the blood was to work my spell, but I don't think I will."

"No, ma'am," Cashel said. "Liane wouldn't like that, so we won't do it."

He was glad Rasile had decided that herself, but he'd have told her just as clear as he needed to. He figured Liane would rather die than be saved by blood magic. Cashel didn't feel that way himself, but he could see that she had an argument on her side.

"We'll put it where she dropped it, then . . . ," the wizard said as she placed the sandal back on the sod. She reached into her basket and brought out the yarrow stalks.

"Why do you want to find her anyway?" asked a woodsprite unexpectedly.

Cashel looked up. She was perched in the crotch of a sumac bush just inside the circle of trees. She rose and stretched, giving him a pixie grin.

"You could do *much* better, you know," she said. "A bull like you deserves the best."

"Ma'am," Cashel said. "Liane's my friend, and she's the intended of my best friend. Do you know where she's gone?"

The sprite hopped to the ground and sauntered toward Cashel through the grass blades. "Then you're free?" she said. "Come with me, bull man!"

"No ma'am," said Cashel, straightening up. She wasn't any taller than his ankle, but size didn't mean much here. He'd been in these places often enough before to know that. "Tell us where Liane is, please."

The sprite made a face at him. Small as she was, he saw her clearly. He supposed he wasn't seeing with his eyes.

"You're no fun!" she said. "Well, you can just forget about your skinny little girlfriend. Milady's servants took her, so you'll *never* get her back!"

"Do you mean that Gorand took her?" said Rasile. She'd set her basket on the ground, but she still held the yarrow stalks.

"Keep away from me, cat!" the sprite said, darting between Cashel's feet. "Don't let her hurt me, big man!"

"Rasile isn't going to hurt you," said Cashel, wondering if that was true. Well, it shouldn't be necessary. "But ma'am, you need to tell us where Liane is."

"Milady isn't Gorand," the sprite said scornfully. She moved out from cover warily, but she still kept to his other side from the Corl. "She's here, and Gorand just *rules*. Gorand wouldn't care about the skinny girl!"

Rasile bent close to the ground and wrinkled her nose. Cashel misunderstood for a moment, then realized that the Corl was catching a scent.

"The apes were here recently," she said, rising. "I should have noticed that before. While I was busy with the elementals."

"Of course Milady's servants were here," the sprite sneered, bending forward to watch the cat woman while keeping Cashel's body between them. "I *told* you that. They took her to Milady in the castle, and you'll never get her away again."

"Where is the—" Cashel started to ask. He looked up, following the line of the sprite's eyes. A tower and a crumbling wall stood against the sky.

The ruin can't have been as much as a bowshot away.

Maybe it was the angle so that Cashel now saw through a notch between the tops of the funny trees; but maybe it really hadn't been there before.

"Why don't you come with me, handsome?" the sprite said. "Just for a little while, if you like."

Figures moved on top of the tower. Two were hulking apes. Between them—

Haze shrouding the moon drifted away. The apes were holding Liane.

"Cashel!" she called.

He was already striding toward the ruin, his quarterstaff slanted across his body. Rasile was beside him.

LEAVES BRUSHED SHARINA'S cheek. She sat upright and flailed mentally for an instant, trying to remember where she was.

She'd been sleeping on the bench in the roof arbor, a soldier's cloak rolled under her head for a pillow. It was near dawn; the eastern stars had faded, though the sun was still below the horizon. The grape leaf had tickled her because—

"Hey, what's that!" a Blood Eagle said.

"Belt up, bonehead!" said Trooper Lires. "That's the princess's pet rat, don't you see?"

Burne, squatting on a wrist-thick vine on the back of trellis, lowered the scorpion he'd just trimmed to harmlessness. "I prefer to think of myself as her colleague," he said, then finished his meal with two more clicking bites. He disposed of the remains over the porch railing.

"Was it about to sting me?" Sharina said. She kept her voice calm, but that was an effort of will. She recalled the chitinous mass writhing on Platt.

Burne squirmed onto her side of the trellis. Sharina's slender hand wouldn't have fit through the diamond-shaped openings, but the rat had no difficulty.

"Oh, no," he said. "He was listening, spying. They all

were. There were three of them when I came back, so I disposed of them before I told you what I'd learned."

The guards were watching in all directions, including the pair at opposite ends of the trellis. They hadn't noticed the—three, apparently—scorpions creeping along the brickwork, but Sharina didn't imagine any human being would have. Except for the Blood Eagles, no one else was present.

Sharina had taken off the Pewle knife when she stretched out to sleep. Now she stood and wrapped the belt around her waist again. She still wore her sleeping tunic as an undergarment, but Diora had brought up a pair of sandals and an outer tunic.

"Tell me," she said quietly.

"The cult's headquarters is the Temple of the Lady of the Grove," Burne said. He sounded quite pleased with himself. "Clever, weren't they? All the priests used to worship the Shepherd, but the leaders are in the oldest temple of the Lady here in Pandah."

"Oh, they're clever," Sharina said grimly. She fitted the tongue of the sealskin belt through its loop. "But thanks to you, Master Burne, not clever enough."

"If you send troops quickly, you may catch them inside," the rat said. "But every scorpion is a spy, and they share each others' minds."

"I'm not *sending* anybody," Sharina said. "Captain Ascor, a company of Ornifal infantry was with us on last night's raid. Where are they billeted?"

"Right here in the palace, Your Highness," Ascor said. "What with the riots, Lord Tadai thought there ought to be more than just the usual guards on duty here. I think, ah . . . it might've been the regiment's camp marshals who suggested that to him."

"Yes," said Sharina. "I rather think it may have been also. Well, Captain, let's go find Prester and Pont. They already know the route."

Prester and Pont often said that they'd become old

soldiers by not taking chances, but they weren't men who'd hide if it looked like there was a prospect of action. The fact they'd chosen to be on duty here meant either that they'd thought somebody was likely to attack the palace, or that they'd expected something like what was happening. They'd seen the princess Sharina use her big knife, and they probably figured that she'd use it again given half a chance.

They were right about that.

Three aides stood at attention outside the first landing. The sound of voices on the roof had brought them to alertness, but the courier hadn't buckled the lid of his sabertache; a dice cup poked out of it.

To him Sharina called as she went past, "Tell Lord Tadai I'm going out with the ready company!"

That was as much information as she was willing to give openly. She doubted it would be of much value to Tadai, but at least she would have something to point to when the city prefect complained bitterly that she'd disappeared without warning. The notion that a princess could do anything she pleased was only true for epic characters who didn't live in a real human society.

"No, left!" Lires shouted from the back of the guard detachment as the leading squad turned right at the ground floor hallway. "They're in the west garden!"

The little entourage changed direction with a degree of stamping and confusion. Sharina herself was in the lead for a moment before Ascor ran to the front, snarling a litany of curses.

Burne rode on Sharina's left shoulder with a tumbler's grace; he laughed, but she thought as much from excitement as for the humor of it. This was exhilarating, especially coming after the formless threat of riots.

The loud scramble provided a useful warning to the Ornifal company. "Stand to!" bellowed a voice through the shuttered windows lining the hallway. Sharina was sure it was Pont speaking.

The door at the end of the hall slammed open before the leading guard reached it. Prester looked down the hallway with a lantern held high, then stepped back out of the way.

"It's the princess, boys!" he shouted to his men. "By the Lady, if you're not on your toes, you better hope you're killed! I'll ride you harder than the Sister will if you screw up now!"

The troops were shouldering their shields, donning their helmets, and falling into ranks. They were already wearing body armor; they'd been ready to react at a moment's notice, which was just what was happening now. . . .

"Marshal Prester," Sharina said. The squat veteran carried a good deal of fat, but he carried it over more muscle than most men could claim. "We're heading for the graveyard where we caught the priest last evening. We'll be following the same route as we did then."

"Things being as they are tonight, Princess . . . ," Prester said. He gave Burne, still perched on her shoulder, a funny look but didn't say anything about him. "We'd likely get there faster going widdershins along the new Boundary Road."

"We're going straight through town," said Sharina, not raising her voice but holding the veteran with her eyes.

"Right you are, Princess," said Prester. He turned to the company, some sixty men drawn up in four ranks.

"Your Highness, I don't think you understand," said an eighteen-year-old ensign. He was a hereditary nobleman who reasonably expected in five or six years to command a regiment. "There've been widespread riots tonight, and the route through the city center may be—"

Pont lifted the ensign's helmet off. The boy jerked his head around and shrieked, "What are you playing at, you fool?"

Prester slapped the back of the ensign's skull with

fingers hard enough to drive tent stakes. The boy yelped and staggered forward.

Pont caught him and said, "Listen, you puppy! The next time you want to talk to the princess, you wait till she asks you!"

He dropped the helmet back on the ensign's head. Prester turned him around and bellowed in turn, "And then you ask us, so we can tell you if she really wants you do open your mouth—which I doubt she does."

"Face left . . . ," Pont said, rattling the palace windows. "Face!"

The company crashed around to the left. "Forward . . . *march*!"

Sharina had seen troops in motion many times now. It thrilled and amazed her every time. She always compared them in her mind to a herd of sheep, since nothing in her life while growing up involved so many human beings doing any single thing.

Sheep were never so organized. Not even bees or ants were organized, compared to what soldiers did daily by rote.

"Double time, *march*!"

Hobnails sparking, spears rocking back and forth at a slant, the troops jogged along the stone street toward the center of the city. The ensign, his helmet straightened again, was at the head of the company, but the two marshals were with Sharina and her section of Blood Eagles in the rear.

She made a platform of her left arm and said, "Burne, hop down."

"I can see better up here," the rat said.

"Yes, but I can't!" Sharina said. She was blind on her left side with the rat perched where he was. Grumbling, Burne dropped onto her arm.

Sharina moved up between the veterans. "Marshals?" she said, hoping she was speaking just loud enough to be heard over the clash of hobnails. "You remember the

Temple of the Lady of the Grove that we'll pass in six blocks?"

"The big one where the two-copper girls hang out after dark, that one?" Prester said.

"I don't know about the girls—" Sharina said, smiling.

"Of course she don't!" Pont growled. "Prester, don't you have nothing but bone between your ears?"

"But the big temple, yes," Sharina resumed, trying to take charge of the discussion again. "We're really going to raid it instead of going back to the graveyard, but I don't want them to have any warning. It's important that none of the people inside get away."

"Shouldn't be a problem," Pont said. "You want prisoners?"

"Some, if you can," Sharina said. The rhythm of her feet punctuated her muttered words.

"Guess we can manage some," Prester said cheerfully.

"Prester?" Sharina said. She scowled at the thought. "Pont? I don't know what we're going to find in the temple."

Pont chuckled. "Princess, we're soldiers," he said. "We never know what we're going to find. Except that there's bloody few *good* surprises in this life."

"I guess . . . ," said the other veteran. He and his friend both carried javelins tonight in place of their batons of office. He eyed his point and went on, "That it's not going to be a good surprise for the folks in the temple neither."

Chapter

14

ILNA WAITED WITH her palms closed before her, holding a neatly folded pattern between them. She hadn't woven the yarn for Princess Perrine's arrival: her fingers had woven it because she had time and the situation might become unpleasant.

Ilna found most situations more or less unpleasant. The only time she was regularly content was when she stood at her loom with no concerns but the work before her. Even before her trip to the Underworld she'd been able to create wonderful pieces, pieces that she could look on with pride.

But instead of doing that, she was in a grove on northern Blaise, looking for a man she'd never met to help a man she didn't particularly like. Well, be fair: she didn't particularly like most people, men or women both. And though this was uncomfortable, she was usually uncomfortable.

Ilna os-Kenset liked to make things work. She was so skilled a weaver that even a complex fabric didn't really stretch her talents. Making people fit together properly was much more of a challenge—

She gave Ingens a cold smile that made him stiffen.

—and one where she was by no means sure of her success.

A pair of apes wearing peaked caps and red vests walked through the dogwoods on their hind legs, lifting the lower branches out of the way for those following. Even upright they were shorter than a man—shorter than her, as a matter of fact—but their shoulders were broad. Ilna knew from experience that the apes' muscles were more like wire ropes than they were to the flesh of humans.

The apes looked as dull as field hands in the middle of the harvest. Not harmless, exactly: in Barca's Hamlet there'd been brutal fights in the evenings every fall, some of them ending in cracked skulls or fatal stabbings by the knives all peasants carried. Well, the apes weren't drunk at the moment.

A youth and girl of twenty or so—they looked younger, but Ilna suspected their delicate features were fooling her—followed the leading apes. There were as alike as twins. Another pair of apes shambled behind them on all fours.

"That's the princess Perrine," Ingens whispered hoarsely. "I don't know who the man is."

"I'm Ilna os-Kenset," Ilna said. "I'm here to return Master Hervir or-Halgran to his family in Pandah. Will you bring him to me, please."

No one listening to her tone of voice could've mistaken the final sentence for a question.

"Mistress Ilna!" said the youth in apparent delight. The leading apes stopped and dropped forward onto the knuckles of their hands; he strode past them with his arms out and his hands spread. "I'm Prince Perrin and this is my sister Perrine. We're *so* glad to meet you!"

"And Master Ingens," said the girl, mincing toward the secretary with quick little steps. She too extended her hands, but her arms weren't spread so wide. "I was so afraid I'd never see you again. Oh, it's wonderful that you've returned, Ingens."

Brother and sister wore matching shirts with puffed sleeves, red vests like the apes' outfits, and baggy pantaloons. Their scarlet slippers had up-curling toes; there were little silver bells on Perrine's, the only difference in their garb.

"Master Perrin!" Ilna said, raising her hands slightly; she didn't open them yet. "Please don't come closer!"

The youth halted as abruptly as if she'd pointed a pitchfork at his eyes. Either her tone had drawn him up, or more likely he at least suspected what the pattern between her palms would do to him if she displayed it.

"Please, mistress," the girl said, dropping onto one knee and tenting her hands toward Ilna before rising again. "We didn't mean to offend you. We were just delighted to have visitors so pleasant as yourself and Master Ingens."

"Princess, we're here to find Hervir," Ingens said. "He didn't return after he went off with you."

"Why, of course he returned," Perrin said in apparent surprise. "We offered him refreshment and showed him the crocus fields, but he went back to the waking world by midafternoon."

"He was supposed to visit us again before nightfall," said Perrine. "To have dinner with us and our father."

"And to close the deal," said the prince. "He said he'd bring the money when he came back."

"Though . . . ," said Perrine, turning her face away but looking sidelong at the secretary. "I shouldn't say this, but . . . I was hoping that he might send you instead, Master Ingens. There was something about you that, well . . . I'm embarrassed to say what I thought. What I'm thinking."

"Hervir didn't come back," Ilna said. "Fetch him to us now."

Part of her mind wondered what she'd do if the couple simply walked through the brush the way they'd come and vanished; she very much doubted that their plantation was on the other side of a band of dogwoods and aspens. But the fact they'd come in the first place showed that they wanted *something* from her and Ingens.

"But mistress," Perrin said, his face scrunched with

worry. "We can't 'fetch,' as you say, someone who's already left us."

"Brother?" said Perrine, looking even more concerned. "You don't suppose . . . ?"

She looked from Ilna to Ingens and turned her palms up. "We offered to escort him to the waking world, Perrin and I," she said earnestly. "There are . . . well . . ."

"There *can be* dangers between the planes of the universes," said Perrin, "but not often. Still, we offered to guide Master Hervir."

"Hervir wouldn't hear of it," said Perrine. "Why, you know how headstrong he was, Master Ingens. He slapped his sword and said he didn't need a nursemaid."

"I think he was showing off for my sister," Perrin said sadly. "Master Ingens, I don't want to say anything against a friend of yours, but Hervir was clearly taken by Perrine. Understandably, of course, but he was distressed, distraught even, that she didn't reciprocate his affections."

"He was a nice enough boy," the princess said. "If I hadn't met him first at your side, Ingens, I might not have found him so hopelessly callow."

She touched the secretary's wrist, her face shyly turned to the side. Ilna glowered at her; Perrine jerked her hand away.

"Please, we're very sorry if anything's happened to Hervir," Perrin said. "I don't know how we can convince you that he was in rude good health when he left us. Perhaps if you'd care to visit the plantation yourselves . . . ?"

"Oh, please!" said the princess. She grasped Ingens' hands, only to drop them quickly under the lash of Ilna's eyes. "Our father would be so glad to meet you both!"

"Mistress Ilna," said Perrin. His hands lifted slightly, but he jerked them back to his sides before she could react. "I . . . it's painful to me that you doubt our good faith. If you would come with us, you could see that we're innocent farmers, unarmed—"

He gestured with both hands to the broad golden sash holding up his pantaloons. Neither sword nor dagger were thrust through its wraps.

"—protected only by our separation from the waking world."

Ilna glanced at the apes seated on the ground nearby. One was combing the fur of another for fleas; a third had found hickory nuts and was cracking them at the side of his massive jaws, then spitting out the debris. As best Ilna could tell, he wasn't swallowing the contents; ordinarily, any nut that the squirrels left was wormy. The last scratched both armpits simultaneously and hooted softly to herself.

"All right," she said. "We'd like to see your farm. Perhaps we'll find some clue to Hervir's disappearance."

Perrin and Perrine gabbled their pleasure. Again their hands lifted but were snatched back before they touched Ilna and Ingens. "Oh, Father will be *so* pleased!" the princess said.

"Yes, come this way," said Perrin. "It's quite simple, really, and perfectly safe."

"Come along, Ingens," Ilna said. The secretary looked less than enthusiastic until the delicate princess stood on tiptoe to whisper into his ear.

Ilna frowned but said nothing as she followed Perrin around the big oak. Usun was a solid weight in the rolled cloak, but he remained silent and as still as a sandbag. He was a hunter, all right.

So was Ilna, she supposed. She wasn't sure what her prey was this time, but she expected that she'd learn before long.

GARRIC WALKED INTO the temple, holding both fillets in his left hand. Behind him Tenoctris sat cross-legged on the ground, chanting into a circle she'd outlined in finely divided metal—silver, he thought, but he hadn't asked. The amber athame rose and fell as she spoke the words of power.

King Carus was poised in Garric's mind, keyed to the edge of berserk violence. Carus had never been comfortable with wizardry, and being drowned in a wizard-raised maelstrom hadn't made him like it better. He knew that Tenoctris was a friend and he accepted that what she was doing was necessary—

But he still didn't like it.

It bothered Garric that Tenoctris used an athame now. She'd always done her incantations with slivers of bamboo which she discarded after using only once. She'd said that because athames and wands collected power with each further spell, they were likely to muddle the work of all but the greatest wizards.

By risking her life and soul, Tenoctris had become one of the most powerful wizards of all time. Her bobbing athame reminded Garric both of the danger she'd undergone and of the danger to mankind which had driven her to take that risk.

His boots tapped on the marble floor. The stone was highly polished, which meant it didn't get much use—if any. Marble is soft.

The golden nymphs watched Garric from just outside the entrance, standing beside the plinths on which they'd been set as caryatids. Were they real women who'd been turned to metal, or were they metal brought to life?

But that didn't matter.

Garric looked down at the massive skeleton. The bones were completely disarticulated; not even shreds of cartilage bound the joints together. How long had Munn lain here?

But that didn't matter either.

Rather than simply lift the bone of the upper arm, Garric worked one of the fillets over the fingers and wrist, then up the forearm. Only then did he slide the silver band onto what would've been the biceps of a living man.

Tenoctris had told him what to say, but she hadn't suggested how he should place the fillets. This just had seemed right to him when he faced the task. When he faced the bones of the ancient hero.

He walked around the foot of the catafalque, holding the remaining fillet. He thought he heard the bones rattle. Perhaps there'd been an earth shock, perhaps it was just his imagination. The light which curled through the solid panel was disturbing as well as deceptive.

Garric had thought that he'd be more comfortable facing away from the rainbow flood so it couldn't trick him with what he *almost* saw in its light. Having it behind him was actually worse. Carus' instincts kept trying to spin him around with the sword ready, certain that something hostile was poised to leap.

"There is, *lad!"* the ghost said. *"There's something and it's an enemy!"*

That may be, thought Garric. *But my job is to put these arm rings on the skeleton, and I can only do that with my back to the light. I will do my job.*

King Carus laughed. *"Death isn't so bad,"* he said as Garric worked the fillet up Munn's left arm as he had the right. *"Maybe running away because you're afraid to die wouldn't be too bad either, but people like you and me are never going to know that. Sorry, lad."*

With the second fillet in place, Garric returned to the entrance. He stood just inside, where he could see both Munn and the panel of light without blocking the wizard's view. She continued to chant, shifting now onto a rising note. The nymphs looked back at him with cold, sad eyes.

"Eulamo!" Tenoctris shrieked in a near falsetto. Instead of thrusting her athame into the ground as Garric

had expected, she turned the point straight up. A blast of scarlet wizardlight suffused the interior of the temple, glowing in and through the walls.

Garric stepped back reflexively, bumping the doorpost. He blinked, though he knew it wasn't his physical eyes that the flash had dazzled.

Lord Munn rose from the bier, hefting his great iron sword. He wore a simple garment of green wool with a black zigzag along the hems. A carved wooden pin over the left shoulder closed it, leaving his right shoulder bare.

The marble catafalque shivered into dust motes, dancing and settling in the illumination of the wall panel. Munn raised the sword high and boomed out laughter. His hair and beard were black and full and curling.

He lowered the sword and let his eyes rest on Garric. "So . . . ," he said in a voice that rasped like thunder. "You, boy? Are you the one who called me from the sleep that I have earned?"

He was a giant, easily seven feet tall; the crude sword was in scale with him.

Garric laughed in turn. It wasn't an act: Carus was in his element here. They wouldn't have needed Tenoctris' coaching to know how to handle *this*.

"Lord Munn," said Garric, standing arms akimbo. "When you speak to me, remember not only that you speak to a king, but that you speak to *your* king. I am Garric, prince and ruler of this world. I have called you to do your duty."

"And what is my duty, then?" Munn said. There was nothing pacific in his tone, but he lowered the sword and rested its rounded tip on the floor in front of him. Even for him, it was a two-handed weapon.

"When you speak to your king, milord," Garric said, "do so with proper courtesy!"

Munn bowed over his sword, then rose to meet Garric's

eyes again. "What do you say my duty is, Your Majesty?" he said.

In Garric's court and when he addressed the citizens of the kingdom he ruled, he kept the fiction that the king was still Valence III, who lived in a dream of the past in his quarters in Valles. Here, though, he accepted the honorific "Your Majesty" due a reigning monarch.

"Milord," Garric said. "The Gate of Ivory is open. The sleep of the dead is being disturbed to aid the forces of Evil against the Good. Close the gate."

The big man's laughter boomed. "What do *I* know of good and evil?" he said.

"You know your duty, do you not, Lord Munn?" Garric said. He didn't try to out shout the giant, but no one could doubt either the power of his voice or the authority in it.

"Yes, Your Majesty," Munn said. "My worst enemies have never denied *that*."

He smiled, an expression that Garric had seen often on the more chiseled features of the ghost in his mind. It had no humor, but there was a fierce, unquenchable joy.

Lord Munn raised his sword to a slant across his chest, his right hand leading. Turning, he strode toward the flood of light. His bare feet whipped swirls from the exiguous remains of what had been a block of marble.

Tenoctris was chanting again. Garric wasn't sure she'd ever stopped: he'd been so focused on Lord Munn that anything less threatening—

"I've seen bloody *few things that were more threatening than that fellow,"* Carus said.

—might have gone on without his notice.

Munn halted, his massive body silhouetted against the radiance, and shrugged to loosen his muscles. He hunched slightly. Then to both Garric's surprise and his ancestor's, Munn strode forward and vanished in the blaze of light.

Garric opened his mouth to call, but closed it in silence.

Shouting at a rainbow-lighted slab of marble seemed pointless even in his present state of surprise. He turned to speak to Tenoctris. She sat as she'd done from the start, chanting in the soft rhythm of a lullaby. He shouldn't—and probably couldn't—disturb her.

I could ask the nymphs.

"Watch the place he went through the wall," said Carus harshly. *"It may not be him that comes out. And it wouldn't hurt to have your sword ready."*

Garric grinned wryly. He left his sword in the sheath, knowing how swiftly his ancestor's reflexes could clear it if need arose, but Carus was right that they weren't here to ask questions.

There was a change. At first Garric thought that it was his imagination or an overload on his eyes, but the stream of light through the wall really was growing fainter. He risked a glance back at Tenoctris. Her eyelids slumped and her body swayed, but she continued to chant softly.

Lord Munn stepped out of the wall. He too swayed. Without thinking, Garric strode to the big man's side and steadied him, a hand on his left elbow and a hand on his right hip. The play of sinews and muscles beneath Munn's skin was more like that of a horse's body than a man's.

The light stopped, leaving only its memory and darkness. The wizard's incantation ceased as well.

"Have I done my duty, Your Majesty?" Munn said in a voice of rusty thunder.

"Yes, milord," Garric's lips said, but it was the king in his mind who was speaking. "The ones who send our sort know that we'll always do our duty, don't they?"

Lord Munn laughed. "Help me outside, Your Majesty," he said. "It's been a long time."

He laughed again. "It's been ages, hasn't it?"

They shuffled through the doorway. Garric was supporting much of the big man's weight, but Munn still carried his sword. It had come back with a violet sparkle on both edges, but that faded by the time they were out of the temple.

Tenoctris got carefully to her feet. Normally Garric would've been helping her, but his present duty was to Lord Munn.

"I'll sit here," Munn said. Garric squatted, continuing to take more than his own weight on his shoulders. The big man bent with a caution that was painful to watch.

"Milord?" Garric said. "What can I get you?"

"You can return me to my rest, Your Majesty," Munn whispered. He leaned back, at first on his elbows, then lowering his back to the turf. He sighed and closed his eyes.

He said, "Take off the armlets. You have to do it yourself—I can't."

"Yes, milord," Garric said. He was whispering too. He carefully worked off one silver band; Munn took that hand from his sword hilt, then gripped the weapon again when his arm was bare.

"Give the armlets back to the girls, though, Your Majesty," Munn said. His voice was scarcely audible. "Because you may need me again. I will do my duty if you call me."

Garric pulled the second fillet clear; the muscular body fell again into a rack of bones. Garric rose to his feet.

"Of course, milord," he said softly. "Your worst enemies could never doubt that."

Garric held out the fillets to the nymphs. They giggled and traded the bands; he'd offered each the wrong one. They whispered among themselves, but Garric turned his back on them: he only wanted to get out of this place.

"Tenoctris?" he said. "Are you ready to go?"

"Yes, Garric," she said. "Though you may have to help me."

"Yes," said Garric, putting his arm around the wizard's waist and letting her grip his shoulder. "That's my duty, after all."

Together they walked through the woodland to where the boat would be waiting to return them to the waking world.

UP CLOSE, CASHEL saw he was looking at more of a palace than a castle, though just the same it was built to make it hard for anybody to break in. The windows on the ground floor and the one above were too narrow for anything bigger than a cat to squirm through.

Those on the top floor used to be barred with thumb-thick iron. Now several grills sagged in the moonlight, meaning the hinges had rusted through. Cashel didn't have to worry about climbing up there and wrenching an entrance, because the front door was ajar. The edge stood a hand's breadth out from the jamb, and blue light flickered through the crack.

He grinned. It'd been a stout door when it was new, but age and lack of care had been hard on it too. There were statues in niches to either side of the doorway, slender stone demon-looking figures with pointy faces and nasty smiles. One was male, the other female; and while Cashel didn't think much of them as art, either one would make a fine battering ram for a man strong enough to lift it off its base and slam it through the swollen wood and corroded iron straps.

Cashel guessed he was that strong.

He glanced down at Rasile. "Ma'am, are you ready?" he said. He noticed the Corl's nose was wrinkling, so he added, "Do you smell anything?"

"Besides the brimstone, you mean, warrior?" Rasile said. "Not to notice. Apes have been here, but your little friend had told us that."

"Right," said Cashel. Instead of putting a hand to the

door, he worked the end of his staff between the panel and the stone doorpost, then pulled it fully open. There was a short alcove, just wide enough for a doorman to stand. Nobody was there, and the inner door was already swung back into the vestibule beyond.

Cashel walked in, his staff slanted and ready to strike in any direction. The wall facing the vestibule had a doorway to both the right and left; the blue light was coming through those openings.

Between the openings was a solid wall painted to look like a view into a garden. The plants looked like they'd been shaped from human bodies, and instead of birds flitting among them, there were lizards with a lot of teeth walking on their hind legs.

On low pillars were marble busts of a man and a woman, facing each other instead of looking toward visitors coming through the doorway. They'd been handsome people, both of them, but they had nasty expressions.

"Ready, ma'am?" Cashel said, glancing toward his companion. Rasile held her athame in a fashion that reminded him that it really *was* a knife even though it'd been carved from black stone.

She nodded curtly. Cashel strode through the right-hand door into the circular room beyond. The floor was onyx. There were several closed doors off it, framed in colored marbles. The walls were otherwise plain, and there wasn't any furniture.

A woman's head was set into the center of the floor. Flames as blue as sulfur blazed from her nostrils as she breathed; that was what the light came from. She'd been the model for the marble face in the vestibule.

Another statue. It only seemed to breathe.

"Have you come to help me?" the head demanded, spurting blue fire with each syllable. "Help me and I will help you . . . but you *must* help me."

"We were told Milady had taken our friend Liane," Cashel said. "We're here to bring Liane back."

Milady laughed like glass breaking. "I'll let your Liane go when I'm ready to, hero!" she said. "The woman came to me, and she'll stay with me till you've done my bidding. Help me and I will help you!"

Cashel looked at the head, just looked at it and thought. Rasile was standing back a little from him, but he didn't say anything to her till he figured things out for himself.

"Don't think you can strike me!" Milady said. From the way her voice went up in pitch, *she* thought he could do that and also thought he might try. "It wouldn't help you anyway! My servants will hurl her from the top of the tower if anything happens to me."

Every time Milady's mouth opened, another gout of flame licked out and the sharpness of brimstone got thicker. It might have been a mercy to dish in her skull with the quarterstaff, but Cashel wasn't going to do that to a woman without better reason than she'd given him so far.

Then again, he wasn't sure that smashing Milady's head would kill her. More was going on here than ordinary life and death.

"Ma'am?" Cashel said. "What is it that you want me to do for you? If I can, I'll do it. But you have to let Liane go."

Milady spat half of a coin onto the floor; it chimed cheerfully on the polished stone squares. Breaking a coin in two was a common way to seal a pledge in Barca's Hamlet, but Cashel had always seen bronze used when it was done there; this coin was silver.

"The matching half is through the door to your right," Milady said, turning her head and nodding. "Bring it to me and I will release your Liane."

Cashel picked up the coin. It was so hot that despite his calluses, he bounced it a few times in his palm. It had a man's head on one side and a pillar with two wings sticking out of it—they looked like wings, anyhow—on the other. He didn't say anything for the moment, but he tucked the pledge into a fold of his sash. As a boy he'd have carried something as valuable as this in his mouth, but—

He grinned.

—he'd seen a lot more silver now than even a rich man would in the borough. Besides, even if he cared about money, he didn't think he'd put *this* coin in his mouth.

This door and the one across from it had white panels set out with gilt borders, the sort of fancy thing you'd expect in a place like this. It hadn't weathered at all, though, despite the door standing ajar and the house on the edge of falling down.

Cashel pulled it open. The room on the other side looked pretty much like this one, though it was a rectangle instead of round and the floor was a pattern of brown and tan tiles instead of squares of black stone. There was a little marble shelf sticking out of the far wall, supported by scrollwork. The glitter on it was likely the rest of the coin in his sash.

Cashel looked back at the head; it had turned to watch him. "All right, ma'am," he said. "I'll do my best to fetch you the pledge, but you have to let Liane go now. She can stay with Rasile till I come back."

"You'll get your friend when you bring me the coin!" Milady said. She had a voice like an angry squirrel. "Go on, hero! Get the coin!"

"No, ma'am," Cashel said. He turned and spread his feet out to the width of his shoulders. Rasile was watching from just inside the doorway from the vestibule. She'd laid her yarrow stalks but she wasn't using them for anything just now.

Her tongue wagged in a laugh. The Coerli sense of humor was a good fit for this sort of business.

"Ma'am," Cashel said to the head, "you'll bring Liane back now or I'll look for another way to get her free."

"There is no other way!" said Milady, even more of a squirrel.

"Maybe, maybe not," said Cashel. "But you won't be around to learn which of us was right. Now, bring Liane down to us, please."

"Are you threatening *me*?" Milady shrieked, her face a mass of anger.

"No, ma'am," Cashel said. "I'm telling you to hand Liane over to Rasile here and then I'll go fetch your pledge."

"Doomed one?" Rasile said. "You picked this warrior because of his strength. You will underestimate that strength at your peril."

"Bring the woman here!" Milady said. She spoke in the same voice she'd done before, no louder, but Cashel wasn't surprised when the door on the other side of the circular room opened.

An ape shambled in on its hind legs. It reached one long arm behind it to hold Liane's wrist. She walked as straight as she could, but the second ape behind had the other wrist and they weren't in step with each other.

Cashel's face went very quiet. He'd swipe the head in the floor as he brought the staff around, then take two strides and with the second ram a butt cap into the—

"Let her go!" Milady said.

Her voice wasn't any more pleasant than it had been, but at least she was saying the right thing. The apes obeyed quick as quick, dropping down onto their knuckles.

Liane darted around the beast in front of her and started toward Cashel. She'd lost the other sandal too, or more likely kicked it off because she could move better barefoot than half shod.

"No ma'am!" Cashel said. She stopped: he hadn't meant to shout like that.

"Ah, Liane," he said. "I've got business to tend to in the next room. Stay with Rasile, please, and I'll be back just as soon as I can."

Cashel walked to the door to where the pledge piece

was waiting. He skirted the head without looking down at it.

It wasn't right that Milady take Liane hostage to make him do this, but Cashel was a peasant. Talking about what's fair isn't going to put food in your belly during the Hungry Time in March. This was something he could do that got Liane free, so he was doing it.

There wasn't anything about the room beyond that looked funny, but if it was as easy as it seemed, Milady would've sent her apes to fetch the coin. Cashel poked his quarterstaff through the doorway and tapped the floor. It clacked duller than it would on stone, showing it really was pottery like it seemed.

But it also popped a bright blue spark every time the iron touched. There was wizardry involved, which wasn't much of a surprise.

Cashel smiled, sort of, the way he generally did before a fight. He wasn't one to start trouble, but nobody'd seen him run away from it yet.

Sideways with his left hand leading on the slanted staff, he strode through the doorway. All his hairs stood up.

The room was gone. Cashel stood on a narrow crystal bridge over a chasm of blue flames. In the depths beneath him stood the tiny figure of Milady, bathed in unquenchable fire. She laughed like a madwoman.

A man with the face of the other bust in the vestibule was coming across the bridge toward Cashel. He held a long crystal wand in either hand and chanted words of power.

FIRST SECTION WITH me!" bawled Prester, who'd trotted to the front as the company approached a plaza where five streets met. He slanted the leading troops to the right rather than following the boulevard they'd been jogging down thus far.

A group of men—mostly men—were sitting and drink-

ing on the display windows of shops they'd wrenched the
shutters from. When the troops appeared, most of the
looters either ran up the street or vanished into the gut-
ted shops in hope of hiding among the debris. The ex-
ceptions were two men lying on their backs with their
arms linked, singing, *"She was poor but she was honest. . . ."*

Sharina kept close behind Pont, jogging to the side of
the second section. As his portion of the company started
around the plaza he shouted, "Guide left, Selinus, Sister
take you! Come on, Second Section, don't embarrass me
in front of the princess!"

The stone curb of the fountain in the middle of the plaza
was crude, but the centerpiece was a delicate bronze
statue of a nymph pointing one hand to heaven and the
other toward the basin at her feet. She'd originally been
gilded; swashes of gold remained as highlights in the
folds of her tunic. The pirate chiefs of Pandah had looted
the lovely nymph, but brute force didn't give them the
skill to place her in a worthy setting.

"Are they going to get lost?" asked Burne, leaning
forward in the cradle of Sharina's arm. She wondered
if the rat was worried or if he was just keyed up with
excitement like her. Like all of them, she suspected,
though the two camp marshals certainly didn't give any
sign of it.

"Naw, not Prester," Pont said, dropping back slightly
to return titular command to the ensign who'd stayed
with this section. "Me, now, I'm no good in cities and
neither's Selinus, the file closer, but—"

He gestured with his javelin. "Abreci there in the first
file, he's from Valles and he never gets lost in a city, not
even in a back alley when he's blind drunk."

"There shouldn't be a problem for us since this street
takes us right past the temple," Sharina said. "But Prester trying to arrive from behind."

Pont chuckled. "Don't you worry about Prester," he

said. "And if anything should happen, well, I figure me and the boys can handle whatever a passel of priests throw at us."

Sharina started to object, then shut her mouth again. That was the right attitude. They had a plan, a good plan: to divide their force and surround the temple before those inside were aware of the troops' presence. If it went wrong, and even good plans did sometimes go wrong, they'd carry on with the force available.

And yes, thirty soldiers trained by Prester and Pont ought to be able to handle as many priests as you could cram into a temple, even a big temple like that of the Lady of the Grove.

As the troops jogged, they held their shields out from their bodies. Simply hanging by their straps, the cylinder sections of laminated wood would have battered the men bloody by the time they'd gone a mile. Each soldier's slanted javelin pumped back and forth, and the studs on their leather aprons jangled together with each stride of their hobnailed boots.

The section clashed into Convocation Square. The court building, a basilica whose eaves were decorated with painted terracotta dragons, was to the right. The walled compound that'd been the slave lines—slaves were most of the loot which pirates captured—was to the left; the contents had been sold weekly at auction in the square. Now it had been converted into barracks for the laborers engaged in Pandah's expanding building trade.

Directly across the plaza—it wasn't a square or even four-sided—was the Temple of the Lady of the Grove, now without a tree in sight. The sanctum was a narrow building surrounded by a pillared porch. There were six sharp-fluted pillars across the front and the shadows of six more just behind them.

"All right, troopers!" Pont roared, lengthening his stride to put himself ahead of the front rank where the whole section could see him. "Follow me! Prisoners if you can get them, but nobody escapes!"

"Yee-*ha*!" somebody called in the near distance. Prester's section appeared from a side street behind the building. They rushed toward it with their javelins lifted. The troops were in shadow, but their boots kicked sparks from the cobblestones.

A door thudded shut beyond the rows of pillars. Sharina drew her knife. She had to be careful not to sprint out ahead of the soldiers as they spread into a skirmish line. Even against priests, she ought to leave the fighting to the men in armor if she possibly could.

Pont's right arm came forward in a smooth, swift motion, loosing his javelin at the peak of the arc. *Why's he throwing at a building?* Sharina wondered.

A man wearing a priest's black robe—but without the usual white sash—lurched from the shadows between the pillars. He'd flung away his bow when the javelin transfixed his upper chest; his quiver spilled arrows as he sprawled down the three-step base.

"For the princess!" Pont cried, drawing his sword.

At the back end of the temple, Prester was shouting, "Come on troopers, show the princess what you're made of!"

The dead archer had been the only man outside the sanctum. The leading soldiers jumped over his body and bashed their shield bosses at the closed door, making peevish thuds. Several men dropped their javelins to draw their swords, but instead of hacking at the wood, Pont sheathed his blade.

"Selinus, with me!" he said, unstrapping his shield so that he could hold it by the edge. "The rest of you scuts keep back!"

Sharina watched in puzzlement as the two non-coms faced one another, turning the shield endwise and gripping what had been the top edge. "On three," Pont said.

They leaned back together, one leg forward against the lintel and the other well back to brace them. "One, two, *three*—"

Together the men used used the whole strength of their upper bodies to slam the shield into the right-hand door valve, just inside the edge where a stiffener would be. The panel was massive but centuries old; the curved shield was of triple-ply birch, inches thick and bound with gilding metal. It smashed a hole a hand's breadth deep where it struck the door.

Instead of rearing back to batter the door again, Pont dropped the shield and thrust his sword through the split in the panel.

Sharina frowned, at a loss as to what the veteran thought he was doing. Pont gripped the sword hilt with both hands and jerked upward, lifting the crossbar from its track before the priests inside understood what was happening.

"Hit it, boys!" he shouted. Six soldiers threw their shoulders against the valves, shoving them inward.

There was a brief struggle in the doorway. The priests had swords or iron-studded cudgels, but the troops' armor and superior training ended the fight before it began.

Sharina jumped the wrack of bodies as she followed the first squad into the anteroom. She thought there'd been four or five priests, but she couldn't be sure: the short, stiff infantry swords made terrible wounds when driven by excitement and strong arms.

She burst into the nave with the troops. The lanterns hanging from brackets on either side still burned, but predawn light, entering through the rose window in the pediment over the entrance, dimmed them. At the back was a pierced bronze screen which could be opened to display the tall statue of the Lady.

Sharina hadn't been in this temple before; she wondered whether the image would be an old one of painted wood or if that had been replaced by a gold and ivory masterpiece. How ready had the pirate chiefs been to spend their looted wealth on the Queen of Heaven?

There were half a dozen priests in the nave. Three with swords had been running toward the entrance when the soldiers appeared: javelins sent them sprawling on the mosaic floor without an order. Sharina already knew that Prester and Pont taught their men always to use missiles when that was an option: it wasn't as heroic as wading in hand-to-hand, but it did the job and saved the right kind of lives—your own and your buddies'.

The remaining priests were unarmed, an old man with wild white hair and two young aides. They halted when they saw the troops. The old man raised his hands in the air and cried, "Sacrilege! Sacrilege!"

"We want prisoners!" Sharina said as she sprinted toward them. Burne sprang from her bosom and hunched over the floor even faster than she did. The nave was easily a hundred feet long, and the soldiers' hobnailed boots skidded dangerously on the polished stone.

The priests started back toward the wicket in the bronze screen. Sharina closed on the old man. One of the aides threw himself at her. She swatted him across the forehead with the square back edge of the Pewle knife; the heavy steel rang, knocking the priest to the floor, stunned and bloodied.

The old man flung his arms out and pitched onto his face with a gabbling cry. Burne jumped clear of his legs.

The remaining priest ran through the wicket into the sanctum. Sharina was only a hand's breadth behind him.

The screen was perforated, but it shadowed the interior. For a moment Sharina couldn't identify the dark mass crouching where the image of the Lady should have been.

It started toward her. It was black and the size of an ox, and it was a scorpion.

Sharina retreated through the wicket. "Get back!" she screamed. "It's a scorpion! Get—"

The bronze screen ripped open. The scorpion, its huge pincers high, stepped over the ruin and into the nave. Its claws clacked on the mosaic floor.

ILNA WATCHED THE leading apes push in single file between two clumps of evening olive, then fade away. It was as though night had fallen and shadows had swallowed them. Perrin walked after them and also vanished; the stiff, upslanting olive stems closed behind the youth's body, but that body was no longer in the waking world.

Ilna made a sour face and followed. She hadn't known what to expect, and now that it was happening she wasn't any wiser. She ducked instead of spreading her arms to keep the olive from slapping her cheeks. She had to keep both hands on her pattern to be able to open it instantly.

Her skin prickled. She was behind Perrin again. The liveried apes led them down a track toward a sprawling mansion a furlong away at the base of the hills. For as far as she could see to either side, there were planting mounds between shallow irrigation ditches. On them grew crocuses in purple profusion, and occasional pistachio trees. Widely scattered among the rows were apes bending to pick the flowers and toss them into baskets.

Ilna stopped. She started to count the laborers, then realized it was a hopeless task. The whole broad valley was a single field. There were more tens of tens of apes visible than there were sheep in the borough where she'd grown up.

Perrine, Ingens, and the remaining pair of apes walked out of the air behind her. There was nothing to see where they appeared except the rows of plantings stretching into the misty distance.

The princess was leading Ingens by the hand. Ilna

wasn't sure he even noticed that they weren't in the world where the gong hung.

"You see, Mistress Ilna?" Prince Perrin said, turning with a welcoming smile. "We are at peace here in our valley, because we've withdrawn from your world. No one can threaten us, and we threaten no one."

"Except the flowers," said his sister with a pleasant giggle. She waved her free hand across the purple expanse. "But they grow back from the bulbs and we tend them, so I don't think they grudge us their pollen."

Ilna stepped two rows away and laid her rolled cloak in the ditch; it was dry at the moment, though when her feet disturbed the stony soil she noticed that the undersides of flat pebbles were wet. They must run the water at night.

The others walked past, putting Ilna's body between them and the cloak. She knelt and looked closely at a crocus to explain why she was delaying here.

Ilna had never been interested in flowers. Their bright colors didn't fade, which was impressive; but they couldn't be transferred to cloth either, and besides—she preferred earth tones and neutrals. People didn't appreciate how pleasing neutrals could be until they'd seen a garment Ilna'd woven solely from gray shades.

The crocus petals pleased her well enough, but the yellow and deep red pistils from which the spice came thread by tiny thread were garish and intrusive even by themselves. In combination with the purple flowers—

Ilna smiled—broadly, for her. Feydra, her aunt by marriage, would have found the yellow/red/purple combination attractive. There might be a more damning comment about the flower than that a fat, cloth-headed slattern would have liked it, but that would do.

"Aren't they lovely?" Prince Perrin said, kneeling across the mound from Ilna. He smiled. "I was just thinking how much you remind me of a crocus, mistress, with your grace and beauty."

Ilna looked at him without expression. She might have gotten angry at his attempts to make himself agreeable, but he was so remarkably clumsy at it that she was on the verge of laughing instead.

In a mild voice she said, "My colors are more muted, I believe."

She stood, fluffing her tunics slightly, and picked up the rolled cloak. As she'd expected, the bundle was lighter now. She didn't look back to call attention to Usun, though she doubted that even she could've found the little hunter if he'd had a few moments to conceal himself. "Shall we go?" she said.

"Of course," said Perrin. He seemed to have no expressions but a half-smile and a smile, though it seemed to her that a hint of fear underlay the jollity.

He offered his arm. "May I take your hand, mistress?" he said.

Ilna glowered. "Certainly not," she said, returning to the track by stepping from ditch to ditch in two long strides. Ingens and Perrine were in close conversation a few paces beyond. They broke apart as Ilna approached; the secretary with a look of embarrassment, the princess turning her face away.

"Our father will be so pleased to see you both!" Perrine said brightly as she and Ingens led the way toward the house. The sprawling mansion of stuccoed brick was probably no more than one story high, but a tall false front over the central section made it look more imposing. The pillars of the full-length colonnade were each of three twisted strands supporting arches, and the roofline had curlicues that suggested battlements but served no purpose but decoration.

Which meant no purpose at all, so far as Ilna was concerned. Well, her taste rarely jibed with that of other people.

More apes in livery were holding open the valves of the front door. They were of fruitwood, carved in a pattern of acanthus vines growing through a lattice. The design was a trifle florid for Ilna, but it had been well executed and she liked the shades within the russet wood.

The field hands hadn't looked up as the entourage passed. Ilna wondered what they—and the attendants—thought of the human beings they labored for. They seemed completely placid, but not even sheep were really spiritless if you knew them well.

Sheep generally had unpleasant personalities. Well, so did human beings, in Ilna's experience.

A middle-aged man with a worn face stepped onto the porch. He bore an obvious family resemblance to the twins.

"Father," Perrine called. "We're back with Master Ingens. You remember me telling you about him? Oh, I'm so happy!"

"And this is Mistress Ilna, Father," said the prince. "She's even more wonderful than I'd thought when we saw her through the glass."

The older man bowed, then rose with his hands extended; that seemed to be the fashion among these people. Ilna was uncomfortable with the idea of being embraced by strangers, though this time the distance made it symbolic.

"Ilna and Ingens, I'm King Perus," he said. "We're honored by your visit. I've had refreshments laid out, and I hope you'll be able to stay with us for a few days to see every part of our little kingdom."

"Oh, Father!" said the princess, leading Ingens up the two broad steps to the porch. "Wouldn't it be wonderful if they could stay with us always? That would be marvelous!"

"We've come to find Master Hervir and return with him," said Ilna harshly. "If you'll please bring him out, we won't trouble you further."

"But mistress . . . ," Perus said, turning his palms up

in apparent consternation. "Hervir was only with us for a few hours, and that was weeks ago."

"I thought if we brought Ilna to the valley," said Perrin, "and showed her everything, then she could be sure Hervir is no longer here."

"It's understandable," his sister added sadly. "Things are so terrible in the outer world that even decent people—"

"Wonderful people!" Perrin put in.

"—like Ingens and Mistress Ilna have to doubt the word of those they meet."

"Well, at the very least," said Perus, gesturing toward the open door with both hands, "do take refreshment with us. As I'm sure you've noticed, though one's mind perceives the journey from your world to ours as merely a blink of time, your body is aware that much greater effort was required."

"Thank you," said Ingens, bowing to Perus as he followed Perrine into the house. "I'm indeed hungry and thirsty. And very tired as well."

"Mistress?" said the prince. "Please, whatever you wish will be granted. But at least do us the courtesy of letting us try to demonstrate our valley's innocence."

Ilna grimaced again. She'd come to find out where Hervir was. *Buried under a pistachio tree* might well be the answer, but she had no evidence even of that as yet.

Further, she *was* hungry and thirsty. And tired. The sun was low over the western end of the valley, and her weariness was as great as if she'd been walking the whole time from morning when they entered the grove till the evening which was falling here.

"Yes, thank you," Ilna said, forcing herself to be polite. She was here by her own decision, not because the prince and his family had forced her. She mounted the steps and walked briskly into the building, again ignoring Perrin's offered arm.

A broad hallway pierced the middle of the house, drawing a breeze from the hills. The archways opening off the main hall were open also; the walls above were a filigree of fine masonry, joined by tiles with swirling designs in blue and white. The patterns weren't writing in any form Ilna had seen before, but she was sure they had meaning.

She smiled wryly. Everything had meaning. Everything was part of a pattern, if you were only wise enough to recognize it. She was better at that than most people were, but she didn't pretend that she was very good.

"We have wines and a light repast waiting in the arbor," said Perus, following them down the hall. His silk slippers whispered on the cool flooring, making no more sound than Ilna's bare soles did.

At least the floor was tile, not stone. Apes, all of them silent and wearing livery, waited or cleaned in some of the rooms she passed. Occasionally one happened to look in her direction, but even then they didn't appear to register the presence of a visitor.

The arbor was a frame of braided pillars and brick arches covering a grassy lawn. The broad leaves of the grape vines planted at the base of each pillar shaded the ground, but many tiny droplets of sunlight leaked through. When Ilna looked up, she could see the hills rising steeply only a stone's throw away.

In the center of the lawn was a low table. Instead of chairs, cushions had been laid along both sides and at the far end; apes waited behind each of the five places. Fruit and nutmeats waited on platters, and in a water-filled tub of brass and copper stood a tall earthenware jug.

Ilna looked more closely at the tub. Chips of ice floated in the water.

"We bring ice down from the peaks to make sherbets and cool our wines," said King Perus, noticing Ilna's surprise.

"Mistress Ilna?" said Perrin. He lifted the wine-thief,

a deep-bellied ladle with a long vertical handle, from the narrow throat of the jug. "Allow me to serve you myself."

He filled a goblet, then handed it to her with a bow. "Our finest vintage," he said, "for the most lovely woman ever to enter our valley."

Ilna frowned. Ingens was frowning also, she noticed, though no doubt—and the thought brought a hard smile back to her lips—for different reasons.

She sipped as Perrine showed the secretary how to recline alongside her on the cushions. The first touch of the wine seemed all right—too thick and too strong, but wine was normally diluted for drinking in those parts of the Isles where it was the usual beverage.

Ilna swallowed. Before she took a second sip she noticed the aftertaste of the first and grimaced. She put the goblet on the table and said, "I'm sorry, I don't have a taste for wines. Do you have ale? I'm not—"

What did she mean to say? *I'm not rich? I'm a poor orphan who drank stale beer most of the time but water often because she couldn't afford anything better.* Though nobody in Barca's Hamlet had drunk wine.

"Ale?" said Perus. "Why, no, we don't brew any kind of beer in the valley."

"Water, then," said Ilna. She was beginning to become irritated. She'd never have demanded something rare or expensive for her meals, but it ought to be possible to get something simple even in a palace.

"I'm so embarrassed, Mistress Ilna," Perrine said. She'd taken a filled goblet from an ape and was holding it for Ingens as he drank. "You see, the water here isn't safe. Our servants, I'm afraid, aren't very fastidious about their natural functions."

"We have other wines, Ilna," the prince said with a worried expression. "Perhaps you'd like a white?"

Now she *was* irritated. She took the goblet waiting at Perrin's place and scooped it full of melt water from the brass tub. "I trust *this* is safe?" she said, then drank deeply before her hosts managed a reply.

"Well, yes, if that's what you want, Ilna," the prince said after an exchange of silent looks with the rest of his family. "Whatever you like, of course."

"Thank you," Ilna said, refilling the goblet. "And if you don't mind, I'll sit instead of lying down. I've never learned to eat one-handed on my side, and I have no desire to make myself foolish in front of you."

"Of course, mistress," Perus said. He sounded gracious, but he had the look of a man who'd been kicked in the stomach. "Our only wish is for you to be comfortable here."

"And to convince you of our good intentions," Perrin said with his usual smile. "We'll do anything we can to achieve that."

As Ilna sat primly, Ingens said, "Well, I must say I like your wine very much, King Perus. I don't believe I've ever drunk a finer one."

He glared across the table at Ilna as an ape refilled his goblet. She ignored him and took a pear from the tray before her.

"Try this plum, Ilna," the prince said, plucking one from another tray. He took out a knife with a tiny gold blade and added, "Here, I'll peel it for you. I think you'll find it amazingly sweet."

"Thank you," Ilna said, making an effort to prevent the words from accurately reflecting her thoughts at the moment. Could they *not* leave her alone? "This pear is delicious."

Indeed, it was. So was the hard-boiled egg whose yolk had been ground with spices before being returned to the cup of its white. The ape serving her was silent and alert, bringing bowls of water to cleanse her fingers between courses. Rose petals floated in them.

The lace table covering and the napkins which followed the finger bowls were linen. Their quality was as good as anything Ilna had seen that she hadn't woven herself.

As for the food—food wasn't important to her, but craftsmanship was. The cooks in this valley were as skilled as the weavers. The base of all the dishes was mutton, rice, and lentils, but the spices turned what might have been simple fare into remarkable works of art.

The prince kept offering her dainties. Ilna kept refusing, as politely as one could be in the situation. Perrin was trying to use her courtesy as a way to bully her to his will, which of course made her more coldly certain in her refusals.

Ilna smiled. She was treating it as a game, she supposed. If she stopped feeling that it was a game, she'd snatch the pattern from her sleeve and display it. She hadn't picked out the knots.

Apes hung lanterns whose parchment screens had been dyed in attractive pastels. The sun had dropped below the rim of the mountains and the sky had faded enough for stars to appear. The constellations weren't familiar to her.

The servants brought pistachios, shelled and arranged in swirling patterns on their silver trays. As they carried them away after the guests had eaten, King Perus said, "I've had rooms prepared for you. It wouldn't be entirely safe to return to your own world after sunset, though of course you're welcome to do so if you prefer."

"Oh, I hope you'll stay," said Perrine, covering one of the secretary's hands with her own. "Oh, please stay, Ingens."

"Of course!" Ingens said. He'd drunk a fair amount. There was a challenge in his tone as he went on, "It's my duty to stay until we find Hervir. Isn't that true, Mistress Ilna?"

Ilna looked at him. This wasn't a game anymore, but that meant it was even more important that she not lose her temper.

"Yes, I suppose it is," she said evenly. "For tonight, at least."

"Then allow me to conduct you to your room, Ilna," said the prince as he hopped to his feet.

Ilna rose, ignoring the offered hand, as usual. "Yes," she said, "I'm ready to sleep."

The room she'd been given was off a cross hall, midway down the palace's right wing. Rugs and cushions were arranged for a bed; she'd certainly slept on worse.

Perrin, as expected, tried to delay her at the door. Also as expected, she dismissed him without difficulty.

The full moon shone through the row of windows just below the roofline. Ilna glanced at it, then used a tripod table to wedge the door. It wouldn't hold long, but it would awaken her.

She left a lamp burning. She'd sleep with a pattern bunched in her left fist. Any person who saw it would wish that they were being disemboweled with hooked irons, because *that* would eventually be over.

Ilna smiled grimly as she lay down. Of course, she could be completely wrong about the danger here.

And perhaps one day pigs would fly.

Chapter

15

℃OMORROW . . . ," SAID THE voice at Ilna's ear.

She jerked upright, raising her hands. Usun stood beside her pillow; she tucked the pattern into her sleeve.

". . . you won't be able to drink the melt water either," the little man said, grinning like a fiend from the

Underworld, "but I don't think we'll be here long enough for that to matter. Are you ready to go, mistress?"

"When I dress," said Ilna, getting up with an easy motion. From the position of the moon she couldn't have been asleep very long.

She'd slept in her inner tunic. She slipped the outer one over her head, then cinched the silken lasso around her waist. "Shall I take the cloak?"

"No," said Usun. "We'll be going down, so you'll want to bring the lamp. Another cave, I'm afraid, but you seem to do well in them for all your dislike."

Ilna sniffed. "I dislike most things," she said. "I certainly wouldn't find that an acceptable excuse for doing them badly."

"We'll go out through the door," said Usun, noticing her glance toward the missing lattice in the row of high windows. "I came in that way because I figured you'd have blocked it from this side. They didn't put guards in the halls, and they'll wait till the third watch, I'd judge, before they come for you."

"All right," said Ilna, lifting the table and setting it out of the way. She took the lamp from the terra-cotta ledge built into the wall.

"Ilna?" the little man said. "Is there any acceptable excuse for bad workmanship?"

She looked at him. "No," she said. "There isn't. Not to me."

Usun giggled. "That's what I thought," he said. "Brincisa was *such* a fool when she tried to make a pawn of you."

"Are you ready to go?" Ilna said flatly, her hand on the latch lever.

"Yes, mistress," Usun said. He giggled again. "We'll turn right and go almost to the end of the hallway."

He trotted past her as soon as she had the door open a crack. He wasn't tall enough to reach the latch even by jumping, though she didn't doubt that he could've gotten up there if he'd had to. He prowled along the right-hand side, blending amazingly well with the painted band at the base of the wall.

Usun held a stick the length of his outstretched arm. It had a short, sharp iron point and looked useful either for throwing or stabbing. She had no idea where it came from, because the little man hadn't had it when they were in the burial cavern.

Apes curled up, often two or three snuggling together, on rugs on the floors of rooms that Ilna passed. One smacked his lips in noisy delight at something in his dreams. A few may have been awake, but even so they didn't track her with their eyes.

Usun reached the second door from the end on his side of the corridor. Facing it, he thrust the point of his staff into the lower panel and lunged upward. The staff braced him as he turned the latch.

The door swung inward on his weight. Usun's arms were quite strong despite being as spindly as a spider's.

The steps beyond led downward. The little man took them in a series of controlled jumps, going down off his left leg, striding to the edge of the next step, and then down again.

Ilna hadn't needed the lamp in the hall since plenty of moonlight came through the open doorways. It was pitch dark after she closed the door behind her and followed Usun, however.

The stairs were made of bricks which had originally been glazed. Lamplight gleamed on edges where the finish had been protected, but elsewhere they'd been ground to their coarse rusty core. Ilna wondered just how old the stairs were.

Her feet whispered. Usun bobbed down ahead of her. He made less sound than even the bird he resembled as he hopped and paced and hopped. What he was doing required a good deal of effort, she realized, imagining herself going down steps of comparable size. He was certainly a wiry little fellow.

A moan came up the passage. Ilna thought it was some natural sound, a steam vent or the rush of air through a crack, distorted by its own long echoes. She had to admit that it sounded like a living thing in pain, though.

Ilna'd gotten into the rhythm of the descent, so that it was her feet rather than her eyes that told her when the steps changed from brick to being chipped from stone. It was granite and unexpectedly slick. Though the rock was hard, feet had polished it to a high gloss which the porous brick wouldn't take.

How many feet, and how many centuries, had been down this passage?

Usun led onward. He'd shifted so that he stepped off his right leg, letting the left side of his body lead. Ilna nodded in approval: she'd learned to vary her posture when she was throwing a heavy loom. You could hurt yourself badly with repetitive work like that; and it was work, no mistake, for the little man.

The passage had been squared to begin with; farther down it became rough save where generations of shoulders had brushed it. She didn't think it had been cut with metal tools: at this depth the stairs seemed to have been battered through stone by other stones.

Had there been a crack or a natural vent which the human builders had merely enlarged? She didn't know much about rocks—by choice—but she didn't remember ever having seen a vent in granite.

"Master Usun?" Ilna said. How long had it been since they started down? She was never good with time, and the stone all around had robbed her of such facility as she'd ever had. "How much farther does this go?"

"It goes this far, Ilna," the little man said. "We've arrived."

The stairs ended in a small anteroom, not a landing as Ilna had thought at first. She stepped out to stand beside Usun, facing an iron door. It was at least double her own height, but it was relatively narrow because it had a single valve instead of being double like most doors raised on this scale.

She couldn't see either latch or hinges; indeed, from the look of it this might be a panel set in the living rock as decoration or to be worshipped. A polished smear along the left edge at shoulder height suggested that it had been pushed open regularly, but how did you unlock it?

Ilna frowned. With only the light of a single lamp wick, the details of the full-length design cast into the black iron weren't very clear, but she could see enough to make her dislike it. A woman in closely fitted armor glared at them. Her face and form were strikingly beautiful, but the expression on the molded features was cruel beyond anything Ilna could recall. One iron hand was closed into a fist; the other held a short trident whose points were barbed.

"That's Hili, Queen of the Underworld," said Usun. "A handsome wench, isn't she?"

He giggled. Ilna's frown tightened into a grimace. "How do we open the door?" she said. "Since I presume we need to get to the other side."

"Just open it, Ilna," said the little man. "Or here, I will."

He put his left hand on the edge of the massive iron panel and pushed. She knew the little man was strong beyond his size, but the way the door swung on hidden hinges was only possible if it had perfect balance.

Yellow-green light, the color of a will-o'-the-wisp or the mold on a corpse, crawled out the opening. With it came the dying echoes of a sound Ilna had never imagined, a rustling that was initially louder than any thunderclap.

"Come, Ilna," Usun said. "We must go in."

He knows more about this than he's telling me, Ilna thought; and smiled. She wasn't one to discuss her plans either, and the little man had shown himself to be a friend at every past occasion where it mattered.

If Usun had worn clothing, she could have stroked its fabric with her fingers and learned a great deal about him. She doubted that she'd have learned anything to change her belief that he was skilled, determined, and completely trustworthy; all the virtues she saw and cultivated in herself.

Ilna strode into the green glow. The door closed behind her.

The scale of the chamber was beyond her eyes' ability to grasp immediately. Faces turned toward her. The only time she'd seen so many people together was in great plazas when Garric was addressing the whole city. Their clothing was of all manner of styles, many that she'd never seen before, but their expressions were uniformly dull and empty. They—mostly men but some women, and a mixture of ages from children to doddering oldsters—stood around the edges of the chamber, rubbing the walls.

"Is Hervir or-Halgran here?" Ilna called. She raised her voice with each syllable till by the end she was shouting, but even so she could scarcely hear her own words in the vast chamber. So many people breathing in an enclosure made a sound like the rage of a windstorm.

"I am Hervir," replied a middle-aged man standing not far from the entrance. He lowered his hands; they held a rounded block of stone which was about half the size of his head. He walked deliberately toward Ilna and Usun.

The big room had been cut out of the living rock. It was granite here, just as it had been on the higher levels through which the stairwell descended; Ilna could tell that from the speckles of quartz and other things mixed with the basic material. It was a dense, supremely hard mass. The granite itself was the source of the glow whose shadowless presence filled the chamber.

Ilna set her lamp on the floor. She might need it again, but at present she wanted her hands free to knot a pattern. She'd have pinched out the wick, but she hadn't brought a flint and steel to light it again. The oil would either last or it wouldn't; she was concerned with more important things now.

"What are you doing in this place?" she demanded. A thought turned her face stiff; she reached behind her to the massive iron door and pushed. It shifted noticeably: it would be as easy to open from the inside as it had been from the anteroom.

"We are building the throne room for the King of Man," Hervir said with mild unconcern. He lifted his stone slightly to call attention to it. "Expanding the room, that is. Rubbing away the walls to make room for more worshippers until the King of Man becomes the God of All. Have you come to join us?"

"I've come to take you back to your family," Ilna said, thinking, *And how am I going to manage that even now that I've found him alive?* "But why haven't you escaped yourself? All of you? Why do you stay down here?"

"It's necessary that we enlarge the throne room," Hervir said. "Though there may be enough of us now worshipping the King of Man; the time is near."

He looked toward the center of the circular room. A granite pillar with steps circling it like the threads of a screw stood there, looming over the crowd. Because of the green light filling the stone, Ilna saw it clearly.

"The king has been gathering worshippers for many ages, waiting for this moment," Hervir said in a musing tone. "I was the last to join him, till you came. I thought perhaps it was my destiny to be the final worshipper, the one who brought him to godhead, but that was not to be."

"I'm not a worshipper!" Ilna said. "And you're not staying here. None of you should stay here!"

"But it's our duty," said Hervir with a faint smile. "Some of us have worshipped the king for millennia, but the time wasn't right until now. Until after the Change."

Ilna looked at the assembly. Some had been sleeping

while others ground at the walls or swept powdered rock into sacks of sisal fiber. They too were awakening to stare at her and Usun.

"Don't you die?" she said. "There can't be people thousands of years old!"

"No one dies here, mistress," Hervir said, smiling again. "The King of Man must be worshipped, and the dead can't do that."

"What do you eat?" Usun said. He was twirling his staff slowly through the fingers of his right hand; the iron point winked each time it came around.

Hervir looked down and frowned in puzzlement. "What a strange little man," he said. "I saw pygmies on Shengy in the days, in the days before. . . . But they weren't so small as you."

"What do you eat?" Usun repeated.

"The king's servants bring us wine and rice," Hervir said. "It's a wondrous vintage. Like nothing I'd ever drunk before I came to worship the king."

"A drug in the wine, wouldn't you say, Ilna?" Usun said, turning his head toward her.

She shrugged. "I suppose," she said, "but that doesn't explain people living forever. Or anyway, for however long."

She looked sharply at Hervir. "Come along," she said. If her hands had been free, she'd have gripped him by the shoulder. "You're coming with us. And when we have you safe in the waking world, perhaps Master Usun and I will return to find this King of Man."

"You needn't look for the king, mistress," Hervir said with his gentle smile. "He's here now."

The swirl of air warned her. She turned quickly to see the tall door opening on its silent hinges.

Perrin and Perrine came in, holding hands. They gaped in surprise.

"Mistress Ilna!" the princess blurted. "We thought you'd left the Valley of the King!"

"I thought I'd failed," said Perrin. The bleak horror of his tone suggested what failure would mean.

Two liveried apes entered in single file; Ingens walked between them. His face tightened when he saw Ilna. "Have you come to worship the King of Man also, mistress?" he said.

"No," Ilna said. "I've come to dispose of him and free the lot of you!" Her fingers were knotting again at the pattern she'd already formed, adding to it as the situation changed and became clearer.

"Will you indeed?" said a great voice.

A huge ape paced into the chamber on his knuckles, then stood upright. He was dressed in crimson silk and wore a golden crown set with rubies; a silken strap passed beneath his brutal chin. He was several times as massive as the ape servants.

"The king!" whispered the assembly thunderously. "The King of Man has come!"

CASHEL LOOKED AT the squat, angry-looking wizard advancing toward him along the shimmering bridge. The fellow's elbows were out and he held his crystal wands like knitting needles. Skeins of scarlet wizardlight spun from them, forming a pattern beyond the tips.

"Sir?" said Cashel. "I don't wish a problem with you. I just need to get the pledge coin on the other side."

He put his quarterstaff into a slow spin. Duzi! there was a lot of room. He couldn't see anything to right or left except a black horizon, and there was nothing overhead. Below, pale blue flames licked across the bottom of the chasm and gave the air the dry rasp of brimstone.

The wizard kept weaving his spell like Cashel hadn't spoken. He was chanting words of power, too, which was pretty much to be expected. A snake of plaited wizardlight curled slowly toward Cashel the way a honeysuckle vine stretches along a pole.

Cashel stepped forward and thrust one tip of his staff to where the strands of ruby light wrapped together and formed the snake. There was a bright blue flash and the air *crack*ed like nearby lightning.

"Hoy!" the wizard shouted. His arms flew apart and he staggered back. He'd been angry before, but now he looked like he was ready to chew rocks. Nothing remained of the pattern he'd been weaving.

Cashel took an easy step forward. This crystal bridge might look narrow to some, but it was a lot wider than some of the logs he'd crossed in thunderstorms, often enough carrying a ewe who'd gotten bogged.

"Sir," he said, "I'll give you a fight if you want one, but that's not what *I* want."

The wizard wore flowing silver robes with symbols in black around the hem and the cuffs. Cashel couldn't read those markings—or anything else—but he knew from the shapes that they weren't the Old Script or the New Script, either one.

The wizard got his composure and began weaving his wands into the same pattern as before. He went back to mumbling words of power, too. He hadn't said a thing except to chant.

Past the wizard's head, the gleaming bridge stretched farther than Cashel's eyes could follow. He wondered what he'd see if he looked over his own shoulder. The same thing, he guessed, but only for as long as it took the wizard to knock him into the fiery abyss because he hadn't kept his attention on the fight.

Maybe that was it: maybe the only ways off the bridge were through the other fellow or down into the brimstone. Well, Cashel hadn't made this place. Chances were the man trying to knock him off the bridge had more than a little to do with why it was like it was, though.

The snake of wizardlight crawled toward Cashel again. He'd struck high the first time, his left hand leading on the quarterstaff. This time he brought the staff up from below with his right hand forward; again there was a flash and a *crack!* The wizard jolted back in startled fury.

Cashel felt a faint tingle all the way up to the bunched muscles of his right shoulder; he worked that out with a few more spins of his staff. The ferrules had glowed when they hit the wizardlight, but that faded in no time. The iron wasn't burnt through, as sometimes happened. He'd had to replace the butt caps several times after fighting wizards, but that didn't matter so long as the hickory he'd shaped with his own hands remained.

"Are you frightened now, Allarde?" shrieked Milady from the chasm below. Her voice was as tiny and insistent as a mosquito in the night. "You should be, husband! You *should* be afraid!"

She was still wrapped in blue fire. Cashel shouldn't have been able to see her, let alone hear her voice from up on the bridge. She was as sharp to look at as a painted miniature he held in his palm, though.

The wizard—Allarde, if that wasn't a curse word in some language Cashel didn't know; Milady had made it sound like a curse, for sure—backed a step and then another step. He started moving his wands again, though this time in a different pattern.

Cashel supposed the wizard could retreat any distance on the bridge, though if you weren't used to backing on a narrow track it wouldn't be hard to go over. He stepped forward again, not rushing but making it clear that he was going to keep right on going to the other side unless Allarde managed to stop him—which he surely didn't look like doing so far.

"You're doomed, husband!" Milady shrieked. "You were so clever, *you* thought. But I have you now!"

Cashel frowned. He didn't like it to sound like he'd hammer somebody just because Milady said to. It was sort of working out that way, sure, but only because

Allarde wouldn't let him fetch the pledge piece without a fight.

Instead of stretching a stout braided tendril straight at Cashel, the wizard was curling a pair of threads like calipers from the tips of his wands. They spread into a circle wider than Cashel could've touched with one tip of his staff reaching out at the end of his arm.

He frowned, rotating his staff in slow figure eights to keep his muscles loose. It looked like a crazy thing for Allarde to do, so it had to be a trap. Except—

It was pretty clear by now that the wizard wasn't used to people who fought back and who knew *how* to fight. No boy in the borough could grow up without knowing that, and a poor orphan who hadn't got his growth yet was going to learn quicker than most. It must not be the same way with wizards.

"Numa quadich rua!" Allarde shouted. The scarlet curls started to hook back in.

Cashel strode forward, left foot and right foot, then lunged with staff out like a spear. Allarde crossed his wands before his chest to block the thrust. The ferrule smashed through them in a blue flash. Bits of crystal flew in all directions, blazing as they fell like sapphires in sunlight.

The staff punched the wizard in the breastbone, flinging him back for a double pace. He bounced onto the bridge, then slipped off and dropped into the abyss. He screamed all the way down.

Cashel recovered his staff. He felt like he'd fallen from a high cliff into the sea, shocked and stunned. He could still handle himself if push came to shove, though. He hadn't planned what he was doing, just did what seemed right at the time.

It *had* been right, but there'd been a cost. Well, it wasn't the first time he'd been bruised and achy after a fight.

"Join the halves of the coin, hero," Milady called.

She'd wrapped her arms around Allarde. Blue flames continued to lick from her mouth as she spoke and from the wizard's as he screamed without end. "There's a doorway in the back of the room you're in. Give the coin to the man in the hut behind the castle. He'll show you to Gorand."

Cashel spun the staff, sunwise and then widdershins; getting his balance, working the stiffness from muscles that'd felt like they'd been frozen when Allarde's wands shattered. He was all right now, or close enough.

"Thank you, ma'am," he called to the tiny figure laughing in the hellfire. He started toward the bridge ending in the far distance, wondering how long it would take him to get there.

His foot came down on polished stone, black and white almost-squares laid in a swirl pattern that matched the floor of the anteroom where the busts were. The bridge was gone, the chasm was gone, and half a silver coin gleamed on the little table against the far wall. It was the room he'd seen through the doorway before he'd entered.

Cashel looked over his shoulder. Liane and Rasile were walking toward him. The head, Milady's fiery head, had vanished. His lips pursed.

"Cashel, you saved me," Liane said. "You and Rasile. Your expression, though . . . is there something wrong?"

Cashel smiled. She was due an answer, though, so he said, "Allarde wouldn't have been a friend of mine, I guess, no matter what else was going on. But being yoked to Milady for, well, forever . . . seems pretty hard."

"He's probably regretting not having considered that before," Rasile said, her tongue laughing. "Before he mated with her and then betrayed her, that is. But we have work to do, companions."

She walked across the room and waited by the table till Cashel and Liane joined her. Gesturing to the bit of silver, she said, "This is your task, warrior."

Cashel fished the half coin Milady had given him out of his sash, leaned his staff into the crook of his arm, and picked up the rest of it. The edges mated with a dusting of blue wizardlight; the coin was whole again.

"This way, I think," Rasile said, walking toward the door in the wall to the left. It was heavy and cross-braced, but the bar had been withdrawn from the staples it rode in.

"A moment," Cashel said, folding the coin back into his sash. He hefted his quarterstaff, then stepped in front of the women and pulled the door open. He strode out into a sun-dappled forest.

SHARINA RETREATED A step but bumped her heel into something. She leaped high, bunching her legs beneath her to keep from sprawling backward as the scorpion advanced on her.

"On command!" Prester shouted. The nave of the temple had excellent acoustics. "Aim at the eyes!"

Sharina landed on the squirming body of the priest Burne had hamstrung. He squealed shrilly. She hopped to the side now that she was upright again.

"Loose!"

Six javelins flickered into the monster's headplate. Two clinked together in the air but penetrated anyway. Cracks spread in pale webs across the black chitin.

The slender steel points obliterated the two large eyes set close together in the center of the plate, though when the scorpion shook itself Sharina saw that there were three more eyes along each side of the head. The wooden shafts rattled together.

"Keep your guard up, boys!" shouted Pont as he rushed in. The scorpion's pincers were each the length of Sharina's outstretched arm. One reached out and closed on the top of the veteran's shield, crunching it into separate layers of wood. Pont stabbed up, into the joint. The other pincer grabbed for his head, but a soldier blocked it with his shield and Prester's sword cut through that joint as well.

The scorpion's tail curled, ripping with it the upper part of the screen that had closed the sanctum. The creature snapped the bronze backward and forward as it tried to shake it off. The perforated plating flexed like thunder in the vaulted temple.

Sharina poised. Ascor bellowed a warning, but she ducked between the first two of the four legs on the creature's right side, chopping right and left. The Pewle knife cut through both joints from the inside.

Yellow ichor that smelled of vinegar spurted from the wounds. The scorpion's massive body sagged, battering Sharina to the stone floor. Ascor and Prester each grabbed an ankle and jerked her back on her belly. The tail flicked down, free of the screen, and stabbed the hooked six-inch sting into the shield which Pont had interposed.

Pont slid his arms from the straps and backed away, his sword lifted on guard. With his left hand he drew his sheathed dagger.

The scorpion shambled forward. Soldiers hacked at the legs on the left side, but the outside joints were protected by stiff hairs and plates flaring above and below the flexible part of the case.

Sharina rolled away and scrambled to her feet. The white-haired priest was trying to get up also, but each time his foot flopped under and he fell down again. The scorpion stepped on his torso and pinned him screaming, then stepped on him again. Blood sprayed from the priest's mouth and he finally fell silent.

Pont and Prester moved in together. The scorpion slashed at them with its right pincer, though the lower blade couldn't close anymore. Pont lunged to meet it with the edge of his sword. The blow slammed him down, but he'd bought his comrade enough time to cut twice. Prester didn't have the advantage of being underneath, but his arm was strong and his sword was much heavier than the Pewle knife. The creature's two hind legs collapsed, dropping it helpless to the ground.

Dawn, flooding in through the opening in the eastern pediment, painted the nave the dusty red of blown roses. Soldiers enthusiastically cut at the legs on the left side, gashing chitin and spraying ichor in all directions without doing real harm. The scorpion was working itself around. Its remaining legs clacked sharply to get purchase on the polished stone.

Sharina gasped to breathe, bending over slightly. Fatigue and the stink of the monster's fluids made her stomach churn.

"Out of the way, farmers!" Ascor shouted. He had a javelin, perhaps the one Pont had dropped on the temple porch; he held it behind the balance. The heels of both his hands were forward as though it were a harpoon.

One of the regulars turned and gaped at the Blood Eagle. Prester grabbed the man's swordbelt and hauled him clear with careless ease. Ascor took a long stride and lunged, thrusting the spear with all his strength into the scorpion's mouth. It sank to the wooden shaft.

Ascor backed away. The scorpion's body arched together. The stinger was still stuck in Pont's shield, a curved section of plywood that delivered a crushing blow to the creature's head plate. The great body shuddered, but its movements were as mindless as ripples dancing on a pond in a sudden squall.

Sharina straightened as she got her breath. She stood in a pool of dawn light. Men were shouting, and her arms were covered with ichor that thickened as it dried. Her skin itched.

She heard, she *felt,* a buzzing sound; the light about her changed. Dawn had become the cold ruby insistence of wizardlight.

"The time is accomplished, Sharina," boomed Black's voice. *"Now you must come to me!"*

The last thing she was aware of as she dropped out of the waking world was Burne, leaping from the floor to her right shoulder.

THANK YOU," GARRIC said to the boatman as the vessel grounded in the cypress grove. Rather than hand Tenoctris over the high gunwale, he took her satchel.

"It's a rare pleasure to meet a scholar," the boatman said with a wan smile. "But I made a conscious choice. It wasn't a bad one, all things considered."

The smile faded somewhat. The boat dissolved in mist and shadow as soon as Garric's boot touched the forest loam, but he thought he heard the boatman add, "And I've had a very long time to consider."

It was midmorning by the angle of the sun through the leaves. Tenoctris appeared beside him—out of thin air, it seemed. She wore a cheerful expression, but the lines of strain at the corners of her eyes hadn't been there when the two of them entered the grove the night before. If it was only one night.

"Your Highness?" called Lord Waldron from just beyond the circle of trees. His presence here, a mile from the camp, was as unexpected as a troupe of dancing girls and it suggested much worse possibilities.

Waldron swung himself into the saddle. "Marstens, bring the mounts for his highness and Lady Tenoctris! Your Highness, I'm *very* glad you're back."

He rode to Garric's side; it was only five or six doublepaces, but Waldron couldn't imagine walking if there was a horse available. He continued, "The enemy's approaching, about three days south of our present camp, and this isn't the best terrain to meet them on. We couldn't, of course, displace until you'd returned."

"You say 'the enemy's approaching,'" Garric said. He felt buffeted by the change from discussing ancient historians on a boat sailing through the cosmos to planning a battle with an unknown enemy, but he supposed that was what it meant to be king. "The main body, you mean?"

The king in his mind laughed merrily. *"That's what it means to be a soldier, lad,"* Carus said. *"Though I could've done without arguments on Poleinis and Timarion."*

"Yes, and the Emperor of Palomir himself is with them," Waldron said as his aide trotted up with two horses—a powerful bay gelding and a cream palfrey wearing a side-saddle. "At any rate, there's a green banner with a white wedge that the scouts haven't seen before, and the pole seems to have a crown on it."

Tenoctris lifted herself easily onto the palfrey and wheeled it around so that she faced the men again. "Yes," she said, "that's the imperial standard. It's Mount Sebala rising above Palomir City. I can easily do a divination to make sure the emperor's really present, of course."

"No, no!" said Waldron with more than a touch of impatience. "We have to get back immediately and give the order to march. I've made the preparations, but of course the order—"

He looked at Garric, now mounted beside him, and dipped his head in brief deference.

"—will come from you, Your Highness."

He gestured to the trumpeter beside him. His quick, silvery Advance was echoed by the deeper notes of the cornicenes of the individual troops. The cavalry squadron started forward.

Garric prodded his gelding into motion to keep up with the army commander. "Milord?" he said, not quite as irritated as King Carus but not pleased with the situation either. "Before I give any orders, *what* do you propose to do?"

"Haft has a range of mountains down the spine, Your Highness," Waldron said. "Not so high as Blaise, but there's only one pass for fifty miles in either direction from the east coast to Carcosa."

He must've noticed Garric glancing over his shoulder,

because he added with the same impatience, "Your guards will follow at their own pace. I've given Lord Asterpos his orders."

"I know Haft has hills," said Garric, controlling his exasperation in part because the boiling fury of the ghost in his mind was so obviously excessive. "And I've crossed from Barca's Hamlet to Carcosa, so I know the pass as well. Are you proposing to retreat to Carcosa?"

"Your Highness, I forgot you were from Haft," said Waldron in startled contrition. Though it wouldn't be obvious to anyone who didn't know him, the army commander had just bestowed a great compliment: he had been thinking of Garric as a noble from northern Ornifal like himself, not as a hick peasant from a backwater island. "And no, not retreat to Carcosa, but if we hold the pass the rats will have to come at us on a narrow front where they can't use their numbers."

He cleared his throat and went on, "The Palomir army is larger than we'd expected. Lord Zettin estimates there are at least forty thousand rats. I find Zettin a bumptious upstart, but his scouts seem to have a good grasp of their duties."

"From previous reports it looked like the rats would come from the south rather than due east," Garric said. King Carus was sifting the data with a quick precision that his descendent would never be able to equal, but they'd come to the same conclusions regardless. "Is that still the case?"

"Yes, Your Highness," said Waldron, visibly pleased that the camp was in sight. "They seem to have planned to overrun Cordin, but they turned north when they realized we were marching on them."

Horns were calling from the camp. The ghost of Carus scowled and said, *"And I bloody well hope the artillery in the gate towers either isn't cocked or doesn't have bolts in the troughs, because they're pointing them at us."*

"Right," said Garric. "So we don't have to worry about Palomir maneuvering around us—they want a battle. We'll march half a day south into the dry grasslands between what used to be the coast of Haft and the reefs paralleling it. We'll give them their battle there, but I don't think it'll be the battle they want."

"Your Highness!" Waldron said. "I don't want you to think that I'm afraid—"

Though the army commander had personality defects, *nobody* who knew him would suspect him of cowardice.

"—but the safety of the kingdom depends on this battle. There'll be time for the people in your home village to evacuate. And even if there wasn't, there'll be no hope for them anyway if the rats surround and destroy the royal army."

The ghost in Garric's mind had a dangerous expression, but Garric gave Waldron a lopsided smile. "Milord," he said mildly, "if I ordered you to expend all your efforts in protecting Barca's Hamlet, what would you do?"

Waldron frowned like a thundercloud; then his face slowly cleared. "You wouldn't do that, Your Highness," he said slowly. "I . . . I hadn't thought or I wouldn't have suggested that your plans were based on where you grew up. Your pardon."

After a further moment he added, "Though of course if you did, I'd obey my orders. I hope I know my duty as a soldier, Your Highness."

"Much as I thought, Waldron," Garric said with a warmer grin. "My actual train of thought is this: the rats are more agile than we are. In broken terrain they'll always have the advantage. In the hills in particular, they'll be able to get around and above us, even our light troops."

"But our troops are stronger man for man," Waldron agreed with increasing animation, "and we've got discipline that I certainly didn't see in the rats when we engaged them earlier."

He frowned. "But they *will* surround us, Your Highness."

Garric nodded. "Yes," he said. "We'll win the battle or die, no question about that. But milord, that wasn't really in question to begin with, was it?"

Lord Waldron's expression remained fixed for a moment. Then he barked a laugh and said, "No, I don't suppose there was, Your Highness. This isn't like fighting the Earl of Sandrakkan, is it? Yes, we'll give the rats a battle—but as you say, it'll be *our* battle, not the one they want."

"Put the men in heavy marching order then, milord," Garric said, echoing the words of the ghost in his mind. "I want a week's rations and water, though I don't think we'll have that much time. We'll have to pack it or push it in handcarts, because we won't be taking any horses and mules."

Waldron sighed, then brightened as they rode together through the east gate of the camp. "Well," he said, "I don't mind marching for a day if there's a chance to kill rats at the other end."

King Carus laughed. *"I'd have gotten along with Waldron, lad,"* he said. *"At least until I lost my temper and took his head off. He's got the right idea this time, by the Shepherd."*

Garric didn't have his ancestor's enthusiasm for battle, but sometimes there was no other choice. He grinned wryly at Tenoctris, then said to Waldron, "I don't know that I'd make that a general rule, but in the present circumstances, milord, I completely agree."

ILNA SMILED COLDLY as she wove and knotted the long strands. The sisal from a captive's basket was stiff and had a harsh texture, but that made it even better for what she had to do. Not that she really needed more than her own skill.

"You've come to worship me, Ilna os-Kenset," said the king, "though perhaps you didn't know it at the time. You have no choice, you see. Your former gods are gone since the Change, but I've been preparing for this moment for longer than you can count. The Gods are dead, and the King of Man is God!"

Usun spun his armed staff like a baton and laughed. "If living in a cave for thousands of years makes you a god, then Mistress Ilna and I just spilled another god into a canyon. Do you have any canyons here, ape boy, or do we need to find another way to dispose of you?"

Ingens was talking to Hervir; they seemed to be paying no attention to the giant ape or their present circumstances. The secretary's posture suggested a degree of deference, but they were still old acquaintances meeting in unexpected circumstances.

"Nothing can harm me here!" said the ape with booming certainty. "You call this a cave, little doll? My congregation has been polishing away the living rock for millennia, creating this sanctuary in which to worship me. I rule men now, but from their prayers in this sacred vault I will rule the cosmos!"

The apes who'd brought Ingens to the cavern were waiting to either side of the doorway, as dull-eyed and motionless as a pair of marble statues. Ilna was glad not to have to deal with them. They were each about the size of a man, but they'd be far stronger. She wasn't sure what effect the pattern she was weaving would have on them.

"Please don't judge us harshly, mistress," said Perrine with a look of misery. "We had no choice."

"The King of Man rules this valley," her brother said. He wouldn't meet Ilna's eyes. "There's no will but the king's."

Together the twins whined, "We had no choice!"

There's always a choice, Ilna thought, but folk like these wouldn't understand that sometimes it's better to die. Her fingers wove and knotted. She'd done worse things than Perrin and Perrine had, but she'd never pretended that she'd been forced to them. Out of hurt and anger she'd surrendered herself to Evil, and for a time thereafter she'd been one of Evil's most subtle and effective tools.

She gave the twins a look of hard appraisal. They weren't even *good* tools . . . though they'd apparently been good enough to trap Ingens and Hervir and—

Ilna let her eyes drift across the huge cavern. Polished out of nothing! Unless the king was lying, and she didn't see any reason he should be.

—tens of tens of tens of men and women. Human beings were no better than sheep! But neither sheep nor humans would be left as prey for wolves while Ilna and her brother were in the world.

"You can put that rag away, mistress," the king said contemptuously. "Nothing harmful to me can exist in this vault. Pray to me and it will go easier for you."

"I don't pray," Ilna said as she wove. "And 'easy' isn't something I've had much experience with, so you needn't expect that that offer would get me to change my mind even if I believed you. Which of course I don't."

"Mistress," said the prince. "The king really can't be attacked here."

"Anywhere in the valley," his sister agreed sadly, "but especially here in his chamber of worship."

Sheep! thought Ilna. To the great ape she said, "You're afraid that I'm going to make you tear your eyes out, is that it, monkey? No, that isn't what I have in mind."

"Are you too stupid to understand?" said the king. "You can do nothing to me! No fabric of yours can touch me. I cannot be attacked!"

The lungs in that huge chest gave the words the volume of an ox bawling, but the hollow chamber drank it nonetheless. The captive humans fell to their knees in terror, the prince and princess along with the others. Perhaps that was an effect of the drugged wine too.

Ilna met the beast's gaze squarely. The beetling brows and massive jaws would've given it an angry expression anyway, but she didn't doubt that it was really angry. Stiff silvery bristles stood up along its spine. She hadn't actually *done* anything, but the mere fact that she wasn't bowing and scraping was enough to infuriate it.

There were human beings like that, of course. She had a short way with them too.

"I'll give you a final chance," Ilna said. She wondered if she'd make the offer if she thought there was the least chance the beast would take it. Perhaps, perhaps she would . . . but the creature *wasn't* going to accept. "Release all these humans. Take no more. And I'll let you live here and rule the little monkeys for as long as you please."

"I will pluck your limbs off," said the king. There was a touch of rumbling wonder in his voice; he was no longer shouting. "I will pluck them off, and as your torso writhes on the floor you will pray to me for the mercy of death—which I will not grant!"

"When people learn my skill with patterns . . . ," Ilna said in a conversational voice. She had a sufficient fabric already, but since the time was available she continued to embellish the present design. "They often ask me if I could foretell the future."

She gave the king a hard smile. Her mind was considering what would happen next, and after that, and the next thing following . . . but that was out of her control. What she *could* control was what would happen to the beast before her, the one who'd enslaved humans for . . . well, the ape was probably correct in saying it was more years than she could count. That would end.

"And I can, of course, or at any rate I could," Ilna said. "I don't do that because I've genuinely been trying not to injure people ever since Garric freed me from Hell, not to mince words. I'm going to make an exception for you though, ape king."

"You cannot harm me here!" the king said, stepping forward. His legs were dwarfishly short, but the arm that reached toward her was twice the length of a man's. The fingers ended in claws like plowshares.

"Is it an attack to show you the truth?" Ilna said, spreading the pattern she'd knotted.

The king stumped another step forward. Ilna realized with a sudden shock that his eyes were closed.

Usun jabbed the pointed staff into the ape's instep. He bellowed and opened his shrouded eyes in surprise, then went stiff. It was like he'd been struck by lightning.

Ilna backed. She folded the pattern between her hands so that none of the human slaves would see it. It would have a different effect on them than it did on the King, but she presumed it would be a different *bad* effect. The details of the future depended on the person, but the basic facts would be the same: everyone died. Everything died. All existence ended in death.

"It cannot be," the king said in a wondering voice. "This is a dream, a sending from an enemy."

Ilna sniffed. "It's quite true, whatever you've seen," she said. "That's the future, *your* future."

She hadn't been sure how the ape would respond, but she hadn't expected denial. Partly because avoiding the truth wasn't something she would do herself, but largely out of pride: Ilna assumed that a pattern she wove would penetrate to the soul of whoever saw it, beyond the ability of his conscious mind to deny.

Her mouth quirked into a wry smile. Perhaps she'd been wrong and would very shortly pay for that pride with her life. Mistakes should be punished, so she wouldn't complain.

"It's a dream," the king said. "A *dream!*"

He lowered his arms to his sides, but his muscles were knotting and his fists clenched into hairy mallets. Spittle bubbled at the corners of his jaw. It appeared that the pattern had worked after all.

The prisoners kneeling in adoration began slowly to get to their feet and move back. They'd drifted forward since Ilna entered, but the behavior of their king and god was visibly repelling them.

The king screamed like a rabbit in a leg snare, but louder. Even in this vast chamber, the impact of the sound made Ilna want to clasp her hands to her ears. She continued to hold the folded sisal pattern.

The great ape shook his head as though he'd been hit on the forehead with a mallet. His ruby crown winked in the foul green light; he raised his hands to it.

"Your Majesty?" said Prince Perrin. "Your Majesty, what should we do?"

The king flexed his arms, pulling the gold wires of the crown apart. He flung the pieces blindly to either side, the silken strap fluttering behind one half. When they hit the wall, rubies popped from their settings and clicked across the stone floor.

Princess Perrine fell to her knees and began to cry. Ilna sneered at her in disgust.

The ape grasped his robes and ripped them off with a jerk. Ilna raised an eyebrow. She knew it took strength to tear metal, even a soft metal like gold, but she *understood* how tough silk brocade was. This beast could have pulled her apart by main strength if he'd grasped her by thigh and shoulder.

The king's scream turned to a series of explosive grunts. He fell onto all fours, then lunged forward as suddenly as a racehorse when the bar lifts.

Ingens shouted and jumped aside. The ape's shoulder caught him a glancing blow nonetheless. He sprawled into Hervir, who'd been running for the wall even though he hadn't been in the way of the beast's charge to begin with. The men spun spread-eagled in opposite directions on the polished floor.

Perrin and Perrine screamed. The king's thunderous grunts smothered that human sound. The prisoners flattened against the wall; some of them faced the stone, others covered their eyes with their hands.

The king's lowered head smashed into the pillar left when the chamber was pounded out of the living rock. Bone cracked like a maul pounding a cliff face, only louder.

The ape bounced back and onto the floor in a sitting position. Blood smeared the black stone, and the beast's face was a mass of blood. Prisoners bawled in horror and amazement.

The king rose slowly onto his hind legs. Ilna fingered her lasso. It wouldn't be of the least use against the huge ape, but if he came at her she'd try to drop it over his tree-trunk neck regardless.

The other choice was her utility knife. She wasn't sure its blade was long enough to reach the beast's vitals. If she had to choose between two useless weapons, she'd pick the cord.

The king had stopped grunting, though his breath blasted like that of an angry ox. Instead of turning to Ilna, he lurched forward and gripped the pillar between his spread arms. With his hands to anchor him, he slammed his head against the stone, slumped, then whipped his head into the pillar again. This time there was a splintering overtone to the hollow *whock!*

The beast collapsed slowly, its long arms still about the pillar. Its legs, no longer gripping the floor, splayed to left and right until the massive chest lay flat on the stone. Blood and brains leaked from the broken skull.

There was a moment of silence. Then the prisoners began to keen in amazement.

Interlude

Nivers, high priest of Franca, chanted, *"Erebani akuia pseus!"* and stabbed with the dagger of gray-green volcanic glass. The man faceup on the altar shrieked in the grip of four rat men.

Nivers dragged the blade from neck to belly along the victim's breastbone, where the ribs were still cartilage; the victim's screams gurgled to silence. The rat men carried his body, still sloshing blood, to the edge of the terrace and flung it as far out as they could into the fire filling the plaza below.

The priest slumped, waiting for the next sacrifice. He'd had to use the strength of both tired arms to finish the cut. He'd need a fresh knife soon, another fresh knife. The rat men kept bringing them, but only Nivers could carry out the rites since Salmson had accompanied Emperor Baray and the army.

Gangs of rat men carried timbers—whole trees, often enough—to the tops of the buildings on the other three sides, then hurled them down into the great fire in the plaza. Though the wood was green, the fire's immense heat exploded it into instant ravening life.

The corpses of the victims flung from the fourth side burst, then shriveled in black, oily smoke. Even the bones burned.

Rat men were bringing another victim up the steps on the back side of the pyramid. The blaze sent its red glow through the crystal of all the surrounding structures. When Nivers looked down, it was as if he were standing above a lake of fire instead of being on the topmost terrace of the Temple of Franca.

It didn't matter to Nivers where he looked or what he saw; the waking world existed for him only as a problem to be solved. The ash and stench of the holocaust swirled, and the heat of the fire hammered him even though he was shaded from its direct radiance.

This was a crisis which threatened the return of the Gods. Nothing mattered save that.

Four rat men carried the next sacrifice, one on each limb; they'd given up trying to get the victims to climb the steps by themselves. The smell of burning flesh made their coming fate obvious; indeed, many of them fainted before they reached the top.

"Your Holiness, it's me, Marisca!" this one screamed. She still wore the short jacket and diaphanous pantaloons she'd been given when she became a member of the high priest's harem. "You remember me! You can't do this!"

Nivers did remember her when he cast his mind back, though he couldn't have put a name to her. Names didn't matter, and she didn't matter.

"I *love* you!" the girl said. Her eyes were open but empty, cold blue chips of terror.

The rat men threw her onto the altar which the fires below jeweled garnet and topaz. *"Erebani akuia pseus!"* Nivers chanted. He chopped down, then ripped the knife toward himself.

A spurt of blood blinded him. He tore off a leg of Marisca's pantaloons to wipe his face, then blinked until tears had cleared his eyes enough that he could see again.

The rest of his harem had gone before. There were almost no humans in Palomir save Nivers himself. On those few potential sacrifices depended the return of the Gods.

One more sacrifice being carried to the top of the temple. The steps were steep, but the rat men seemed indefatigable. Their individual strength wouldn't be enough, though, not now that the Gate of Ivory had been closed. Only the Gods Themselves could tip the balance.

The rat men reached the terrace; Nivers straightened and took a firm grip on the glass knife. It would do for one more sacrifice, and that a slip of a girl.

"You senile old pervert!" the victim said.

He blinked. The girl was Anone; he remembered her from the days he'd been only Nivers the high priest, not the avatar of Franca. Anone had been his favorite, the youngest and freshest of his harem. But now . . .

The rat men spread-eagled her on the altar. It was crystal like the rest of the temple, but days of blood baked by sunlight and fire had coated most of it with a crusty black. Her body gleamed in nude white contrast.

"I'd rather die than have you touch me again!" the girl cried. "I'd rather die! I'd rather—"

Nivers stabbed. Anone belched blood, blinding him again. The hot, black smoke of the pyre wrapped and raised Nivers, filling him with the immanence of godhead.

Smoke and the thunderheads lowering above Palomir merged into a mighty figure in the sky. His beard streamed with storm clouds, His fingers crackled with the lightning. He turned and strode purposefully to the west.

No eyes but those of rat men were present to watch Him go.

Chapter

16

CASHEL TOOK TWO steps out from the castle door, far enough that the women could follow him, and then stopped to take stock. Three or maybe four double paces away, a man sat on the stoop of a log cabin; he had one foot up on the railing. There wasn't anything unusual about the cabin or him, either one, save that they were a bit outsized: the man was easily two hand's breadths taller than Cashel, and the cabin was built to its owner.

There was a door in the middle of the front wall and a window to either side of it. The roof was board underneath from the ends sticking out at the eaves, but it'd been sodded over; buttercups now grew in the grass.

Pines with chestnuts and a smattering of other hardwoods spread toward the distant mountains behind the cabin, and the usual little trees—sweet gums, dogwoods, and the like—filled in the spaces. Behind Cashel and the women was a lake; he could see across, but it stretched out of sight to right and left.

A dugout canoe was drawn up on the mud shoreline; the pair of milk cows standing knee-deep in the shallow water looked back at him. The castle and the door Cashel had come out of were nowhere to be seen.

A loon called from the invisible distance. You might think it was a lost soul if you'd never heard the real thing.

Cashel laid the quarterstaff into the crook of his left arm instead of holding it ready for use. He smiled and called, "Hello the house!"

"Hello yourself," the big man said, lifting himself from

the puncheon bench he'd been sitting on. He was taller than he was broad, but his shoulders were pretty impressive. "I don't get many visitors here."

He paused for a moment, clearly considering his next words. "Come and set," he said at last. "You and your friends."

Cashel walked up slow and easy, keeping the smile. The man wore a leather tunic with no weapons in sight. As big as he was, the bench itself would make a club if he thought he needed anything. Cashel hadn't any wish to make the fellow think that.

"My name's Cashel or-Kenset," he said, stopping at the edge of the stoop. He nodded to the women. "This is Lady Liane, and that's Rasile. She's a Corl."

The cows had gone back to drinking. They were in milk so there must be a bull around somewhere; maybe it was corralled in a clearing deeper into the forest.

"Rasile," the big man said, letting the syllables roll on his tongue. He wasn't a giant, but even Garric would have to look up to meet his eyes. "I haven't met a Corl before."

Returning to Cashel—a man talking to a man, not presuming to talk directly to the other fellow's women—he said, "Can I offer you anything? I've got milk cooling in the springhouse, and water of course."

"Sir," said Cashel, fishing in his sash. "We were told to give you this. We've been sent here to release a man named Gorand. He's a hero and he's needed back in Dariada."

He held the coin out in the palm of his right hand. The silver had joined perfectly, like it had never been broken.

The big man took the coin between thumb and forefinger; he held it up to view one side, then the other. He spun it in the air, caught it, and said, "I don't have much to do with money now."

He quirked a smile at all his visitors, not just Cashel. "Well, I never did," he said. "I was a warrior, not a merchant."

He spun the coin again, then squeezed it in his left

hand. His face hardened in appraisal. "I'm Gorand," he said, "and now you've released me. Why?"

"Master Cashel?" Liane said quietly. "Would you like me to join the discussion?"

"Yes, ma'am," Cashel said, feeling enormous relief. "Master Gorand, I'm a shepherd. Liane, ah, Lady Liane's able to tell you about all this better than I ever could."

He stepped aside gratefully. Gorand looked him up and down, then grinned. "It seems to me that you might just be able to tell me something, boy. *Might.*"

Cashel spread his stance a little without thinking about it. He kept the staff as it was, though, looking about as innocent as a solid, iron-shod length of hickory could.

"Sir," he said and paused to clear his throat. His voice had gotten thick; the words sort of growled out. "Sir, I've got business to take care of right now. Afterwards if you want to look me up, sure. If that's what you want."

Gorand laughed. "No, that's not what I want, boy," he said. "At least not with a quarterstaff. Did you ever use a sword?"

"No sir," Cashel said. He hated swords, always had. Given the choice he'd pick a round iron bar before he would a sword. "But if that's what you want, we can try swords."

Rasile gave a ripping snarl. "Males posturing!" she said. "Are we not all the same clan today? Stop this!"

"Sorry ma'am," Gorand muttered at pretty much the same moment as Cashel was saying, "Sorry, Rasile," with his face turned toward the hard-tramped ground at his side.

"Yes," said Liane firmly. "Lord Gorand, the city of Dariada is being menaced by an army of pirates."

"And?" said Gorand. "For in my day, Dariada had walls that no mob of masterless men could threaten."

"There are still walls," Liane said, giving Gorand a little nod to show she appreciated his mind. "But the pirates have a Worm. They would say they control a Worm,

I suspect, but you know better than anyone else that no one controls a Worm."

Gorand laughed long and savagely, waking a smile from Cashel's lips. Cashel had met big men and strong men in the past, but this fellow was a *man,* right enough.

"*I* controlled one!" he said. "The Shepherd knows I did, lady!"

"Yes," said Liane. "And the Tree Oracle of Dariada said that we must release you to save the city this time also."

"Ah, the Tree Oracle," Gorand said, chuckling without the fierce passion of a moment ago. He gestured to the bench and added, "Won't you sit, milady?"

"Thank you, no," Liane said primly. "Milord, will you return with us to Dariada now?"

"The citizens of Dariada sent me here after I settled the Worm the first time," Gorand said, letting his eyes rove over the forest on the other side of the lake. "They were supposed to leave me with this—"

He tossed the silver coin and caught it by the edges as it spun, a neat trick.

"—so that I could return when I pleased. But they didn't."

He met Cashel's eyes. "They gave it to you instead," he said.

Cashel didn't speak; he'd put this in Liane's hands. If there was something for him to deal with, well, he'd do that.

"The coin was in the hands of a pair of wizards," Liane said, just as coolly as before. "We don't know how they came by it. One of them took me prisoner. Master Cashel—"

She nodded at him.

"—freed me and took the coin from them."

"Did he, now?" Gorand said, flipping the coin and looking at Cashel. "So, Cashel . . . do you think the good people of Dariada didn't mean to strand me here? That it was all just an accident?"

Cashel shrugged. "Sir," he said, "I don't know. I didn't much take to the folk of Dariada when I was there, but it's not the same ones as in your time, not by a long ways. And anyhow, I'm not from a city myself. I don't like any city I've been in, and I don't generally warm to the people who live in them."

Liane was looking at him with no expression at all. She wanted to break in, but she was afraid to. Gorand had asked Cashel, not her.

Cashel knew how she felt, but he was going to tell this his own way. He and Gorand were both men, and they didn't see things the way women—and city folk—did.

"But none of that matters, sir," Cashel said. "We're shepherds, you and me. Not because we like the ones we're looking after, maybe, but because we're the ones who *can* look after them. Right?"

Gorand chuckled. "That's so, isn't it?" he said. He tossed the coin from one hand to the other, then stepped forward and clasped Cashel, right arm to right arm. "All right, Cashel. I'll go back to Dariada."

They leaned back and parted hands. "Warrior Gorand," said Rasile. "Take us with you, if you will."

Cashel looked at her. He'd been expecting they'd be taking Gorand back, not the other way around. Though how, he now realized, was a good question what with the door and the castle not being there anymore.

"Yes, wizard," said Gorand; he bowed to her. He hadn't been told Rasile was a wizard, but it seemed like he could see as far through a stone wall as the next fellow.

Gorand strode out from the cabin and raised his arms. His hands were clenched, and the coin was in the left one. He seemed to swell, and as he did Cashel felt something scoop him up and rush him forward.

There was a roaring sound in the sudden blackness.

* * *

I'D BE BETTER with a short sword! Garric thought, holding the scabbard of the long horseman's weapon. The long blade would beat him black and blue if he let it flop as he ran along with the infantry regiment.

"Not when it came time to use it, lad," Carus said. The ancient king watched through his descendant's eyes with the smiling anticipation of a cat with prey in sight. *"Though we'd make do with a butter knife if we had to, I suppose."*

Well, I'd be better off with sandals than with these boots! thought Garric, and that at least was inarguable. He'd become used to wearing riding boots, so he hadn't bothered to change back to sandals when they left the horses behind.

It hadn't occurred to him how awkward they were to run in until whim sent him trotting off with a thousand men from the phalanx to escort in a supply convoy which had fought off a band of Palomir raiders. Lower heels would've been much less uncomfortable.

He heard a horn blat in the near distance—a shepherd's wooden trumpet, he was sure, not a brass or silver military instrument. Rear Admiral—the phalanx was organized in naval ranks because the pikemen had doubled as oarsmen—Ditter called, "Your Highness, the wagons are in sight!"

There was no longer a royal navy, because the Inner Sea had vanished at the Change. Pikes were useless too, against the agile rats. The men of the phalanx had leather cuirasses, short stiff swords, and wicker shields that were longer and stouter than those carried by skirmishers, however. These—and the troops' exceptional discipline—were the perfect combination for fighting the new enemy.

Attaper pounded along beside Garric, looking as grim as if he were presiding over an execution. Though fit, he was older than his prince by twenty years, had shorter legs, and hadn't grown up tramping the length and breadth of his home borough on foot. He held the pace only by the dint of iron determination.

Carus chuckled with a combination of affection and exasperation, his usual mix of feelings toward the commander of the Blood Eagles. He respected Attaper as a soldier, but the ancient warrior wasn't the sort to react well to a bodyguard's niggling concern for safety.

"At least he doesn't have breath to tell you that you shouldn't be doing this," Carus said. The ghost pursed his lips and with unusual seriousness—Carus was often angry but very rarely thoughtful—went on, *"A king who only does what other people think he ought to do isn't much of a king, it seems to me. And he's going to lose a lot of battles too, or at least lose one battle for good and all."*

Because Garric was in the middle of the regiment, it wasn't until the relief column was almost on top of the supply train that he got a good look at it. All twenty wagons were intact, but some of the oxen had been lost and half the surviving animals bore cuts that'd been stanched with mud for the time being.

"It's the prince!" a wagoneer shouted. Garric wasn't wearing his gilt-winged helmet, but his features had been spread across the kingdom on any number of paintings, statues, plates, napkins, and so forth. Most of the likenesses were crude or worse, but this supply train was from eastern Haft where both interest and the opportunity for an accurate portrayal were greater than the usual.

"Hail Prince Garric!" rattled out with, "Haft and the Isles!"

The Coerli trumped that with a screaming battle chorus that brought nervous bawling from the oxen. If the teams hadn't been so exhausted and frightened by the

Palomir attack they'd just survived, some of the teams would've tried to bolt.

A heavyset man was trying to climb down from the seat of the lead wagon with the help of a guard. His head, right arm, and right thigh were bandaged. He wore a tabard embroidered with the Ornifal eagle; the front panel was ripped and bloody.

Garric reached him at a run, no longer aching from his five-mile jog. He shouldered the guard out of the way.

"Sir, stay where you are!" he said, catching the wounded man by the hip and under his left arm to lift him forcibly back onto the seat. "You're the wagon marshal?"

"Sister take you, you bloody rogue!" the marshal shouted. He was older than Garric had thought, closer to sixty than fifty. "The prince is coming! I have to get down!"

"You have to do what your prince tells you, sir!" Garric said. "And right now I'm telling you to stay where you are."

"It *is* the prince, Marshal Kucros!" said the guard. He was probably a former shepherd. He wore a fleece jerkin skin-side out and carried a short wooden bow; his belt quiver was empty, as was the scabbard which should've held a utility knife. The bowstaff would make a decent club.

"Your Highness?" Kucros said in amazement. Seated again, he could see Garric instead of staring at the wagon as he tried to lower himself with as little additional pain as possible. "What are you doing with the likes of us, Your Highness?"

"When I heard that a supply train had fought off an attack by raiders close to the camp . . . ," said Garric. "I thought I'd join the regiment that was going to escort you the rest of the way in. You men are heroes."

The chieftain of the Corl hunting band came up, accompanied by two of his warriors. They'd led the reaction force patrolling the supply route. All three had fresh rat tails dangling from their leather harness. The maned chief was the size of an average man, while his companions had the willowy slimness of twelve-year-old girls.

There was nothing girlish about their fanged smiles and bloody weapons, though. Now that they were allied with humans, they carried steel in preference to their native wood and stone.

"And you Coerli are heroes as well," Garric said, giving the cat men a deep nod. "You were outnumbered, but you attacked and saved the supplies."

The chieftain fluffed his mane in pride. There was a matted cut on the right side of his head; not all the blood spattering him had come from the rat men.

"We are the True Men!" he said with a boastfulness that would've irritated Garric under other circumstances. "Shall we run from rats?"

"I'd had my doubts about the cats, I don't mind telling you," said the guard who'd been helping Kucros. Ditter was organizing a review of the wagoneers and guards, but nobody was going to intrude on Prince Garric's informal discussion. "I wasn't sure which side they'd take if push came to shove, you know what I mean. But by the Lady, it was like a fox in a hen coop what they did to them rats."

"I thought the rats was quick," agreed Kucros, nodding three times at the end of each phrase. "It could've gone hard with us, I'll tell you. Even with the wagons circled like we had them. But then the cats come in and the rats, they didn't have time to run, a lot of them."

"Your monkey folk were holding," the Corl chief said. "I thought monkeys would be no more than the cattle we ate in the old days, fit only to tend fields and muck out our huts. That was not so: they are warriors. I, Raelert, chief of chiefs, say so!"

"It looks like this Palomir business is going to be really

good for getting people and cats to work together," said the ghost in Garric's mind with a broad smile. *"Which isn't something I care much about, but you do; and you're generally right about things, lad."*

It'll help if we survive, Garric agreed silently.

"But Your Highness . . . ," Kucros said, scowling as he wrestled with a thought that was too big for him. *"You* shouldn't . . . I mean—"

He straightened, as much as sitting down and the pain of his wounds would allow. "Your Highness, I was with your father—"

Which meant Valence III, Garric's father by adoption and officially still king.

"—at the Stone Wall when we beat the Sandrakkan rebels back into their kennel. But I was just a file closer, never got higher than that, and I only been called back to the colors now to put a little discipline in shepherds and wagon drivers. You've got no business wasting time on us!"

"I've driven oxen," Garric said, smiling but feeling the sadness of the youth and innocence he'd lost, "though they were yoked to plows rather than wagons. I've watched my share of sheep as well. Also I've fought rats, like you men—"

He turned and nodded, to include the Coerli in the word "men."

"—just did. When I decide that I'm too good for any job the kingdom requires, then I'll have stopped being the prince that the kingdom needs."

Garric turned and cleared his throat. His eyes fell on the guard who'd been helping Kucros. The fellow straightened in a parody of a soldier coming to attention.

"A good bow," Garric said. He'd carried one like it in the pastures south of Barca's Hamlet. The short, stiff yew staff was a useful prod and lever, and strung it would see off wildcats or even the sea wolves which sometimes rushed out of the surf to claim a sheep.

"Your Highness, I didn't, I mean I couldn't take time to look for my arrows," the fellow blurted nervously. He wasn't someone Garric knew, but he knew the *sort* of man he was. Garric had been, or thought he'd been, one of them. "We had to get going. And we're short-teamed now, from the rats."

"There're additional oxen on the way from camp," Garric said. "They won't be long coming even at the pace an ox moves, since you're so close."

They were using the heavy infantry to guard the transport and food animals in stockaded camps. Their equipment wasn't suited for fighting rat men, but they had a great deal of experience in building and holding fortified positions. The noblemen commanding what had been the elite infantry regiments hadn't liked what they saw as a demotion, but Lord Waldron—a cavalryman now on foot because of the nature of the new enemy—had even less sympathy for their complaints than Garric did.

"There's somebody coming now," said Kucros, looking to the east. "Is that them?"

He rose on the wagon seat, forgetting his wounds until the pain jabbed him—and then standing nonetheless. King Carus nodded grim approval: Kucros was an old soldier. He wasn't especially bright or talented, but he was a man you could count on to hold firm no matter what it cost. An army needs those men, almost as much as an army needs commanders who won't throw these men away.

"It can't be," Garric said, hopping onto the wagon step to get a little additional height. "No, that's a battalion of scouts."

He frowned as he stepped down. "And Lord Zettin himself is with them. Attaper, something's happened."

The scouts, two or three hundred of them, loped toward the halted supply train. They were spread to sweep half a mile or more and to reduce the chance of an ambushed enemy catching the whole unit. Garric knew that some scouting formations segregated humans from

Coerli, but in this battalion javelin-carrying woods rangers alternated man for man with the cat men. Lord Zettin was in the center, running easily beside a chieftain with a brindled hide.

"What happened to Zettin?" said Lord Attaper. Then, in fury and amazement, "Sister take me, *what* does Zettin think he's playing at?"

Carus chuckled. *"Attaper hadn't seen his boy in field uniform, I guess,"* he said. *"Yeah, that might be a bit of a surprise."*

Zettin was a former Blood Eagle and Attaper's protégé. He'd done a very professional job as commander of the royal fleet, and he'd obviously thrown himself into his new duties as commander of the scouts. Instead of a gilt breastplate and a glittering helmet, Zettin wore an iron-studded leather cuirass and a leather hat. In the loops of his cross-belts were two throwing axes and several knives; but he didn't carry a sword, and the salt-cured tails of five rat men dangled from epaulets sewn for the purpose onto the shoulders of his jerkin.

"Your Highness?" Zettin said. He wasn't breathing hard. "The rats are moving faster than we expected. Their main body is fifteen miles to the south."

"How far away are the additional draft animals?" Garric asked, letting the king in his mind sort the priorities with the ease of long experience.

"The oxen?" Zettin said in surprise. "Half an hour, I suppose. But Lord Waldron hopes you'll return at once, with my men as escort."

"First things first, milord," Garric said. "Admiral Ditter, hand over escort duties to the heavy infantry when they arrive with the oxen, then return to the camp as quickly as possible. Not until you've been relieved, though. We're not leaving Marshal Kucros and his men without an escort."

"Yes, Your Highness!" Ditter said. "But we'll be back in time for the real action?"

"Have no doubt of that, sir," said Garric. "Lord Atta-per, are you ready for another run?"

"Yes, Your Highness," Attaper said curtly. He didn't say, "or I'll die trying," because death would be failure and he didn't intend to fail. Anger at the situation burst out, though, when he snarled, "Zettin, who told you to dress like that? A jester?"

"You have your uniform, milord," said the younger officer. "So do we in the scouts."

Holding Attaper's eyes, he flicked the dried rat-tails with his thumbs. "And I lead my men from the front," he added, "as you taught me to do."

"Let's go, gentlemen," Garric said, his grin a mirror of the ghost in his mind's. "With luck and the help of the Gods, we're going to make these rat men extinct before sunset!"

INVISIBLE BRIGHTNESS PRESSED Sharina from all directions. Her skin prickled and her mind, not her eyes, felt squeezed. Then—

She stood in the temple precinct of her nightmares. Her feet were firmly planted on the pavers of black granite, and Burne balanced on her shoulder. She couldn't move her limbs, and the rat was as still as a furry statue.

Before them stood Black, hooded and ten feet tall. He held a codex in his left hand and an athame of black crystal in his right. On his shoulder, its hooked stinger raised, was a scorpion; its body alone was longer and broader than a man's hand and extended fingers.

At one end of the colonnaded plaza beyond the tall wizard was the temple on whose triangular pediment a figure robed like Black strangled a bull, while a great scorpion drove off a horde of tiny humans.

To Sharina's right—she could turn her head, though her arms were petrified like her legs—she could see above the portico that a series of mansions with gilded entablature climbed the natural slope. To her left, past Burne, was a multistory building with ranks of glass windows in bronze casements on the upper levels. Sharina had looked at the design of a similar central records building with Lord Tadai and a trio of architects, though the one they planned would've been in white marble.

In the sky roiled a figure molded from storm clouds, a scorpion which stood upright instead of sprawling. Lightning flashed behind its many eyes and dripped like poison from the tip of its stinger.

Black laughed in the same thunderous rumble as he had in her dreams. "You've caused me difficulties, Princess," he said. "That's ended, now. Nothing can prevent the rise of Lord Scorpion, the only true God."

The scorpion on the wizard's shoulder drew a complex pattern with its pincers; the figure of cloud lowering over the black city mimicked—mirrored?—the same gestures. Sharina tried to grasp the hilt of her Pewle knife. Black was too far to stab from where she was frozen, but she could throw the weapon.

Her arms didn't move any better than her legs did. She strained anyway. She had to do something.

"Lord Scorpion will appear in the sky of Pandah, your Pandah, as soon as I speak the final incantation," said Black, "and the city will worship Him. When Lord Scorpion becomes manifest, you and I will return to the waking world as His high priests. We will live and reign forever in Lord Scorpion's black radiance!"

"I'll never join you," Sharina said. "I'll fight you until I win or I die. Never!"

"You won't have a choice," said the wizard said with another boom of laughter. "Your mind and soul belong to Lord Scorpion, Princess, and your body is mine!"

Holding the book out, Black chanted, *"Skirtho athea darbo. . . ."* Instead of dipping and rising over words written around a symbol, the athame in his right hand drew a pattern in the air. It wasn't identical to the move-

ments of the scorpion on his shoulder, but at the fuzzy
edges of her mind Sharina realized the figures comple-
mented one another.

"Milio mili . . . ," said the wizard.

"Mother?" chirped Burne. "I know we've had our differences, and I'm no more ready to concede than you
are. But if you'll still admit that you have a son, this
would be a good time for you to show it."

Sharina turned her head toward the rat, her mouth
open to speak. Her arms and legs tingled.

Burne leaped to the codex in Black's left hand and
with that as a platform sprang upward. He arched down
with the wizard's scorpion in his forepaws.

Sharina's fingers closed on the horn grip of the Pewle
knife. She stepped forward, watching for her opening.
She didn't need to hurry. Black had long legs, but he
moved awkwardly; she could catch him easily.

"Lady, aid me in your service," she whispered.

"What are you doing?" Black said. *"What are you
doing?"*

Sharina stepped close. The shell of the big scorpion
crunched like eggshell in the rat's jaws.

Black threw the codex at Sharina; she blocked it with
her left elbow. It was a small volume but leather-bound,
with iron corners and a hasp. It would have stung if she'd
had time to think about it.

Sharina lunged. Black screamed and jabbed with the
athame. The long crystal blade could've been a dangerous weapon but the attempt was clumsy, like all the
wizard's other movements.

She caught Black's right wrist with her left hand. He
tried to jerk free, but he wasn't strong enough. She
chopped at the side of his left leg to where she thought
his knee should be under the robes. She missed the joint,
but a bone cracked anyway at the stroke of the sharp,
heavy blade.

Burne's clicking teeth spewed out bits of chitin. The

fragments gleamed in an arc against the duller black finish of the pavement. Overhead, the cloud wrack was dissipating, shredded by gusts which seemed to come from every direction.

Black lurched sideways and fell. Sharina landed on top of him, still holding his wrist. The fall drove the point of the athame into the pavement, chipping the granite and jarring the knife from the wizard's hand. The crystal didn't shatter: it must be black diamond instead of quartz or some lesser material.

Light spread through the plaza, bleaching the temple and porticos without blinding Sharina. Black mewled and squirmed like a salted slug. She thrust upward: from below the wizard's ribcage she thought, but the heavy steel grated through bone this time too. Dragging the Pewle knife free, she stabbed him high in the chest.

There was a stench worse than a long-dead mule bursting. Sharina rolled away from the body and got her feet under her. Holding her breath, she wiped the blade of her knife on the wizard's robe and backed away.

Black's hood slipped off. His flesh was dripping away as a foul liquid. The bared skull was neither human nor that of any animal of Sharina's experience. Its bulbous cranium sloped sharply to narrow jaws which hinged sideways instead of vertically.

Burne looked up from the remains of the scorpion and chuckled. "I'll bet mine tastes better," he said. He lifted his pointed snout and added, "Thank you, Mother!"

Things were . . . changing. Sharina stood in light that neither blinded nor dazzled her. She was no longer in the dream Pandah, or not only there.

She heard voices, prayers; more than she could count but each distinct and meaningful. *"Lady, preserve us from evil. Lady, save me/us/mankind. Lady, grant us your mercy in this hour of trial."* Many voices, desperate but hopeful. There were people kneeling before temples, pausing in fields as they scythed grain, and standing before the windows of huts to look in the direction their men had marched off.

Lady, preserve us!

The world turned beneath Sharina's feet. Armies were massing for battle. She slid the Pewle knife back into its sheath; its time was over.

The storm that had gathered in the south now rushed toward her, taking on human shape. It was cloaked in cloud and the lightnings flashed from its hands.

Lady, preserve us!

IT'S NOT OUR fault," Princess Perrine begged.

Ilna felt a sneer, though she didn't let it reach her lips. In her experience, nobody said that unless they were sure it *was* their fault.

"We were prisoners too," said Perrin. "Even when we went to the waking world, our parents remained here in the king's hands. We had no choice!"

An old woman in silk and gold lace had come out of the throng to embrace King Perus. They were crying hopelessly, helplessly. That was weakness; Ilna had only contempt for weakness. Nonetheless, the old couple weren't whimpering lies like their offspring were.

She began to pick out the knots of the pattern whose truth had destroyed the King of Man. She hadn't cried when Chalcus and Merota were killed. Would it have been better if she could have?

Hervir knelt before her, touching his forehead to the floor before rising. "Your Ladyship," he said, his tongue stumbling over the emotions that thickened his words.

"I'm not a lady!" Ilna said. There was little enough she was sure of, but that she knew.

She looked again at the chamber, partly to avoid seeing the devotion in Hervir's eyes. "Why did that monkey imprison so many people underground?" she asked. "Was it just out of cruelty? Because with the drug he was giving you, he could have put you all to working in the fields and you still wouldn't have escaped."

"This is only incidentally a prison, Your Ladyship," Hervir said. Ilna didn't correct him again because that would obviously be a waste of breath, but her fingers started a new pattern—which she picked out unfinished with a look of self disgust. "It's the throne room of a god. By polishing the walls outward, we slaves of the king— the monkey—worked our very souls into the stone."

Ilna's face worked on the sour thought. "It must be the drug," she said, as much to herself as to the fawning merchant. "To worship a monster like that, an ugly beast!"

Usun had sauntered back to her, twirling his staff. He chuckled and said, "Surely you've seen more of people than that, Ilna? They'll worship any strong person who orders them around. If he tells them they're worthless scum fit only to sacrifice and slave for him, so much the better!"

Hands on hips, the little man surveyed the vast, self-lighted cavern. "And they're right, aren't they?" he said. "People *are* worthless slaves."

Ilna stared at Usun in cold fury, her fingers knotting a pattern that would—

The little man grinned at her. He'd caught her out, baited her into a reaction that taught her something about her own feelings that she wouldn't have guessed.

"No, they're not," Ilna said quietly. "As you and I both know. And that's probably less of a surprise to you than it was to me."

She held up the fabric she'd begun, picking the knots out as she spoke. "You're a very clever fellow, Master Usun," she said. "Perhaps too clever for your own safety, sometimes."

"There wasn't any danger that you'd act without thinking," said Usun, still grinning. "Unless I'd misjudged *your* cleverness. If I made a mistake like that, why, I'd deserve to be punished, wouldn't I, Ilna?"

She laughed. She didn't do that very often. She turned and called to the former prisoners, "You're all free now. We'll go back to the surface and then—"

And then what? Return to the waking world? From what both Hervir and the monkey-king had said, some of the prisoners had been in this hole for thousands of years.

"And then we'll decide what to do."

Her voice carried better than it should have; it filled the whole glowing cavern, despite the sighs and prayers of the captives. Maybe when they were out in the light of the valley, those who wanted to stay could set up a kingdom, a something, of their own. Garric would surely help those who wanted to live in the waking world.

"For now, leave this place! Perrin, you and your sister lead them out. Now!"

The door opened. The woman whose image was carved on its outer face strode into the chamber. She stood twice Ilna's height, clad in armor gleaming like black pearl. The points of the trident in her right hand glittered with a vicious absence of color.

"I am Hili, Queen of Hell!" she cried. "Worship me, slaves! You are mine for all eternity!"

THE WIND WAS worse than the storms out of the northeast that sometimes lashed Barca's Hamlet, but this time Cashel was sweeping across worlds and ages, not driven but driving. Mountains swayed beneath him; great seas rose in billowing waves before his onrush.

Cashel laughed with the joy of it, but he kept a firm grip on the quarterstaff. He knew he'd have need for it soon.

With no sense of motion or past motion, Cashel stood on the Stone of Question in the court of the Tree Oracle. Liane was on his left side and Rasile on his right. He didn't see Gorand.

Cashel turned. The women were looking around silently. Neither was the sort to talk just to be working her lips. They were good companions for when things got hard, which they were likely to do any moment now.

There hadn't been anybody else in the enclosure when Cashel first found himself in it, but Amineus and two other plump, middle-aged fellows came walking out of the Priests' House a moment later. One of the strangers led a goat; the other had a wax-stoppered wine jar with a pretty design in blue glaze. Amineus held a bowl, a knife with an engraved bronze blade, and a folded length of red cloth.

They were talking to each other. They didn't see Cashel and his friends till Liane said, "Good day, Master Amineus."

The priest with the wine screamed, "Spirits!" and flung the jar over his shoulder when his limbs spasmed. The goat got away too, bolting across the enclosure. The brick wall there had started to come down, which the goat seemed to have noticed as sure as Cashel had.

"Master Cashel!" Amineus said. "How—where—how did you get here?"

The priest who'd lost the goat sat down on the ground like a little boy and put his face in his hands. "Oh, may the Lady help us!" he said, then started to cry.

Cashel heard the *WHACK!*/thump of a catapult loosing, a big one. The bar hit the stop to release the stone, then the back legs of the frame slammed back down on the battlements. Not long ago he wouldn't have recognized the sound.

He'd been around armies a lot since he left Barca's Hamlet; way too much, in fact. Cashel didn't mind a fight, but war was more like a slaughteryard than fighting. He didn't like slaughteryards even when it was sheep being slaughtered.

"The pirates are here?" he asked.

"Yes, yes!" Amineus said. "They haven't released the

Worm yet, but we know that it's only time before they do. We—my colleagues and I—came here to beg the Tree to send the champion Gorand to us, but everyone else is in on the walls."

"Gorand brought us here," said Liane, looking in the direction where the catapult had shot. When Cashel concentrated, he could hear clangs and the snap of bows from that way too. It was just skirmishing this far, though. "We don't know where he is now, though."

"I'm here, Your Ladyship," said a voice behind them.

Cashel turned, smoothly and not in a panic, but he wasn't wasting time either. Then he lowered his staff with a bit of a smile.

The pod had opened; the eyes of the human face in it were open too. Even with the bark-brown color of the skin, Cashel could tell now that the face was Gorand's. He felt foolish not to have seen that when he first met the tall man sitting on the stoop of his cabin.

"Hello, Master Gorand," he said politely. "Thank you for bringing us back so quick as this."

The man in the pod—Gorand—chuckled. "It wouldn't been worth coming if we'd waited much longer, would it, Cashel? Not if I'm hearing what I think I am. I haven't been so long in the woods that I've forgotten what a siege sounds like."

"They figure the pirates'll bring out the Worm pretty quick," said Cashel. "Which is likely enough. Rasile here—"

He nodded to the Corl wizard.

"—showed me what they did to Ombis on Telut, and it was pretty bad. But I guess you know that from your own time."

Gorand nodded. "I guess I do," he said.

"Oh, mighty champion!" said the priest who'd dropped the wine. The first time they'd been in this place, Amineus had said one of them was Conwin and the other was Hilfe, but Cashel hadn't any idea which was which. "Tell

us how to vanquish our enemies in this day of great
trial!"

"For a start, you greedy little toad," said Gorand,
"you—all three of you—can shut your mouths. I'm going to take care of this, but the less I think about you and
all the other city scum, the better I'll like it."

"What's he saying?" said the goat-priest. Amineus
clasped the bowl and other gear to his chest. With the
hand thus freed, he tried to hush his fellow.

Who wasn't interested in being hushed. He pushed
Amineus' arm away and said, "The oracle's not supposed
to talk like that! There's something wrong, I—"

A branch of the tree curled down and slapped the noisy
priest across the back of the head. He yelped and threw
himself on his belly, covering his scalp with both hands.
He was bald now that his feathered hat was knocked off.

Things got really quiet for a moment. Liane turned to
face the pod, but Cashel decided he'd better keep an eye
on the priests just for now. Rasile walked over to the
ancient temple and spread her yarrow stalks.

The priest who'd dropped the wine jar started moving
back toward the house; the fellow who'd been knocked
down looked fearfully over his shoulder and gathered
his knees under himself to run. He'd be running away,
though, nothing for Cashel to worry about. . . .

"That's right, Hilfe, time to flee," said Gorand with so
much contempt that it made Cashel think of his sister.
"Let somebody else do the dangerous part. That's what
you Dariadans are good for, isn't it?"

Amineus tossed his paraphernalia on the ground and
faced the pod with his hands at his sides. He said, "What
would you have me do, Lord Gorand?"

Gorand laughed. "Go or be silent, Amineus," he said;
there wasn't the edge in his voice that there had been a
moment before. "All of you priests, go or be silent."

Conwin walked away, taking a longer stride and quicker
one each time his legs moved. Hilfe stayed on the ground,

lifted his knees to his chest, and began to cry. Amineus folded his arms and said nothing.

Cashel turned to Gorand. "Sir?" he said, leaning his staff into the angle of his elbow just like he had when they stood in front of his cabin in the woods.

"The people of Dariada were very pleased that I'd saved them from the Worm, back all those years ago," Gorand said. He was talking quietly, but Cashel could hear the anger returning to his tone. "And they were pleased at the Tree Oracle, too. It wasn't long at all before somebody figured out that they could make a very good thing out of that. They're merchants, you see."

"Yes, sir," said Cashel, just showing that he was paying attention.

"But they didn't want *me,* or that's what I think happened anyway," said Gorand. Another branch of the tree waved; just a wave this time. "They're nervous around my sort when it's all peaceful again. *Our* sort, Cashel. You'll need to watch out too, you know."

Cashel shrugged. "Sir," he said, "I trust my friends. But anyhow, I miss peace myself. I'm not, well . . . I'm a shepherd."

"The obol struck in my honor, that was the key," Gorand said. "My face is on it, not the gull's head for Dariada . . . or now the Tree, but in my time the gull was the symbol of the city. With that in my hand, I could go or stay as I liked. But they didn't put it in my hand, did they? Not till they needed me again!"

"Sir," said Cashel, "I don't know what happened in your time. Neither does Master Amineus, I'll warrant. But like we said back at your cabin, it doesn't matter."

Gorand laughed again, but this time he sounded sad. "You needn't worry, shepherd. I gave my word that I'd deal with the Worm, so that's what I'll do. Just like you would if you could. But there's something else that I'm telling you because of who you are. You can think of it as a free response from the Tree."

Gorand's brown eyes shifted—to Amineus, Cashel guessed, but he didn't take his attention off the man in the pod to make sure. "Ordinarily a response from the Tree would be worth the taxes of your whole borough. Though as you can see, I wouldn't have been the one spending the wealth that came in."

"Sir," said Cashel, just a placeholder like before. He'd rather have all the answers straight out, but the tall man was angry and it sounded like he had reason to be. Letting Gorand talk himself out was better than pushing the business . . . though he would still do what he said. Cashel didn't doubt that in the least.

"I'll take care of the Worm," Gorand repeated. "But Archas, the pirate chief who's handled the Worm in the past, he's left it to his one-armed lieutenant this time. Archas is in the city now. He arrived with the last group of refugees fleeing the terrible pirates. He'll be coming here, Cashel."

"Coming to the Tree?" said Cashel, frowning as he thought of all the things the words could mean. "Coming to you, Master Gorand?"

"I won't be here, Cashel," Gorand said. "He's seeking the temple that was here when the Tree was planted. If he's allowed to stay there, you and your friends will rue it for the rest of your short lives."

Cashel glanced at the stubs of the ancient stone columns. Just how old was it really? Though that was the sort of thing Garric and Sharina thought about, not any business of his.

"Thank you," said Cashel, turning. He shifted the quarterstaff into both hands, slanting it on-guard without thinking. "I guess we'd best not let him stay."

There was a rattling and cracking, then a long, drawn-out crash as the brick wall around the enclosure crumbled into bricks and brick dust. Had the Worm . . . ? But the Worm couldn't have torn the whole thing down all at the same time.

The Tree was rising, out of the ground and out of the wall too. Over the centuries, hair-fine tendrils had dug away half the mortar, but they'd wrapped the individual bricks in a web that held them firmer than the lime could. When the roots pulled away, what had been masonry collapsed into rubble.

Amineus and Hilfe ran together into the Priests' House. Cashel couldn't blame the priests—there was nothing holding them here, after all—but he wondered how much shelter they thought the building was going to be from what was happening.

The Tree trembled. Cashel thought it was tipping into the street, but the roots nearest him bent away like legs. The huge creature stepped toward the southern edge of the city—toward where the fighting was going on. The pod with Gorand dangled high in the air, looking down on Dariada and the battle.

"Good luck, Master Gorand!" Cashel called, raising his staff. The noise was tremendous, worse than the crash and boom of a thunderstorm.

"Good luck to you, shepherd!" called the man in the pod. A branch waved goodbye to Cashel.

Chapter

17

CHE SUN'S GOING to be in our eyes by midafternoon," said Lord Waldron gloomily, eyeing the army of giant rats to the south.

"That man would complain if we hanged him with a golden rope!" King Carus said in half-serious exasperation. Waldron wouldn't run even from certain death, but

Garric didn't recall the army commander ever making an optimistic assessment.

They were lurching along on a platform raised from the bed of a cart drawn by eight span of oxen. An artificial vantage point was the only way you could see any distance on these rolling prairies. The oxen were slow, but the army was advancing in battle order and wouldn't have been travelling faster than this anyway.

"The sun was in your eyes at the Stone Wall, milord," Garric said mildly. "And you won there."

To the south, Palomir's forces moved like a swarm of ants; more ants than a tax clerk could count in an afternoon. Dark-furred, steel-glittering companies appeared on hilltops, trotted down grassy slopes, and vanished again in the swales.

"The Stone Wall was a bloody near thing!" snapped Waldron. He blinked, thought about the verbal exchange, and managed a smile.

"But as you say," he added, "we won."

A second oxcart ambled along beside the first. Tenoctris sat cross-legged in its bed with her paraphernalia laid out before her on a white tarpaulin. A solid-looking man, one of Liane's agents, squatted in a corner in case the wizard needed something fetched or other help. Normally Garric or one of his friends from Barca's Hamlet would be with Tenoctris, but they had other duties today.

Duzi, preserve my friends, Garric thought. *Duzi, keep Liane safe.*

Even if Duzi existed, he was a little god who couldn't affect great affairs. He'd been the god of Garric's youth in Barca's Hamlet, though, and a prayer to him gave comfort to that boy whom the world now called a prince.

How many rats are there really? Forty thousand, Zettin's scouts had guessed, but it might be more than that. It might be impossibly more than that.

The royal army advanced in a shallow V formed by

troops of the former phalanx, now arrayed only four deep instead of sixteen. The skirmishers with bows, slings, and javelins extended the wings of the V, and the heavy infantry closed the back of the formation to turn it into a triangle.

To either side moved the scouts, humans and Coerli in ragged bands no more formally organized than the rats they were facing. They took the place of the cavalry which would've flanked the army in a normal battle.

The rats would envelop both wings of the royal army. The heavy infantry would have horrendous casualties, but there was nothing to do about it. There simply hadn't been time to reequip those regiments and train them in a wholly new style of warfare.

"They won't break, lad," Carus said. *"Sometimes that's the thing you need most: men who won't break even when they know they're going to die if they stand. They'd die if they ran too, of course, but that isn't what'll keep them in their ranks."*

A company of giant rats came over a hill barely a half-mile away. Waldron gestured to his trumpeter, riding in the bed of the cart and looking upward. The silvery Prepare to Engage rang out, followed by the trumpets and horns of all the regiments.

The scouts didn't have instruments, but they let out a yipping ululation. It was apparently a compromise that fit both human and Corl throats.

"Sister take them!" said Carus. *"I don't know what that'll do to the rats, but it'd bloody well raise the hair on the back of* my *neck. If I had hair, or a neck."*

The Sister will have her share of them, I have no doubt, thought Garric. *And the rest of us. But that's the job.*

Garric adjusted his ornate, parcel-gilt cuirass. "Milord, I'll leave you to it," he said to Waldron. "May the Shepherd be with you!"

He dropped down the ladder, impressed again by

how rigid the apparatus was. The platform's pole frame
had been cross-braced by guy ropes—stays, in nautical
parlance, since the work had been done by former sail-
ors of the royal fleet. The result was makeshift and
the additional twelve feet of height amplified the cart's
every jolt and wobble, but there was nothing flimsy
about it.

The Blood Eagles—the hundred and ten men who remained of the regiment besides the section in Pandah
with Sharina—were waiting for him. They wore the
leather padding without the bronze cuirasses that would
normally cover their torsos, and steel or leather caps in
place of full helmets. They carried skirmishers' round
wicker bucklers with linen facings instead of their usual
massive shields of laminated wood.

Lord Attaper's grim expression had very little to do
with the coming battle and a great deal to do with where
his prince intended to fight it from. "Your Highness," he
said, handing Garric the silvered helmet with flaring gilt
wings. "This isn't a normal battle where your armor can
give you reasonable protection. I know you like to lead
from the front and—"

"And I'm going to lead from the front again, milord,"
said Garric. "Attaper? Please. This may be the last conversation we ever have. Let's not make it an argument, eh?"

He lowered the massive helm over his head and cinched
the chin strap. He would've liked to wear a cap like the
phalangists and reequipped Blood Eagles, but if he was
going to do this, it was important that he be seen doing it.

And he *was* going to do it.

For an instant, Attaper's face went blank as a stone
wall. Then he grinned—slightly—and said, "All right,
we won't argue, Your Highness. After all, if anything
happens to you, I won't be around for people to complain to."

They trotted to the point of the wedge. The leading

companies of the phalanx had spread their rear ranks left
and right during the advance; now those troops slipped
back behind their fellows, making room for the Blood
Eagles and Prince Garric.

The vanguard of the rats bounded down a grassy slope
toward the humans; their stink curled on the breeze. Archers loosed arrows from the flanks, and the Blood Eagles readied their javelins to throw. Garric drew his long
sword.

"This isn't a bad place to be in a hard fight," said the
ghost in his mind, musing with the odd dynamic relax-
ation Carus always fell into before a battle. *"There's no
safety anywhere, whatever Attaper says; and looking for
safety is the quickest way I can think of to get killed."*

He laughed like a cheerful demon. *"I've killed my
share of folks trying to do that. I'll tell the world!"*

"The kingdom!" Garric shouted.

"The kingdom!" the army snarled. Skirmishers and the
Blood Eagles launched their javelins, and the rats were
on them.

A chittering rat rushed Garric, then hunched instead
of lunging. Garric—King Carus—thrust. His long arm
gave him an angle over the top of the rat's little circular
shield.

The beast gurgled and vaulted backward. Garric
couldn't tell whether the jump was the rat's death throes
or a vain attempt to escape. It was gouting blood from
severed arteries.

A rat came in from Garric's left while he was extended
for the lunge. He had his long dagger ready to defend—
Carus preferred to use two blades rather than a shield in
this sort of melee—but a Blood Eagle in the second rank
had kept his javelin. He jabbed, taking the rat through
the chest just below the shoulders.

The initial rush was over. There'd been about a hundred rats in the company, but they'd rattled against the

wedge like hail on a slate roof. A few men were down, but human discipline and close ranks had told. More rats—judging from the sound, half a dozen similar companies—had attacked at about the same time, but with no greater effect. The army marched forward, maintaining its formation.

More rats bounded onto the ranks of swordsmen, yipping and clicking. They threw themselves against the front of the wedge like a wave hitting a seawall.

Garric used his sword's length, thrusting for the beasts' wrists before they were able to strike. The dagger was a help, but Blood Eagles saved him repeatedly by forcing themselves in front of the rats' weapons.

Some of the bodyguards went down or fell out of line, cursing and trying to bandage their own injuries, but the army trampled forward over a carpet of quivering Palomir corpses. Carus had been right when he directed his descendant to wear the winged helmet and silvered cuirass: by drawing the rats' sole attention to him, he left a broad swath of the beasts open to slaughter by the disciplined soldiers surrounding.

It would only work for as long as the glittering prince remained standing, but so far, so good. Garric's left thigh was bleeding, his dagger was badly notched—he'd have to replace it, but when?—there was a dent in the back of his cuirass, and a sword spinning from the wielder's dead paw had lopped off part of his helmet's right wing.

That was nothing at all in a battle of this magnitude, but the battle was scarcely begun. Carus, in his element, laughed in Garric's mind. As for Garric himself—

Garric was tired and knew he'd be more tired. He disliked slaughter, even slaughtering beasts, and the stench was even worse—far worse—than that of a human battlefield.

It didn't matter. The rats wouldn't surrender, but they died. Garric would stride forward and kill for as long as there was an enemy to kill. It had to be done.

The rats swept in a third time, separate war bands spreading themselves like a sticky fluid across the front of the wedge. Lord Waldron commanded the army. Prince Garric was the champion, the warrior, and the Isles had never known a greater warrior than the ghost who now controlled the prince's body.

Garric's eyes saw only movement: a whiskered face— *dimpling before a sword tip; a sword swinging in from the left—blocked but the bloody dagger broke, left leg kicking the rat's feet from under it, right heel flattening the pointed helmet and crunching the narrow skull;* rats on three sides—*lurching forward, powerful human body shoving the lighter beasts away, slash, stab, fur spouting bright blood in arterial arcs, grabbing a sword in the air and blocking a stroke with it despite the rat's severed paw locked on the grip.*

The rush was over, drowned in its own blood. Garric stood on top of a hill, looking down into a swale and still another mass of rats tramping forward.

The green-and-white Palomir standard fluttered on the ridge opposite. Beneath it stood a human warrior in black armor, his sword drawn. Below him was another human, a wizard in blue robes of some thin fabric. He gestured with a wand and chanted words lost in the intervening distance.

"Your Highness!" Attaper said, gasping with effort. His shield had been hacked so often and deeply that part of the outer layer of wood had sprung away. "Your Highness, I *can't* follow you if you run into the middle of them that way. I can't, nobody can!"

"I didn't . . . ," Garric said, looking around dully. His every muscle ached or stung. His arms were red to the shoulders, and some of that blood had to be his own. "Did I . . . ?"

He tried to remember what had just happened in a connected sequence. He had—Carus had, wearing the body of his descendent Garric or-Reise—burst into the tight Palomir ranks, cutting a path ahead of himself and largely ignoring the rats he'd left behind.

He'd actually ripped through the wave—and survived, because the rats hadn't expected what was happening any more than the Blood Eagles had. Attaper and his men had had to butcher their way forward, taking reckless wounds as they tried to save the prince they were sure had committed suicide in front of their eyes.

Men fell in beside Garric as the wedge re-formed. Half of those in the ranks were dismounted cavalrymen who'd formed the reserve in the center of the triangle. Waldron had ordered a troop to the front to replace the Blood Eagles who'd fallen in their desperate haste.

The sky to the south throbbed with black clouds. Lightning crackled from thunderhead to thunderhead, and the rising wind hissed with waiting violence.

Garric looked at the slope behind them. The ground was as thick with bodies as a wheat field with stubble after the harvest, and hundreds of those lying still or moaning were human.

The ancient king viewed the scene through Garric's eyes. *"We're just tools, now, lad,"* he said in a tone of cold appraisal. *"You and me and them. Tools break, but only the work matters."*

Briefly taking control of Garric's body again, he threw down the clumsy Palomir sword. "Give me your dagger," he said harshly to the cavalryman beside him.

"Your Highness," the man said. He already held his shield and his drawn sword, so he lifted his elbow. Garric pulled the dagger from his right-side sheath.

Tenoctris sat in her cart as it trundled forward. From the pentacle before her, a mist of wizardlight spurted upward like smoke. Scarlet and azure strands mixed in a delicate netting. She paid no attention to the carnage about her. Garric smiled at his friend with gentle affection and returned to his own business.

"They're coming," muttered Attaper. The sword he now carried was of infantry pattern, not his own horseman's sword. Waldron's trumpeter blew Prepare to Engage!

The rats bounded up from the swale. As they did so, the Palomir wizard pointed his wand into the sky. A bolt of wizardlight crashed upward, turning all the clouds the sullen red of a banked furnace.

The storm struck, lashing the faces of the human army with hail the size of pigeon's eggs among the icy rain. Men cried in surprise and the fear of wizardry, and the chittering rats raced upward.

THE TREE WALKED south, out of the ruins of its enclosure. Dust from mortar and the broken bricks swirled in a rusty blanket; every time another pile of rubble settled, more choking powder spurted up. Cashel turned his head slightly to breathe through the sleeve of his tunic.

He expected the Tree to smash a path through Dariada the same way as the Worm would, though of course the Worm wouldn't stop with making the one track. Instead Gorand picked his way along like an octopus walking across the sea bottom on the tips of its arms, only he had more legs than *anybody* could count.

The gnarled trunks, dangling roots, and vines furred with green mosses reached and placed themselves with rippling ease. Cashel could tell there was a pattern, though it wasn't something he saw with his eyes; it was more the way he judged the swirl of a fight with quarterstaffs, but a lot more complicated.

Chimney pots fell and shards of roof tiles rained off the eaves as the Tree passed, but the only real destruction was what happened to the enclosure itself. Though Gorand now was a whole forest walking, he chose where he put his legs. The cobblestone streets took most of his weight, and though they twisted like sheep tracks, the roots/stems/vines spared the houses from any but brushing contact however the streets turned.

Cashel grinned in delight. It was always a pleasure to watch somebody who really understood craftsmanship, whatever his craft happened to be. What Gorand was doing now was beyond the slickest dancer Cashel expected to see ever.

The Tree passed out of sight. It hadn't been tall as trees went, and even lifted up on its roots the houses blocked the view by the time it had gone more than maybe halfway to the city walls.

Cashel turned, wondering which direction this Archas was going to come from. He didn't doubt the pirate *would* come; not because Gorand was an oracle, but because he wasn't the sort of man who'd say something he wasn't sure of.

Rasile was chanting. To Cashel she sounded like a pair of screech owls courting, but she knew what she was doing. Liane stood beside the wizard, looking alert and ready to help if she needed to. To look at Liane you'd never guess that she'd just watched a big grove of trees lift up from around her and walk over the roofs of the city.

Cashel grinned. She'd seen other stuff just as amazing, he guessed; but he'd bet she'd look just as cool and unworried now if she'd spent her previous life chatting with other fine ladies in the palace. She was a good friend for Sharina, and she'd be a great queen for Garric.

Rasile yipped, then made a funny twitch in the air with her slate athame. A slanted image of Dariada hung in the air, not dimmed by the sunlight nor smothered by brick dust still settling over the ruined enclosure.

From this angle the Tree looked like green surf sweeping across a beach of red roof tiles. The soldiers and citizens on the battlements were ant-sized; Cashel could tell what they were only because he already knew. There were lots more ants on the plains to the south of the city, but he didn't see the Worm. It would come soon enough.

Cashel went back to looking out for Archas. He wondered if the fellow would be alone. Well, he had to be stopped. No matter who or what was with him. He spun his quarterstaff, getting the kinks out of his shoulders.

"You can watch this, Warrior Cashel," Rasile said. Her voice was a bit harsh, but she sounded strong.

"Ma'am," he said, "I think I ought to keep an eye out for the pirate that's coming here."

"I will let you know when Archas nears," Rasile said. "Until then you may watch your fellow warrior. You are much alike, you and Warrior Gorand, you know."

"Yes, ma'am," Cashel said, turning toward the image. "I do know that."

The Tree was climbing over the city walls. Gorand had gone off to the left instead of heading straight to where the pirates were. Which made sense when Cashel thought about it, since Gorand would've been trampling on people for sure if he'd crossed the wall where they were thickest. There were only a few stairs down from the battlements for folks to get out of the way.

The picture was clear as clear, even sharper than what the wizard had showed him back in Pandah. She didn't seem near so wrung out as she'd been then, neither.

Rasile smiled. "This is a good place for my sort of art, Cashel," she said. "Almost a uniquely good place. That is why the Warrior Archas is coming here."

Cashel nodded; he could feel the prickle of wizardry all over his body. It wasn't just Rasile's little chant to make the picture of what was happening on the walls.

The Worm squirmed out of the air like a maggot twisting from the sore it'd raised on a sheep's back. Its solid parts were gray, and it was purple with mixed wizard-light in the splotches that hadn't yet come out of the place it was from. The Worm had a round mouth, and the spike it pointed to the city wall was as long as a boat's mast.

The defenders had to have known about the Worm, but they must not've understood. There was a rush to get off the battlements right *snap!* when the creature started toward the walls. People fell and pushed each other off; even soldiers were running, some of them. Cashel grimaced, but he couldn't have done anything about it even if he'd been there.

He started the staff circling again, slowly though. This wasn't for any purpose besides working his muscles while he watched what he couldn't change. He wondered if he and the quarterstaff would've made a difference down there on the walls. He didn't suppose they could, though he'd be willing to try.

An angle of the walls poked out to the east, following a wedge of land between two gullies that were dry at least at this time of the year. The Tree was crawling toward it.

Rasile's image showed things so well that Cashel could see that the fields—they'd been planted in maize—were torn up behind the Tree. It looked like a whole village of drunken plowmen had driven oxen through them. Gorand was doing what he could to spare people, but anything else had to take its chances.

The ground trembled even here in the center of the city. It was a constant shudder, enough to keep dust motes dancing over the piles of brick where the walls used to be. Cashel thought it was Gorand, but then the Tree walked around the corner of the wall. The shiver in the ground changed as the Worm turned toward the new enemy.

The pirates had been standing well back from the Worm. When Gorand appeared they just ran: south back where they'd come from, or west away from the Tree.

Rasile didn't seem to do anything, but Cashel found he was seeing the Worm and the Tree up close as they slid together. The Worm had been big when he watched it smash through the walls of Ombis, but it'd gotten a lot bigger since. He wondered how long Archas figured to control it if it kept on growing; but maybe that was why the pirate chief was coming here to the temple.

The Worm reared, swelling its mouth open the way a whirlpool spreads in still water. It puffed black smoke across a broad swathe of the Tree. Foliage fell away like leaves killed by a late freeze. Even bark sloughed, leaving branches dry and as white as old bone.

The Worm drove forward, slashing with its murderous tusk. Wood seared by the creature's poisonous breath crackled and splintered before its attack. Nothing could've stopped that onrush, but the long flanks of the Tree closed about the gray body. Cashel could hear the Tree's movement, a vast hollow sigh like a storm sweeping through a forest in springtime.

Branches slid across the granite-speckled skin, gripping and lifting it. The Worm twisted, stabbing again. Vines and creepers looped the tusk from all directions, using its leverage to lock the creature's head.

The Worm's mouth opened. More branches caught at the circular lips, pulling them wider and wrestling the creature's head up. Again the maw spurted black smoke, but this time into the air like a whale blowing. The gout drifted back on the breeze, settling slowly. Some vegetation withered, but patches of the Worm's tough hide blistered to an angry red also.

The Worm thrashed, hammering the ground and shaking down houses that the Tree's passage had weakened. The branches didn't lose their grip, though, and the long gray body began to stretch.

The Worm's tail was still free; it twitched up and slammed repeatedly. Cashel felt the ground throb to the dull hammerblows well after each stroke, the way thunder follows distant lightning.

The Worm tried to coil, dragging part of the Tree along for a distance. The roots dug down to bedrock, scraping up soil in a growing ridge.

Even the Worm's strength failed after a time: the motion slowed, then stopped. The Tree's foliage rustled, but for a moment nothing happened; Cashel wondered if maybe Gorand had worn himself out in the grapple too.

Portions of the Tree strained in opposite directions, still holding the Worm like algae to a rock. The long gray body stretched and stretched further. The maw spurted liquid, not the corrosive smoke, and the tail twirled in a desperate spiral instead of drumming the ground.

The Worm tore open, pouring out sluggish fluids and fat coils of intestine; Cashel heard a ripping sound like nothing in his experience. The skin at the edges of the tear pulled back.

The Worm shrank like a slug which the sun caught on bricks. Though Gorand released it, the gray corpse continued to shrivel.

The Tree, still bearing white scars from the battle, reformed itself into a compact mass instead of the hollow circle it'd been here in the enclosure. It walked slowly toward the west.

"Isn't it coming back?" Liane asked quietly.

Cashel shrugged. "Gorand spent a lot of time in that cabin where we found him," he said. "He's took care of the Worm the way he said he would, but he's holding the coin himself now. I guess he wants to see some of the world, or anyway a part of it that isn't Dariada."

"Warrior Cashel?" said Rasile is a raspy voice. "I said I would tell you when the Warrior Archas neared. He is here now."

She pointed her short, hairy arm toward the east side of the enclosure opposite where the Priests' House stood. A big man with a braided blond beard climbed over the pile of rubble. His chest was bare except for leather cross-belts hung with weapons, and he held curved swords in both hands.

He crossed the empty ground, drawing circles with his sword points. "I am Fallin, God of the Sea!" he shouted.

"No," said Cashel, stepping into the ruined temple, "you're not."

He began to spin his quarterstaff. The butt caps crackled spirals of blue wizardlight.

PUT THAT FISH spear down," snapped Ilna to the armored woman, "or I'll take it away from you!"

Hili laughed and pointed the trident at Perrin and Perrine, the humans nearest to her. They cringed and clung together, too frightened even to run.

Ilna had been poised to reknot the cords whose truth had driven the great ape mad. She threw down the strands of sisal. Everything had suddenly become clear to her; the real pattern stretched in all directions.

It was perfectly beautiful—it was *perfect*. Everything was obvious, woven into its proper place. She was disgusted with herself not to have understood it before. She began to weave again, not with her hands and not needing anything material to work with.

Hili's trident jabbed toward the prince and princess, a motion rather than a real thrust. Black, crackling lightning twisted from its points. The twins flew back screaming, their silken garments smoldering where the sparks had touched them. The armored giant laughed merrily.

"You prancing fool," Ilna said, coldly furious. She hadn't really thought the giant would listen to her, though. She stepped forward, casting the new pattern before her.

Hili turned toward the movement in surprise, then stabbed at Ilna with a expression of rage. Her lightning sizzled and caught in Ilna's pattern. Its meshes curled around Hili like a minnow net and closed.

Hili shrieked, ripping her trident through the encircle-
ment. She was no longer a giant. The place they fought
wasn't the cavern either, but in a corner of Ilna's mind
she could see the door to that stone prison standing open.
The captives were streaming out behind Usun. Perrin
and Perrine were being carried by the ape servants, while
the twins' aged parents stumbled along behind.

"No one can oppose me!" Hili shouted, gripping her
trident in both hands and shoving the points toward Ilna's face. "I am God!"

The trident blasted glittering black fire again. Ilna's re-
formed pattern tangled the bolts, stretching as it dragged
them to silent oblivion.

Ilna stepped forward, weaving a new pattern. She
smiled coldly. What the other woman meant was that nobody could *successfully* oppose her, which the recent
past should've taught her was a lie. But just to oppose
this ranting bully—Ilna would've done that if it certainly
meant her life. You didn't give into bullies.

And it wasn't as though life meant a lot to her anyway.

Hili danced aside, her handsome features suddenly as
cold as a statue's. Hair-fine needles rained from the trident's points. Ilna's net caught most of the cascade, but
pain shivered across her skin and under her eyeballs. She
could see nothing but black pain.

Ilna drew her pattern tight. She didn't ignore the
pain—it couldn't be ignored; it was her whole being—but
she did what was necessary anyway, as she'd always done.

There was a squawk of surprise; the pain stopped and
a moment later Ilna could see again. Hili was struggling
in Ilna's net, slashing at it with the trident though the
meshes fouled her limbs. She broke free at last and stood
glaring at her opponent.

Ilna had been breathing hard. She straightened and
began to repair her pattern. There wasn't as much damage this time. She considered making the strands thinner

and the meshes tighter so that they would better protect her, but that wasn't really necessary. It was only pain, after all.

She started forward, her pattern swirling before her.

Hili hunched, holding out her trident. She screamed like a trapped wildcat, then retreated instead of attacking.

Ilna smiled without humor and continued toward the other woman. She didn't know how this was going to end, but she was going to keep on going until she'd ended it.

The trident spat a net of sparkling blackness that pressed against Ilna's pattern instead of trying to stab through it. Ilna paused, not stopped by her opponent but stopping to measure Hili's strength. Yes, this would do. . . .

Ilna's pattern enveloped the pulsing black and the trident it sprang from. The cosmos twisted. Hili gave a despairing shriek; her protection and power vanished as if thrown into bottomless quicksand.

Ilna paused, breathing hard again. "You should have listened to me," she said. "But you're not the first one who didn't."

She started forward.

Hili retreated, her face desperate. "I yield!" she cried. She threw down her helmet and fumbled for the catches of her body armor. "I surrender to you! I am your slave!"

"You're mistaking me for my brother Cashel," Ilna said as she continued to advance. "He's a much nicer person than I am."

Ilna spread the pattern that had just crushed the trident out of existence. Howling, Hili turned to run. She stumbled, threw her arms out before her, and fell—not downward but out, shrinking and screaming and finally vanishing into utter blackness.

"Now that, dear heart," said Chalcus, "was as nice a piece of work as I ever hope to see."

"We've been waiting for you, Ilna," said Merota. "I'm glad you've come."

Ilna embraced them. She was crying. She never cried.

"Sharina needs help still, of course," said Chalcus, "but that can wait for a moment. Dear heart, dear love, dear life of my life."

The King of Man's former prisoners had reached the surface of the valley. With little Usun standing on an overturned cart to lead the cheers, they shouted, "Honor to the Sister! All praises to the Sister!"

Ilna cried and hugged her family.

CASHEL SPUN HIS staff sunwise in a figure eight as he walked forward, then switched the hand that led on the shaft and reversed its rotation. He wasn't being fancy and he sure wasn't trying to spook the pirate; Archas pretty clearly wasn't the sort to spook. Cashel just needed to be sure his muscles were ready for whatever happened.

Archas, Fallin as he called himself now, laughed. "If you get out of my way, you stupid ox," he said cheerfully, "then I'll kill you quickly. If not, I'll take my time . . . and I'll let you live in pieces. Forever."

His swords did a pretty dance in opposite directions to each other, spinning off wizardlight as bright as necklaces of rubies. He stepped in and, though his lips were still laughing, his right-hand sword thrust at Cashel's heart.

The quarterstaff blocked it with a ferrule and a *bang!* like a ram battering an iron-faced door. Wizardlight spewed out in a mixed shower. When red sparks landed on Cashel's wrist and arm, they stung and the little hairs shriveled up. Archas jumped back, though, swearing like the pirate he was; the scattered blue light had sprayed him too.

Cashel grinned and held where he was for a moment,

keeping the staff moving widdershins. Archas didn't look much like a god now.

The pirate came in quickly, his right hand stabbing again but chopping with his left a half-heartbeat later. Cashel was moving before the strokes even started. Even so he couldn't have blocked both, but his quarterstaff met the thrust. The blast knocked him and Archas back, just like it had before.

The air had the burned smell of nearby lightning. Cashel wasn't in the old temple anymore, and Liane and Rasile weren't anywhere about.

He got his quarterstaff back into a rhythm. This time he stepped forward instead of letting Archas come to him.

"I am Fallin!" the pirate shouted again.

Cashel straightened the staff into a thrust, left hand leading. Archas brought his swords together like scissor blades on the straps of the butt cap, catching it and stopping the stroke like Cashel had punched the side of a cliff.

The shock hurled them apart again. Cashel's palms tingled all the way to his elbows, and there were blisters on both forearms.

Cashel set the staff spinning, sunwise this time. He was breathing through his mouth. He stepped in again, just moving forward. The tips of the quarterstaff knitted a round of vivid blue before him, like the sky on a cloudless summer afternoon.

He and Archas circled on a featureless black plain. The stars gleamed above, not the familiar constellations but all stars, a universe of stars, each shining with a subtle difference in color.

Archas tapped his sword points against the sparkling blue shield in a pattern as careful as a spider placing the lines of her web. Part of Cashel's mind knew that what he saw—the staff and the swords—wasn't really what was happening anymore, but it was easier to imagine it in the fashion he was used to.

Cashel felt growing pressure. His arms ached like he was pushing a board through sand, heaping up the pile in front of him. His shield dimpled with each touch of a sword, and spots of heat swelled behind the dents. He kept walking forward, slower now but still moving. He wondered how long this could last.

Archas' blond hair spread like a halo. His beardless face was smiling, but there were beads of sweat on the pirate's clear brow.

Cashel took another step, as slow as ice creeping down a roof under its own weight. It was like pushing a mountain.

People thought fighting was about how strong you were. That was part of it, sure, but there are other strong people around. Then it came down to timing.

Cashel twisted and thrust like he held a spear. Archas might even have seen the stroke coming—he was that good—but this time he couldn't shift his swords to block it. The butt of the quarterstaff smashed into a blazing blue sun that filled the black cosmos.

It seemed like Archas—Fallin—was screaming, but maybe that was a marsh hawk. Cashel stood on a hill under an ilex tree. There were ever so many sheep in the meadow about him. The sun was bright, and insects buzzed among the flowers.

Cashel stretched, smiling lazily. There was one more thing to take care of before he got back to the regular business of watching his flock.

Still smiling, Cashel strode off to find Sharina. He began to spin his quarterstaff in slow arcs, staying loose for when he needed his strength again.

SHARINA WALKED TOWARD the cloud-wrapped, thunder-roaring figure Who lashed rain and hail onto the army below. Franca might be god of some skies, but the heavens have many moods. The slashing violence of a storm was only one of them.

Franca's eyes flashed fury beneath His black brows. "Are you here to fight me, child?" he boomed. "Go back to your cradle!"

He extended His arms, spreading His fingers toward her. Lighting rippled from His palms and dissipated in the air between them.

"I'm not here to fight," Sharina said. She smiled at Him. She'd loved thunderstorms as a little girl, standing thrilled in the rain and delighted to be part of their power and flashing radiance. "I'm here to bring peace, for you as well if you'll accept it."

Beneath her, flowers bloomed on the rolling hills. Grasses sprang up to recover the royal army's broad, muddy track; they were a brighter green than that of the meadows to either side.

"Peace?" said Franca, and the land shuddered. "The peace of the grave, you mean!"

His lightning blasted, this time in a continual torrent; ripping from all sides, tearing the cosmos apart in thorny crackling chaos. Sharina's bright comfort met the violence and washed it away like dust sluiced from windows by the spring rains.

She extended her hand toward Franca and said, "Real peace, for you and for everyone. Take my hand."

"Never!" Franca said. He launched another rush of lightning to push her back.

Sharina spread her arms, bringing warm sunlight to the soil. She didn't budge from the spot, but she couldn't advance either.

She thought of the big knife in her belt and smiled in soft amusement. There was a place for violence; but not for her; not now.

"Death!" cried the thunder. "Death and destruction and chaos! Chaos! As it was, so shall it be forever!"

"I might have been able to agree about death," said Ilna. "But not destruction. And as for chaos, if you're so fond of that—we'll send you there."

A net wove itself around Franca. He roared. The world would have shattered, but Sharina sheltered it beneath her cloak of light.

Franca's lightning tore Ilna's pattern, but it rewove even as the blazing edges of His power passed on.

Sharina looked at her friend and thought, *She isn't cruel. But she has no more mercy than the turning stars.* Ilna wore a cold smile, though her pleasure was in the craftsmanship rather than the result of that craft.

Cashel joined them. "This is the last one, then?" he said.

"Cashel, you're here too?" said Sharina. She'd felt peace and contentment, but now joy swept the cosmos.

"Yes, Sharina," he said, smiling but too embarrassed to look straight at her. He stepped a little to the side, his hands spread on the shaft of his quarterstaff. "This is my business, I think."

The net drew tighter. Franca shouted.

"There's peace even for Him," Sharina said. "If only—"

"No," said Ilna; coldly, quietly. "Not this one. End it, brother."

"She's right, you know, Sharina," Cashel said sadly. "She really is."

"Death!" Franca cried. "Death and destruction and—"

Cashel rammed the quarterstaff home. All his strength was in the stroke. Franca disintegrated into dust motes swirling in eternal chaos.

Sunlight and flowers swept across the world. Sharina stood, linking hands with Her friends.

THE SHOCK OF the rain and scourging hail stunned Garric for an instant. He felt the soldiers around him hunch also; they were tired, bone tired, and the hammering cold tightened their bruised and strained muscles. *It's too much.*

"*Haft and the Isles!*" Carus bellowed through Garric's throat. Technically it wasn't the right war cry, but it was the right one for this moment. "Let's finish these bloody rats, troopers!"

Garric strode down the slope, swinging for the face of the leading rat man. The beast got its sword up in time, but Garric's long wizard-forged blade sheared it and the rim of the rat's bronze cap on its way to the brain beneath.

The rat fell. The royal army surged ahead—hacking, stabbing and shouting a variety of things. The former cavalrymen used the Ornifal war cry, "Forward the Eagle!"

The storm vanished, driven back on a brisk north wind. In the clear air Garric saw that the slope ahead and the hills beyond to the horizon were covered with swarming rat men. There were too many to kill, too many even if they'd been a forest of birches and there was nothing to the business but chopping.

The wedge staggered forward, one sword stroke at time. Garric and the army would go on as long as they could. That was all that mattered. Scholars could discuss the battle in the future, if there was a future for human beings. This was soldiers' work.

A rank odor swept southward on the breeze. Garric chopped backhand to crush a rat man's skull with the pommel of his dagger. The blow missed, because the rat fled with a terrified squeak.

Garric stumbled, twisting left to keep from sprawling. He'd been counting instinctively on the stroke to balance him. He was wide open to the nearest pair of rat men. They could chop high and low, at his neck and his right ankle, and he could only block one.

But those rats and more rats in a wave spreading southward were running. *All* the rats were running. The dark-furred mass turned like barley bending away from a storm.

Garric fell to his knees. He'd kept going on willpower; his body had been played out long before.

He was gasping. He tried clumsily to push his helmet off without letting go of the dagger in his left hand. He'd forgotten about the chin strap. Even after he remembered, he couldn't force himself to drop either of his weapons.

The rats fled in panic. Their swords lay where they'd stood, and they'd thrown away their helmets and breastplates as they ran. They littered the hillside with equipment all the way to where the Emperor of Palomir and his wizard stood.

Garric looked back. Tenoctris stood on the hilltop, chanting with her arms spread. The smoke mounting from her cart swirled above her into the figure of a giant weasel. The beast's harsh musk swept across the battlefield.

The weasel opened its mouth in a rasping shriek. Despite Garric's exhaustion, the sound brought the hair up all over his body.

He got to his feet. "Come on, troopers!" he croaked. "Let's finish this now!"

Carus chuckled. *"It's never a bad idea to keep a sword in your hand,"* he said. He was probably joking; but he was Carus, so maybe not.

Garric started up the hill. Once he got moving, it was bearable. This close to the end, it would've been bearable if he'd been barefoot and running over swords.

He grinned. It felt good to grin, though the rat-blood caking his face cracked and pinched his skin. It wouldn't be long.

The Palomir wizard dropped his athame and turned to run. The emperor leveled his sword at him and said, "Stop them, Salmson! This isn't supposed to happen!"

The wizard shouted, "Run, you fool, it's all over!" He dodged past; the emperor stabbed him through the ribs from behind. He tumbled on his face, coughing bright blood.

"This isn't supposed to happen!" the emperor repeated as he turned. "I am Baray, Emperor of Palomir!"

He wore full armor and he'd been merely watching while Garric and his men fought their way through a landscape of rats. But—

Carus laughed. Garric thrust over the shield and in through the open visor. Teeth clicked as the point drove through the brain of the late Emperor of Palomir.

The sun shone on the grass, and the scent of flowers washed the breeze clean.

Epilogue

ILNA WAS WEAVING in shades of gray. The pattern was subtle, perhaps too subtle for anyone but herself to really see, but everyone could feel it.

She smiled: it was attractive, very attractive. And if that was boasting, well, it was *still* very attractive.

"Dear heart," said Chalcus, "you should put in some color. People like color."

Ilna looked at him, though she continued to work. His smile waked a smile from her too, as it always did.

"There's color enough in life," she said. "Here there should be peace, which the living see little enough of."

"Chalcus is right, Ilna," said Merota, snuggling closer as she watched the fabric grow. "A *little* color."

"Tsk!" said Ilna, but she thought about the problem. There were ways to keep the pattern whole but, yes . . . to add a little color. If you were good enough, of course.

"There's never been a better weaver than you, dear heart," said Chalcus.

The Sister smiled as she wove. Her fabric showed touches of color, now; just a little color.

CASHEL STOOD WITH his back to the ilex, watching his flock as it wandered. He rubbed his shoulders on the rough bark, then shifted so that he didn't neglect any of his charges.

Duzi, but the silly things some of them got up to! But that was all right; that was what people did. A good shepherd didn't meddle except when he had to. The flock wouldn't thrive if you kept pestering it.

At the end of the day, there'd be Sharina. Cashel smiled wider. There was *always* Sharina.

Until then, if a sea wolf wriggled out of the waves, well, it'd find the Shepherd standing in its way.

SHARINA SMILED TO think of Cashel as she checked the furnishings of the inn. They were already in order; or anyway, as much in order as they could be with people.

"I wouldn't call it order," said Burne critically. "Tumblers would break their necks if they were as sloppy as most people."

Sharina laughed. "People aren't statues to be set in place and polished," she said. "But they deserve to be treated decently."

She thought for a moment and added, "People ought to be comfortable, too."

The rat sniffed. "Coddled, you mean."

Sharina shrugged. "There might be other opinions on what's a reasonable degree of comfort," she said. "But mine is the one that counts here."

"Well, I don't say but you might be right," admitted Burne. He hunched, then hopped to her shoulder.

Sharina looked the house over yet again, still smiling but with a critical eye. One more thing.

She spread her hand. Flowers sprang up, growing even from the walls. Cashel liked flowers. That would've been reason enough even if she hadn't loved them herself.

The Lady smiled at Her house. She was well pleased.

THE SERIAN ENVOYS insist they must speak to His Majesty personally rather than through an intermediary," Liane said in a carefully neutral tone. "Even if that intermediary should be his consort Lady Liane or Lord Reise."

The sun was barely up, but artisans were already at work on the new Temple of the Great Gods. They weren't just the laborers constructing the temple itself, but also the skilled workmen erecting the three cult statues, which would be too big to bring in after the building's shell was complete.

Each of the Great Gods was the responsibility of a separate sculptor. The three men were present, using lamps to make out the details of the armatures their subordinates were clamping together.

A section of Blood Eagles stood nearby. The men were alert but not on edge. There could be trouble—

"There can always be trouble!" said Carus.

—but they no longer expected it.

Garric laughed. "The Serians are a polite people, as I recall," he said. "We could tell them that they are being notably discourteous in presuming to dictate the actions of a monarch in his own capital. On the other hand, I could simply talk to them. What is it they want?"

Across the plaza, workmen walked up the steps on the outside of a crane's twenty-foot wheel, using its leverage to sway a portion of the architrave into place. The crane's beam squealed as it straightened with its load. The foreman of the specialists waiting on the transom to make the fine adjustments shouted directions to the crane operator.

"Unofficially, what they want is to remain independent," said Liane, allowing herself a smile. "Though of course they can't discuss the matter with anyone but you."

Garric shrugged. "The Serians have never been a problem to their neighbors, not so far as I know," he said. "I don't see any reason why they shouldn't remain outside the kingdom. Do you?"

"There are questions of trading law," Liane said.

"Particularly jurisdiction over mixed cases, that is where a Serian and a royal citizen are on different sides of the dispute."

Garric looked up from his sheaf of architect's drawings. "The Serians have been trading with the other islands for years," he said in puzzlement. "Centuries, I suppose. Why should there be a problem now?"

"In the past, each island had its own arrangements with the Serians," Liane said, taking a codex out of her traveling desk but not, of course, opening it. "There's wide variation."

Garric frowned and started to speak.

"Which will cause problems *within* the kingdom," Liane continued firmly, as though she hadn't noticed her prince and husband's intent. "Now that there's real unity."

Smiling, Garric went back to the drawings. "Give it to Tadai to sort out and bring me a recommendation," he said. "Royhas has his hands full with taxation."

"A committee under Lord Tadai, you mean?" Liane said, knowing full well that he didn't.

"I *could sort it,*" said the ghost in his mind, joking but not entirely. In life Carus had found administration frustrating, and death hadn't given him patience.

"No," said Garric. "But put in someone you trust— one of your father's trading colleagues, perhaps—as Tadai's deputy. I have full confidence in him, but like the rest of us, he's capable of being self-willed."

He grinned. "Tadai's not," he added, "as likely to lop somebody's head off as some of my trusted advisors are, though."

The sun fell across the rising temple. The proportions were strikingly *right* even in this incomplete state. "It's going to be beautiful," Garric said. "It's beautiful now."

"The Dalopans will insist on independence too," Liane said. "They would have even if you didn't grant that right to the Serians. Though nobody in Dalopo was organized enough to send envoys, of course."

Garric snorted. "Freedom to a Dalopan means a chance to loot his neighbor. And then eat the prisoners as well, if he's feeling peckish. Dalopo will have a military commissioner and enough soldiers to make sure the survivors learn to do what he says."

Garric put his arm around Liane. They were in public, but at the moment he didn't care. "It isn't perfect," he said. "But it's pretty good. And with the help of the Gods, we're going to make it better."

He glanced down at the drawings of the statues as they'd be when completed in gold and ivory. The Sister was weaving, of course. In relief on the wall behind Her were the figures of a man and a young girl.

The Shepherd, solid as a mountain but smiling, stood in front of sheep cropping a pasture. His staff was upright in His right hand.

In the center was the Lady. Her right hand touched the Shepherd's forearm, and Her left hand was outstretched in blessing. The rat which had recently entered Her cult gamboled on the ground at Her feet, and the wall behind Her was a mass of flowers.

"With the help of the Gods," repeated King Garric, and kissed his queen.

TOR

Voted
#1 Science Fiction Publisher
20 Years in a Row

by the *Locus* Readers' Poll

———•———

Please join us at the website below
for more information about this
author and other science fiction,
fantasy, and horror selections, and to
sign up for our monthly newsletter!

www.tor-forge.com